Sensuosity

Also by Jamie Laster

Life, Love & Passion: Reflections of My Soul

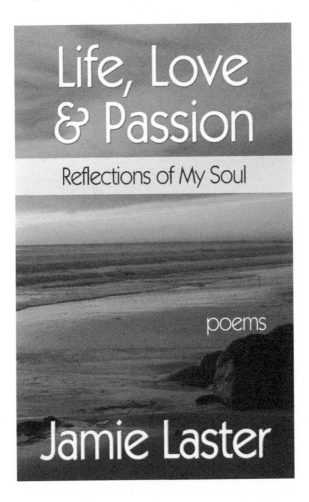

Available on Amazon in Both Print and eBook Formats

Sensuosity

Jamie Laster

Copyright © 2022 by Jamie Laster

ISBN Paperback: 978-1-939229-35-9
ISBN eBook: 978-1-939229-36-6

Flying Donkey Press

Interior Design by Shawn Hansen
Cover Design by Matthew J. Myers

Dedication

This novel is dedicated to my sons for all their love, encouragement, and continued support of my writing. To my father, King James Laster, for always pushing me to be my best, and to my mother, "Alice O.", for always being my emotional rock with unwavering encouragement.

For those cherished and indelible slices in time, my sincere gratitude to, "D", "J", and "R".

To K.D., A.A., and Mark, thank you for enhancing my life with friendships I will cherish for a lifetime.

A special thank you to Matthew for feeling my vibe resulting in his artwork for the book cover, and my WT Shawn, who made publishing this book possible.

The deepest of appreciation to Jordan, "Keyshia", the rest of my family, and all the friends who support my writing.

Sensuosity

sen(t)-shə-'wä-sə-tē

noun

1. Relating to or involving gratification of the senses or the indulgence of an appetite; sensuous enjoyment; sexual attraction

2. Relating to or affecting the senses; sensual and/or sexual experiences

I just may be,
that woman who your mother warned you about.

That elusive and mysterious woman who calls to you in your dreams.

I will make your pulse race,
then steal your breath away.

That woman who brings your body and soul to new heights of ecstasy.

I just may be,
that woman who will ease your mind and soothe your soul.

That woman who can charm you and make you smile,
even on your darkest of days.

I know the path to the rainbow which shines after the storm.

I am not that one in a million woman,
I am that once in a lifetime woman.

Passion is the trump card in my deck,
embrace the danger if you so dare.

As she let the sunroof back and the sunshine in, Mia exulted in the liberation she felt coursing through her body. She planned this getaway at a spectacular, beachfront, hotel months ago, and finally the day had arrived; she was nearly there. As she traveled down California 1 on that gorgeous sunny afternoon, she firmly decided this trip would be the first of many. A wave of exuberance washed over her as she traveled along the coast and the first beach came into view. The beach was her therapy, well, that is besides Retail Therapy. More specifically, new shoes to her already vast collection she thought with a smile. Welcome to the rest of your life Mia, it's finally time to do whatever makes you feel good, and to just take care of you.

It is a fact that being a single mom of two sons for 22 years will take its toll, yet as much of a struggle as it had been, it had also offered Mia an opportunity to tap into inner strength she never knew that she possessed. She had endured 13 years of incessant court battles as well as seemingly unending obstacles, but somehow managed to get her twin boys through private school where they both graduated with honors. Both had earned full athletic scholarships - Marquis in baseball, and Russell in basketball, thank you Jesus. Through the grace of God, her family for support, and therapy for all three, she bravely survived her divorce from hell, the ensuing years' long custody battles, and pulling double duty as both a mother and a father.

It was well worth all the money and emotional price she paid through those long years of court, mediation, and therapy sessions though. Mia had ultimately disencumbered herself of Myron, and in doing so, had liberated her sons as well. Marquis and Russell were free of Myron forever. Her victorious court battles had given them the power to choose to continue their relationships or not. Yes, the struggle had been real all those years, but her sons had grown into strong, loving, and independent men. Her ex-husband Myron on the other hand, had remained a narcissistic, controlling, abusive, and unhappy man. Despite any and all sacrifices Mia had made over the years, she had no regrets whatsoever. With a smirk on her face, she recalled seeing someone wearing a t-shirt last week reminding her of Myron, and why their marriage had to come to an end:

IT IS BETTER TO HAVE LOVED AND LOST,
THAN TO SPEND THE REST OF YOUR LIFE WITH A PSYCHO

Looking back, it all seemed like a lifetime ago, but somehow at the same time, it seemed like only yesterday - as if it had all happened in the blink of an eye. Summer had brought the boys back home before beginning their senior years, but now, once again, the house was empty. Mia loved them with every ounce of her being, but it was time to "exhale", so she was on her way for some much needed me time to collect herself and recharge. After arriving and checking in, she immediately changed into her black swimsuit, tied a black and white sarong over hips, then slid into her rhinestone studded flip flops. She threw her phone and wallet into her purple tote bag, then headed out with only one destination: the beach.

Mia grabbed a beach towel from the hotel bin, settled onto a chaise, then taking a deep breath, literally exhaled. She could already feel her body beginning to relax with the smell of the ocean and the sound of the surf mere yards away. She pushed out all thoughts of things she needed to do or take care of, but more importantly, refused to allow any negative energy or thoughts to seep in. Feelings of contentment immediately began permeating her very soul; she was beyond happy to finally be here. The only things scheduled for the next two days was for Mia to clear her mind and to do whatever felt good, but above all, for her to just relax.

Sitting on the table beside her chaise, was a kiosk to order selections from the bar. Well hot damn - today's technology she thought with a smile. She placed her order then lay back. As she people watched, pangs of regret from not staying consistent with her workouts hit her hard. Just where in the hell had time taken her biceps and triceps like she had back in the day? She surmised wherever they were, they were with her 24" waist. She looked down at her somewhat softened tummy, then nodding her head with pursed lips, she resolutely decided then and there, that consistent gym visits would begin once she returned home.

Thinking back though, she remembered that most of her past lovers did not care too much about her waist or her stomach. The last one in fact loved her body when she was at her heaviest or at her thinnest. She tried not to miss the times with him, firmly believing that if someone is meant to be a part of your life, they will be. If they are gone for a while, but you are truly destined for one another, you will find your way back to each other.

"Spicy, Stoli bloody mary with salsa and chips, Miss?" the server asked interrupting her thoughts.

Mia peered over her blue mirrored sunglasses, "Why yes, thank you. That was so fast, and this is so very much needed," she told him flashing a bright smile.

He smiled and handed Mia her selections on a small glass tray.

"May I see your room key please Miss?"

Mia sat the tray on the table, pulled the card key out of her tote bag, and handed it to him.

He nodded, "Thank you. This charge will be added to your room. Now if you would please just sign there with your finger," he told her while pointing to indicate where.

Mia signed and lay back on the chaise, "All done, thanks."

"Please do not hesitate to let us know if you will require anything else by using the kiosk. Do enjoy your day and your stay here with us Ms. Taylor."

"Thank you."

And with another nod of his head, he was gone.

Mia took three long sips of her drink, then dunked a few chips in her salsa, and it was all so delicious. So much yes. Ahh, she could feel the sun and alcohol beginning to work their magic. The last few weeks began melting away as she lay there slowly unwinding and beginning to relax. Another long sip and her drink was now half-gone, intensifying the magic she was already feeling. Lounging on the beach this Thursday afternoon and enjoying the luxury of time, Mia allowed herself the indulgence of reflecting on those memories the server had interrupted. She could not help but smile, thinking back on some of those times.

Stolen moments.

Unspoken words.

Words we dared not speak,
but were nonetheless shouted by our bodies.

Shouted so loudly, it would seem the entire world could hear us.

Trying to satisfy that unending craving we feel.

Skin hungering to be touched.

Yearning for a satisfaction
that only we can create.

Ignited passion uncontrolled,
like a mind-bending drug.

Bodies aching for release.

Hearts racing, bodies pounding.

Skin drenched and slick with sweat.

Completely engulfed in a frenetic dance of ecstasy.

Our bodies speaking well beyond any words,
that could ever, ever be uttered.

JAVIER

I

Mia was rushing to meet her friend Sandra who was helping her set up her new website. After working in her home so long, Sandra had finally branched out and rented a small space in a strip mall. She finished up her appointment with Sandra, then walked outside to her car. She was tempted to go into the consignment store next door to Sandra's place, but decided to be good, by handling her business of the day without a shopping distraction. She walked straight to her car and threw her black Coach purse and backpack on the passenger seat. She popped on her sunglasses, cranked up the music, but before she could shift into drive, the brake light came on, again.

Well, I will be damned. Can I catch a fucking break?, she asked herself. Feeling exasperated, she looked up, then realized there were at least three auto places right there in the same parking lot: Tires R Us, Smog 'N Go, and Martinez Auto Repair. She grabbed her purse, got out of her car, and began walking towards Martinez Auto Repair. She vaguely remembered hearing Mark, a co-worker and BFF, mentioning that name with nothing but good things to say about his experience.

She walked over and saw several cars and mechanics working in the bays. Hmm, that is a good sign she thought, so let's see what happens. She walked into the office, but unfortunately found it empty. She stepped back out and peered back over where she saw men working, when she heard a deep, melodic voice say, "Please go in and have a seat, I will be right with you."

Mia did not know who had said it, but she turned around and walked back into the office. She looked around this time. Certifications filled the slate blue wall behind the desk. Lots of auto memorabilia on the other walls. Alone in the office, she grabbed a cup of cold water from the cooler and began mindlessly staring outside through the front glass door. After a couple of moments, the phone began ringing. She heard the door open and turned around to see a man rushing in to catch the call. She assumed he was the manager, since the other men were working on cars. Mmm.

What a striking man. Milk chocolate shade of brown, tall and lean, with a well-manicured goatee, and sexy full lips. He looked to be way younger though. Delicious eye candy to be sure. If only I were about 10 years younger, it would be on, Mia thought to herself smiling. He grabbed the phone, gestured to Mia that he would be right with her, and sat down at his desk behind a tall, slate gray counter. Mia could only see the top of his head. His hair was styled in a brush fade, and his waves were on point. Unh, wasn't he having a good hair day? Hell, he could make a sista seasick and whatnot with those waves Mia mused fighting a smile.

Clunk.

Mia heard the phone hang up and that now familiar, deep voice again.

"Sorry for the wait Miss. Hi, I'm Javier, how may I help you?" he asked standing up and making eye contact.

Mia was immediately struck by his eyes; he had the most unexpected azure blue eyes. How was that even possible?

"Uh, Miss?"

"Oh, sorry, I zoned out for a moment. I was just talking to my friend Sandra down the way, got ready to leave, and the damn brake light in my car came on, again. It's been coming on sporadically the last few days, but I have no idea why. It's just an older used car, and the brakes were okay when I had an oil change a month or so ago, or they didn't mention it," she explained rolling her eyes and pursing her lips.

Javier walked around the desk to where Mia was standing.

"Uh huh, I see, "Well, why don't you just drive it over here Miss...?" he said extending his hand.

Mia was already fumbling in her purse for her keys and held up an index finger motioning for him to wait, "Mia. Hi, I'm sorry my name is Mia, and thank you, I will drive it right over. Sorry, it's just so goddamned stressful when those damn lights come on, and you don't know what's wrong or how expensive it will be to fix."

Javier put his hand down and tried to listen to what she was saying. He found it nearly impossible not to get distracted though. What a sexy woman she is he thought, as his eyes traversed her body. He got especially distracted when his gaze met her full, round, breasts. He was trying hard as hell to appear discrete though, hoping that she would not notice his ravenous eyes ogling her luscious body. With his head cocked to one side, he crossed his arms over his chest, and stood there silently staring, totally mesmerized by Mia.

Uninterrupted, she continued on with her rant, "Then you have to find a mechanic who you can trust and who won't take advantage of a woman plus charge you a bazillion dollars. And then, even after all that, sometimes after a few weeks, it has more problems again, so then you have to go back. Oh - sorry Javier. I am not saying that you would be like that. Damn. I am just rambling on and on," she told him as she finally found her keys.

Javier remained standing there staring intently at Mia.

She stopped talking and looked up, making full eye contact. Javier raised his eyebrows but continued to stand there silently.

"Lordy Jesus, I feel so dumb. Bet you probably don't really want to shake my hand now huh?" Mia said extending her hand out to Javier.

Javier extended his hand once again. They both gave a nice firm shake. Javier's hands were not too soft, just a little on the rough side. That's just how a man's hands should feel Mia thought.

"No worries over here, I get you."

That voice though. It curiously did not sound Hispanic, not in the least. It was hell of deep though. Slightly gravely. Sexy as hell. Damn, this man was sexy as hell. If his last name was Martinez though, there must be a story she decided while standing there.

"Why don't you drive it over so I can give it a quick look?" Javier said snapping her back to reality.

"Really? Wow, thanks so much Javier."

"No worries."

They both stood there staring, not uttering a single word for a few seconds.

"I will drive it right over," Mia said as she walked towards the door.

As she headed towards her car, for some reason, Mia felt that Javier was watching as she walked away. She glanced back over her shoulder and sure enough, Javier had a slight smile with his head cocked to one side watching her booty as she walked away. Mia's imagination took flight as she walked to her car. Oh my God, that man has to be at least five, hell maybe even ten years younger than me. And on top of everything, he's married; I noticed his ring when he shook my hand. Hmm, what a pity. Not that he'd necessarily be interested in me if he were single, but goddamn - there is something so sexy and electric about him. Well, maybe I still "got it," and not just to men my age, after all, he was sneaking a peek while I was walking away. Feeling sexy her damn self, Mia got into her car while making up her own Evil Kermit Meme in her head:

Me: He's married.

Inner Me: But you ain't – Girl get after it!

The thought made Mia laugh out loud. She started her car up and drove over to where Javier was motioning her to go.

"Can you pop the hood please Miss, I mean Mia, and let's see what we have going on here?"

Mia turned off the car, popped the hood, and then walked to the front as he lifted the hood, as if she knew what she was looking at.

"I'm sorry, but you really can't be here in the bay. Would you mind going back inside to wait? It is not technically safe, liability issues and all. I will give it a quick check and see if I can figure out what the problem is going on here, so try not to worry okay?" Javier said with a wink.

"Oh yes, of course. Sorry. Thanks Javier," Mia replied while walking back inside and trying to shake the feeling of dread from an expensive and unexpected repair bill.

She heard her car start up and a few moments later shut down. Since there was nothing that she could do, Mia decided trying to decompress while waiting. She grabbed a Car and Driver magazine off a small, wooden, gray table, then sat in one of a pair of black club chairs which she found to be surprisingly comfortable. She got so carried away in an article on restoring an old Mustang, that she actually lost track of the time.

Ba-zing, ba-zing, ba-zing.

Her attention to the article was broken by noise from the shop as Javier opened the door to the office. She looked up to see him walking in carrying a brown clipboard, jotting on it while walking. He stuck the pen behind his ear and walked over to where Mia was sitting. The door automatically closed with a *shooosh.*

"Well Mia, not sure how this news will hit you, but your brake light has been coming on because you need brakes. Your pads need to be replaced, but I think your rotors are okay. Today is Thursday, so did you want me to order the pads? I can have them here in the morning. You can either leave the car here tonight or drop it off in the morning. I can squeeze you in and have it done by this time tomorrow, then you will be good to go for the weekend. Of course, there is always next week, but I would recommend you get this taken care of ASAP to avoid future issues. If you give me a minute, I can give you an estimate for the parts, and my labor is $115 an hour. My guys are working on finishing up two jobs, so your timing is spot on. I'll have them working on your car as soon as the pads come in. I got you covered," Javier told her with a smile.

Mia stood there momentarily stunned trying to absorb the news, then looked down at the floor shaking her head.

"Honestly, it's not a major issue, I promise you that."

Mia slowly looked back up at Javier, "I'm sorry. I know you're probably good at what you do, I mean wow, look at your wall, it's just that I'm kind of in shock. I was not expecting this, at all."

Nodding, "I understand," Javier empathetically replied.

Mia stood there silently for a few seconds more, then after rolling her eyes in disgust, "It just figures that it wouldn't be brake fluid or something simple like that. Thanks for checking it out for me so fast though. It would be better to leave it here tonight so I can get it taken care of, but I would need to get my sister to pick me up, and your shop is about to close," Mia told him before a heavy sigh.

"Well actually, I have a lot of paperwork to catch up on. I will be here for at least another hour, and you're welcome to stay. Timing is everything in life, is it not?"

Stepping back and slanting her eyes towards Javier, "Oh, I see. I see what's going on now. I see what you're trying to do."

Frowning and looking totally confused, "Huh? Trying to do?" Javier asked with outstretched hands.

Mia smiled. "You, are just trying to get me to leave you a glowing review on Yelp or something huh? Guess what? You're gonna get one!" she said pointing at Javier with both index fingers.

Looking relieved and pretending to wipe his brow, Javier began laughing and told her, "Wow, you got me on that one Mia."

She began laughing.

Shaking his head, "I was thinking, what in the hell is this woman talking about?" Javier joined in Mia's laughter.

"Sorry Javier, I have a crazy, bad girl side that pops up at times."

Javier's eyebrows raised in surprise, "Oh... do you now? Hmm, well maybe you should let that side "pop" up more often. I mean, I wouldn't mind," he replied with a wink.

Not missing a beat, Mia responded, "Hmm, time will tell, yes? Endless possibilities and whatnot," giving him a wink right back.

Javier smiled; eyebrows still raised.

"And yes, I will take you up on that offer Javier and call one of my sisters. She passes by this freeway exit on her way home from work, so hopefully I can catch her,"

Mia stood up looking Javier in the eye, "Seriously though, thank you Javier, you are very kind."

"No problem Mia," Javier told her before going back to his paperwork.

Mia grabbed her phone out of her purse and stepped outside. She called her sister Juanita and gave her the address of the shop. When she walked back in, Javier was busy working.

Clack. Clack. Clack.

In the otherwise silent office, the sound emanating from Javier's keyboard was all that could be heard. He seemed to be hard at work, so Mia decided not to disturb him. She stared at all the certificates on the wall again, beginning to feel more confident that everything with her car would be alright. Javier seemed to sense her vibe, stood up from his desk and asked, "So, you have any other questions, Mia?"

"You know, to be honest, I'm actually feeling somewhat relieved about all this car drama after looking at all these certifications on your wall."

"Great, I want you to feel that way. Honestly, your brake job looks to be pretty, straightforward. I will call to let you know the status as soon as your job is done in the morning. Will that make you feel any better?"

"Yes, much better actually. I really do appreciate your bedside manner," Mia told him chuckling.

Javier smiled.

"Seriously though, it's always a struggle being a woman and worrying about getting taken advantage of and paying too much. I know basic stuff about cars, but this is way above my head. I'm not very trusting, but I'm thinking you are one of the good guys, so don't prove me wrong, please," Mia pleaded with praying hands.

"Nah, you're good. So, what is it you do Mia?"

"My side gig is a freelance writer, but the money job is working for the state as a Right of Way Agent. I used to be a Title Officer for many years. You got some property questions for me?" she asked rhetorically and was surprised to hear an answer.

"Well to be honest, actually I do. I'm considering refinancing my home. So, do I need to get an appraisal first? Do I need to find an appraiser on my own or does it get ordered from the escrow person or the loan person?" he asked looking genuinely confused.

"Well, I have always worked on the title side, which is telling you about property taxes, easements, policies, money matters, types of things. Dabbled on the escrow side so I have some knowledge on how it goes. The lender generally orders the appraisal, and yes, you will usually have to pay upfront and out of pocket for it unfortunately. I still have tons of Escrow Officer friends and contacts. I can make a call tomorrow and have comps run on your house to find out what homes in your area are selling for. This will give you a good idea of your market status to help you decide whether it's a good time for you to refinance or not, that is, if you like."

"Wow Mia, yes please, that would be great. I will write my address down right now," Javier told her grabbing a pen.

"Come on now man, really? Feel free to step into this millennium and text it to me," Mia said teasing.

Javier rolled his eyes then laughed and shook his head, lightly tossing his pen down on the desk.

"Oh damn, you got me Miss Lady. I will text you the address. Thank you in advance though."

"Well, some of us do stick together, ya know?" Mia said eyebrows raised.

"I feel you on that Mia. You know, I am feeling pretty damn

fortunate that you happened in here today. I mean, who knows, maybe one day we can form a company and flip houses or something," Javier said with a shrug.

"No way - *O.M.G* - I've always wanted to do that! Hey, you never know, maybe it's our destiny," she said nodding her head in his direction.

"Wow. Yeah, kind of feeling like our paths were meant to cross."

"Right? It's definitely feeling like the universe is at work here. I totally believe in laws of attraction."

"Hmmm, do you now?

So, years ago after my nephew was killed, I felt lost and was questioning life; nothing made much sense anymore. Trying to find answers led me into this metaphysical mode, and I mean like a serious mode. I started with The Conversations with God books, went on to angels, the Seth books, Sylvia Browne, Goddess, I could go on - but I'm truly convinced that thoughts do create. Manifesting what you want, or need is real. Laws of attraction and all that you know? It doesn't always happen when you want or think you need it, but it does come," Mia said nodding her head affirmatively.

"Absolutely. Yes. Yes Mia. I totally agree with all that you just said about thoughts, the universe, and laws of attraction, it is real."

"Well, honestly, most people just shake their heads and think I'm crazy."

"Same here, so I keep it to myself for the most part."

"I sure wish I could relax enough to meditate, but I just can't seem to keep my mind clear for it to work well. Done it a few times, but only when I was dead tired. I haven't tried it for a few years now, but after talking to you, it's made me think about trying it again. Have you ever tried it? It's supposed to center and de-stress you."

"I don't really stress much, but I'm down to try it, sounds like it would be helpful."

"Well, I have a book and cd if you're ever interested in borrowing them. I can always drop it off since your shop is on my way home from work."

"Sounds like a plan. Yeah. Uh, yes Mia. I would like that please, thank you."

Mia smiled happy to help. Plus, she had just given herself an opening to pop by and see that sexy Javier sometime in the future should she decide to. Options are always a good thing to have.

"Here's your estimate. If you could just fill out your address, phone number, and sign at the X please," Javier said handing the form to her.

Mia filled out her portion, signed it and handed it back to Javier.

17

"Thanks Mia, and the phone number is your cell so I can text you my address, correct?"

"Yup, sure is."

"Great, so all good then. Any other questions you have for me?"

"Well, I'm good with the car, but yes, I do have another question for you if you don't mind. It has nothing to do with cars though. I'm just kinda curious, well to be honest, nosey, 'cause I know it's none of my business really," Mia said squinting apprehensively.

"Damn, now you have me intrigued. Sure, shoot. I'm an open book," Javier said leaning back in his chair and crossing his arms.

"You sure?"

Nodding, he told her, "Go ahead and ask me anything," before reflexively licking those full lips then flashing a white smile, prompting Mia to smile back and reply, "Ooh, that could be dangerous with a woman like me."

Javier's eyebrows raised with a look of surprise, "Unh, you don't say?"

Mia took a deep breath, then looked down towards the floor, "So, the name of the shop is Martinez. Is that your name, or just the name of the shop?" she asked, then slowly looked up until her eyes met with Javier's.

Javier smiled again and with a shrug told her, "Yes, it is my name, and it is my shop; my name is Javier Martinez. My father is Mexican, my mother is Black, and this is what happened when they got together," he told her while pointing at himself and laughing.

"Hmmm. Interesting."

"My paternal grandmother has blonde hair and blue eyes, go figure. My mom has green eyes. Those women's genes gotta be where my eyes came from," he said throwing his hands up and shrugging his shoulders.

"Well, I must say, they are striking. You have such an exotic look, and your milk chocolate skin makes them pop even more. But man, your lashes are to die for – I am so jealous."

"Thank you, thank you Mia. I will take all that as a compliment."

"You really should."

The air was full of electricity as their eyes met and locked in a gaze.

Mia finally broke their electrical filled pause, "Well, I will try not to disturb you from working. I was lucky and caught my sister, so she should be pulling up any minute," Mia told him then turned to walk back to her seat.

"More like distract not disturb baby," Javier muttered under his breath.

"Huh? What did I miss?" Mia asked turning around.

Looking sheepish and shaking his head slightly, Javier replied, "Oh nothing, just talking to myself, you're fine Mia."

What he was thinking though, was yes baby, you are hella fine - and sexy, as fuck.

"Talking to yourself is good, I do it all the time."

Javier just nodded while thinking that she might not be saying that if she knew what else was going through his mind about her at that moment. The thought made him smile.

Buzz. Buzz. Buzz. Buzz.

Mia heard her phone, checked it, and saw that her co-worker Ashley had texted, confirming that she could take her to work in the morning, and drop her back at the shop after work.

"My friend said she will drop me off after work tomorrow to pick up my car, I would be here between 5:00 and 5:30, will that work for you?"

"Sure will."

Those words were still hanging in the air when her sister Juanita pulled up outside the door.

Honk, honk, honk.

Well, here's my ride. Thanks again Javier, and please let me know what happens tomorrow. I'm going to try not to worry," Mia said while grabbing her purse and backpack off the chair.

"You're in good hands Mia, don't worry. I will let you know what's up tomorrow once the parts come in and we get working on your car. You have a good night, I got you Lady," Javier said standing up.

"I sure am counting on that, and gonna hold you to it. See you tomorrow Javier. Now don't forget to text me your address so I can get those comps run," Mia told him while pulling the glass door open.

"Will do."

She waved as she walked out to Juanita's car. Javier stood there and watched her walk all the way to the car and get in. When he finally sat back down to his paperwork, he had a big smile on his face thinking about seeing Mia again tomorrow.

As Mia got into the car, she was smiling like the Cheshire Cat, prompting Juanita to frown before asking, "Girl, why you looking so happy when you're leaving your car at the shop? What's going on?"

"Oh, it was just the mechanic, Javier, he made me laugh is all. Thanks for coming to get me," Mia said, then gave her a hug.

Raising her eyebrows with a slight scowl, Juanita pulled back and looked at Mia hard for a few seconds.

"Mmm hmm, okay. Let's go then," she said before driving off.

About two hours later Mia got a text from Javier with his address.

She made a call to get paperwork for his house. He was treating her pretty well so far about her car, so she was just trying to reciprocate. Ashley picked her up the next morning and it was such a crazy, busy, morning at work that time just flew by. When Mia thought to check her phone, she saw that she had missed a call from Javier. Panicking, she called back.

"Hey Javier, it's Mia. I missed a call from you. Go ahead and break the bad news to me."

"Hey Mia, how's it going? I was just calling to let you know that there was a delay, but your pads will be here any time, and I should still have it done for you by the time you get here. Told you I would keep you updated, and word is bond, right? See? Told you I had you covered Miss Ma'am."

"Thank you. Thank you so much. Whew. What a relief, you have no idea. Oh yeah, so *your* update is that I reached out to a good friend, and I should have some info about your house in a day or so. Whenever I get it, I will drop it by for you though."

"Sounds great, thanks Mia. See you in a bit," Javier said then hung up with a smile thinking about seeing Mia later. The chemistry with her was off the damn chain.

Ashley got to the shop about 5:40.

"Thanks a billion Ash, I owe you a big lunch," Mia told her while getting out of the car.

"Well, we don't want you going into the 'New Shoe Fund' and all, but sounds good, catch you later," Ashley told her laughing.

Mia laughed and waved as Ashley drove off. She quickly opened the door and rushed over to the counter in front of Javier's desk.

"Hey Javier, sorry I got here so late, bad traffic," she breathlessly explained.

"Hey Mia, no worries, and I would have waited for you. As you can see, I'm just doing my paperwork thing as usual," he said pointing at the stack of paperwork on his desk while rolling his eyes and shaking his head.

"I do have some news for you though," he told her with a serious face.

"I knew it," Mia responded deflated.

"So, here's the scoop, when the mechanic was doing your brakes, he noticed some oil. Have you noticed anything leaking?"

"No, I don't think so. Wait. To be honest, I am not entirely sure. Last time I got my oil changed they did say my oil was low now that I think about it. Dammit," she said throwing her purse down hard on the counter and letting out a heavy sigh.

"Well, we checked it, and it was a little low today as well. I had one of my guys top it off for you though. It will be crucial for you to check your oil level every few days though, do you know how to do that? And I am not being facetious, some men don't even know how to do it."

"Yes, believe it or not, I actually do know how, my father taught me. He told me it was very important to always check it, and now just look at me. Damn. I had a bad feeling you would tell me something else was wrong," she said sadly with another heavy sigh.

"No more negative thoughts now, laws of attraction, remember? We don't even know if it there is a leak yet, but if there is a leak, you know I will take care of it for you, right? Of course, you can always go to another shop, I was just letting you know what we saw."

"Oh no, I will definitely bring it back to you Javier. I trust you. If you were trying to take advantage of me, you would have just told me that I had an oil leak, given me the estimate, and be getting your money right now, am I right?" she asked matter-of-factly.

"True that. Thanks for the confidence Mia."

"Thanks for looking out for me."

Mia laughed and shook her head. Javier looked at Mia with a confused look cocking his head to one side.

She explained, "Well, you're giving me potentially bad news, but I could almost hug you - pure craziness."

With raised eyebrows and sensuously licking his full lips like usual, Javier replied, "Well, I'm sure glad I could instill that kind of trust, but more importantly, elicit that type of feeling."

Silence. No one moved. Electricity radiated throughout the silent room.

After a few seconds, Mia grabbed a debit card out of her purse, "Go 'head on and melt it L.L. Cool J," she said handing it to him breaking the stillness.

Javier laughed, "I see you got jokes."

"Well, I like how he seems to lick *his* lips subconsciously too."

They both just looked at each other not speaking again. This time Javier broke the silence, "Well, I did give you a good price. I won't melt it completely."

"I appreciate that," Mia told him looking relieved.

"I suggest that you check your oil in a couple of days. I mean, if I were you, I would check on Sunday and then again on Tuesday," he told her while processing her card.

"I will be sure to do that, and thanks again for looking out for me Javier."

He handed her card back along with the receipt to sign. She grabbed a pen out of the holder on the counter and signed the receipt.

"Not bad as I thought, thanks."

"See? Hey, would you mind letting me know either way about your oil level?" he asked while taking the receipt back.

"I will be in touch for sure, promise," she said taking her keys from his hand.

"Well, got my fingers crossed for you."

As soon as the words were spoken, this time Javier was the one who laughed, and Mia was who looked confused.

"Why do I have my fingers crossed though, that's taking money out of my pocket," he asked shaking his head.

"It's because you are a decent human being Javier," Mia replied with a shrug and a nod in his direction.

"Nah, it's just my one day a year to be nice."

"Well, lucky me then. I will give you a call next week to let you know Mister Man," Mia said walking to the door.

"Take care Mia."

She opened the door and looked back, "You too," and with a wave she was gone.

Javier sat there staring at the door for a few moments before returning to his paperwork. Mia drove home with Javier on her mind, but not about her car. *I may burn in hell, but damn, that man is fine. The things I could do to him - unh, unh, unh.* She knew it was highly unlikely that circumstances would ever allow her to do any of the things crossing her mind, but then again, there were always those endless possibilities.

II

Sunday morning Mia woke up, got dressed, and hit the gym for her U-Jam fitness class. She stopped to grab a vanilla latte from Starbucks drive-thru on the way home, and as she pulled up to her house, she remembered about checking the oil. Just the thought of something else wrong with her car weighed like a heavy ass boulder in the pit of her stomach. She turned off the car and grabbed a Kleenex from the box in the console. She popped the hood, wiped the oil off the dipstick, then stuck it back in. She hesitated, fearing the worst, but took a deep breath and pulled it back out.

Hmm, Javier told her he topped it off, so it should still show pretty full, but it was not quite as high as she thought it would be. She stuck the dipstick back in, closed the hood, hopped in her car, and started it back up. She backed up then got out and looked. There had always been a stain on the street there, but unfortunately the spot did appear a bit wet. Damn, damn, damn. Well, Tuesday's results would determine whether she would need to take the car back to Javier's or not. At the very least she would call him as she promised. She did promise him, and besides, she loved talking to him. Even better, it appeared he felt the same way.

Monday was busy at work but otherwise uneventful. After a night of insomnia, Tuesday morning found Mia exhausted. She could not count the number of times she hit snooze. Somehow, some way, she dragged her tired ass out of bed and into the shower. Those multiple "snoozes" had cost her though; she had no time for real makeup or to do anything to her hair. She pulled it up in a clip, threw on a little lip gloss and eyeliner, and got dressed in record time.

The morning was a bit chilly. Mia clicked on the seat warmer, cranked the heater and was about to drive off when she remembered the oil. Ugh. She turned off the car and got out to check it. Damn. It *was* lower than Sunday's level. An impending repair bill of who knows how much, caused that gnawing sense of dread to return to the pit of her stomach. She knew Javier would give her the best price, well, at least there was that. Somehow, she managed to grab her vanilla latte from Starbucks and still get to work on time. About 8:30 she summoned up the courage to make that call.

"Martinez Auto Repair, Javier speaking," greeted her on the phone.

His sexy voice brought an instant smile to her lips, "Morning Javier, it's Mia."

"Oh, hey Mia, how's your car? Thanks for following up and calling me."

"All bad. Oil is low, must be a leak as you thought. So, tell me, what's my next step?"

"Sorry to hear, but we'll get it all fixed. I'll need an hour or so to check it out though. When can you bring it in?"

"When do you have time?"

"You can come in anytime. Today if you want, you know I'll squeeze it in for you."

"Appreciate that. I'll go ask my boss about leaving early; it's not like I have a choice really. I will call you back to confirm, is that okay?"

"Of course. Now Mia, take a deep breath, it will be okay. I got you lady."

"Thanks Javier. I will call you back shortly."

Mia emailed Mrs. Johnson her supervisor explaining the situation. She got approval to leave at 2:00. She called Javier and let him know she would be there by 3:00. As Mia drove up to Javier's shop, she saw him walking from a car towards his office. He saw her and motioned her to drive over in front of a bay. He walked over to her car, and she let the window down, "Why don't you let me drive it in and you go in and have a seat? You know the drill," he said with a wink.

"Yes, I do," she told him rolling her eyes then grabbing her purse and backpack from the front seat. She resignedly walked into the office to sit down and wait. After only a very few moments, Javier walked in the office.

"Whoa, can't be done already?"

"I wish, but I'm not *that* good, "Javier said with a big smile.

"Got my guys working on it but it will be an hour or so, need to check a few other things too. Someone coming to get you?"

"Well, I'm sure I can get my sister to pick me up, but she doesn't get off until 5, so I would have to be here for another 2 hours or so," Mia told him making a frowning face.

"Come on now Mia, you know I don't mind your company, and it's cool to hang with your mechanic for a minute, right?" he jokingly asked.

Looking despondent, Mia shrugged and shook her head.

"Go call your sister and just chill here with your boy Javier. Like you said, you don't really have a choice, right?"

Mia nodded, then stepped outside to call Juanita to arrange another ride home. She came back in and grabbed a large white envelope out of her backpack. She walked over to Javier's desk while pulling a stack of papers out, then placed them on his desk.

"So, here's the paperwork I got with info on your house. I don't know what your credit and FICO look like, but the appraisal will be the key piece of info to see how much equity you have. Your FICO will aid in determining what type of loan and interest rate you can get."

"Wow, that was so fast, I really do appreciate this, Mia. When I get a chance to go over it, I will probably need to call you, will that be okay?"

Mia smiled looking at him over her glasses.

"Don't be silly, of course you can. I have connections everywhere, so in this I have *you* covered. Looks like we got each other's back, huh?" she said gesturing with her hand and smiling again.

"Well, like I said, looks like we were destined to meet."

"It does appear so."

They silently stared at each other in another one of their long pauses, both seeming incapable of moving or speaking.

Ring. Ring. Ring.

Sill not breaking his gaze, Javier answered the phone, "Martinez Auto Repair, Javier speaking," before finally looking away at his computer screen.

Mia took that as a cue to walk back to her seat and let Javier work. She waved, he nodded and continued his phone conversation. She plugged earbuds into her phone and listened to her old school playlist while reading her emails and surfing social media. Javier was in and out of the office, and on and off the phone; he sure was a busy guy. Mia decided to begin re-reading an old book she had brought with her, and time just flew by. About a quarter to five, Javier walked over to her.

"Mia. *Mia*," he said louder.

She was in a zone though and did not hear him calling her name, so he stood in front of her and waved.

"Oh, sorry Javier," she said quickly pulling the earbuds out of her ears.

"Okay, so I have info for you. I have some good news, and some bad news."

"Oh hell, let's just rip the damn band-aid off. Give me the bad news first," Mia replied rolling her eyes and slumping in the chair.

"Okay, well the bad news is yes, you do have an oil leak."

Looking visibly upset and throwing her hands up, she looked at Javier, "Lordy Je-*zas*, and the *good news* then?"

"The mechanic already tracked down the source of the leak, so I can get it taken care of for you tomorrow."

"Well, I just paid for brakes only a few days ago. I definitely wasn't expecting another repair..." Mia began, looking extremely stressed out.

"I understand. I'm just saying, I will get it done for you if you want it done now. If you need to wait, you are going to need to keep a very, and I do mean *very,* close watch on your oil level Mia. You will need to keep the level maintained until you get this taken care of, and honestly, the sooner, the better," Javier candidly told her.

"I get what you're saying Javier, and I appreciate your honesty and effort to help me, I really, really do. The thing is, I don't get paid until Friday, and it's only Tuesday," Mia told him shaking her head and looking defeated.

"Okay look, your car is already here and diagnosed. What if I went on and did the repair, and you pay me Friday? It's only an extra couple of days, Friday instead of Wednesday. And it would be late Wednesday so technically Thursday for the bank, you know?"

"You would do that for *me* Javier? *Really?*" Mia asked stunned.

"Now don't go around spreading the word, but yes, I can wait until the end of the week for you to pay me."

"I don't know what to say. I lost my damn debit card and am still waiting for the replacement. If it's not here by then, can I just write you a check and date it Friday? Will that work for you?"

"That will work."

"Oh my God, you have no idea of how much I appreciate your kindness," Mia said looking relieved.

"No worries. Just send business my way if you hear of anyone needing a mechanic and we'll call it square."

"You got it Mister Man," Mia said pointing both fingers at him with a huge smile.

Honk. Honk. Honk.

Juanita was outside again.

"Oh wow, my sister is here, and she told me she would be in a rush," Mia said as she began hurriedly stuffing things back in her backpack, then grabbed her purse.

"Gotta go, but thank you so much Javier, I will see you tomorrow about the same time, okay? And I am going to go by no news is good news, so hoping *not* to hear from you," Mia said flashing a smile then turning to rush to the door.

"Gotcha. See you tomorrow Mia."

Mia got in the car, "Hey Sis, thanks again," she told Juanita while strapping on her seatbelt.

"What - no smiles this time? So, what the *hell* is up with your car? That mechanic isn't trying to rip you off, right? I mean you were *just* here Thursday Mia. So, *what's the deal?*" Juanita asked concerned while driving off.

"*Helllooo.* Yes, I am well aware I was just here. So, last week it was the brakes, but I didn't know then that I also have an oil leak. He's fixing that now. Guess I wasn't paying attention, but there *is* a wet, dark spot on the street underneath where I park," Mia shrugged.

"Oh damn."

"Thankfully, he mentioned the oil being low last week when he did the brakes, so told me to check it for a few days. I did, and sure enough, the oil level kept dipping unfortunately. So nope, he isn't trying to take advantage of me Big Sis, not to worry."

"Guess you're just having a streak of bad luck then, huh?"

"No shit I am. Things go in 3's though, like Mama always says, right? First the unexpected brake job, then last weekend I lost my damn debit card when I went to Costco, so really hoping this is the third thing and boom - I'm done."

Glancing over at Mia, "No doubts sis, sorry to hear all this. Unh, ain't it crazy how things are going along just fine, then one domino falls starting a damn chain reaction, and then everything starts feeling like it's all going to hell? I hate it when that shit happens. But you know what? Sometimes, not too often, but *sometimes*, good things happen in 3's too, so try to remember that, okay?"

"Okay, gonna try," Mia said unconvincingly.

"Well, here's hoping things will start going in a positive direction for you sis. So how are you getting to work and picking up your car tomorrow?"

"One of my co-workers has me covered, but thanks."

"Okay, well let me know if that falls thru, you know I got you."

"Yeah, I know, thanks sis," Mia told her staring out the window a bit detached.

Mia's mind was racing. Juanita sensed she was stressing so just let her be.

As they pulled up to her house Mia told her, "Thanks again for saving me 'Nita."

"Of course."

Juanita observed Mia's body language as she walked to her door. She let the passenger window down and called out to her, "Hey Mia, it's going to be okay. Never forget, I'm always here for you."

Looking back at Juanita, "Thanks, and I appreciate it more than you know. Love you sis," Mia said turning back to open her front door.

"Okay, now don't forget, I'm always just a call away. Love you too," Juanita said before letting the window back up. Mia opened her door, turned, and waved, before Juanita drove off.

The next morning came *way* too soon. Mia had hit snooze three times already, but when the alarm went off for the fourth time, she knew that she had to drag her ass out of the bed *now*. She needed enough time for makeup since she would be picking up her car and seeing Javier after work. The hot shower felt so good, she stayed in way too long but dressed in record time. She put eyeliner, mascara, and a little shadow on, but no time to do her hair. She just pulled it up in a clip as was becoming the norm lately. Oh well, it was not like he was going to notice anyway. Damn there goes that negative thinking again. Gotta work harder on that she thought while she applied some red lip stain and clear gloss. She stood back and looked in the mirror. Hmm, she looked "presentable," as her mom would say.

Mia's ass was still dragging though; it *was* morning after all. She had just never been a morning person, and never would be. Those synapses in her brain did fire nor connect well until later in the day. And conversation? That was a definite no-go. Work was always a struggle, but her co-workers knew this of her, so did not really talk to her until mid-morning. Much gratitude.

Buzz. Buzz. Buzz. Buzz.

It was Ashley texting her, God bless her for all the rides, and the bonus was that Ashley wasn't a morning person either.

Mia locked her front door then got into Ashley's car.

"Hi, thanks again Ash."

"Uh huh," and they were on their way.

It was a busy day at work, so time flew. As the hours passed, there was no call from Javier, *thank you Jesus*. Finally, it was time to leave. Mia still felt a bit nervous about the car. It was almost 5:20 when Ashley pulled up to the shop.

"Thanks for the rides again Ash, I owe you lunch," Mia told her.

"Not a problem, going home to lie down and try to shake this headache from hell. See you tomorrow girlie."

Mia opened the door and Javier looked up over the counter with those smiling electric eyes, she instantly smiled.

"Hi Javier."

"Hey Mia, how's it going? I will be right with you, but do you mind waiting a second? Been a crazy day and I just need to finish up this customer's paperwork, and I'm right in the middle."

"Sure, of course, I mean how could I say no to *you*, uh - that didn't come out quite right," Mia said shaking her head and rolling her eyes.

"It didn't huh? Are you sure about that? Freudian slip maybe?" Javier asked smiling.

They both laughed nervously.

"I'm sorry, that was wrong for me to say no doubt. Best stop being a smartass before I get slapped. Got a Black Mama remember? I know how it works," he said laughing.

"Oh, and why would you get slapped Mister Man? Let me tell you something about me. First, I am a very direct person; I have absolutely *no* time to go around wondering about things. Second, if I have a problem with what someone says or does, I do *not* have a problem telling them right there on the spot. And third, confrontation is not a problem for me. I do not play the 'Damsel in Distress' role, and I am not one of those people who suffer silently. And just so you know, I am a big girl and do not scare much, if at all. So, you're safe; not to worry kind sir. If I don't like it, I will *most definitely* let you know right on the spot, *just sayin',*" Mia told him cocking her head to one side.

"Well damn. Maybe you should learn to come out of your shell and speak your mind woman," Javier said laughing.

Mia just looked at him over her glasses pursing her lips before smiling.

"But you know, I do like the sound of that, 'cause that's how I roll myself. I will keep that in mind *most definitely,*" Javier replied, mimicking Mia's voice and smiling.

"Okay now, don't get yourself in trouble. Were you *not* listening to what I just said Mister Man?" Mia asked with her hands on her hips crooking her neck, replicating the *Angry Black Woman* pose.

"Now, don't threaten *me* with a good time," Javier replied, and they both laughed.

Mia sat down and began checking her email.

"All done," Javier said standing up looking over the desk at Mia.

Mia looked up from her phone, then sat it in her lap, bracing herself for Javier's news about her car.

"So, we fixed your leak, and found nothing else this time. Let me just finish *your* paperwork so I can get you out of here. I know you're ready to get outta this place and get home."

A wave of relief swept over Mia, "No worries Javier, I'm good," she told him exhaling hard.

"Great, will just take me a minute," he said sitting back down to finish Mia's paperwork.

Clack. Clack. Clack.

The sound emanating from his keyboard was the only sound to be heard in the quiet office as he typed away. Mia picked her phone up, but to her dismay, saw her battery was nearly dead.

"Damn," she muttered under her breath.

She stood up, "Hey Javier, would you mind if I charge my phone? I don't see an outlet over here though," Mia said still looking at the walls near where had been sitting down.

"There's one back here, by me," he told her as their eyes met and locked.

"Oh, okay," Mia said hesitantly but did not move.

They continued to stare until Javier broke the silence by joking, "Don't worry, I do bite at times, but I had my shots, so, you're safe, well, in that respect."

Regaining her composure, "Like I said, I don't scare much," Mia replied with a slight attitude while walking over to where he pointed.

She bent down to plug in her phone and pretended not to notice he was watching her. As she was walking back to her seat, Javier rolled over in his chair to the file cabinet and began looking through files. His black Nikes caught her attention. Mia stopped walking, then cocking her head to one side, looked at them harder. Both of her sons had such big feet, clown feet almost. Javier's appeared so much smaller, yet he looked to be about the same height.

"Hey Javier."

Normally Javier would be irritated at being interrupted, but he easily answered without looking up, "What's up Mia?

"How tall are you?

"I'm 6'3'. Uh, that's pretty damn random," he replied looking up with a frown before shaking his head, then going back to looking in the file cabinet.

"So then, what size shoe do you wear?"

Javier looked up again from digging through the files then over at Mia, negatively shaking his head.

"Hey ... *Hey*. It's not true, it's *not*," he told her shaking his head even more intensely.

"*What?*" Mia asked looking confused.

After a few seconds, the reason for his reaction dawned on her.

"Oh. Unh, unh, *unnh. Man* - that's not even why I asked. Lordy Jee-zas. Men and their egos," Mia said rolling her eyes and laughing.

"Really? Uh huh, okay then," Javier replied through narrowed eyes looking at her disbelievingly.

"For real Javier, you and my sons are about the same height, and I am so used to seeing my son's big clown feet. Yours look kind of small, that's all," she said with a shrug.

Javier crossed his arms and blankly stared at her.

Making a circular motion with both hands, and looking down towards his crotch Mia told him, "Now that, all of *that*, has *nothing* to do with me - not at all. Not my farm, not my pig, but I guess I will just have to take your word for it," she said laughing.

Javier was about to respond when he looked over and saw a truck pulling up outside the glass front door.

"Excuse me a moment would you please Mia, I need to grab this part."

Before she could answer, Javier abruptly got up and walked past her to the truck waiting outside the door. Unfortunately, her replacement debit card had still not arrived, so Mia found herself foraging through her purse looking for a pen to write out the check. As luck would have it, there was no pen to be found. Well, doesn't that just figure she thought, tossing her purse down hard on the table. She got up and walked over to the counter in front of Javier's desk to grab one from the pen holder, when she heard the door open. A cold gush of wind blew in causing her body to shiver a few seconds until the door closed shut with a *shooosh*, leaving only dead silence. Mia knew Javier was standing behind her waiting for her to turn around. For some reason, lyrics from a song on that TLC *CrazySexyCool* cd popped into her head. It seemed to be no secret that he had been watching her, and it was apparent that he wanted her, but just exactly what would he do, in order to get to the center of *this* Tootsie Roll Pop?

As much as she wanted to turn and look back, that stubborn streak she inherited from her father simply would not allow her to. Instead, she remained standing there refusing to move, "*CrazySexyCool*". She was trying her damndest to control her breathing; attempting to slow it down so as to appear totally unaffected. Javier continued to slowly and silently walk closer and closer, until she could feel his presence directly behind her. Mia stood perfectly still; her body totally frozen. At this point, she could not have moved even if she wanted to. Incapable of movement, she could only stand there waiting, caught up in the anticipation of the moment. All her concentrating did nothing to slow down her heart; it was beating hard and fast as a locomotive hitting its stride barreling down the tracks. Then wait, was it? Yes. Oh my *God*. She could feel Javier's hot breath softly raining down the back of her neck. She heard him inhale deeply before his deep voice reverberated near her ear, "Mmm, well don't *you* just smell delicious."

Stunned, Mia remained frozen, still unable to move, and now, even unable to speak.

"What *is* that you're wearing Mia?" Javier asked, inhaling deeply again.

Summoning all her strength, "Umm, it's called Pleasures, by Estee Lauder," she answered breathlessly in a rush.

"Mmm, now how perfect is *that*? As is your little up-do hairstyle.

It does leave your neck pretty vulnerable though. But you know what? Someone *I* know just told me that she doesn't scare much. Now, do I have that right?" he quietly asked.

Plunk.

Before Mia could answer, Javier sat the small box with his part on the counter. He then slowly stretched out his other arm on the other side of her and grabbed onto the counter with both hands. Still not touching her, he straddled her body in between his strong arms, and then once again, she felt his hot breath on her neck. Taking a deep breath and trying her best to swallow what felt like a damn medicine ball in her throat, Mia breathlessly but fearlessly replied, "Yes, I did say that, and no, I am *not* scared of you Javier, I'm way too old for that. Why? Are you going to do something that you think is *scary* to me right now?"

There was no answer, just Javier's continued presence behind her, and his hot breath on her neck.

Recovering her moxie Mia continued, "Go ahead and give it your best shot, but I'm still not afraid Mister Man."

As the words rolled off her tongue, Mia was wondering just how far Javier would actually go. From what she could tell of him already, he was *not* going to back down, but then neither was she. The game of chicken was on, and Mia was secretly loving it.

"Hmm, well it all depends on your definition of scary, but that sure as hell sounds like a challenge to me," Javier told her, his body only mere inches away from brushing up against hers at this point.

Mia still did not move.

"Here's a news flash for you Miss Lady, I'm not one to shy away from challenges. You know, I got that Alpha Male thang in effect," he softly spoke in her ear.

Throat thickening, nipples hardening, Mia continued trying to play it cool. She gave a non-committal shrug as she ever so slightly looked back over her shoulder, inadvertently exposing a larger portion of her neck. And then, oh *damn* ... she felt those full sexy lips of his softly graze her neck at that very moment. She reflexively quivered and took a deep breath, trying her hardest to get everything that was speeding up to slow the hell down. Her heart was pounding so hard, she thought for certain Javier could hear it beating. As she closed her eyes to focus, she felt a soft kiss on the back of her neck causing her to involuntarily shudder and arch right back into Javier's body. He did not move. She could feel his hardness pressing against her. Involuntarily she let out a small gasp causing Javier to abruptly step back. Without a word, he began walking around to his desk while shaking his head.

32

"I'm moving before I get that slap. Damn woman. You are so *goddamned* sexy. I knew it from the moment you walked through that door though," he said taking a deep breath and exhaling loudly, while shaking his head intensely as he pulled his chair out. He looked squarely at Mia, not breaking his steely blue stare as he sat down licking those full lips.

Trying to catch her breath and regain her composure, "What exactly do you mean by that Javier?" Mia asked, still slightly winded.

"I would be totally crossing the line to tell you, but if you really want to know, remember it was *you* who asked," Javier said throwing his hands up with a shrug.

"Yes. Yes, please tell me Javier," Mia implored him.

"That day you found the shop and that moment, from that very moment that I saw you, ooh, I was so glad you had come in. I could feel a connection with you - like a magnet drawing me to you. I thought about you after you had left the shop for a little while that night. Being generous, *maybe* about 30 minutes, but I knew then without a doubt – I *knew* that I wanted to fuck you Mia ... *fuck you hard.*"

Mia found herself speechless once again.

"You are an incredibly sexy woman. I have no doubts that you felt *exactly* what you do to me when I was standing behind you right?"

Still not being able to find her voice, Mia could only nod yes.

"And before you give me that *men always want sex thing* – okay *wait.* Uh, so it *is* true with a man like me, because I absolutely *love* sex, I admit it," Javier said pursing his lips with a shrug.

"But to be real, it's rare for me to get turned on like this, well besides all the porn I watch," he said laughing.

Listening intently, Mia did not utter a word.

"I just don't know what it is about you. I feel drawn to you with a chemistry I honestly can't explain. And I have been a faithful man, always," he told her shrugging his shoulders.

"Je ne sais quois?"

"What was that?"

"Je ne sais quois. It's French. It means that certain something. Like it's something that you can feel or sense, but you cannot really describe."

"Absolutely."

Mia smiled, "Anything else to add?" she asked rhetorically and not expecting an answer, especially not the answer Javier was about to give.

"I may as well lay it all out then, I'm in this far and I don't half-ass it. Full transparency," he said holding his hands up in a mock

33

surrender pose.

"My home life is complicated right now," he told her while holding up only his left hand this time, showing his wedding band.

As if Mia had not scoped that fact out already, but she did not stop his monologue.

"Yes, I am married, but honestly don't see it as being sustainable. My youngest, my son, is a junior now, and when he graduates and goes off to college in a year or so from now, well, who knows? My wife and I have been growing apart for years, and honestly, I'm tired as hell of being taken for granted. Our sex life is marginal. I wouldn't even be surprised if she had somebody on the side, because I sure as hell don't get much at home," he told her matter-of-factly.

"Most of the time, it feels more like she's doing it because she feels obligated, and who the hell wants that? And no Mia, sex is *not* everything. I know this, but it does mean *something*, and for a man like me, it helps me to reconnect sometimes, actually, often. But you know, after a while always being the one who wants it, well, that shit gets old, *real* old," he told her not breaking eye contact.

"I can imagine so."

He nodded and continued, "My kids though, I love them more than anyone or anything. I would die for either of them. Look Mia, I am not telling you all of this in hopes that you will ever allow me the pleasure of you sharing your body with me, but then again maybe I am."

Mia was completely captivated listening to the words pouring out of his mouth and could only nod.

"What I *am* doing, is trying to explain my situation as honestly as possible. Sometimes life brings people into your life temporarily, sometimes permanently. Sometimes their time is fleeting, and sometimes they are needed for a longer duration. But I will tell you this, they are most certainly there for a reason. Sometimes you just don't realize at the time what their true purpose is. There is a reason though, there is *always* a reason. But you need to be open to recognize it you know?" he asked with a nod in Mia's direction.

"Yes, I agree."

"I think it's far more than what meets the eye, but if you're not paying attention, you can miss it. The whole laws of attraction at work. So, there you have it. This is where I'm at. I am putting it all out in the universe right damn now, so let the chips fall where they may," he resolutely told her, his fiery blue eyes never breaking full contact.

"Unh."

"We don't have to continue this conversation or ever speak of it again, if that is what you choose. I have been married over 20 years, and yes, I have come across many beautiful women. To be real though, I've never experienced anything like what I feel with you *ever*, to be where I am mentally or physically right now. It's actually blowing my mind if you want to know the truth. I really don't know what it is with you, but honestly, I'm digging it. I'm also apologizing if I did or said anything that you did not want or like," he solemnly told her holding his hands up once again in mock surrender.

Mia slowly began nodding her head affirmatively.

"Well, I do appreciate honesty, and that was a lot to unpack. You do realize though, that now I feel compelled to tell you how *I* feel about it, right? I mean how can I not? So, are you ready?"

"Bring it," Javier said motioning with his shoulders and hands.

"You sure?" she asked cocking her head to the side.

"You already know," Javier replied cocking his head to the side mimicking Mia.

"Okay, so first thing is, I am not upset by anything you said or did to me. As a matter of fact, I feel very flattered that you are so attracted to me. *And*, as you so aptly put it, yes, I could feel exactly *what I do to you*, and to be honest, it's not just one-sided."

Pleasantly surprised, Javier's eyebrows raised in surprise as he barely hid a smile.

"And here is *your* news flash Mister Man. I am so very sorry to hurt that *Alpha Male* part of you, but it *is* a fact I that I could have stopped you at any time you know. But then again, *I* was the one who chose not to, *right?*" she asked raising her eyebrows while staring deeply into his eyes.

Javier shrugged then nodded yes.

Mia continued, "I really wouldn't enjoy playing the role of *the other woman* since my ex cheated on me so many times, but this situation is a bit different. I am not trying to break up your marriage or steal you away, and you are not trying to leave. From what I've seen so far, if you were to leave, it would be for your own terms, not for another, which is how it should be. I learned the hard way that happiness comes from within, *not* from another person. Another person can only enhance the happiness you already feel, not *be* the happiness. I remember a quote, well not exactly, I'm hell of paraphrasing, but goes something like a man with dreams needing a woman with vision to help challenge him. A man who wants to be ordinary will not need to feel any expectations of him by his woman, but a man who wants to be great will expect her to push him, pray with him and invest in him. From what I'm gleaning of your situation, I feel like without your woman really having your back, you are doing what needs to be done, mostly alone, and almost entirely for your kids. You're getting by okay, but not really being challenged to be your best, know what I mean?"

Javier once again nodded in agreement.

"You seem to be self-driven, but who knows, maybe I am here at this time to help motivate you. Manifestation and laws of attraction at work as it were. Maybe you summoned me with your thoughts and needs. Or maybe you were in need of a muse, and that's the reason you manifested me. On the flip side, I could be the one who manifested *you*. Who is to know who, how, or even why?"

"The universe knows."

"That would be correct Mister Man," Mia said pointing both index fingers towards him.

Javier smiled.

"And by the way, I feel chemistry with you unlike any other I have ever felt as well, so it's not just you or your imagination."

Loudly exhaling and shaking her head, "Damn man, we sure got into some heavy stuff huh? Apparently, it was necessary though. Well, those "chips" are definitely falling as you said, are they not? And only time will tell when and where they will land," she said with a wink.

Javier pretended to wipe his forehead in relief then let out a heavy sigh.

"Whew, I have to say that I am pretty damn relieved. Even though I was feeling that vibe really strong from you, I just didn't know how it would end up. I mean you didn't seem upset or irritated really, but for some reason, I don't know why, I just couldn't stop myself, and kept on pushing. But then I started worrying that maybe I might have gone too far, so that's why I came back around the counter to my desk. I was waiting on that "slap" or you to cuss my ass out," he told her with an apprehensive expression, like a child waiting for punishment after doing something he knew was wrong.

Once again there was only silence; the wind howling outside was all that could be heard. Mia appeared to be in a deeply pensive state. Javier let out a huge sigh finally asking, "Come on Mia, tell me, what are you thinking, *please*?"

"No worries Javier. I'm really glad we cleared the air, but I was just wondering, what in the hell did we just set in motion? Guessing endless possibilities?"

"Boom."

Mia smiled.

"Okay, let me pay your bill man, so you know, you can go out and buy a new Armani suit with some matching shoes and whatnot," Mia said laughing.

Javier handed her the invoice. She filled in the rest of her check, and as she was handing it to him, he told her, "Now remember, you have your own mechanic - I'm your guy," he said pointing to himself.

While staring intently into her root beer brown eyes he continued, "Seriously though Mia, please, don't ever hesitate to reach out to me if you need anything, and I do mean *anything*," letting his fingers softly graze hers as he took the check out of her hand.

"You know, I 'm beginning to think you're a bigger flirt, than I am. But after what was said today, I will come to you, *always* – I mean, how could I not?" she asked as she walked to the door, then turned back and gave him a slow wink.

After she walked out the door, she glanced back and saw him staring at her ass again. She got in her car with another huge smile and before driving off, adjusted her panties which had become moist.

Fortunately, over the next year or so Mia did not have too many car issues. She and Javier stayed in touch fairly often though, and she gave him advice on his real estate issues. It was Mia who helped him decide that it was not the right time for him to refinance. Still, she found reasons to come by for even minor things like getting a brake light bulb replaced. True to his word, Javier always took good care of her. He was always glad to see her and would just say, *"It's not a bother, that's what you have me for,"* whenever she just happened by on her way home from work and needed his assistance.

Sometimes she called on the way home just to chat. They spoke often about forming an LLC. He always asked if she was going to stop by to visit, but her answer was almost always that she had passed his exit on the freeway. Mia knew the extent of her willpower. "Flesh is weak," the Good Book does say after all.

Their phone conversations were always interesting to say the least. But those times that Mia did stop by the shop, their conversations were even more dynamic due to that amazing chemistry between them. Those conversations were always fantastic. They could speak on anything from sports to politics, and in doing so, this unique bond formed between them. Of course, there was always a whole lot of innuendo and flirting going on. Those *falling chips* as it were. Mia always found it hard to leave as much as Javier regretted watching her leave. Then there was that transmission leak which changed, *everything*.

III

Mia had taken a sick day and took care of some appointments, but on that afternoon as she was pulling up in front of her house, she noticed another dark spot on the ground where she parked her car. What in the actual fuck, no, *not* again? She went into the house, grabbed a paper towel then went back outside. She wiped the dipstick, stuck it back in, and apprehensively, pulled it back out. Whew, the level was normal. As she was on her way to work the next morning, she found it difficult to turn the wheel. Well, I will be damned. What in the hell is going on now?

She made it to work, but knew she had to make that call. She dialed the number while unconsciously holding her breath until she heard, "Martinez Auto Repair, Javier speaking."

She exhaled, and her lips instantly formed a reflexive smile before she replied, "Hey Javier, it's Mia. I know it's been a while. How have you been?"

"Oh, hey Miss Lady, long time no hear, I'm good, but I'm just going to take a wild guess that maybe your car isn't?

"Well, on the way to work, my car was kind of hard to turn, and this time I looked, and unfortunately noticed a wet spot on the ground where I park my car. My oil level is good though. I don't know what you've got going on, but is it possible for me to swing by later today?"

"Sure, come on down, you know I will *always* fit you in. I do recall telling a certain someone that I was *her* mechanic, am I right?"

"You did."

"Now, just letting you know that after 4:00 would be better because you would have a shorter wait. I will definitely check that out for you, can you bring it by?"

"Whew. Then I will see you about 4:00 then. You know me, I am stressed as fuck though. Thanks Javier. Appreciate you man."

"I got you lady. See you later."

They both hung up smiling, each of their imaginations racing.

As Mia drove into the parking lot, Javier's garage appeared packed full of cars. She felt a little guilty bringing hers in seeing how slammed he was. She was thinking about leaving a message saying she would try next week, when Javier appeared from one of the bays and waved her over. She drove over to him and let the window down as he walked around to her door.

"Hey Miss Lady, do you mind if I take over and drive the car in to have it checked out?"

"You look so busy; I was almost about to tell you maybe I could come back next week and..." she began.

"Now don't be silly. Told you - *I got you*. Now if you would be so kind as to open the door, please," he said gesturing at the door.

Mia opened the door and got out, although Javier did not give her much room. With a mock disapproving glance, she wiggled through the tight squeeze as he laughed.

"It's been a while. You know, a brotha was just trying to get all he can outta this visit," he said winking.

Mia smiled, secretly loving his boldness and went into the office to wait. Damn, it *had* been a while since she was there, but it all looked the same, it all felt the same; she could have been there just yesterday. Those sparks that she and Javier generated felt the same as well, highly intoxicating. Their connection remained intense as fuck. Mia sat there experiencing a strange mixture of apprehension for issues with her car, the cost, plus the anticipation on what would transpire between her and Javier. Coming to his shop was usually interesting, often enlightening, but always exciting.

She sat in her favorite chair and began tripping kind of hard about Javier. Although she tried resisting, thoughts began swirling around and around, in her head. She got up and looked through the window into the shop. Javier and a mechanic were doing something to her car, so she sat back down to wait. She finally succumbed to the thought tornado whirling in her head and got lost there until Javier walked in. He walked over to her looking serious.

"Okay Mia, so here's the scoop on your car. You have a transmission leak this time. You barely had any transmission fluid which is why it was so hard for you to turn the wheel earlier. I can probably get it done for you by the end of tomorrow if you can leave it again."

Looking defeated Mia shrugged with a heavy sigh, "Well, once again, guess I don't really have a choice."

"Aww come on now Mia, you know I will take good care of you," Javier told her looking empathetic.

"I know, I know Javier. And I appreciate it, really, I do. There is another problem though," she said sadly.

"And what is that?"

"Well, I'm sure I can get my sister to pick me up, but she doesn't get off until six today, so I would have to be here for another hour or so," Mia told him frowning.

"That's *it*? Come on now Mia, you know I do *not* mind your company, and not like it would be the first time. You know how we roll. Besides it's cool to hang out with your mechanic for a minute, right?" he jokingly asked while prodding her with his elbow.

Mia smiled and just shook her head.

"Go on and call your sister and then just chill. Like you said, you don't not really have a choice, *right*? You know I got you. Let me go see what needs to be ordered and get it taken care of. And on the real, you know that I love your company," he slyly told her.

"Thanks Javier, you're right. I'm going to go make that call right now," Mia told him before stepping outside to call Juanita.

She walked back in feeling a bit sad, but resigned to her situation, so sat down without speaking. Javier saw her come in, felt her energy, and decided she needed space. He pretended not to notice and kept working. She was grateful. As usual he was busy on the phone, in and out of the office instructing his employees, and troubleshooting issues they could not solve.

Finally, 5:00 rolled around, and the mechanics rolled down the doors to the bays and left for the day. Mia was deep into another book when she looked up to see Javier standing in front of her holding a cold bottle of water. She looked up from her book, her eyes filled with gratitude as she took the bottle of water he offered.

"*You*, are a jewel Javier."

Javier batted his eyes and then winked. He looked both ways, then put his finger over his lips before telling her, "Shhh, don't tell anyone. And if you do, I will deny it."

Mia shook her head and smiled.

"There it is - there's that smile! I mean *damn* girl; I have been waiting to see that all day."

Mia rolled her eyes and shook her head no.

"Hey, I know that you're worried, but you do know that I will take care of you, *right*?"

"Yes, I do know. You are a good person, Javier. *Oops* ... there I go again, huh?" Mia asked covering her mouth with one hand and laughing again.

"Yeah, you need to watch that," Javier told with a nod before heading back to his desk.

Mia's eyes followed him. He turned around before sitting down and caught Mia watching him. Looking like a deer caught in headlights and feeling a bit embarrassed, she held her head down, "Oh man," she mumbled to herself, shaking her head no.

Javier licked his lips, à la L.L. Cool J as per norm, and smiled.

"See anything you like," he teased in that deep, melodic voice.

Mia instantly recovered, lifted her head, and somewhat defiantly replied, "*Hellooo.* I thought we went through this already."

"Uh, not exactly Miss Ma'am. It was more of me saying how *you* make *me* feel. It was specifically about your effect on me. Your little lecture as I recall, was more in general, not specific to me," Javier replied with attitude.

"Oh."

"Right. So, care to elaborate? Thinking nothing has changed, as in you don't *scare much*. Am I correct in my assessment?" Javier teased.

"Okay so look, I told you I felt an incredible chemistry with you though, right? Normally that is simply not possible, if you are not attracted to the person, correct? So, sue me. I'm just sayin' a sista can look at that menu you got over there even though I'm not allowed to order from it, if you really want to know how I'm feeling about it at this moment in time," she replied matter-of-factly, pursing her lips and cocking her head to one side.

"Unh. I sure do like the sound of that, well the looking part. The ordering part, not so sure I agree. I'm thinking that maybe you might just be pretty damn hungry and need to eat somethin'."

"Oh - is that right? Well, possibly. But I have no doubts that there are many young "thangs" that come through here, so, why me? I don't get it, really, I just don't," Mia said with absolute seriousness.

"Well, maybe because they are too ready to give it up, I mean just *way* too easily. Maybe because they don't even take into account the fact that I'm married, they just think about what *they* want. Maybe because they don't make me feel the way that you do. And maybe, just *maybe*, it is all about *you*. You are sexy as fuck Mia. You *do* know that don't you?"

"So, it's the thrill of the chase?"

"Is that all you got from what I just said?" Javier asked shaking his head.

Mia just shrugged.

"Well, I'm sure that's probably part of it, but most of it is all you. It seems like I've been chasing for quite awhile now, but you know what? I am a patient man, as well as tenacious."

"You don't say."

"I *do* say. And since you like to point out our age difference so often, by me being younger and all, I got that stamina going on, might want to take advantage, just sayin'," he told her staring intently into her eyes.

"Unnh, maybe *I* like the sound of that."

"Do tell."

"I just did," she said with a smug expression.

"Queen of evasiveness this evening, aren't you? What happened to being direct and all that?"

"Look Javier, if I were younger, no wait - I'm not even going to use the age card again. It's because you're *married*, whether happily or not, it's wrong. But I must admit, it *is* very tempting. You are an incredibly sexy man, Javier. I'm just trying to be a good person is all."

"Well, perhaps being a good person is enjoying your life and helping me enjoy mine. I have given this some thought, and it's not like you are going to try to ruin my marriage, and I'll come home to a bunny being boiled on my stove in a big ass pot, right?"

Mia tried not to laugh, "You watch a lot of movies as I do I see. I do get your point. Life really is so damn short; you just never know when your time is up. Umm, so, it kinda sounds to me like you're offering me something?"

"No idea why are you even asking me that, 'cause you already know."

"I see."

"Anytime."

"Anytime huh?"

"Did I stutter? I don't believe I did, so yes, you did hear me correctly the first time. But just so there is no confusion, let me just say it again for you - *anytime*."

The air in the room ceased to move. Speechless, Mia stared at Javier, as if in a trance.

Honk. Honk. Honk.

The horn snapped Mia out from her momentary hypnosis.

"Oh damn, my sister is here, I totally lost track of time. I better go before she gets all pissy," Mia told him grabbing all of her stuff.

"I will give you a call tomorrow about your car Mia. You guys drive safely."

"Will do, talk to you tomorrow Javier," she said biting her lip, her imagination running away with her.

Javier stood up watching her. As she grabbed the handle on the door he told her, "I said what I said."

She opened the door, and shaking her head with a sly smile, gave a quick wave, before running over to her sister's car and getting in. Javier sat back down feeling some sort of satisfaction knowing that tomorrow, Mia would be back.

Insomnia decided to visit, so Mia did not get much rest. Around 5:00, she decided to go on and get up since sleep continued to evade her. At least it gave her more time for makeup since she would be picking up her car after work and seeing Javier. Juanita came by to pick her up and drop her off at work.

"Got my fingers crossed your car won't be too expensive," Juanita told Mia as she was getting out.

"Thanks for that and all of the rides sis, you are a lifesaver. Love you."

"Back 'atcha," Juanita said mouthing a kiss and drove off.

The day at work was passing without much drama when her phone rang around 1:00 p.m. She saw it was Javier and tried not to panic.

"Hello."

"Hey Mia, it's Javier."

"Yes, your name popped up on my phone. Oh Lord, *please* tell that you aren't calling to tell me something more is wrong?" she cautiously asked.

"No, no, no, nothing like that," he laughed.

"There was a slight delay with a part being delivered, but your transmission leak is almost fixed, the mechanic is working on your car right now. It will be done by closing time today. Just checking if you still wanted to pick it up today? I close at five, but I can wait for you if you like. I have paperwork as usual to catch up on anyways. Plus, it's Friday, and I'm sure you want your car for the weekend, am I right?"

"Yes, I would love to pick it up today. I would so appreciate if you could wait for me, I will owe you big-time man. I can get one of my co-workers to drop me off probably between 5:15 and 5:30, if that's not too late for you?"

"Nope, that works, I will be right here, see you later then."

"Yes, see you then, and thanks so much," Mia replied, and they both hung up with smiles.

Relieved, Mia sat at her desk anticipating being at Javier's shop later. She loved their conversations; they could talk about anything. Not to mention the man was sexy as hell, and ooh, that chemistry. Lord give me strength she thought smiling.

Mia texted Ashley:

> *Hey Missy, you said to let you know, so can I bum a ride to pick up my car from the shop again after work? Pretty please with brown sugar on top????*

Ashley replied:

> *Gotcha covered but be ready to roll at 5:00 sharp. I can't wait for this day to be over!*

Mia:

By the time 5:00 rolled around, a storm had rolled in, and it was pouring rain. Par for the course, there was horrible traffic due to the inclement weather, and accidents due to people driving batshit crazy. Why don't people ever get a clue and slow down when the weather is like this Mia wondered. Since she had flat ironed her hair the day before, she was happy that she had the foresight to put that beret in her purse this morning. After all that work, she sure as hell didn't want it getting wet and frizzing all up. She twisted her hair and slipped it on.

"Ash, thanks again for yet another ride for this *got-damn* car."

"No worries Mia, I got you covered girlfriend. Hopefully, it won't be too expensive."

"Right? He gave me an estimate, hopefully it won't go over."

Mia tried calling Javier to let him know she was running late, but no answer. She tried again a few minutes later but still nothing. She tried not to panic.

"Damn, he's not picking up."

"Don't worry Mia, if I get there and he's gone, I can take you home. There is a good chance that he *is* there working, and just can't get to the phone though, don't you think?"

"Yeah, you're right. It is so unlike him to leave without telling me. Reason number 225 why I love you to pieces. Well, looks like you are going to have free lunches for a week," Mia said winking.

"Uh, Miss Thing, you have a car repair bill to pay for, so let's just play it by ear," Ashley said pursing her lips.

"True that girl, true that. Well, I owe you a *big* favor, just let me know when, and I got you, *promise*."

"One day, I'm gonna hold you to that too," Ashley said pointing her finger towards Mia.

"*'Cause word is bond,*" they both said at the same time and laughed.

Buzz. Buzz. Buzz. Buzz.

Alarmed to see Javier calling, Mia picked up right away, "Hey Mia, it's Javier, are you still coming? The power went out here for awhile but just came back on. Fortunately, we finished your car first."

Hey Javier, I called you a few times and didn't get an answer to let you know I was running late from this crazy storm. We just pulled up though. I'm about to come in thanks."

She grabbed her purse, "Ashley you're an angel, thanks again," she told her before opening the door.

"No worries, now hurry so you don't get all wet. See you Monday Mia."

As she reached the door she turned and waved, and Ashley drove off.

"Hey Javier, I'm finally here," Mia said rushing through the door.

In the short distance from Ashley's car to the shop, Mia had still managed to get wet. She walked over to her usual chair and sat her purse down, immediately taking off her black coat and hanging it over the back of the chair. Next, she took off her black beret, then she shook out her hair. Finally, she unwrapped the red cashmere scarf wrapped around her neck and sat it on the small wooden table. Javier had just been watching her the whole time from the distance of his desk, his chin resting in his left hand. Mia finally looked over and noticed him staring.

"May I *help* you?"

"Oh, I don't know, *may* you? Maybe you can. I was just wondering when and if you were going to ever stop stripping. I mean, I don't have a pole or anything like that, but I can always put on some sexy music for you if you like," he told her with a smirk.

"Smartass. Fortunately for you, I find it to be a great character trait of yours," she told him with a mock kiss.

"Mia, Mia, Mia. If only you knew."

"Knew what? Cat got your tongue? If you have something to say man, spit it out why don't 'cha?"

"Hmm not sure if it's something to say or ask. Could be both," Javier replied pensively looking at the ceiling with a finger over his lips.

"Well, I *am* a big girl Javier, I can take it. I am a very direct person, *remember*? If I dish it, and you know I can - I can take it as well. Life is far too short to go around wondering, or missing opportunities. I am not one whoever wants to say, *I wonder if I had only tried longer or harder,* or, *if I had only asked.* I figure the worse that will happen is that someone will tell me no, and then I am no worse off, right? We have gone way past that business/customer type relationship *long ago,* have we not?" she asked him, throwing her hands up.

"True that."

Walking over to his desk Mia began, "So me being the older, more mature one and all, what I am saying is, that it has been my experience, that there is more of a chance that you will get a yes, rather than a no, so well worth the risk, at least *I* think so, Mister *Javier*," she said blowing on her nails and mock shining them on her sweater.

Javier sat there silently, his arms crossed over his chest.

"But 'cha know, that is just *my* school of thought about things - I'm *just* sayin'. Plus, I'm a great deal older than you are...." Mia began.

Javier quickly cut her off, his hands gesturing a time out signal, "Okay, okay, let's get this age thing out of the way right here and now Mia. You *always* bring that up, so let's just squash it right here and now. I was born in 1976 so that makes you how much older than me?" he asked pursing his lips.

Taking a deep sigh with and rolling her eyes Mia answered quietly, "10 years. 10 years and change. Damn, that's so bad. Worse than I thought. Looks like I'm in Cougar territory then?" she asked looking down.

Javier stood up and walked over to Mia lifting her head up, then smiled and looked deep into her eyes.

"It doesn't bother me at all, and I have to say Miss Lady, 56 looks great on you - you wear it well. I mean *damn,* I wouldn't have guessed your age. I know a lot of women who are younger than you but who sure in the hell *wished* they looked like you do, trust me on that. Is *that* your concern?"

"Well *duh.*"

"Mia, you are a woman who seems to know what you want and what you need, and to me that's exceptional. *Plus,* you are sexy as hell. And the cherry on top, is that you are smart as fuck. Intelligence is such a turn on. The thing is though, most intelligent women are simply *not* sexy, and definitely not sexy on *your* level. Look at you girl, *unh!* I mean you just *ooze* sex appeal. And then you got that sass on top too? *Bam!*" he told her looking her up and down.

"Oh, stop it."

"Dems the facts. Mmm hmm," he said gesturing with his palm upwards.

"Well damn, there go those "chips" still falling, huh?

"And ain't nothing wrong with that. I don't have a problem with it do you?"

"No, not at all, just an observation Mister Man."

The rain started coming down harder. The wind picked up as well, sending a box tumbling that hit the shop's glass door startling Mia.

"Damn, the storm is coming in hard now. Let me stop running my mouth and get your paperwork done so you can get home."

Boom. Boom. Boom, Boom!

Thunder sounded and the lights flickered as soon as he spoke, leaving those words just hanging in the air. They looked at each other, both waiting apprehensively to see if there would be more, but the only sound to be heard was the pitter-patter of the rain dancing on the roof.

"Damn, you're right – but if you're so clairvoyant, can you pick the winning Lotto numbers for me so I can retire and travel now?" Mia joked.

Javier laughed and continued working on Mia's invoice. He looked over and saw Mia shiver a little.

"Kinda chilly huh? Let me bring the space heater out of the back room, be right back.

Mia walked to the window and watched the rain. Javier came back in, plugged it in, and the heat began circulating.

"It has a really short cord unfortunately, so you will need to come closer to get warm. You look like you may need some uh ... warmth," he told her with a smirk.

"I am too old to be afraid of you Javier. Besides, you wouldn't do anything to me that I didn't *want* you to, of that I am quite sure, because you are a gentleman," Mia told him as she began walking over to his desk.

Javier nodded in agreement, but still cocked his head to one side with a smirk on his face. Mia shook her head as she walked around his desk to get closer to the heater, and Javier found himself unable to take his eyes off of her. She felt him staring and turned around to face him.

"Are you undressing me with your eyes Mister Man? 'Because I almost feel naked right now with that look on your face."

"And if I were, and I answered yes, how would that make you feel?" Javier asked standing up to make room for her by the space heater.

"I'm good with it, I just hope you like what your imagination is showing you is all."

"Just so you know, I may be younger and all, but I do know what I like, and most *definitely* what I want," Javier said as his eyes first traveled down, then slowly back up to her face, gazing intensely into Mia's eyes.

Mia looked surprised raising her eyebrows, but before she could respond, Javier told her, "I'm going into the next room to get your invoice off the printer, excuse me please."

Mia merely nodded as she was barely able to swallow let alone speak. Trying to step out of the way, Mia backed right into Javier at the same moment thunder boomed again making her jump. Instinctively Javier embraced her, "You okay?" he asked but did not let go.

"I will be, seems I have someone protecting me."

Unable to resist, Javier softly kissed the back of Mia's neck, sending ripples down her spine. Reflexively reaching back, Mia's hands found his thighs and pulled him closer. Javier did not miss a beat, as his hands squeezed her ass, then slowly began traveling up under her sweater.

Mia's heart rate continued to climb by the second in anticipation of that first touch of Javier's hands on her breasts; her breathing quickly became labored. Javier's hands continued their ascent, expertly unhooking Mia's bra on the way to their destination. Simultaneously, he snaked one hand under her sweater cupping her left breast, as the other softly but firmly pulled her head back by grabbing a handful of hair. With more of her neck exposed, Javier wasted no time continuing his passionate assault on her neck. Mia was melting under his touch.

He turned her around and pushed her back and down in one motion; she was now sitting on his desk. Her full, brown breasts were mouth level. He pushed her bra and sweater up, and slowly began kissing them. Mia could barely catch her breath. With a breast in each hand, Javier unleashed the full power of his carnal appetite over both of them. She pulled her sweater off over her head, then flung her bra to the floor. Javier never stopped. He delighted in squeezing and kissing her full breasts, then softly sucking on one of her nipples. He increased his intensity of his oral loving as he softly nibbled, first one, then the other, over, and over, and over.

"Definitely in the mood for Hershey Kisses, are we? Looks like you're a breast man then?" Mia breathlessly asked.

Looking up at her, Javier smiled, grabbing both round brown breasts in his hands and shaking them, "Absolutely, and your breasts are fucking amazing Mia. You have no idea how long I've fantasized about being able to do this."

"And how does it compare to those fantasies?" Mia raspingly whispered to him.

"Not that great."

Mia looked away feeling a little dismayed.

"Mia, what I mean is, my fantasies did *not* do justice to what I am actually experiencing for real. They are beautiful, and so responsive," he said then lightly nibbled on one of her nipples, making Mia close her eyes and shudder from the pleasure/pain derived from Javier's teeth and tongue.

"See? I love it," he said, then softly kissed that nipple before sucking on the other one, stretching it a bit outward before his mouth finally let it go, then looked up at Mia.

"If you love it so much, then don't ever stop," she told him grabbing him by the hair and pulling his face back into her breasts.

Javier picked up right where he left off causing Mia's internal meltdown to continue.

Javier stopped, then stood up and pulled his t-shirt and hoodie off over his head revealing a smooth, lean, and delicious, milk-chocolate body, with a sexy, flat stomach. Mia kicked off her short boots, then got off the desk but when she tried to stand in the small space behind his desk, she stumbled and fell into his chair. At that precise moment, the electricity died, and the lights flickered off, leaving them in complete darkness. Stunned, they both froze for a moment. Javier quickly grabbed his phone, flipped it upside down, then turned the flashlight feature on.

"Well look at you MacGyver. *Clever*," Mia said laughing.

"Now check this Ol' School shit out right here," Javier said as walked over and grabbed a boom box out of the bottom drawer in his file cabinet.

"See? People always have jokes about my shit, but it's coming in handy right about now. A brotha keeps fresh batteries too, just for such situations," he said winking as he hit play.

The Commodores *Brick House* came on as he sat it on the counter.

They both laughed as Javier said, "Well, see? They know, 'cause they sure ain't wrong babygirl - you got it going *on*."

As he walked back around to his desk, Mia swiveled around in his chair to face him, "Well, well, well, look what we have here," she said as she began untying the drawstring on his pants.

Excitedly Javier said, "Well let me help a sista out why don't I?"

"Yes, why *don't* you?" Mia asked seductively looking up at him.

This time it was Javier whose heart was racing and who was finding it impossible to swallow. He accomplished pushing his underwear down along with his pants in one push, breathing heavily, his eyes closed in anticipation.

"Mmm. I do love gummy worms," Mia told him wrapping her fingers around his rapidly hardening dick.

"Do you now? I have one for you. Sure, am hoping that you will like it."

"Mmm. Trust me, I do. But you know, my daddy always said talk is cheap, so ..." she said right before she began softly licking the bottom of the shaft, then slowly working her way up.

Javier had a strong intake of breath and held onto the counter with one hand to steady himself, as he looked down while Mia swirled her tongue around the head of his dick, then slowly engulfed it and just held it in her mouth. He could feel her tongue softly lashing against it.

Mia pulled back and looked up at him, "Just so ya know, I really enjoy doing this, and I am more of a giver than a taker in this realm," she told him before resuming her oral aerobics right where she had left off.

Javier found his voice and breathlessly told her, "I'm seeing that you are, and oh – *oh,* feeling that you do. Damn Mia. This feels so good. Oh. My. God. *Mia.*"

With the fairly diminished lighting, Javier's vision was limited, and only increased his sensitivity. Mia slowly engulfed his dick, inch by inch, and as her saliva dribbled down the side, she slowly began stroking him in rhythm with her sucking. Her oral skills were incredible, and the desire for him to be deep inside of her was intensely growing. His hand found its way back into her hair, softly but firmly grabbing a handful to help increase her tempo until he could take no more.

"Mia, I love what you're doing to me. It feels *so* good, but I want to be inside of you so bad," he told her, his voice having grown husky.

Mia looked up, pulling his dick out of her mouth, and with full eye contact, licked him from his balls all the way to the tip before asking, "Are you sure you want me to stop?"

By now Javier's dick was so hard, he was surprised that Mia could not hear it throbbing. Before he could answer, she stuck the head back into her mouth, swirling her tongue slowly around and around, then softly sucking on it before pulling it back out. She slowly looked up at him for the answer. Their eyes met and locked. Silently, in almost one fluid motion, Javier quickly pulled her up to standing, turned her around, and bent her over on his desk. It happened so fast that Mia had to catch her breath.

"Talk is cheap, the lady says," Javier told her as he reached around unbuttoning and unzipping her jeans.

Mia stood up straight and began trying to help Javier pull the jeans down over her hips. She was only able to get her right leg out, leaving her jeans crumpled around her left foot, as Javier bent her back over his desk.

"So ... you ready for me Mia?" Javier whispered in her ear then began kissing her neck again.

"You tell me Javier, am I"? Mia answered reaching back to pull his thighs closer. Javier pushed forward and slowly rubbed his throbbing dick against her slit, finding it smooth, hot, and oh, so very wet.

"Mmm Mia, so smooth and wet. So much better than all the times I have ever, *ever* imagined. Damn woman," Javier's deep voice reverberated near her ear.

"I think you found the answer to your question. But you just gotta wiggle it a little bit," she breathlessly told him, while rotating her hips and backing onto him.

Javier grabbed her hips, wiggled a little, found the sweet spot, and with one hard thrust, slammed it home.

"Aahh. Oh, *fuck*. Javier moaned.

"*Yessss*. Oh, damn Javier," Mia breathlessly replied.

"This has been building for such a long time, but it was so worth waiting for."

"Timing is everything," Javier said picking up speed as Mia slammed back into him, over and over. He reached around grabbing a breast and pinching a nipple. He continued his pounding, and though she tried to hold herself back, she found that she could not, and was pushed over the edge.

"I tried to wait for you, but damn, you feel so good, I just couldn't wait."

"I love it, I absolutely *fucking*, love it. I love making you cum Mia. I want to make you cum over and over again. Don't ever stop."

After a few more strokes, he pulled out, flipped her around and sat her back on his desk. He pushed papers out of the way, and they fell to the floor. He grabbed her by the hips and pulling her towards him then penetrated her again. Mia wrapped her legs around his waist. He held her by the back, "I got you lady, you're not falling or going *anywhere*, I promise you that," he whispered in her ear as he slowly began moving in and out again.

"I have fantasized fucking you for so long, you don't even know. You're such a sexy, motherfucker, you know *that*? Do you know that, Mia? Unh, it feels so good to finally be inside of you," he breathlessly said in her ear.

Mia began nibbling on his neck, which added more fuel to his fire that was already burning white hot.

"Damn I'm so close Mia, too damn close. I don't want it to ever end, it just feels too good."

"Come on, give it to me. Fuck me. Fuck me *hard* Javier."

Her words made Javier do just that, and he instantly increased the tempo and intensity.

Clink. Clank. Clink. Clank. Clink.

The increased intensity from their pounding, sent car keys in the box sitting on Javier's desk clattering to the floor.

Clunk. Clunk. Clunk. Clunk.

A few clipboards joined the keys finding their way to the floor as well. Javier and Mia never slowed down.

"I don't think I can hold on anymore ... it feels too good, but I'm trying."

"No, *no*. Please don't hold back. Cum for me one more time Mia. I always want to make you cum," he breathlessly told her, then pulling her head back by her hair, he smothered his face in her neck.

"Come on Mia, give me one more," he whispered in her ear.

"I can if you show me how much *you* wanted it. Come on Javier, show me. I want it. Give it to me, fuck me hard Javier," Mia whispered in his ear before biting the lobe.

"Oh Mia. Can't. Hold. Back. Anymore. *Oh Mia!*" Javier moaned loudly.

Hearing him calling out her name sent Mia over the edge, joining Javier's explosion.

Their bodies hot and slick with sweat, Javier blew on Mia's chest to cool her, gingerly brushing her hair back with his fingers. Breathing heavily, they both worked on catching their breath.

Shaking his head in disbelief, "Oh my God woman."

"Yeah, that was something else, wow. Well, I guess I am officially a Cougar now," Mia said laughing.

"Well, *I ain't mad at 'cha*," Javier said laughing before kissing her softly on her décolleté.

Finally, their breathing slowed down to normal and Mia got off the desk.

"Well, babycakes, your desk will never be the same, and what in the hell did we just break?" Mia asked looking intensely over at the desk.

Javier laughed, "Oh nothing broke, it was some keys that fell down, that's all...we're gonna have to find them all though," he said laughing.

"I'll help you, but probably best to get dressed first, ya think?" she asked lightly slapping Javier on the ass.

Mia looked at Javier while scrambling to find her clothes, "Wow. Man, that was beyond intense."

"I knew it would be, I've always felt it," Javier said her handing her his phone with the flashlight.

"Don't want you to trip on anything, gotta protect all *that*," he said as she walked by her, this time he slapped *her* on the ass.

"Hey."

"I give as good as I get Miss Lady. That *is* some good stuff right there," he said laughing as she walked away.

After dressing in the bathroom and a little clean up, Mia walked back into the office about to hand him his phone when the power magically came back on.

"Great. Now it's my turn," Javier said as he grabbed his phone and walked to the bathroom.

Mia slipped into her boots, then began attempting to straighten up the mess they had both made of his desk.

Javier quickly returned, "It's okay Mia, I can get it."

"Well, it *does* take two to tango, so I'm down to do my part," she replied as she continued to pick up the strewn papers from his desk.

Javier looked at her body language, then walked over to her. She looked up and they both stopped and stared at each other. Mia shook her head and looked down.

"What? What are you thinking right now?" Javier asked, taking her head in his hands.

He stared into her eyes, "Tell me Mia."

"I'm a horrible person. I should have never done this."

"So... so you didn't like it?" Javier asked apprehensively.

"You're kidding, *right*? I feel bad because, well I know that what I did was so wrong. But I would be lying if I told you that I didn't like it. If you hadn't noticed, my body seemed to fucking love it. How many orgasms did I need to have for you to know this?"

"Okay, I'll give you that."

"All I know is, that was some great sex, and we weren't even comfortable in a bed."

Javier grabbed her by the ass, pulled her to him and gave her a big hug.

"Mia, but just don't tell me that was it though. Please don't tell me that was the only time we will ever do this."

"It should be."

"That's not what I asked. I'm already looking forward to you sharing that caramel brown body with me again."

"Lord help me because I can't tell you that I won't. My mind tells me it's the right thing to tell you no, that this was a one-time thing, but the rest of me, well..."

"Well?"

"I just can't honestly say right now that I will never do it again, but I am going to *try* to be good," she told him while wrapping her arms around him.

Javier pulled her face up towards him, "Better be careful now, because *your* definition of good and my definition are apparently two different things. Saying you are going to be good means to me, that you will be back and fuck my brains out again, and again, and again. *That's* what "good" is to me. And yes - I am hoping sooner rather than later Mia. I fucking loved it, and I can't wait to fuck you again."

Words escaped her so Mia burrowed her head in his chest and held him tight. Javier held her back and they stood there in that silent, tight embrace for a few seconds.

53

"Okay we better find those keys before the lights go back out again, and I'm on it," Mia told him as she got down on her knees and found 3 keys underneath the desk.

Javier picked up a few keys near the heater.

"Well, my desk is definitely christened now as well as my chair, but there *are* more rooms," Javier told her with a wink.

"You are just terrible," Mia said throwing one more key to him.

"You know the thought of that turns you on a little."

Mia looked over at him then slanted her eyes, "If it does, I'm not telling."

"Girl, you better watch it, or you will be facing round two. Let me give you your invoice and get you outta here, or I can't be held responsible for my actions."

Mia laughed, "Yes, I do need to get going, but this was the best diversion, *ever.*"

Mia paid Javier, then headed for the door. Neither one could stop smiling. She stopped before opening the door, then glanced back over her shoulder, "I will be in touch."

"And if you don't, I will," Javier told her suggestively licking his lips.

That night would be the first time of many at the shop. It was also the first domino to fall in the chain of many stolen moments, and many more secret rendezvous times, filled with intense ecstasy and great desire. Javier's shop and office seemed to be a challenge that they so often embraced. They found a way to "christen" pretty much each, and every room.

IV

It began slowly, once every few months or so. Quite unexpectedly, Mia's father passed away, sending her into a tailspin and making her feel extremely mortal. From then on, she decided that until the day she joined her father on the other side, when an opportunity presented itself to bring her joy, happiness, or pleasure, she was going to take it. More often than not, the opportunity which presented itself for pleasure, was Javier.

After several "shop visit's", Javier mentioned how much more comfortable it would be in her bed, and so it began in earnest. At first, it was about once a month. Their sex was so good, it seemed the more they had, the more they craved. Their *secret rendezvous* times became more and more frequent until it was weekly, sometimes twice in a week if they were lucky. It was as if they just could not get enough of each other, and if their schedules allowed it, they took advantage of it. They were incapable of staying away from each other.

It was more than their great sex though; their connection was indescribable. That unique bond between the two of them only continued to intensify with each passing week. They found themselves to be cut from the same cloth as it were. They were both *grinders* – those who never stopped working until they accomplished exactly what was needed to get done. Both of them had goals for financial security in real estate, and neither one had ever given up on those dreams over the years. They had different skill sets, yet they complemented each other extremely well.

They were both the total package as it were, but there was the factor of timing - Javier already belonged to someone else. He had long outgrown her in addition to him being taken for granted, especially for his income. Javier was not merely a good man or a father, he was a good person. For the life of her, Mia simply could not understand how he was not appreciated more or treated with the love and compassion he deserved at home. It was his life though. He was a grown ass man after all. He continued to stay, and this was the reality of the situation.

Unfortunately for Mia though, this reality also meant that he could not be hers, now, or probably ever. It was highly doubtful that they would ever be that great power couple which often seemed to be their destiny, but then again, you just never know. Mia accepted these facts, but also weighed it against how extremely short life really is. She remained true to her decision, that not only should you find as much joy and pleasure as you can in life, but you should find it *as often* as you can. It went against her values, but at this time in her life, she decided to do what felt good to *her*, and to ride that wave until it crashed against the shore. No way of knowing when or if the day would come when Javier's seeming fascination with her would come to an end. He too was riding his own wave - having his cake and eating it too, but without having any idea when, or if, Mia would ever tire of their arrangement. If those stolen moments and limited time to spend with him was no longer enough for her and would force her to let him go.

They both realized those facts but never vocalized them, instead, they instinctively chose to continue along the path they found themselves on. The proverbial chips continued to fall - tumbling down without either of them knowing when or where they would eventually land. Weeks turned to months, and months into a few years of unequaled ecstasy and passion. But change being the only constant thing in this life, events from work to family slowly seized control, and their *secret rendezvous* times began slowing down, becoming father and farther apart.

They went from weekly, to bi-monthly, then monthly, and then even less than that. It became quality over quantity, because their times together were always, *always* fucking fantastic. There were various reasons from work schedules to family issues on both sides, but Mia sensed there was also some other dynamic going on, perhaps with his wife. Javier told her it would be hard to only be friends with her if their special relationship ever ended. Mia did not understand why but felt it would be unfortunate. The thought of it saddened her, but she respected his feelings. One day after a lull between them, she stopped by the shop after hours. The door was still unlocked, and he looked up from his desk surprised to see her, his luminous blue eyes glowing.

"Hey Mia," he said smiling, looking happy to see her.

Mia was equally glad to see him, "Hey Javier, we really need to talk. I need to know what's going on," she told him taking on a serious tone.

Javier slumped back in his chair, "I know. I'm sorry for my lack of communication. Let's talk, sit down."

She pulled a chair up to his desk so they could have a heart to heart. They were always honest with each other, *always*.

"So, I agreed to try counseling with Maria. We have gone twice, but it's not helping, maybe even the contrary. I wasn't sure how to tell you. It's making me question quite a bit within myself to be honest. I am trying not to let it overwhelm me, but it ain't easy," he told her looking down and shaking his head.

Hearing those words broke her heart as well as being the breaking point for Mia.

"Javier, I never knew when or if this day would come. I want you to know that I wish you the best if this is what you truly want. I honestly think that this thing we do, it has to come to an end in order to give yourself a full chance to see if you can save your marriage. As much as I will miss this, and you know I will, it looks like it is time to go back to our business relationship, if that's even possible at this point," Mia said sadly but with resolve.

Javier remained silent and just shook his head in disbelief.

"It is unfortunate for me that you told me that you would not really want to be friends without being able to be the way we are, or *were,* I should say. I had hoped we could form that LLC one day soon, but it is what it is," Mia told him with a heavy sigh.

"I don't know what to say Mia, maybe you're right, but I'm really not so sure."

"Well, we both know it's *always* great when we are together, but lately I feel a distance that seems to be growing. Maybe the lack of communication is because you may feel torn. I have always appreciated your honesty, but lately communication has been, I don't know, murky?" she asked with a shrug.

"Yeah, it probably has been. Definitely not my intention."

"Yes, I know. But it kind of makes me feel taken for granted, and I absolutely *hate* that feeling. I cannot and will not allow that to ever happen to me again. I realize that you are probably confused with your situation, but that is why communication is vital. That is why I came by, so we could sort this out, face to face."

"Oh Mia, no, that would *never* be my intention. I'm really, *really* sorry if I have done anything has made you feel that way, or if maybe I kind of - damn, *did* I take you for granted?" he rhetorically asked, looking at her intently.

Mia shrugged and shook her head, looking sad.

"Damn I did. I didn't mean to, please believe me. Mia, you are the *last* person that I would want to make feel that way. You definitely don't deserve that at all. I am *so* sorry Mia, really. I *never* meant to do that," he told her looking down and ashamed.

"I appreciate you telling me this. It's just that for me, without clear communication, it's hard to know, and you know that I do not like going around not knowing," Mia solemnly said.

"Yes, I do know, and again I apologize Mia. My communication skills have been lacking, no doubts there. You are right, I have been confused, but should have let you know where my head was."

"I can imagine it's been hard for you with this juggling act you have been doing with me for a while. I'm thinking those chips have finally landed, and if not, they are hovering pretty damn close to the ground," she said throwing up her hands and hunching her shoulders.

Javier just sat there silent, words escaping him.

"You know that I would never want to be the reason you leave right? Only *you* will know when and if leaving is what you need for your soul. For *you*. Not to be with another, but to allow yourself to become whole again. And only you will know when it's over and it's time to move on. But, it's also best that if you do decide to go, that you know you gave it your all, and have no regrets," she said as she traced her fingers along his goatee, then softly kissed him on those sexy lips.

Javier sat there remaining silent and unable to move.

"I have been down this road before, remember? I have walked this path, so I really do understand how you are probably feeling at times. But listen, sometimes things get heated, strained, just downright impossible, so if you ever find yourself in that predicament, no matter what time of the day or night, call me, and you can always stay in one of my spare bedrooms."

"Damn, that is very righteous of you, I appreciate that offer more than you know."

"My offer is on an unconditional basis. Look Javier, sometimes when things like that happen, you just don't really have the energy or desire to talk to anyone, let alone explain your situation, you know? You can think of it like a "Safe House" situation - no demands, no explanations, and no judgments. Before anything else happened, we had built a pretty strong foundation on friendship, right? I truly believe that this is why we have such a deep level of intimacy, and I would like to think that facet of our relationship will *always* remain intact, even if the rest fades away," Mia told him gazing intently into his aqua eyes.

"I...I don't even know what to say right now, besides thank you Mia. You are an amazing woman, and I feel fortunate for what we have shared. Honestly, I cherish it."

"As do I, and like most everything else, we are aligned on this fact as well. It's like that line from one of Tina Turner's songs about time easing the pain and something beautiful still remains. I really believe that what our friendship evolved into, however morally wrong it may have been, was a *symptom* of what was wrong with your marriage, but *not* the cause. I've told you before, I'm not a one in a million, type of woman – I'm a *once in a lifetime* type of woman. So, you know, *how* in the world could you have resisted me? Me being the best wife you've never had and whatnot," Mia said fluttering her eyelashes and laughing.

"Hmm, you know, I'm thinking that is pretty damn accurate."

"Undoubtedly," she said with a wink and a smile.

"So then, it's looking like it's time for us to continue on our paths without doing that "thang" that we've been doing, as much as I will miss our stolen moments and secret rendezvous times. Whether our paths can intersect again at all is going to be up to you. As much as it pains me, and please trust me on this one, it does more than you can *ever* know - it just feels that this is the right thing to do, well, given where you are right now."

"Mia, I don't know what to do or say. So, what are you saying - that you're *leaving* me?"

"It no longer matters what I may have begun wanting or telling myself that maybe I could have, the fact is, that you were never really mine to have *or* to leave Javier."

Javier sat there pensive and looking sad. They sat in silence for a few moments.

"Well damn, I don't think there is anything I can say that would stop the way things are going at this point. It looks like your mind is made up, and part of me knows that you are probably right, but I'm having a hard time accepting this," Javier told her slumping down in his chair.

"I'm just reading the writing on the wall Javier; I would be a fool not to. I understand where you are and what you may need to do."

Javier sat there silently, slowly nodding yes. Mia got up and pushed her chair back to its place. She walked back around to Javier's desk, then bent over and softly kissed his forehead. He looked up and she found herself unable to resist those full sexy lips of his and gave him one more soulful kiss. She turned to walk away, but he grabbed her by the arm and pulled her back. Without uttering any words, he quickly stood up and hugged her hard and tight. Reluctantly, he released his embrace after a few moments to let her go.

"I always say there are those endless possibilities, right?"

"Right."

"And at this point, neither one of us knows what the future may bring. If we are meant to be together, we will re-connect, the universe will see to it that it happens. But then again, there is more of a chance that we have already served the purposes for which we crossed each other's paths.

"Mia I ... I don't know what to say."

Mia walked over to the small magazine table, grabbed her purse, then turned and said, "You know how to find me. Take some time, who knows? You may eventually decide that leaving is what is best for you, but like I said, only *you* can make that decision - no one else. If that ends up being the case, after you get grounded again, you might find yourself missing a sista one of these days. Maybe we might decide on trying to see if what we have is still there. Only time will tell, but right now, it seems that there is a good chance that you are right where you need to be."

"I just can't bring myself to say goodbye," Javier told her sighing heavily. He rested his chin in his hands and sadly looked up at Mia.

"It's because it's not goodbye, it is only, *see you later*," Mia told him.

"I just can't bear the thought of no longer seeing you anymore, and most especially not making love to your sexy body anymore. Damn. I know everything that you are telling me is right. I just never wanted to hear those words because of what would happen *after* they were spoken."

"It is what it is Javier, but look, we have given each other priceless gifts, and like I said before, I will always cherish the times we have spent together. My life has been enhanced by our relationship, and I will keep that with me always. I hope you feel the same."

Nodding yes, Javier quietly replied, "You already know."

Mia slung her purse on her shoulder, grabbed her keys and walked to the door.

She turned back, "Take care of yourself Sexy Man."

"You take care of yourself too, Sexy Woman."

She blew him a kiss, then gave him one last wink before opening the door and walking out. This time she did not look back. That was nearly four months ago. She did get a long text a month or so later, saying he was back East helping to take care of his brother who had fallen ill. They texted a bit back and forth sporadically, but he spoke nothing of their *secret rendezvous* times, so in turn, Mia did not mention them either. They seemed to be friends again, contrary to what Javier had told her.

Mia had found it extremely difficult in the beginning - no longer being able to call, text, Messenger, or see Javier anymore. Those long, and often fascinating conversations were to be no more, so it would seem. As the days passed, she found herself missing the sound of his sexy voice, and even more, missing that indescribable feeling from the chemistry they generated. The void from his absence ran much deeper than she ever imagined would even be possible.

Her body missed his touch, his kiss, his unrelenting passion. She ached too, from missing the best sex she had ever consistently had; it was hard to get through, but she had no choice not to. The days slowly morphed into weeks, the weeks into months, and the depth of the void from his absence in her life began to grow shallower. Maybe those chips they once sent falling had finally landed, then again, maybe not. At this point in time though, only the universe knew their true paths. As she so often said, *time will tell.*

Not supposed to get into heavy thoughts, but oh well too late, Mia thought as she ordered another bloody mary from the kiosk. The only thing in life that is consistent is change, and if you do not adapt, you can get lost and lose your way. Mia decided to keep an open mind and take it as it comes, that was really the only way to view things, as a whole anyway. And although no one person may know what the future will bring, Mia *did* know that she must keep *on keepin' on.* She still had so much work to do if she was ever going to achieve the goals that she had set for herself, which would in turn, allow her to live her dreams. And Mia *had* to do it, because no one and nothing else was going to do it for her.

Fully back to reality after having been lost in the *Land of Javier,* Mia became aware of her surroundings once again.

"Spicy, Stoli bloody mary?" a different server asked.

"Yes, thank you. Sign the kiosk again, right?"

"Yes please, thank you. Anything else I can get you?"

"I'm good for now, thank you."

"Very good then, enjoy," she said walking away.

Mia took a few long sips and began working on her erotica novel, jotting ideas down about a beach fantasy. She found it enjoyable to sometimes write by hand, the old-fashioned way. She got lost for quite some time in her writing, sending her mind off on a different track.

Maybe it was the sun, maybe it was that second spicy bloody mary that she was sipping, but she began having an uneasy feeling that that she was being watched. She turned her head slightly to the left. Diagonally, a few hundred feet away on the patio, under a red umbrella emblazoned with *Cinzano* in white lettering, an older gentleman sat alone sipping a drink. Their eyes met, he nodded, then raised his glass in a toast to her. She could not help but to smile. In response, Mia returned the gesture, nodding and lifting her drink in their now joint mock toast. He smiled this time, showing a flash of white teeth. He had full lips, with a close shaved, well-manicured, and brilliant white beard. His thick, lustrous locks matched in hue. It appeared he had been spending some time at the beach, as his hair was a nice contrast to his smooth olive, tanned skin. Hmm, very striking. I wonder what *his* story is Mia mused. The author in her soul almost began making a storyline for the *Mystery Man*, but she chose to just allow her mind to relax for once.

Chance meetings.

Drawn together by an irresistible force.

Serendipity or synchronicity?

Smoldering passion
intensifying to white hot flames.

Skin anticipating his touch.

Body hungering for his.

Heart pounding.

Breath catching.

My body wanting to feel,
his kisses,
his caresses,
his tongue.

I overflow in anticipation,
of pleasures yet to come.

GIOVANNI

I

Taking a brisk walk in the surf had been one of Mia's better ideas of the day she decided; it felt absolutely, phenomenal. The surf and sand seemed to nourish her very soul. The beach at sunset though, now *that,* was Mia's very favorite thing in the world. Above all, her heart felt happy thinking of how blessed she was to be Marquis' and Russell's mom. So many thoughts began running in and out of her mind as she trekked along the surf.

For so many years, she had been relegated to a life playing dual roles of mom and dad. She was always at home, if not at one of the boy's school or sport activities. Looking back, she had absolutely no regrets whatsoever for having sacrificed her personal life in order to *raise* two men, instead of trying to find one for herself. In an attempt to offset her lack of a personal life, she had begun writing erotic stories of a fantasy life she would like to lead herself. With her recently found freedom, she decided that she would now be open to doing more things like the heroine in her stories, Cassandra.

She could remember back in the day, being like one of those hard-bodied women out there on the beach in bikinis. All those years of modern and jazz dance, plus years of bike riding and roller skating until she had to come in before it got dark, (saving her from an ass whoopin' from her mama), had served her well though. Even at this age, her long, brown legs were firm. Still, she did possess a modicum of modesty, and chose to wear a sarong tied over her hips. Thanks, Mama, for the great genes though she thought with a smile.

People were beginning to thin out as dinner time was fast approaching, and for that, Mia was grateful. As she began walking back to her chaise, she looked over at the red umbrella where the *Mystery Man* was sitting earlier, but he was no longer there. What the hell was I thinking, she laughed to herself. A 56-year-old woman with a mature body might be a distraction, but not likely to keep someone's attention for too long.

The Tiki torches from the hotel were being lit as sunset was fast approaching. Mia returned to her chaise, sat on the end, and placing her hands palms face up on top of her knees, tried to feel the energy of the day ending and the night beginning. She sat there watching the ebb and flow of the surf and began feeling a bit mesmerized by it all, when she felt a presence looming close. At that same moment, what was left of the sun became mostly blocked, snapping her out of her trance-like state. Coming into focus was the *Mystery Man*, who was now standing almost directly in front of her. He was wearing white gauze pants, a white gauze shirt slightly unbuttoned with the sleeves rolled up, and beige suede loafers. He was a striking image against the impending sunset.

She looked up as he smiled and said, "Hello, I am Giovanni. I was hoping that you might be returning to your spot. Are you a guest at the hotel as well my dear?"

"Possibly," Mia replied dryly, peering at him over the top of her sunglasses.

"I know you were no doubt taught *not* to speak to strangers, but I assure you that I am not too dangerous – I bite but I have had *all* of my shots."

Mia tried not to roll her eyes. Javier had used that same line; maybe it was a standard pick up line for a guy? Must have been that second bloody mary which made her humor him and go with the flow though, "You don't say? I'm Mia," she noncommittally replied, while quickly giving him a more thorough going over top to bottom.

It was great that he could not see her eyes scrutinizing him from behind her mirrored sunglasses.

Giovanni held out his hand, "Well I am quite happy to meet your acquaintance Ms. Mia."

As Mia held out her hand to shake his, he swooped down and kissed her hand politely. "My, oh my, a gentleman - and quite a smoothy I might add," she said with a slight smirk.

"Well, the rare times that I see something or someone substantial enough to attract my attention, I try to not let that be a missed opportunity. For what? Who even knows? But *always* worth inquiring is my school of thought. I hope you do not find me too direct Ms. Mia, but I find it unwise that by a certain age, one does not know what one likes, wants, or needs," he politely told her.

"As a matter of fact, I appreciate a man, or actually *anyone* who speaks what is on their mind," Mia spiritedly replied.

"Well, to the point you just made, and not to be completely forward, but looking at your hand, I do not see a ring. I would be dishonest if I told you that I was not in hopes that this symbolizes you are single and not otherwise committed," he said gesturing with praying hands.

Mia sat there silent and aloof. She zoned out as thoughts swirled about in her head while Giovanni continued talking. Where is he going to take this, she wondered? Well, it certainly is a different approach, I will give him that she thought. As she continued sitting there, mute but somewhat listening, he continued speaking, seeming intent on engaging her in the conversation. His tenacity made her begin to dig the fact that she had taken up so much space in his mind. Bonus points given for the *cojones* he had, summoning up the courage to approach her and tell her exactly what he was thinking about her.

Mia tuned back into the conversation.

"And if that is the case, of which you can tell I am wishing for, I am in great hopes that you might bestow the honor of accepting my sincere invitation to dine with me this evening, here at the hotel?" Giovanni asked nodding his head respectfully.

"Hmm... do you *always* ask strange women you meet on beaches out to dinner?"

Gesturing to his hand, "By the way, I noticed that *you* are not wearing a ring either, and so I pose the same question to you?" Mia asked raising her sunglasses above her eyes.

"From your reply then, I think that the answer I was hoping for is yes."

A slow smile spread over Mia's face.

"Tenacious. I *like* it," she said nodding towards him.

Pushing her sunglasses atop her head, she squinted her big brown eyes with a mock disapproving look before continuing, "You do realize that I could be an assassin? Or a spy? For God's sakes man, I could even be an alien sent down to earth to take over *your* world and take *you* to my leader. In other words, I could be quite the *dangerous woman* you know. Perhaps you should be afraid, *quite* afraid. So, my dear sir, how about you enlighten me - are you just very brave, or just very curious?"

Giovanni smiled.

"I would say it is both. And just so you know, I am *especially* brave. If I *am* to suffer at your hands, I will take the punishment valiantly Ms. Mia. Also, full disclosure, I am not married or otherwise committed," Giovanni answered, nodding once again in Mia's direction.

Digging on his sharp wit and surprisingly feeling a connection with this stranger, Mia began nodding her head and replied, "Hmmm, I see."

"And, if you answer yes to meeting me for dinner this evening, I will answer any, and all questions you may have now, or possibly think of later. How does eight o'clock at the steakhouse sound Ms. Mia?" Giovanni asked slyly.

Her inner voice spoke up:

So, what would Cassandra do? He is presenting you with your first opportunity girl, what the hell are you waiting for? Damn,

71

Mia took a deep breath, "Well, *I* would be dishonest if I told you that you have not piqued my interest, and that does *not,* happen often. Besides, my witch like sixth sense is not indicating that you are a serial killer, nor stalker material, so yes, Mr. Giovanni, I will meet you at eight o'clock for dinner," Mia said her head cocked to one side and eyes slanted.

"Thank you, Ms. Mia. I am quite looking forward to dining with you this evening."

Their eyes met and locked.

"I will be seeing you later then," Mia said as she grabbed her towel and beach tote.

As she rose to stand up, Giovanni offered his hand to assist her, then adeptly caught her fall as she stumbled getting her flip flops on.

"How embarrassing, but thank you, Giovanni."

"Not a problem my dear."

Their eyes met once again, and time stood still for a few seconds.

Buzz. Buzz. Buzz. Buzz.

Giovanni's cell phone vibrated at that very instant, snapping them both out of their momentary trance. He pulled his phone out of his pocket to answer it, so Mia turned to walk away. After only taking a single step, she heard him say,

"Do you mind holding a moment?"

Giovanni called out to her, "Ms. Mia, I do sincerely apologize, this is a business call that I have been waiting on all afternoon."

Mia stopped and turned back around, "No worries," she replied.

He continued, "I cannot put into words how much I am looking forward to dining with you this evening. You have captured my attention *and* my curiosity which is a rarity for me. But trust me my dear lady, you will have my undivided attention when again we meet."

Shaking her head and smiling, "Well that was the smoothest damn brush off to take a phone call *ever.* You go on ahead and handle your business, and I will meet you for dinner at eight. But be forewarned, I *will* have more questions, so get ready for me," Mia told him with a wink.

"That I will. Until eight, Bella Signora," he told her and waved.

Mia waved back and he remained staring after her before resuming his phone call. She turned around and began walking back to her room. Wow, what the hell just happened, she pondered with a huge smile on her way to the elevator. Did she just manifest this meeting, sitting on the beach earlier? The fact that it was totally unexpected only added to the excitement and anticipation.

Mia made it back to her room, threw all her stuff on the dresser, and lay back on the bed with a huge Cheshire Cat smile spreading across her face. What an unexpected twist; she loved the adrenaline pump stemming from looking forward to an evening out with a man. It had been far too long without it. She wondered how long Giovanni would be staying at the hotel, as she was only there for one more night. Another detail she planned to ask over dinner that evening.

She found herself floating in her clouds of thoughts once again, and nearly panicked when she glanced over at the clock. Just where in the hell had the last 40 minutes gone? She dashed to the bathroom and began running a bath, then grabbed her long black skirt with the sexy side split, and a V-neck leopard print top to wear. Just to think, she had almost not packed this outfit since she was flying solo on this trip. At that moment she was quite relieved that she listened to her inner voice telling her to add it at the last moment. Of course, being the *Shoe Diva* that she was, she had also packed a pair of black, sexy, high heeled sandals to go with. How could she not? If she *were* to wear the outfit, she would need them to compete the ensemble after all. The universe at work she decided.

As she sat soaking in the tub, Mia's mind began traveling down the all too familiar Mia's Fantasy Road. She could think of several erotica short stories she had written but never published, and how Giovanni would fit perfectly into a few of them. If only she were younger - oh wait, Giovanni was no spring chicken himself. That thought brought about a spirited laugh out loud.

Ooh, that delicious anticipatory feeling was completely enveloping her now, and she was enjoying it immensely. She got out, dried off, and slathered Kiehl's from head to toe. She decided to go light on the makeup - just liner, mascara, blush, and red matte lipstick. She fluffed her curls out into a sexy come-fuck-me look, then spritzed on a little Estee Lauder Pleasures. She stepped into the hallway, but just before closing the door, a thought went through her mind, so she stepped back inside to grab her purse.

She fished around, found, then opened her business card holder, but was immediately dismayed to see her that only her work business cards were inside. There were none from her website. She grabbed one anyway, thinking that there was a high possibility that she and Giovanni might really click. She had no idea what would happen, but an opportunity just might present itself. The heightened anticipation she was feeling continued, and it was absolutely exhilarating. She stuck the card in her pocket along with her room card and Driver's license, then quickly headed back out the door.

She got downstairs to the restaurant with about four minutes to spare. Giovanni was already there waiting. Well of course he would be there she thought, trying not to smile. He was standing near the entrance clad in navy slacks, a lavender shirt, and navy loafers. He looked quite pleased when he saw her walking towards him.

"*Bellisima*," he said smiling and flashing pearly white, perfect teeth.

"My, but don't you look lovely this evening Ms. Mia. Come this way. Our table is ready, but I wanted to wait here to see you walk in and greet you before escorting you to our table," he told her motioning with his arm to walk with him.

As they were heading towards the table, Giovanni walked closer to her, bent down, and whispered, "Although I must admit, watching you walk *away* a bit earlier was quite pleasurable as well."

Not missing a beat, Mia teased, "Well feel free to speak your mind now, you really *must* stop holding back so much Giovanni."

Giovanni smiled, "I will definitely keep that in mind. Now if you would follow me this way, please, we are almost there," he said motioning with his arm to bear to the right.

They arrived at the best table in the restaurant. Giovanni pulled out Mia's chair, but sat next to her instead of across from her. She wondered how long he had actually been there, as lying neatly across the back of one of the chairs on the other side of the table, was a navy jacket which matched his slacks.

Occupying the center of the table was an exquisite, clear crystal bowl, with white tealight candles and fresh, tiny, pink flowers, floating about in blue colored water. The table was situated smack in the middle of an enormous picture window; the view was to die for. The seascape of waves rolling onto the shore caught Mia's attention, and made her feel immediately at ease. The scenic Cypress trees and the waves crashing over the huge boulders was truly mesmerizing.

"Wow, this view is out of this world. I could just sit here and stare at it forever. Thank you for the dinner invitation Mr. Giovanni," Mia enthusiastically told him.

"I know this may be tired and quite cliché, but it's honest … the pleasure is *all* mine. Please trust me on this," Giovanni replied smiling at her delightedness.

Mia looked over at him and smiled back.

"By the way, you smell delicious," he said with a wink.

"Why thank you, and your scent is quite intoxicating as well," Mia quipped back.

"Ooh, intoxicating, is it? I am seriously considering scooting closer then, so that you can become *truly* inebriated Ms. Mia," Giovanni said with raised eyebrows.

Pursing her lips, Mia cocked her head to one side staring at Giovanni, grooving on their chemistry.

As if reading her mind, "I am feeling that we are pretty evenly matched in wit, would you not agree?"

Mia did not utter a single word. She just raised one eyebrow and looked at him, then gave him a slow wink.

The waiter approached just at that moment.

"Good evening, I am Walter, and will be your waiter for the evening. May I get you something to drink or some appetizers to start with?"

"I would like water with a slice of lemon, but haven't quite decided on a drink as yet, thank you," Mia answered.

"Yes, I will have the same," Giovanni replied and then turning to Mia, "As dangerous as it may be, I am going to assume that you enjoy champagne, yes?"

"Yes, you have guessed correctly my dear sir."

"Wonderful. We will also have a bottle of Cristal, the fruit and cheese platter, and two shrimp and crab cocktails for now, thank you very much," he told Walter.

"Very good sir," he said nodding then briskly walking away.

"Well now, good thing I am not allergic to shellfish. You *do* realize that you could have just ordered my death due to anaphylactic shock," Mia said throwing her hands up and rolling her eyes toward the ceiling feigning exasperation.

"Well, my dear, were you allergic, you strike me as the type of woman who has the sense to speak up. Brains *and* beauty are truly a powerful combination. In your case, possibly lethal I am thinking, but *oh*, what a way to go," Giovanni said decisively nodding his head.

"You know, I think there is a compliment hidden in there, so thank you. Now, as I recall, I was told that I would have free reign of questioning if I agreed to dinner, am I correct?"

Before Giovanni could answer, Walter was back with their water, champagne, and glasses. Another server laid out the fruit and cheese platter, as well as the seafood cocktails along with warm sourdough bread and butter. All very synchronized. Mia was quite impressed. After it was all set down and the champagne poured, Giovanni picked up his glass and motioned Mia to join him in a toast, "To California sunshine, beaches, and chance meetings."

Mia picked up her glass and added, "Good food, drink, and intriguing company," before clinking her glass to his.

They both took a sip, but Mia's nervousness made her take another. She drank half of the glass before she realized it. Giovanni discretely smiled.

"So, Giovanni, I have to say that although I find myself going with the flow here, I'm quite curious with all those young, nubile, hard bodies on the beach this afternoon, as to why you asked *me* to dinner. I mean, although it's flattering and all, you have *got* to admit, it seems a bit strange - *don't ya think*?" Mia asked squinting.

"Feel free to call me Gio, Giovanni is quite a mouthful."

"*Touché.*"

"Indeed."

Shaking his head and smiling, Giovanni picked up where Mia had left off.

"Hmm. Strange you say, how so? In what way?"

"Seriously? Come on now, let's be real here. A man, of it appears your stature and apparent *means*, can probably have his choice of dinner dates, yet you chose *me*? And by the way, as you can see, I am also a very direct person. I find that life is far too short to beat around the bush, so I say what I mean and mean what I say. And in your case right now, I'm asking what I need and want to know."

Looking over her glasses for emphasis Mia continued, "As someone pointed out to me earlier, it would not be wise to *not* know what one likes, needs, or wants at a certain age. So do tell, how is it that I was the one who caught your attention, hmm? Maybe you have an affinity for caramel or milk chocolate?" Mia asked with raised eyebrows and a smirk.

While waiting for her answer, Mia picked up her champagne flute and swiftly drank the rest of her champagne, then sat it back down on the table with a smug expression. Staying on task, and ever the gentleman, Giovanni picked the champagne bottle up out of the bucket, refilled Mia's glass, topped off his, then returned the bottle before turning to Mia and saying one word,

"Wow."

"Wow is *not* what I was expecting nor looking for as an answer kind sir," Mia shot back slanting her eyes.

"Molta Bella, you did not give me a chance to finish, now did you? I was merely beginning my monologue. My dear, physical beauty can be overrated as I am sure you know by now. Not to say that without it, there is not that initial attraction, however, the depth of that beauty, the perception and interpretation of that beauty, is as they say, in the eye of the beholder, is it not?" he asked before taking a long sip of champagne.

Mia shrugged, "So it is said."

"I am 64, a widower, I have a 40-year-old son, and am a fairly adept business executive. No prison record whatsoever, I promise," he said holding up his hands in mock surrender.

Mia opened her mouth to speak, but before she could reply, he added, "I was merely saving you from asking."

"Why thank you, so kind of you."

"My pleasure," he told her smiling, before continuing.

"I watched you writing in your notebook, and looking quite in the zone, so did not want to intrude on your solitude. Yet watching you, it was almost as if you belonged right there on that particular beach, at that particular time. And quite fortuitously, I was in the perfect vantage point to take it all in. I watched you seemingly oblivious to everything but your imagination for quite some time. The longer I watched without you feeling my gaze, the more intrigued I became. I felt incapable of leaving my seat as I became captivated by you. Sitting there I desired more interaction with you besides our "toast". So, right then and there, I decided that before you left, I *must* make contact with you, or at least try."

Intently listening, Mia told him, "Please continue."

"I began wondering how your voice would sound, how your eyes would look, what type of energy surrounded you up close. When my curiosity got the best of me, I left my table to come introduce myself, but you were gone. That initial panic I had of missing my opportunity to meet you passed when I saw your notebook, tote bag, and towel still there. I was relieved, and decided to go back to my chair, bide my time, and wait for your return."

"I see," was all Mia managed to croak out. She picked up her glass and took another long sip of champagne before she could speak further.

"I do not know of how long I was at the beach earlier. I could not tell you if my life depended on it, which is rare for me. I am normally on a tight schedule, but it was nice to just let go without responsibility for anyone besides myself for a change. I felt your gaze once, and enjoyed our "toast", but honestly, I was lost in my own thoughts. I am stunned hearing your words ... that I could still have this type of effect on a man like you. I'm nearly speechless, and that almost *never* happens," Mia told him laughing.

"Well, as you said earlier, life *is* very short, so I decided that we should meet. Lady luck was on my side, as you accepted my invitation. Now sitting next to you, your scent lightly wafting in the air, feeling your energy, and your undeniable and scintillating sexiness, I am feeling a bit overwhelmed, but loving every moment. Another toast to chance meetings."

"And all those endless possibilities," Mia added lifting her glass.

Giovanni raised his glass once again. He and Mia clinked glasses.

At that moment, she had no choice but to drink the remainder of the champagne in her glass in order to try dissolving the enormously large goose egg that had now lodged in her throat. She unfolded her napkin, took her silverware out, and told Giovanni, "I think we should eat our appetizers now, while I also try to digest your words."

"As you wish," he replied, and they began eating while watching the surf pounding the shore through the window.

They ate in silence for a few moments until Giovanni said, "So…what's a nice girl like you doing in a place like this?"

Mia peered over her glasses at him, "You could not come up with your *own* line or question? *Really* Giovanni?" shaking her head with a mock disapproving face.

"Oh, trust me, I can, but not so sure it would be entirely appropriate," he told her pursing his lips.

"Well, aren't you an ace at setting traps? I'm sure you already knew that I would take the bait and say, '*Oh really, inappropriate like what?*'"

Giovani smiled before replying, "Thank you for indulging me, and remember, you *did* ask as it were, so here is your answer. I wondered if your skin feels like the satin it appears to be. I wondered how it would feel to hold you in my arms while dancing. I wondered what your lips would feel like, and what your mouth would taste like," he told her with a penetrating gaze from his hazel eyes.

Mia's head was spinning. She could do nothing but sit there silently absorbing his words while trying not to smile. Giovanni stared at her inquisitively, waiting for her to speak.

"I sense that the wheels *are* turning, but it's fine, I am quite the patient man I can assure you," he told her, then took a sip of his champagne, sat the glass back down and folded his hands in front of him, never once taking his eyes off of her.

Mia began shaking her head slightly while finding her voice, "Well my dear sir, I am finding it pretty damn ironic, that besides our names, and only our first names at that, we know nothing about each other, not really. Yet here we are, having what is turning out to be an erotically charged conversation over a dinner, in a fabulously romantic spot. But alas, unfortunately for you my dear sir, I cannot really address any of that you mentioned, as all of that is more of a *hands-on experience,* so to speak."

"Hmmm. Fair enough. That was an answer given in response to *your* question. Moving on, so tell me, what is it that you do for a living? Do you live here in California or are you here on vacation?"

"Yes, I do live here in California, and work for the State as a Right-of-Way Agent, but I am also a free-lance writer. I write articles, have self-published two self-help books, and am currently working on two novels. My mood and state of mind dictates which novel I work on," she told him with a shrug.

"One is a mystery, and the other, *erotica*," she told him with deliberateness watching for his response.

He merely nodded.

Mia continued, "At this moment, I feel as if though I am trapped in the erotica novel, and to be quite honest, I am enjoying experiencing a scenario like my main character Cassandra might find herself in."

"My, what an interesting woman you are. That is just absolutely fantastic. I will have to pick up your books, and who knows ... maybe I can get the author to autograph them for me. I will be able to say I knew you when, you know when you are a rich and famous author. And where might I find them, please?

"They are self-published on Amazon, just search for Mia Taylor."

"Duly noted. Now, on another note, I am thinking that I just may need to get inside the head of Cassandra, and see what she is thinking, and hopefully planning or anticipating," Giovanni told her with raised eyebrows.

"Now, that is privy to only a select few, and only to a certain degree. After all, if you can figure such things out, where is the fun in that? Uncertainty can have its advantages, and most definitely adds to a heightened sense of anticipation, wouldn't you say?"

Giovanni just smiled and shook his head. "I must admit, I am loving the sparks flying off this electrical current we are creating, and the intensity seems to be growing stronger by the moment. It appears that we both appreciate an intelligent mind, and we both possess a sharp and witty tongue, no?"

"Well, a tongue though sharp and witty, can have quite a few other uses as well," Mia told him with a wink.

Giovanni could not hide the surprise expression from his face.

"Now *where* is your mind, Gio? I was speaking of me playing the clarinet of course. I was *always* First Chair in band after all," Mia said laughing.

Giovanni exhaled, "My dear, whatever am I going to do with you, *and* more importantly, where have you been all my life?" he asked before breaking into laughter.

"You did not really just ask me that - *me*? As if I did not have an answer. Not to fear, I will give you an out and just say it was rhetorical. Besides, how do you know that it will not be *whatever will I do with you*, hmmm? A little food for thought Mister Man," she asked while batting her eyelashes rapidly with a demure face.

Giovanni burst into soft laughter once again.

Mia continued, "Although I must admit, and I do not think all of this is the champagne talking - but most certainly is probably a large part of it - I think that I could honestly sit here chatting with you all night long."

"Then why don't we do just that my dear Mia? I mean I honestly cannot think of anything I would rather be doing with anyone else in the world at this moment in time, well, maybe doing *one* other thing. You most certainly ..." he was saying when Mia interjected.

"Wait. Did you say one other thing? *One*? Only *one*? Come now, I would be disappointed if your imagination gave rise to only *one* thing," Mia said slyly.

Shaking his head and smiling Giovanni told her, "My dear, you are ever the formidable one, and I am loving it. I am thinking that facet of your personality may just be one of my favorites of your many qualities so far. If Lady Luck remains on my side, perhaps I might even be able to wade into the depths of that formidability. In a perfect world, sooner rather than later."

"Is *that* right?"

"One can only hope. You most certainly appear to be the total package: intelligence, beauty, grace, and sexiness, the likes of which I have not encountered for ages, if at all. May the good Lord help this weak man," Giovanni told Mia throwing up his hands and shaking his head trying to look forlorn and lost.

"Time will tell, will it not?"

They both laughed and agreed to decide on what to order before the waiter came back.

"Hmm so many choices, but I am in the mood for something with a little punch or spice, and you, kind sir?"

"Well Ms. Mia, it certainly does appear that this man has all the spice he can handle already at this very table, but as someone I know has told me, *time will tell*. You know, I may just be that predictable kind of man and order some type of surf and turf combo, you know to get a little of both. Then I can enjoy more - you know, *more* than one thing," Giovanni said with a wink.

Before Mia could reply Walter appeared as if on cue.

"In case you have not decided and/or perhaps you have, but need to be confused even further from all the choices, may I tell you tonight's specials please?"

Mia and Giovanni both nodded to each other.

"Why yes, you may," Mia replied.

"Very well," Walter continued, "The specials for tonight are our seafood fettuccine alfredo, which has lobster, crab, shrimp, and clams in an Alfredo sauce. We are also featuring an herb crusted salmon, served with a cream lemon sauce, asparagus, and garlic mashed potatoes. And our soup du jour, is loaded baked potato. Was I able to tempt you with any of those, or have either of you already made up your mind on some of our other fantastic choices?"

Giovanni motioned to Mia, and she told Walter, "I will have the jambalaya, and the small crab salad with the Louie dressing on the side please."

"Very good Miss, and what can I get for you this evening sir? Walter asked turning his attention to Giovanni.

"I will have the prime rib, medium rare, the lobster tail, and a cup of soup if you please. Can you also bring another bottle of champagne, we seem to be running low," Giovanni replied glancing over at Mia and giving her a quick wink.

"Of course," Walter said motioning to another server.

"Sir, may I point out that there is a combination that has both the prime rib and lobster tail for a better value on the next page?" Walter asked Giovanni.

"Why yes Walter, I did see that, however, I am sure that particular lobster tail is smaller than what I have ordered. I may want to share mine with my beautiful companion here. Your lobster is quite delicious, and I am sure that once she sees it served to me, she will be curious and want to try a sample. I have no doubts, that just one bite will make her hungry for more,'" Giovanni said staring directly into Mia's sparkly brown eyes.

"Very good then. I will have your soup sir, your salad Miss, and more champagne out momentarily."

As he was clearing the bowls from the seafood cocktails, an additional server brought out another bottle of champagne.

"Ahh, and here it is, right on time," Walter said.

Once again, it was all extremely well-coordinated. The other server refilled both of their glasses, sat the bottle in the champagne bucket, and they both walked away within seconds.

"What exceptional service, but my, my, my, don't you have a gargantuan appetite tonight Mister Man?"

"Well Ms. Mia, to be honest, it has been a gratifyingly productive day, and I am finding that to end such a day, the meal must be nothing less than outstanding. Of course, the meal pales in comparison to the exquisite company it is my pleasure and privilege to entertain this fine evening. Our meal is merely a period ending a sentence, and hopefully not in the final paragraph of the Mia feature in my day's story. I am very much hoping that this is a chapter in say, Cassandra's mind and not the entire story."

"Well damn, once again, I have to say that you are smooth as can be, I will give you that. You know, even though I am an author, you certainly do have a way with your choice of words, and most definitely know your way around an innuendo. Hmmm, possibly one of *your* more redeeming qualities, no?"

"Well, I am most hopeful that it is. And from your words it seems that perhaps like me, you are feeling a scintillating chemistry growing between us?"

"Well as a matter of fact, the answer to your question is..." Mia paused holding up her right index finger as she took a long sip of champagne, frowned, rolled her eyes upward, and then put her chin in her hand as if in very deep thought.

Giovanni stared intently waiting for her to finish her thoughts and/or speak to answer his question. Mia simply smiled in all her smug splendor, delighting in holding Giovanni in a state of suspense awaiting her answer.

Giovanni smiled, then finally asked, "Well Ms. Mia, are we waiting for dear old Santa Claus to bring me the answer?"

Mia laughed then motioned him closer with her finger. Giovanni came closer as Mia bent over and softly whispered in his ear, "Oh yes."

She let her moist lips lightly graze the side of his clean, shaven cheek above his beard. Giovanni felt as if the hairs on his neck were standing on end. This time it was Giovanni with the goose egg in his throat. He reached for his glass of champagne and drank it down.

Mia leaned over again, and with a slight smirk on her face softly told him, "Yes, I must say, champagne has really helped in certain situations for me this evening. Are you finding that out to be true for you as well Mister Man?"

Giovanni merely took a deep breath and exhaled, then shook his head and smiled. Their soup, and salad arrived at that very moment, breaking them out of their spell momentarily. The electricity between them hung heavily in the air as they both ate in silence, with only admiring and *curiosity killed the cat* glances between them every now and then.

Mia finally broke the silence asking after finishing her salad and setting her fork down,

"Well, looks like we both are a bit speechless. I find it ironic that it happened at the same time."

Giovanni smiled, "Yes, but at times being in one's presence is all that is needed, and words are not a necessity," he told her as he pushed his soup bowl away.

Walter appeared as if on cue once again and began clearing away their dishes and replacing them with their meal. The aromatic scent of the garlic butter being heated by the warmer was amazing; all the food looked delicious.

"May I bring you anything else?" Walter asked them.

Mia nodded towards Giovanni who replied, "No for now, it all looks wonderful."

"Very well then, I will leave you to dine. Please do not hesitate if you have any other needs," Walter told them before walking away.

"This looks wonderful but also looks like two weeks of Zumba to work it off. Maybe I should just save time and spread dinner on my bubble butt now," Mia teased.

"Hmmm. Now you know there are *so* many things I could say to that comment, but I will only say that your "bubble butt", is another one of your redeeming qualities my darling. You may complain about your age, but there is something to be said for a mature, firm body, so you must be doing something right. Now eat your dinner like a good girl," Giovanni said in a mocking stern voice.

"Well, you sure don't miss a beat, and seem to know just how to diffuse me, now don't you? Of course, maybe it is *you*, and then again maybe it could be all the champagne I have been drinking tonight," Mia said before laughing.

"Diffuse? *Diffuse*? How is that even possible? Wait - are you telling me that you are *not* wearing your superhero suit under your clothing tonight?" Giovanni teased.

"Now, what makes you think that I am wearing *anything* under my clothing tonight Mister Giovanni?" Mia asked winking.

Giovanni was actually stunned for a few seconds before shaking his head once again and smiling, "Wow. One for Mia. Now, may I interest you in a sample of this delicious lobster tail Signora?"

Mia's eyes lit up, "Why yes you *may* sir, as long as it gets dunked in that heavenly warm butter first. When in Rome and all that you know."

Giovanni pulled the lobster from the shell, cut a few pieces, squeezed lemon on them, and motioned to Mia to partake of her choice of the pieces. Mia reached over and selected a medium sized piece as Giovanni moved the butter closer to her. She dipped and swirled it in the butter, then put it in her mouth, slowly chewing it to savor the flavor before swallowing.

"Mmm. Absolutely delicious. You chose well. And yes, you were correct. When I saw your food arrive, I regretted not ordering lobster myself, thank you for your thoughtfulness. One for Giovanni. Looks like we're even now."

Giovanni smiled and ate a piece himself. Once again, they ate in silence. Mia was deep in thought until she heard, "*Open wide*, here comes the airplane."

She looked up and Giovanni was holding one of the last pieces of lobster soaked in that glorious butter on his fork near her mouth. She smiled, and reluctantly opened wide to accept the lobster. Some of the butter drizzled down her lip near the corner of her mouth. Giovanni reflexively wiped it with his thumb at the same moment that Mia reflexively licked out her tongue to catch it, in the process licking Giovanni's thumb. Sparks flew as their eyes met and held and they both smiled. Then they were back to eating in silence again.

"Thank you, Giovanni. It was delicious, I am so full, I think I may just burst. I need to excuse myself for a moment please," Mia told him.

"Of course."

"All that champagne though, sure hope I don't fall off my high heels," Mia giggled as she stood up before heading towards the restroom.

Giovanni watched her walk away with a slight smile and a heart beating so fast it forced an unexpected deep breath. When Mia returned, Walter had cleared away their dishes and was placing coffee and a slice of key lime cheesecake for them to share, along with a small plate of fresh fruit.

"Are you trying to spoil me or what?"

They looked at each other, before both saying at the same time, "Another redeeming quality," then broke into hearty laughter.

Giovanni grabbed her hand, kissed it, and told Mia, "Thank you for one of the most enjoyable afternoons and dinners I've had in ages."

"No *really* ... thank *you*," Mia quipped back.

They drank their coffee and dabbled with the desert and fruit, both surprisingly speechless.

Mia finally broke the silence, "Well, I am guessing it is time to part ways as hard as it is to leave. Thank you again for a wonderful meal and truly, *truly*, amazing company."

"Well, if you do not mind, I am *not* quite ready for my evening to end; it is only 9:40 for Christ's sakes. Will you indulge me a bit longer and take a walk with me beautiful lady? Pretty please?" Giovanni asked extending his hand to her.

"I don't see how I can refuse, and how lovely for you to ask," Mia said as she took his hand.

He took her hand, then kissed her on the cheek before they began walking hand in hand on the cement walkway adjoining the beach.

"Smoothy."

"Ooh la la. But is it *working* my dear?"

Mia smiled, "Well, I *am* walking hand in hand with you when I was supposed to be on my way back up to my room all alone, so you tell me."

They walked along the bike trail for a stretch, then sat in silence on a small bench and mindlessly watched the waves. It had been a gorgeous and very warm day, however after the sunset, thick, gray fog had begun rolling in and there was a slight chill in the air. Mia reflexively snuggled close to Giovanni for warmth, shuddering a bit. Without a word, Giovanni took off his jacket and draped it over her shoulders.

"Such a gentleman, thank you," Mia said then kissed his cheek. Giovanni turned his face and softly kissed Mia on the lips. They paused, then Giovanni planted a soft kiss on Mia's neck, then another and another. They paused again, but this time it was Mia who initiated the kiss. Their kissing became more intense, as their passion seemed to be overtaking them both, until they broke away, both looking around to see if others had noticed. Not that there were many nearby, but those that were there did not seem to notice, or if they did, they did not seem to care. They both turned and looked at each other.

"Feels like we are in high school, doesn't it

"Yes, it does," Mia replied and snuck another quick kiss on the neck, catching Giovanni completely by surprise.

"Mia, I would so love for us to be more than friends, not *that* – I mean of course I would *love that*," Giovanni said rolling his eyes.

"What I am trying to say and apparently not so eloquently, is that when this night ends, however it does end, I would like to be able to contact you, and possibly see you sometime. What do you think about that?"

"I think that is a very distinct possibility."

"You know, I am in the Sacramento area for business time to time, what do you think about me calling you to have a quick lunch, or coffee on your lunch break on one of those times?"

Reaching into her pocket Mia told him, "Well, something told me that the evening might go well, but not to the degree that it has, which has pleasantly surprised me, so here ya go Mister Man."

Giovanni reached over and took the business card Mia was offering to him out of her hand.

He looked down and smiled. Mia smiled back and shrugged, "I try to be prepared for opportunities that may come my way, what can I say?"

"I am glad that we seem to be in sync on how this evening progressed. It does appear that we seem to be birds of a feather speaking directly what is on our minds - I *like* it. And yes, I know we just met and all, but I do not want you to think that I have wined and dined you, just get you into my bed, but I would love to...."

Buzz. Buzz. Buzz. Buzz.

Giovanni stopped midsentence as his phone vibrated startling them both. He pulled the phone out of his pocket and looked.

"Damn. What is with this terrible timing? I'm sorry, I'm afraid that I must take this call, can you please excuse me for a moment Ms. Mia?

"Of course."

Giovanni stepped away while Mia sat on the bench staring out at the waves crashing against the shore. Even at night it had a calming effect on her. God, she loved the beach. The crisp air was helping to clear the haze generated from the champagne a bit. Giovanni finished up his call and came back walking towards her. Unfortunately, his body language was the exact opposite of only a few moments ago.

"Everything okay? No bad news or anyone hurt I am hoping?" Mia asked looking concerned.

"No, nothing like that thank goodness, but yes, there is a business deal needing my attention. I must throw a bag together and catch a flight to help the negotiations conclude. I am so sorry Mia," Giovanni told her as he took both of her hands in his and stared into her eyes.

"I had hoped that we were about to embark on an even more pleasurable way to end this evening. I do have an hour or so leeway if you are interested. I do hope that I am not being too forward."

"I must admit that I am a bit disappointed that our evening is ending, but I am more relieved that it is only for business reasons. And by the way, no, you were not being too forward. We both felt the direction our bodies were leading us and how tonight would most likely have ended."

Giovanni nodded in agreement.

"But yes, I will pass on the hour. I appreciate the offer, but I would rather it end this way, rather than everything being rushed."

"You have *no* idea of my disappointment, but I am putting you on notice, that whenever I am on the West Coast, I will move heaven and earth trying to find you and get back to where we are right at this moment."

With a smug expression Giovanni reached into his pocket and handed Mia *his* business card telling her, "I try to stay prepared as well, you know, great minds thinking alike and all that."

Mia took the card from his hand, and chuckled before telling him," Yep. Definitely on the same wavelength."

"Please send me a text or a give me a call, so I have a way to reach you my dear."

"Will do. I look forward to spending more time with you Mister Gio. Come, let us go so you can get all packed and ready to go save the world," Mia told him extending her hand.

"Quite gracious. You are so very beautiful my dear Mia. Just know that tonight, this is merely a pause in the music – our song is not over yet. There are at least two more choruses to be sung," he told her as they walked back to the hotel elevators.

When the doors opened, Mia walked in, turned back around, and quietly said, "Goodnight Giovanni."

"Goodnight Mia. I will dream of you."

"Endless possibilities," she said with a wink as the doors closed.

II

Mia awoke from the sunlight streaming in through the window, pleasantly surprised that she was not suffering from a headache after all the champagne from the night before. She stretched for a moment, then rolled over on her side, hugging her pillow tightly under her chest. She closed her eyes, letting the events from yesterday and especially last night, run freely through her mind.

So where was a man like Giovanni all those years while she was busy fighting her ex-husband from hell for custody? Or during all those years of her struggling as a single mother? Wait, I am getting way ahead of myself. Deep within her heart, she knew that she did not want a "permanent man" in her life. She needed to find herself and get centered, then begin working on her real estate goals.

Almost inevitably during all those years of being a single mom, there was a certain area of her life that became quite neglected, her sex life. Actually, it was more of her lack of a sex life she thought sadly. The fantasy/erotica stories she wrote, with scenarios she would love to act out, had filled in the missing moments for her somewhat. During most of those single mom years when the boys were still young, she unfortunately had neither the time, confidence, nor the man, in which to enact any sexual fantasy she may have even imagined.

Her mind once again drifted back to Giovanni. She still found it hard to believe that he was so drawn to her, a total stranger. She wondered too, if a man of the means he appeared to be, could just crook his finger, wine, dine, and dazzle his way into the hearts of many women. No doubts that his *dazzle*, had the capability of also landing him into many women's beds.

Last night. Ahh, last night. Had she decided differently, it would have been her chance to end this insanely long sexual drought she found herself in. Giovanni was an oasis in her desert of a sex life, but she chose not to venture into that body of water last night. She asked herself again, why? Deep down, it just did not feel the right time; it would have been far too rushed.

Giovanni was willing to miss any sleep though, he had made that abundantly clear. Mia wanted his mind as well as his body all to herself, without having any business distraction hanging over his head. Whatever problem or issue that he had to fly away to solve, would have still been on his mind. Still there was a slight feeling of regret. Well, he is thinking about what might have been last night just like I am *right* now, at least that is what it is she told herself with a smile.

She rolled over on her back and stared up at the ceiling. So, what is it that I really want? Do I want another husband? No. Do I want a permanent relationship with all that responsibility again? That would be *hell no*. The thought of it all made anxiety rear its ugly head and she caught her breath, then exhaled slowly. *Woosa* Mia. She took several long, deep breaths, reminding herself to relax, and that is when it really dawned on her. That was when she realized that at this time in her life, she just wanted great sex, pure and simple. Great company, maybe friendship, but *no* strings.

Immediately she felt somewhat ashamed, until her inner voice chimed in:

> *Girl, men have done this shit for centuries. No guilt, just pleasure. If men can do it, then why can't you? Live your life and fuck what others think, it's your life Mia. Do what feels good to you. Have no fucks to give and live your life girl.*

It's not like she wanted to just go out and have one night stands all the time, but maybe get to know someone a bit? Hmmm, but would that lead to a relationship? There needed to be something more than sex, but not a true commitment, some type of hybrid would need to be worked out she decided. If someone were to intrigue her as Giovanni had though, who knows? The key was to learn to go with the flow.

Her tagline, *endless possibilities*, summed it up she decided, then laughed out loud at that thought. Maybe she could act out one of those fantasies she had in her head, or one she had already written about. Maybe she could become a character in one of her own novels. You are so lucky you are miles away Mr. Giovanni, or I would literally eat you alive, Mia spoke out loud to no one. She began to giggle to herself, until it evolved into hearty laughter.

She got up, dressed, and then hit the hotel gym. While on the elliptical, her thoughts kept taking her back to last night. Working out always helped her clear her head, but this morning it already felt surprisingly clear. Thoughts drifted back to last night again. Too bad she had not poured champagne all over her naked body and asked Giovanni to lick it all off, very, *very*, slowly. Teasing her until she begged him to take her - hard. So it begins, Mia mused. If thoughts really do create, then I can make a life full of erotic and fantasy filled days and nights, right? I am going to be open to new opportunities from what I manifest. I am going to do what I want and live every moment from now on Mia vowed.

She had a great workout, and upon opening the door to her room found that it had already been made up. There was a cart from room service near the window. On the table next to it sat a vase of beautiful, long-stemmed, and very aromatic, lavender roses. Mia stood there frozen, looking bewildered and unable to move. This has got to be in the wrong room, I did not order room service, *and roses?* Giovanni maybe? No. Couldn't be. Hmm, could it be though? She did not tell him her room number. Did she even tell him her last name? No idea. That champagne haze blurred her memory.

Her inner voice spoke up:

> *"Well DUH, why don't you just walk over there and read the damn card? Go find out instead of just standing here wondering, dumb-dumb."*

Mia shrugged and walked over to the roses. There was an envelope with no name on it, she opened it and inside was written:

My lovely Mia,

Thank you for one of the most enchanting evenings of my life.

My apologies that I had to take that call and leave.

I will visit you in my dreams.

Until we meet again,
Giovanni

Mia smiled. What a lovely and totally unexpected surprise. But her soul told her, that even in the right circumstances of what seemed to be a wonderful man, she just would not be able to commit to a relationship. Oh well, he managed to make me feel special, no wait, *extraordinary* this morning, so appreciated. She walked to the room service cart, and there was another card. She opened it and began smiling as she read it:

Ms. Mia,

Yes, I know you told me you were not big on breakfast, however if I were there, I would hope we might be eating this in bed.

So, this means without my presence, you must eat heartily to make up for my absence. I hope what I chose pleases you.

Bon appétit,
G

There was coffee, teas, juice, milk, and sparkling water for beverages. The first chafing dish held sausage, ham, bacon, and potatoes. The other contained eggs, waffles, and toast. There was a delicious bowl of cut fresh fruit, as well as all the accoutrements for the food. Mia was overwhelmed but at the same time delighted. She had only met Giovanni yesterday, yet he had already stamped an indelible impression in her psyche.

Mia poured herself a cup of hot water and dropped in a couple of Earl Grey tea bags to steep. She grabbed a small bowl of fruit, then headed with them into the bathroom to run her bath. She turned on the water and squeezed some Amazing Grace gel into the running water before undressing. She caught a glimpse of herself in the mirror. Hmm, not *too* terrible, but consistent gym time was definitely in her future she firmly decided. She grabbed her tea and fruit before slowly sliding into the water, of which felt heavenly. She sat there feeling delightfully decadent, eating her fruit, and sipping her tea as she luxuriated in the tub. After finishing, she sat her dishes on the floor, then lay back in the tub, relaxing in the soothing and scented, warm water.

Determined not to think about much, she shut her eyes and tried to picture herself in Hawaii on a beach. Inevitably, her thoughts returned to Giovanni with a whole new scenario coming to mind. She closed her eyes and let her imagination run wild. Their chance meeting on the beach a day ago, morphed into quite a different spin than what happened yesterday.

Giovanni was tired from conferences all day, so thought he would relax at the poolside bar. He found a chaise mostly in the shade with just enough sun. He ordered an appetizer sampler and his libation of choice then settled onto the chaise. He was halfway through his drink when he saw her. She was not very tall, about 5'4", but she had these long brown muscular legs which caught his eye and made him wonder what was under her sarong. She had a towel draped around her shoulders and a book tucked under her arm.

Hmm. Giovanni wondered what her eyes looked like under those dark sunglasses as well. He wanted to go over to her but that was not his style. A man approached her, and they began chatting. Damn. Maybe he should have tried to strike up a conversation after all. An attractive blonde sat on the chaise next to him attempting to start up a conversation, but he kept looking at *her.* Not capturing his attention, and finally tiring of the lack of conversation, the blonde gave up and lay there in the sun silently. Giovanni finished his drink, then not taking his eyes off of her, signaled the waiter for another. He watched her raise her sunglasses atop her head and smiled at the man she was chatting with. She possessed sparkly, root beer brown eyes, and a bright smile. Very lovely. Very enticing. Very sexy.

The pool area was beginning to become crowded. Still watching her, Giovanni saw a woman appear and *yes*, she seemed to be with the man. They all chatted and then the couple left together. Giovanni took a deep breath, feeling relieved. Now, if only he could get the courage to say something to her. The sun was shifting a bit. The blonde got up and left, vacating the chaise next to him.

At that precise moment *she* started looking around and seeing the empty chaise began walking towards it. She reached the chaise at almost the exact same moment as a brunette in a bright blue swimsuit, who attempted to claim it by placing her towel on it. Quickly thinking, Giovanni said, "Oh, I am sorry, but this chaise is saved for my guest," as he nodded towards Mia.

The brunette looked up and saw Mia standing there.

"Oh sorry, I didn't know," she replied grabbing her towel and walking away in her quest to find another chaise.

Mia flashed him a smile and said, "Thanks a billion, my name is Mia and yours?"

"Giovanni," he replied.

The waiter came over at that very moment.

"Gin and tonic please, and whatever the lady would like," he said motioning to Mia.

"Grey Goose Martini, dirty. *Extra dirty.* Two olives and one onion please."

"Very good, I will be right back with your drinks," the waiter told them before heading to the bar.

"I've been here on a conference, and this is my last evening here, just wanted to relax a little before heading home," Mia said.

"Same here," Giovanni replied.

He tried not to be obvious when she took the towel from around her neck and laid it on the chaise. She had on a bright yellow suit that was high cut on the legs with a zipper running down the front. It was partially unzipped revealing her ample cleavage. Mia rubbed suntan oil onto her legs and arms.

"Looks like you already have a most beautiful natural tan."

"Thank you, but I like enhancing it a bit more in the summer."

The drinks came and their conversation flowed easily. They chatted about everything under the sun. Giovanni ordered another round. Feeling relaxed, Mia flipped over.

"Hey Giovanni, would you mind rubbing some oil on my back please?"

"But of course," he told her jumping at the chance.

He immediately moved to her chaise. Her halter swimsuit was tied at the neck, and when she began untying it, Giovanni thought he would die. Not that he could see anything but the images running through his imagination were extreme. He began rubbing the oil onto her back.

"Thank you. That feels wonderful."

"At your service. Anywhere else?" he asked thinking it was a rhetorical offer, not one she would ever answer to.

"That would be fabulous. The back of my legs, are in desperate need if you don't mind please, and thank you," Mia replied taking him up on his offer.

Giovanni could barely believe his good fortune and wasted no time. He started at her ankle and worked his way up, first one leg then the other. Her skin felt so smooth, and along with the oil, sun, and those drinks, he found himself getting highly aroused. He began imagining kissing her back, fondling her and then flipping her over and kissing her lips.

"Giovanni. *Giovanni*? Mia said snapping him out of his dreamlike state.

"Oh, sorry Mia."

"I was telling you that I have a favor but feel free to say no."

"Go for it."

"Well, I really, hate tan lines, so if I pull my suit up a little would you mind putting more suntan oil right here," she asked while grabbing the bottom roundness of her ass.

Trying to swallow an invisible goose egg he found in his throat, Giovanni answered without hesitating, "But off course, M 'lady, I'm here to serve you. Your *every* wish, is my command."

"Now that could be very dangerous you know," Mia said with a sly grin looking back over her shoulder.

"I just don't have enough nerve to wear the thong type of

swimsuit in public, yet here I am a total stranger ...."

Giovanni did not hear anything else as he poured the oil onto his palm, rubbed his hands together, and began to massage it onto the roundest part of her ass. He massaged it in, while imagining kissing her there, his tongue there, licking, kissing, nibbling, sucking. How he wanted to make love to this total stranger right now. Instead, he finished and excused himself to the men's room. He was wearing baggy shorts, thank goodness, as he had a hard on like he was a teenager. He considered not going back, but he *had* to go back; there was just no way that he could not. He got a grip, returned, and they chatted a little more. Mia retied her suit and slipped a sarong on.

"I feel like taking a walk along the beach, care to join me?" Mia asked.

"Sure."

By now it was sunset.

"This is my favorite time of night, and sunset at a beach is the ultimate for me," Mia told him.

Someone had left a bamboo mat under a tree, and they settled there. A man pedaled by selling snow cones and Giovanni bought them two cherry ones.

"I am so buzzed from the sun and those drinks, but hey, it's my last night so better make the most of it."

"Here, here," Giovanni said, and they toasted their snow cones.

They started chatting again and Giovanni made a hole in the sand and saved his snow cone there. They sat there until the sunlight totally diminished, and Tiki torches began lighting up the darkness.

"Was a beautiful sunset, but I guess we better head back," Mia said attempting to stand up.

Giovanni grabbed her by the arm, gently pulling her back, and before she could say anything, kissed her softly on the lips. She looked somewhat surprised and then kissed him back. He pushed her down onto the mat and began kissing her neck. As he unzipped her suit, he continued to slowly kiss his way down until he finally reached one of her chocolatey nipples. He licked around the areola slowly teasing her. He grabbed his snow cone out of the sand and splashed some of the cherry juice and melted ice on her breasts. The coldness made Mia shudder at the same time as his hot mouth sucked on both nipples causing her body to undulate.

Mia found that her hand had snaked down her body during her fantasy, and that her body undulating was not just imagined. She laughed to herself feeling good. Too bad that had not *really* happened, but who knows what the future holds she mused, *time will tell.*

She got out, dried off, massaged in some Kiehl's lotion, and threw on the hotel robe. She found she was starving, so made herself a lovely plate of the scrumptious food. She ate it outside on her small patio, feet up on the ottoman, relaxed, and without a care in the world. The sun felt wonderful, but took its toll, and Mia soon found herself sprawled on the bed again. She lay there feeling extremely lazy, like a full, fat, contented cat. She fell asleep almost instantly. Nearly three hours later she awoke to a sharp knock on the door. She sat up and heard it again, but before she could reach the door, she saw an envelope being pushed underneath it. She bent down and picked up the envelope but still opened the door, peered out and looked both ways. She saw no one in the hallway. She stepped back in, closed the door, and opened the envelope:

Ms. Mia,

It appears that I am cyber stalking you, does it not? As you are reading this, I am on my way back, and once again am requesting the presence of your lovely self to dine with me this evening.

If you choose to accept my invitation, you have two options:

Option 1. Meet me in the lobby at 6:00 p.m., and we will leave to dine at a nearby restaurant, returning in a few hours.

Option 2. Meet me for dinner in my Penthouse Suite on the top floor to dine al fresco on my patio.

Here is my cell number 510-555-7892.

If you decide to accept my dinner invitation, please choose an option, and text me the number, so I may plan accordingly and give you instructions.

I cannot seem to stop thinking about you my dear Mia, hope to see you in a few hours.

Regards,

G

Mia stood there reading and re-reading the letter again, at least two more times, with her heart beating wildly. Talk about romantic. This is the stuff a girl fantasizes about. Two options? Umm, no, not really - just one as far as Mia was concerned. She almost ran to get her cell off the nightstand. She typed in Giovanni's number, texted the number 2, and hit send. Before she could set the phone down, she received a text:

I can barely wait to see you at 6.

When you reach the top floor, get out and please have a seat in the red chair, and you will be escorted to my suite.

G

Well hell, Giovanni sure knows how to evoke excitement in a girl, Mia chuckled. I will give him that. Damn, but what to wear? She had already worn her sexy skirt last night. Hmm, that black, jean skirt with buttons down the front was packed in her bag. That could work, but she still needed a top that she could work the skirt and sandals with. She decided to run down to peruse the gift shop downstairs. She threw on some sweats and headed down. As she walked in, she was of course drawn to the black clothes, and lo and behold, she found a black burnout blouse in her size. A little pricey, but worth it. She charged it to her room, then headed back upstairs to get ready for her big date.

From all appearances, Giovanni was quite a successful businessman, but Mia was certainly in high hopes that he would turn his phone off this time. Well, she would just have to make sure he stayed distracted, at least for three or four hours she thought with a smug expression beaming across her face. It was already 4:50, so Mia decided to start getting ready, allowing more time to do her make up this go-round and go a little more "glam". She decided to just wear her hair in its natural curl again. She threw on a little conditioning gel and fluffed it a bit for that wild child look, fitting since it was her mood after all. She pulled out her clothes and laid them out on the bed.

She took extra time doing her eyes, doing an ultra-smokey-eyed look, gold shadow under her brows, highlighter on her cheeks, and two coats of mascara. She finished with scarlet red lipstick in matte, no shine. Decided against a necklace, opting instead for the large bling hoops in her cosmetic bag. She threw on her clothes and had just fastened her sandals when she looked at the time, it was now 5:55. Good thing dinner was only upstairs. Mia absolutely hated being late for anything.

III

Mia rode the elevator to the top floor, got off, and sat in the red chair as instructed. Within what seemed mere seconds, the elevator doors across from her opened; it was 6:00 on the dot. Giovanni stepped out, dressed in black slacks, ultra-polished black shoes with a small tassel, and an muted olive, cotton sateen shirt, which closely matched his eyes. Mia stood up. Giovanni seemed to hesitate for a few seconds before beginning to walk over to Mia, giving her pause.

"Everything okay?" she asked apprehensively as he drew nearer.

"It is now, seeing you again. All is well, I was merely admiring the lovely view. I know this may sound a bit cheesy, but you have been on my mind all day."

Mia inhaled his cologne as he softly kissed her on the cheek and knew this evening would be special. They got into the other elevator and went up one floor. The doors opened revealing a glorious atrium. Taking Mia by the hand, Giovanni led her inside where everything was decorated in white, accented by navy, and steel gray.

"Would you care for something to drink Ms. Mia?" Giovanni asked as they walked into the kitchen area.

"Yes please, I am feeling like tequila tonight, if you have it."

With a nod he replied, "Which would you care for, Patron Gold, Silver, Anejo, or Reposado? Mixer, lemon, lime?"

"I will have a double shot of Patron Reposado please. Neat."

Giovanni walked over to the bar, poured her drink, and handed her the tequila along with a glass of mineral water infused with cucumber.

"I brought you a glass of water as well," Giovanni said nodding towards her.

Mia threw back half the tequila to help stave off the nervousness that was beginning to creep up.

With raised eyebrows Giovanni smiled and clapped, "Well atta girl Mia," he teased then walked back to the bar to pour himself a drink.

"Encore performance," she replied, giving him a quick nod before putting the glass back up to her lips and downing the remaining tequila.

Clunk.

Mia slammed the empty glass down on the table.

"Impressive. So, tell me Ms. Mia, will you be dancing on the bar soon, à la Coyote Ugly? If so, please let me grab my phone so I that I may record and upload it to YouTube. I am betting I would get lots and lots of hits," Giovanni said laughing as he walked back over to Mia.

"Smartass ...I like it," Mia responded patting Giovanni lightly on the back.

She took a sip of the water and instantly loved it.

"Mmm, this is absolutely, delicious," she told him while looking squarely into his eyes and slowly licking her lips after taking a sip.

Gulp.

Giovanni took a huge swallow of his Hennessey in an attempt to clear the enormous lump in his throat, before leading her out to the patio.

Mia walked over to the railing and looked out, "What an amazing view, it's just beautiful Giovanni, it takes my breath away."

Giovanni sat his glass down, then stood behind her to see the view from her vantage point, and softly told her, "As do you – you take my breath away."

"Is that right? Is that what I do to you?"

"Absolutely."

The tequila was already working its magic. Mia could sense Giovanni's body was only a few inches from hers, so holding onto the railing she slowly leaned back until their bodies made contact. Giovanni took her cue and wrapped his arms around her waist, planting a soft kiss on her neck. Mia shuddered, her nipples hardening at the touch of Giovanni's lips. At that moment, Giovanni's phone buzzed, once again giving Mia pause, but he took her by the hand telling her, "The food has been set out. Come, let us go have a bit of sustenance."

Mia smiled, feeling relieved as they walked over to a small round table laden with fresh bread, veggies, fruit, cheese, and accoutrements. Mia swirled a strawberry in a bowl of whipped cream, then slowly licked the cream off before putting the whole strawberry in her mouth while staring at Giovanni. He slammed the rest of his Hennessey.

With a smug expression, Mia gave him a quick wink, as she stood staring at an adjoining table which contained a variety of seafood dishes and salads, as well as a pitcher of that heavenly cucumber water.

"Am I in a fairytale or a dream?" Mia asked looking at the spread of food set out before her.

Giovanni smiled, "I am glad that you are pleased."

Mia cocked her head to one side, straining to listen to the jazz which was softly playing, "Is that Brian Culbertson?"

"It is," Giovanni replied.

"Would you mind turning it up please. I love this song," Mia told him.

Giovanni poured Mia another drink and sat it on the bar before picking up a remote to turn the music up. He walked over to her, "Ms. Mia, may I please have the pleasure of a dance?"

"Absolutely,"

Giovanni grabbed her hands and spun her around. He was a wonderful dancer, and they danced for several songs before stopping.

"I don't know if that dancing helped you to work up an appetite for dinner, but I am absolutely starving," Giovanni told her.

They walked to the table spread with the food and he passed her a plate, "Now let's see you eat like you drank that tequila."

While patting her ass lightly she told him, "Well I'm sure you couldn't help but to notice that I definitely do not look like a girl who lives on celery and carrot sticks."

"As a matter of fact, I did notice - thank goodness for that - now let's eat."

They both chose the crab leg salad, lobster fettuccine, and French bread. As they reached the dinner table, tiny white lights came on throughout the patio. Mia looked curiously around, and before she could say anything, Giovanni chimed, "They're on a timer."

They sat down, and as Mia was placing her napkin in her lap, she looked over at Giovanni shaking her head in disbelief.

"Giovanni, I feel like a queen. This, all of this, is just simply amazing," Mia told him motioning to the patio with her arms.

Giovanni smiled.

"You have no idea of how magical all of this is, and how happy my soul feels at this moment. Thank you. Tonight, is truly the stuff that fairytales are made of."

"You are more than welcome my dear, now eat up, who knows you may need the energy," Giovanni told her with a wink.

"Those endless possibilities again," Mia told him winking back.

Of course, there was champagne with dinner, so Mia was feeling no pain whatsoever. Their conversation pretty much covered everything from A to Z, lasting through a beautiful sunset. It was a magical evening, and as night ultimately fell, a crescent moon and a sprinkling of stars presented themselves.

"I imagine you must be exhausted, working earlier and flying back, but I must tell you, none of your effort was lost on me. Tonight, is going down in the history book of the greatest dates ever," Mia said smiling and squeezing Giovanni's hand for emphasis.

"I am quite pleased that you are so happy my dear."

"The only thing missing is water, but the beach is too far away and too cold by now anyways. I find water to be extremely sensual, I can't explain why, I've just always felt this way."

"Duly noted. We have already enjoyed the sunset, but shall we continue to enjoy this lovely evening under the stars by having our coffee relaxing over on the chaises?"

"Yes please, that would be lovely. I'm light with two sugars," Mia called out as she walked over to a chaise. Giovanni brought out two cups of coffee and sat them on the small glass table in between them, then with a click of a remote, turned on the patio heater.

"My, my – the host with the most, no detail left out. I am feeling so pampered, so relaxed, but especially so grateful that our paths have crossed Mister Gio. Not to mention being beyond flattered that you flew all the way back here for 'Lil' Ole Me," Mia said batting her eyes then winking at Giovanni.

"Well worth any effort on my part."

Mia sat up, "Will you excuse me for a moment, please? The bathroom is in this direction?" Mia asked pointing towards a hallway.

"Yes, down the hallway to your right."

Mia excused herself briefly, and as she was returning to her chaise and walking past his, Giovanni grabbed her by the hand, "Thank you, mio caro, for spending another evening with me."

"You don't need to thank me Giovanni, I have enjoyed your company immensely tonight, and last night. I feel so spoiled."

"As you deserve my dear."

As his eyes swept over her body in admiration, he noticed one of the buttons on her blouse was unbuttoned.

"You may need to button your blouse," he told her pointing towards her chest.

Mia looked down, "Well, this did not stir too much excitement, so, guessing that you are not a breast man then, huh? Hmm. What is it? Let me guess. I know, legs! Wait. No, changing it to ass. I bet you are an ass man," she told him snapping her fingers twice and smiling.

"I like them all," Giovanni answered, matter-of-factly.

With her hands on both hips, "Now come on, that, is a bullshit answer, and you know it. Okay, okay, okay. Which one do you like on me then? Which one is your favorite?" Mia asked striking three different poses, and ending with a big, exaggerated wink and bow.

Giovanni clapped once again and laughing at her antics told her, "My dear, with you it would be quite impossible to choose only one, as you seem to have cornered the market on all three."

"Lordy Jee-zas, that's still no answer. You gotta have a favorite.

Hmmm. Maybe I could help you decide if I just unbuttoned the rest, you think?" she asked while biting her bottom lip.

"Is that a trick question?" Giovanni asked narrowing his eyes.

"Hmm."

Mia looked at him, her brows furrowed as if in deep thought, then nodded affirmatively and strode over to the bar. She picked up the shot of tequila Giovanni had poured for her earlier, made eye contact with him, then threw it straight back.

Giovanni found himself totally enthralled watching her. She grabbed a quartered lemon, sprinkled salt on it, slowly licked one side, then sucked some juice from it before sensuously licking her lips.

Looking at Mia, Giovanni's imagination began running away with him, "Oh, I wish you would," he muttered under his breath.

"What was that you said?" Mia asked looking up from the lemon.

Giovanni hunched his shoulders and shook his head, "It was nothing,"

"Nothing?" she asked slowly unbuttoning the rest of the buttons.

Giovanni was lying back on the chaise, but quickly sat up, speechless.

"Well, my dear sir, I am quite sure I heard something," she told him while sauntering over to his chaise, her blouse softly billowing behind her.

Still speechless, Giovanni stared at her in wonderment. She stopped a few feet away, her blouse now totally unbuttoned and hanging off her shoulders. He could see her dark brown areolas and nipples clearly through the black, sheer mesh of her bra.

"You do realize, that by not answering my questions, you have become complicit with what is going on," she told him as she let her blouse fall completely off her shoulders and down to the ground.

Giovanni began unbuttoning his shirt, and finally finding his voice replied, "Is that right?"

Mia cocked her head to one side with and raised her eyebrows.

"Oh my God, you are so damn sexy," Giovanni told her with his shirt wide open now as well, revealing a smooth and lean, but muscular chest.

"Oh, you think so, do you?" Mia asked, while slowly unsnapping the silver buttons running down the front of her skirt. After the last button was undone, she let her skirt fall to the ground as well, leaving her clad in only her bra, the skimpiest, sheer black panties, and those sexy, black patent leather sandals. She slowly stepped over her skirt while maintaining full eye contact with Giovanni.

"Well words without action and all that," Mia replied as she walked a few steps over to Giovanni's chaise and straddled it. She tenderly kissed him on the forehead, both eyes, then softly on the lips.

Giovanni effortlessly unhooked her bra, letting it fall off her satiny brown shoulders freeing her round, caramel breasts. He moaned as they rubbed against the now exposed skin on his chest. He kissed her neck and nibbled on her ears while squeezing them and running his fingers across her already erect nipples. He sat forward and began kissing her breasts, then licking and nibbling, until finally sucking one of her chocolatey nipples into his mouth. First one then the other, over and over and over. He could feel her body undulating until she grabbed him by the hair and held his face against her chest. He did not move his face away until they were both able to slow down their breathing. He had not felt desire for a woman like this for so long, if ever.

He finally looked up, "Can you please excuse me a moment Bella? I believe it is now my turn to go down the hall, but I promise to be right back," he said as he stood up to excuse himself.

"Of course, Gio. No worries. I will be right here enjoying all this loveliness," she told him gesturing with her arms of the patio and smiling as he walked away.

Mia got up and walked back to her previous spot to gaze down at the beach below again. As she stared down at the waves, her soul and spirit felt pleased and contented. As he returned, the mesmerizing vision which met Giovanni was of Mia standing at the railing, slightly bent over staring out at the sunset. It took but a very few seconds of seeing her standing there in those black, strappy sandals, and those sheer, black panties, for him to know exactly how he wanted this evening to end. With aging things had slowed down, but tonight he was most certainly having a different experience. He had not been this aroused for quite some time, years really. His erection was definitely harder than it had been since he could remember. He walked over to Mia and stood behind her, his hardness pressing against the roundness of her ass.

"Mmm."

He pulled her hair to one side and began softly nuzzling her neck with his lips. The scent of her perfume only intensified the effect she was having on him. Giovanni inhaled again, deeper this time, and felt transported. He reached down and squeezed her ass as he began softly kissing her neck. His hands reached up and found her firm, round, breasts once more, squeezing them as his body involuntarily began softly grinding on her ass. Mia's body moved in rhythm with Giovanni's motions, and he could feel that she was loving what he was doing as much as he was. He let one of his hands slowly snake down the front of her body and into her panties. He was pleasantly surprised to find it hairless and smooth, causing a sharp intake of breath.

"Oh my dear, I fear that you may be the death of me. But as I have told you before, what a way to go."

Mia turned around and kissed him softly on the lips.

Giovanni softly whispered in her ear, "Ms. Mia, would you mind coming with me now?"

Without uttering a word, Mia simply raised her eyebrows to signal yes.

"I have a surprise for you. Come Bella," he said to her extending his hand.

"How lovely, but you do realize that we got uh, side-tracked, and never drank the coffee you brought out for us, right?" Mia asked as they walked past the untouched coffee sitting on the table.

"Well, perhaps the universe is telling us that we are not finished with drinking something stronger then?

Giovanni led her down the hallway then stopped at a door across from the bathroom. He opened it, revealing a spacious Jacuzzi tub filling with water that was about half full already.

"Wow!" Mia said looking amazed.

"The lady said she likes water, did she not? We do aim to please here."

"Oh my God, Giovanni. It seems that your thoughtfulness knows no bounds. Well, this lady is extremely pleased," she said enthusiastically hugging him and walking into the room.

"I am so glad that you are," he said smiling and following Mia inside.

"Since one is not supposed to assume, I am asking if you would care to join me? It did seem that our trajectory was heading to a more intimate ending this evening, but..." she said with a shrug.

"Oh yes. I am looking forward to relaxing in here with you as much as you are, if not more so, of that I can assure you," he told her while dimming the lighting.

"Listen, I need to grab a few things and will be right back. If you so desire to put on a robe until the water fills, there is one for you on the vanity where you may also leave your clothing, or what is left of it," he said with a smirk.

"Good point, thank you so much, Giovanni."

"No worries, I won't be but a moment," he said with a wink and left the room.

This is definitely a chapter from one of Cassandra's adventures

Mia happily decided. She wiggled out of her skimpy panties, unfastened her sandals, and sat them on the black marbled vanity. Of course, she did not choose to take the option of wearing a robe and climbed into the tub even as it was still filling. She sat on one of the molded seats facing the window. Once again stars could be seen twinkling in the night sky. Just like the table at dinner, it sat center of a large window that extended up to the ceiling.

Giovanni entered the room pushing a small cart with both a glass of tequila and of Hennessey, the pitcher of cucumber infused water, and two empty glasses. There was the bowl of the fresh fruit left over from earlier, as well as the whipped cream. On the bottom shelf was Mia's clothes she had left on the patio.

Mia sat there shaking her head.

"So Gio, I am thinking you want to take over all the top spots for best dates ever? I have had two "official" dates with you now, and they have pushed any others down on the totem pole quite significantly."

Giovanni took a bow.

"How is the temperature?

"It could be just a tad bit warmer, but you have not gotten in as yet, and we both know the temperature will kick up when that happens," she said pursing her lips in a mock kiss.

"She shows no mercy," Giovanni said chuckling and pushing the cart next to the tub, then handing Mia her drink.

"You ain't seen nothin' yet," Mia said before taking a long sip of her drink.

Giovanni undressed, grabbed his drink, and settled in next to Mia.

"Just how fabulous is this? Mia said resting her head on his shoulder.

"More than I could have hoped for."

Mia slammed the rest of her tequila, sat her glass on the tray and dipped her finger in the whipped cream.

She looked over at Giovanni, who was watching her, then slowly sucked her finger in her mouth, sucking it clean, and slowly pulled it back out, never breaking eye contact.

He gulped down his cognac in one swallow, sat his glass back on the tray, and closed his eyes reveling in the warm water, when he felt Mia softly kneading his neck.

"Oh my dear, this feels heavenly."

"Well, we aim to please as well my dear sir."

Mia continued to massage his neck, moving onto his shoulders for a while, until she felt his body finally relaxing.

"Thank you for that," he told her with a kiss before grabbing Mia's foot and began massaging it.

"Ahh. Now this is heaven. Seriously."

"Well now, you never know what tricks I may have up my sleeve. I would like to believe that with my age comes wisdom," Giovanni laughed.

"Well, you absolutely nailed it on this one right here."

"I do believe that over the past 48 hours, I have gotten a good read on what you may like. Guess we will soon find out, will we not?"

"They looked at each other and in unison said, "Endless possibilities," and broke into laughter.

Giovanni increased his intensity, exacerbating Mia's meltdown. He grabbed her other foot and repeated the same thing.

"I feel like melted *buddah*," Mia said laughing.

Staring directly into her eyes, "Oh I don't know if you're melted completely though, let's find out, shall we?" Giovanni asked while grabbing one of her feet and placing it on his chest.

He slowly began kissing her ankle with teeny tiny kisses.

He heard a sharp intake of breath and saw Mia close her eyes, which he saw as signaling a green light. He continued his kisses partially up her calf, then back down to her ankle where the kisses turned into soft licks. Ever watchful of her body's reaction, Giovanni began the teeny tiny kisses from her ankle to her foot. Mia's reaction was stronger, and kisses there turned into soft licks as they had on her ankle.

"Ooh Giovanni, that feels so good," Mia told him breathlessly.

Giovanni paused, then lifted Mia's foot slightly bringing it to his mouth, moving his mouth down to her toes. He ever so slowly began sucking on her big toe, increasing his intensity until he saw her body begin to tremble.

"Oh my God, oh damn. Ahh," Mia moaned her body convulsing from what Giovanni was doing.

Giovanni gave her a few more seconds of his effort then placed her foot back into the warm water. He picked up her other foot and repeated the same thing, loving her reaction. Then silently stared as her body slowed down.

She opened her eyes with a big smile on her face, "I like what your wisdom has taught you."

Giovanni softly chuckled, "You just let me know, when you're ready to get out, it's your call my dear."

"Oh I'm quite ready," Mia told him and without waiting, climbed out, dried off and began putting on one of the robes. Giovanni quickly followed suit.

He took Mia by the hand and led her to his bedroom. She looked around and saw that the closet doors across from the bed were mirrored, how perfect.

"Would you care to lie down?" he asked before her imagination had a chance to start rolling.

They both walked over to the bed and lay down. Giovanni picked up a remote dimming the lights, and jazz began softly playing.

"Ms. Mia, I see that you have an affinity for jazz, and this would probably be a stretch, but can you guess this tune?" Giovanni teased.

Mia cocked her head to the side listening, "Sure hope there's a fabulous prize for the correct answer."

Giovanni looked at her amused, then folded his arms across his chest.

"Tick, Tock, Bellisima," he said wagging his right index finger.

"Ha! Got it. It's Straight No Chaser by Monk, thankyouverymuch," she said with a curtsey.

Giovanni's eyebrows shot up in surprise, "It's before your time, so thought I had you for sure."

"My father and I used to put jigsaw puzzles together pretty often, and he always had jazz and blues playing. Guess it just kind of became a part of me, but I didn't really realize until I was in my late teens," Mia told him shrugging.,

Shaking his head disbelievingly, "You just do not disappoint, do you? You are correct. So, now, for your prize,'" Giovanni replied as he pulled Mia downwards from the headboard, opened her legs, and crawled between them.

He slowly crawled up her body, planting kisses and softly licking his way up both thighs, continuing his ascent, until finally reaching his prize. He began giving Mia's bare "kitty" teeny kisses, and then slowly and softly licking her. He could tell from her body language, that she was enjoying it. Mia reached down with both hands running them thru his Giovanni's hair.

"Oh. Oh yessss."

Hearing her speak spurned Giovanni to begin slowly increasing his intensity, licking and sucking the "kitty" making Mia squirm from the pleasure he was inflicting. She was so damn wet, the more he licked the more she flowed, turning Giovanni on even further.

"Oh, damn. You know what's about to happen," she said breathlessly.

"Oh yes. Yes, Mia, I want you to cum. Cum for me Mia, now, he told her as he slipped his hands under her ass and pulled her closer to his mouth, then softly began sucking on her clit until he felt her body spasm. Her grasp on Giovanni's hair became stronger holding his head in place, as he took her over the edge.

She caught her breath then told him, "It's my turn."

She grabbed a pillow to place under his head, then had him turn sideways on the bed.

"Look over there," she told him pointing to the tall, bronze, mirrored closet doors.

Giovanni turned his head to look, "As I said earlier, you do not disappoint."

"For your viewing pleasure I now present..." she said while gesturing towards the closet doors.

Mia was on the side of him closest to the headboard and with his head turned and neck exposed she began her journey there, while once again grabbing a handful of his lustrous hair holding his head in place. She kissed, licked, and nibbled making him squirm this time. As he was catching his breath, she fished a chip of ice out the water and held it in her mouth. She moved back over to Giovanni's body, and with the ice between her teeth moved it slowly down his chest, causing his body to shudder.

"Ahh. Oh Mia."

She then moved the ice to one of his nipples, causing his body to spasm. Finally, she began her descent south to his naval and left what was of the ice chip melting there. She moved back to his nipples and sucked on them. Giovanni could see everything in the mirror and feel it at the same time, which further intensified everything Mia was doing. She kissed her way up to his lips, then worked her way, down, down, down, finally climbing in between his legs. She softly licked on one of his inner thighs while her hands reached up seeking and yes, finding his nipples yet again. She ran her fingers softly over them before pinching them as she simultaneously playfully bit an inner thigh. His breathing began to get more labored. He stopped looking over at the mirror and closed his eyes. Although he knew Mia's endgame, he really had no idea of her method, of which the anticipation was dizzying to say the least. He felt her lightly brushing her breasts along his inner thighs, and then her hot breath on his balls, and finally his dick. His body was wound tight in the anticipation of Mia's next move.

With one lick from base to tip, Mia began her oral assault. She swirled her tongue softly around the head, as she inched more of him into her mouth. She just held it there for a moment, and then he felt her tongue slowly moving against it. She began alternating between tender licks and kisses, to more aggressive stroking and sucking. It was driving Giovanni out of his mind.

"Oh Mia," he said looking down. Mia looked up at Giovanni, and their eyes met and locked, and at that very moment she slowly began engulfing him inch by inch until she could take no more in.

"Oh. My. God."

"I think you're ready for me, are you, Giovanni?"

"Oh God, yes!"

Mia straddled him and very slowly engulfed his dick inch by inch, gyrating her hips and milking him with her muscles, until she was completely impaled.

"Oh my God Mia, you feel so good."

Mia nodded and began riding him faster as he grabbed her ass while watching her ride him in the mirror.

Giovanni sat up momentarily to lick her jiggling breasts, prompting her to increase her rhythm. As he lay back down Mia, bent down and whispered in his ear, "You know that you are going to make me cum all over you, don't you?

"Yes, I want that. Cum all over me Mia."

He grabbed her ass and squeezed it, urging her body to go faster. She sped up and felt him getting closer, so slowed down. She stretched one leg out and slowly began rotating her hips and grinding him hard with long strokes.

"Do you like it, tell me," she asked before pulling her leg back up and sitting astride him.

"Oh My God Mia. I love how you are riding me. I love everything you're doing to me."

She bent down and softly kissed him on the lips.

"This is so much more than I could have ever, ever imagined."

She began slowly moving her hips again with long strokes, and whispered in his ear, "Tell me, what is it you want? Do you want to cum?"

"Oh my God yes, yes!"

Mia began increasing her tempo and could feel Giovanni's body responding.

"I don't want it to end, but I can't hold on much longer."

She sped up, "Oh yes Giovanni, give it to me," she told him as she felt rode hi harder and harder until feeling his body undulating and convulsing,

"Oh my God. Oh Mia!"

His words triggered her yet again and she joined Giovanni in euphoria. They lay in an entangled heap for a few moments afterwards trying to catch their breath and slow down.

"Never in my life, never...oh my God. That was something else," Giovanni told Mia.

Smiling and stroking his hair, Mia told him, "Well, gambling woman that I am, I'm gonna hedge a bet and say that you are going to sleep well tonight," she told him laughing before rolling off of him.

"I am thinking the same of you Ms. Mia."

"Oh, absolutely, but I have to be home early for appointments, so I am not spending the night with you, I hope you can understand."

"Bella, as much as I would love to wake up to your face and body, sadly I am not the man I used to be, especially after you have finished with me. But would you mind indulging me and staying with me just a bit longer, please?" Giovanni asked squeezing her hand as he looked into her eyes.

"Of course, I wasn't planning on leaving this very minute you big silly. I was just letting you know how I was feeling and my intentions."

"I honestly could not imagine a better night to cap off the last 48 hours. One of the phone calls that interrupted us in which I had to leave, was for me personally. I received a tremendous promotion, so tonight was a celebration of sorts for me."

"Oh wow, how wonderful for you. Congratulations Mr. Giovanni," Mia said gently pulling his face towards hers and kissing him softly

"Thank you, but trust me when I say this - none of the perks from this promotion can come even remotely close to this joyous evening I have spent with you. In fact, these last two nights have made me feel more alive than I have for quite some time, you have no idea."

"That is kind of you to say."

"I am just being honest. I was married for 32 years before my wife passed away. She was here one day, and the next day she was not at home when I returned from work. I phoned her several times over the next few hours with no answer, it was very strange, and I began having a bad feeling. About 10 p.m. or so, a Highway Patrol Officer rang the doorbell and broke the sad news to me. My beloved Cecily had been in a car accident. It was a head on collision; the poor dear died instantly. At least she did not suffer much, thank God."

"Oh Gio, I am so sorry for your loss."

"Thank you, but I have many memories with her to cherish. Of course, friends kept trying to 'fix me up', so I could move on, but everyone grieves in their own way, you know?"

"Yes, yes I do."

"Over the years after her death, I have spent time with some female companions, but my sex life has been, well pathetic is an accurate description. I just did not have much desire, that is until you. My dear, you have awakened a part of me that had seemed to die with my dear Cecily, and for that, I will be forever grateful."

"Well, I am glad I made you feel alive again, even if temporarily."

They lay together silently for a bit listening to the jazz softly playing until Mia said, "Well I suppose I should find my clothes and get dressed, I do not think it would bode well to walk to my room in this state."

"Oh, I don't know. If I saw you on the elevator or in the corridors naked, I would not mind at all," Giovanni told her handing her a towel from the nightstand.

Mia shook her head and laughed, then began dressing as Giovanni threw on some sweatpants, a sweatshirt, and a pair of deck shoes.

"I am certain that I will sleep like a rock tonight, thanks to a certain caramel beauty from a chance meeting."

Crooking his elbow for Mia to grab onto his arm he told her, "Come mio caro, allow me to walk with you down to the main elevator where I met you earlier this evening."

They got into the elevator and went down to the landing of the main elevators. Giovanni walked her over to the main elevators, then kissed her softly on the lips. Mia got into the elevator as he told her, "Tonight was priceless, and it will go down in history of one of my greatest dates as well. Sleep well Cara Mia."

"Ditto, and you do the same. Congratulations again Gio," she told him, blowing him a kiss as the elevator doors closed.

What a fairytale evening Mia thought, feeling giddy walking to her room. As she walked into her room, she saw a bud vase with a single red rose and baby's breath. This time she read the card without wondering.

My Dearest Mia,

Thank you for the last 48 hours, and especially tonight. I look forward to seeing you again, and all of those "Endless Possibilities".

G

It all felt so magical. She showered, finding herself constantly smiling of the last 48 hour's events with Giovanni. It felt surreal, as if she had been in one of her own stories, which pleased her no end. She too, found herself feeling exhausted, so jumped into bed. With a smile still on her face, Mia fell asleep almost immediately.

The next morning, she was up at five, and ready to leave, since she had the long drive home. She had appointments beginning in the early afternoon. She called the front desk to get her bags and vase of lavender roses. She grabbed her purse as well as the small vase containing the single red rose, before heading downstairs to the desk to check out.

It was very early, so there was no one else at the desk except for the clerk.

"Morning, I was in room 111, and this is the card you have on file for charges," Mia said as she handed him her card.

"Good morning. I am Daniel, and I do hope your stay has been pleasurable Ms. Taylor. Did our hotel meet your needs and expectations?

"Oh my yes, it was fabulous staying here."

"Excellent. Your belongings will be down momentarily. You may pull to the front and the concierge will put them in your vehicle. Here is the final receipt for your stay. Your original reservation deposit has been refunded, your rooming charge, gift shop charge, and all amenities have been taken care of. I have been instructed to give these to you as well," Daniel said handing her two envelopes marked #1 and #2.

"What? I mean how..." Mia began.

Daniel interjected, "It states here that your stay was comped, by management. I am guessing that the two cards may provide the explanation.

Bing.

The elevator arrived, the door opened, and the Bell Captain began pulling the cart with Mia's belongings towards the front desk.

"Right on time. Here is Jay with your belongings. Please pull up front and we will load them for you. Is there anything else I can do for you Ms. Taylor?"

"No but thank you," Mia replied feeling a bit bewildered.

"And you as well. Please do come back to stay with us again soon."

Mia smiled and grabbed her vase telling him, "Thank you Daniel. Have a good day."

She walked through the glass sliding door, wondering what was going on as she walked out to her car. She drove up to the front, popped the back, and her bag was loaded into her trunk. Jay, the Bell Captain walked over to her window, so she let it down.

"Ms. Taylor, would you like your roses on the back seat or on the floor? I thought they might tip over in the back. We placed them in this box so they would be stable."

"Oh yes, how thoughtful. I can pull the passenger seat up and the box should fit behind it. Thank you so much."

"Almost a perfect fit," Jay replied after sitting the roses down and closing the door.

Mia handed him a tip and grabbed her sunglasses out of her purse. She was ready to hit the road, but of course curiosity got the best of her. She grabbed envelope #1 and opened it.

This card entitles Mia Taylor to a room of her choice for two nights.

All food and amenities included.

Massage and spa package included.

No exclusions or blackout periods apply.

Giovanni Esposito

Mia's head was swimming. How is this possible? Daniel at the front desk said her room was comped by management. She quickly opened envelope #2:

My Dearest Mia,

I cannot begin to tell you how much our chance meeting has meant to me. You are an intelligent woman, and there is a good chance that you have already figured out your surprise at the desk by Googling me. In case you did not, and to save you time, yes, I am now the President of the company who owns this hotel chain. This is the promotion I mentioned to you. I was formerly the Western Divisional Manager. I admit that I also have ulterior motives in card #1, because I am hoping it will draw you back here in the future. I only ask that should you decide to make reservations to return, that you let me know so that I can make sure I am here to spend time with your lovely self. I would appreciate a text or call to let me know you have arrived home safely if you don't mind. Here's to chance meetings.

Until next time,

Mind. Fucking. Blown. Mia sat there for a few moments trying to absorb this reality. Looking back, his suite, the lavish meals, the service, all of that told her he was very wealthy, but wow - the President of the hotel chain! It felt surreal, as if she were living in a fairytale. She could not stop smiling. She knew it was stretching her budget to stay at the hotel, but she always wanted to splurge on a weekend like this, and so finally did it. Meeting Giovanni was a definite surprise. She would have to text him when she got back home. She threw in a Boney James cd, cranked the volume, and began her journey home.

Buzz. Buzz. Buzz. Buzz.

After only a few moments into the trip home, Mia heard the vibration from her phone receiving a text message.

Buzz. Buzz. Buzz. Buzz.

Dang, another text, back-to-back. Well, she was still on her fairytale weekend mentally, and did not want to read anything that might throw off her groove. Besides, she was driving and did not feel like pulling over.

About an hour later, pulling a Classic Mia, she pulled off the freeway and into a Starbucks drive thru. She grabbed a vanilla latte but could not resist checking her phone.

Damn, both appointments had cancelled on her. She could have stayed later and seen Giovanni this morning. On the other hand, she was glad she was on her way home, and that her time with him ended the way it did. Who knows, he may visit her someday as he said, but she was not holding her breath. She did have options now with that "free" weekend at the hotel, bringing along with it those endless possibilities again. Hey now, that should be the epitaph my tombstone Mia decided, bringing a smile to her lips. Well, as they say, "Everything happens for a reason", she ruminated, but before she could shift her car into drive,

Buzz. Buzz. Buzz. Buzz.

What in the actual fuck is going on this morning? And who in the hell is blowing up my phone now, Mia wondered aloud.

She sat her latte in the cup holder, the last text was from Javier. She sat there staring at the phone for a second before reading it.

Hey Sexiness,
Hope you are doing well. Just letting you know that
I am heading back to Cali this month. My brother
pulled thru I am happy to say. There is so much to

*catch up with. I will be in touch soon. Been missing
you, and most definitely, all of "that". You sure miss
what you had when you go without it, then find
yourself wondering what the fuck you did. Jonesin'
like a mofo, but you had to know that I would
somehow right? That magic we create between the
sheets, or the desk or... I always looked forward to
next time. Hope to see you soon.*

Mia sat staring at her phone unable to think or move. Talk about life throwing you curve balls.

She threw her phone in her purse, then took a long sip of her vanilla latte. Ooh, that first sip though, she thought and smiled. She headed back to the freeway homeward bound. Another hour driving and she was almost home, and although she was beginning to feel a bit tired, she decided to make a quick dash into Sprouts for some fruit and veggies. She knew that once she got home, that would be it; there would be no going anywhere for the rest of the day or night. Hmm. Somehow, some way, an apple turnover had found its way into her basket. Well, I will just have to keep it a secret from my thighs she mused, as she put the green grocery bag on the back seat.

Thank God the store was only a short distance from her house. After she pulled into her garage and turned off the ignition, the fatigue of the last 48 hours began to hit her. Yay, I am finally home she thought, and just sat there quietly for a few moments before letting the garage down. Curiously though, as she grabbed the bags out of her car and came back for the roses, she somehow also felt energized from the memories the weekend had generated. So many thoughts of Giovanni floated through her mind.

Last night was so out of character, but then again, maybe it was not. Maybe it was in fact only a facet of her personality that had been in hibernation for the past few decades. She sat the vase of roses on the kitchen table, and the vase containing the single rose on her nightstand. Mia had no regrets and felt free, freer than she had for so long. Glad to be back home, she put her groceries away and began running a nice, hot bath to unwind from that long drive.

She began thinking about her neglected website as she sat on the edge of the tub, throwing some lavender Epsom salt in the water. She really needed to work on it; she had been such a slacker for way, way, too many months now. The tub filled and she turned off the water. Before getting in, she decided to check her emails to catch up on things. She logged on, brought up her email account, and saw that an email via her website had been forwarded to her.

She clicked on the message. She was absolutely shocked to see who it was from. It was sent from a man from her past ... past like almost 30 years ago past. OMG! It was an email from Tony King. Mia had tried several times to track Tony down over the years, but never with any success.

Pampered passion unconditionally given.

Secrets whispered only by our bodies.

Those secrets still lie behind the walls on Alice Street.

Walls which observed our silent dancing and naivete.

They felt the emotions locked within the walls of our minds.

All the passion that was unleashed.

All that we dared not speak of,

in our escape behind those walls,

where time did not seem to exist.

In those slices of time,

no one or nothing else mattered.

Those walls remember us.

They know our secrets still.

TONY

What a blast from the past. Mia clicked to open the message, and the words poured out:

> *Can't explain why I was thinking of you today. Amazing to me how easy Google makes it to find long lost friends. So, you still have the writing bug huh? So do I. Haven't written anything for quite awhile now though.*
>
> *Just wanted to say hello. Connect with me if you would like.*
>
> *Take care,*
> *Tony*

Wow. Mia was floored. What a pleasant surprise she thought while making a big mug of ginger-lemon tea before sliding into her sudsy, warm, scented bath. First Giovanni's, then Javier's text, and now hearing from Tony after all these years, was tripping Mia the hell out. Well damn, maybe Juanita was right, maybe sometimes good things happened in 3's too. She relaxed in the tub until her fingers got pruney. She got out, dried off, then threw on an oversized t-shirt, and settled onto the chaise section of the sofa. She grabbed her fluffy, gray and white chenille throw pulling it up high around her neck. A nap was imminent. As she closed her eyes, memories of Tony came flooding back, postponing that nap. Reflecting on back in the day, she remembered exactly, how she had met Tony in high school. He was that guy who blatantly stared at her whenever he saw her. Then there was that one day when he finally introduced himself.

She was only a sophomore and he a senior, but she can remember how he adamantly told her that did not matter. She was sitting on a bench in front of the 40 Building at Nutrition Break, trying to cram for her economics final the following period, when she felt she was being watched. Out of the corner of her eye, standing in the distance, she saw Tony clad in black from head to toe, staring at her with his arms crossed. She decided to ignore him and continued to study. After a few moments, she pretended to grab something out of her purse to sneak another look, when she noticed he was walking towards her. She closed her book preparing to leave, but accidentally knocked her purse off the bench. She bent down trying to hurry and put everything back in, but she saw his black Timberland boots fast approaching; it was now too late to escape. She picked up her purse, stood up, and there was Tony, standing right in front of her.

"From the moment that I saw you, I wanted to, hell, I just had to come over here to get to know you. I am Tony and you are?" he asked with raised eyebrows.

Feeling a bit overwhelmed, Mia still managed to play it cool.

"Is that right? So that's why I've seen you staring at me sometimes then?

"Ahh, so you have noticed me," he replied smiling.

"Well, when you feel someone staring and undressing you with their eyes, you kind of notice them," Mia replied while narrowing her eyes and throwing off attitude.

"Guilty as charged, but in my defense, just look at you. I mean, how could I help myself?"

Mia gave him a deadpan stare, saying nothing.

"Now, judging from your books, you are a sophomore, and here I am, a senior. But you know, age is just a number - it really doesn't matter in the scheme of things. Plus, I can already tell ... we are gonna be great friends," he told her with a smirk nodding his head yes.

"You think so, huh? Well, we will see if that ever happens. But then again, possibilities are endless are they not?" Mia asked, while picking up all of her things to leave.

Tony just stood there smiling, silently observing. Her items collected; Mia began walking away.

"Hey, come on, can't I at least get your name?" he yelled to her.

Mia slowed her walk, glanced back over her shoulder, "My name is Mia. Au revoir, Tony," she yelled back, with a quick wave.

He made a mock gesture of grabbing his heart as Mia turned back to focus on getting to her classroom.

Who does he think he is? And why in the hell did I even tell him my name? What is wrong with me? Lordt! Mia pondered these questions while walking to class early. Even though he came off somewhat arrogant, she could not help feeling flattered by his complimentary, though shameless attention. There was something magnetic between them beginning on that day, something they both felt but never really spoke of.

After that initial meeting, Mia would see Tony around campus, and he always acknowledged her by nodding her way or with a quick wave. Eventually she began responding by nodding or waving back. Around the same time there was another senior named Arthur, who was becoming stalker material pretty much. He and his brother caught the same bus home as Mia often, and she just could not seem to catch a break from his attention. Unlike Tony though, there was absolutely no chemistry, or physical attraction on Mia's part.

Unfortunately, they both had 2nd lunch, and he often stopped by where she and her bestie Carol were sitting and eating; it was always uncomfortable and difficult to make him leave. Arthur had stalked Carol for a while too, but fortunately for Carol, Arthur knew her brother Ricky. It didn't take long for Carol to grow tired of Arthur bothering her, tell him to leave her alone, and go fuck himself. Because of Ricky, he did not have a choice. Whenever Carol and Mia saw Arthur anywhere near, they quickly dodged him and went the other way; they tried to avoid him as much as humanly possible.

"How can he not know we don't like his dumb ass?" Carol asked Mia one day on the way to English class.

"Girl, I have no idea. I just wish I had a brother who could make him go away like you do," Mia told her.

Unbeknownst to Mia, a brother of another friend found her phone number and gave it to Arthur. Mia and her sister Denise shared a phone, and since back in the day there was no way to tell who was on the other end, you answered the call. One day Denise had answered the phone, heard Arthur's deep voice, and freaked the hell out:

"Hello, can I speak to Mia?"

"Wait a minute, who is this and why are you calling for Mia? How old are you?"

"Oh, uhh, we go to school together."

"How old are you?"

"I'm 18 ma'am. Is this her mother?"

"You don't need to worry who the hell this is. But I am telling you now, that you need to leave her alone and find someone your own age. You just hold on. Mia. Mia. *Mia telephone!*"

Mia remembered walking to the phone, which was in Denise's room, and seeing her standing there with one hand on her hip, and the other hand holding the receiver of the goldenrod yellow, push button phone, and shaking it towards her.

"Who the hell is Arthur, Mia? And how old is he? He does not sound your age at all. He sounds like a grown ass man!"

"He's a senior Niecey, calm down."

"I should tell Mama on you."

"No, please don't. I don't even like him, but he won't leave me alone."

"Wait, what?" Denise asked before looking at Mia, then at the phone, then back at Mia, then slammed the receiver down and hung up on Arthur. They both looked at each other and started cracking up. Unfortunately, this did not deter Arthur in the least – in fact it had the opposite effect. He seemed to take it as a challenge, becoming more determined than ever to try to date Mia. He still randomly called, and if Denise answered she would curse at him and hang up.

One day Mia was at her locker and had just grabbed her books out, but before she could leave Arthur came slinking over, talking some nonsense she was trying not to hear. She had totally tuned him out, and then all of a sudden, Clank!

Arthur slammed her locker door shut – hard, making Mia jump. People that were in the hallway looked over for a second wondering what was going on. Fortunately, she had grabbed the books she needed for her next class already, so turned to walk away. Arthur grabbed her by the arm and stopped her.

"Come on Mia, why won't you give me a damn chance? You should be glad that a senior is even talking to you, a sophomore. What? Think you're too good for me or something?" Arthur sneered at her.

"What is your damn damage, Arthur?" Mia asked snatching her arm away.

"Look, I have been trying not to hurt your feelings, but I am done being nice to you. Never touch me again, and I am not going out with you, not now, not ever! Leave me the hell alone!"

She turned to walk away again, but Arthur once again grabbed her by her arm, stopping her for the second time. Tony had just walked out of a classroom and seen a little of what was going on. He could tell from Mia's body language what was going down was not good, so he decided to put a stop to it.

He began briskly walking towards her before shouting in her direction, "Hey Girl, I've been looking for you, where have you been?"

Mia and Arthur stood still, silently watching as Tony rapidly approached. As he walked over to Mia, he glared over at Arthur with raised eyebrows, "Hey Man, I'm going to ask you nicely, you want to take your hand off my lady?"

Arthur immediately let go.

"Aww, sorry man. I didn't know," he said holding up his hands in mock surrender.

Tony just stared him down and threw his hands up with an exaggerated shrug.

"But like, she never even said she had a boyfriend, so how was I supposed to know?" Arthur asked Tony giving Mia a menacing look.

"She didn't need to, did she? I'm sure she told you that she wasn't interested, I mean that should have been enough. No means no – for everything man - you feel me?" Tony asked him a in a forceful voice.

"Yeah, cool. I got it. I got it, "Arthur told him shaking his head and quickly walking away.

The look of relief on Mia's face said it all.

"Tony, I..."

"No thang girly girl. I have sisters, and I don't take kindly to guys harassing them either."

"Thank you so much, he's been bothering me for over a month. Ugh," she told him rolling her eyes and shaking her head no.

"That's what friends are for. See... I told you," he said nodding his head while pointing at her.

"Okay, okay. Sincerely though Tony, thanks so much."

"You are quite welcome, but can you say that in French please?

Mia rolled her eyes but still smiled, "Merci. Merci beaucoup. Tu es quelque chose d'autre."

Tony grabbed at his heart, "I have no idea what you said, but I loved hearing it – so what did you say?"

"Sillyhead, basically I said thanks a lot, and that you, are something else, basically."

"Yummy. Shoot, I gotta get to my class, but if he ever bothers you again, just let me know. Wait, you know what?" he asked reaching over and grabbing one of her folders. He opened it, then jotted down his phone number.

"Gotcha covered Madame, oops! Wait, hold on now," he told her snapping his fingers trying to think.

"Ahh, got it. Mademoiselle, right?" he said with a wink, then walked away while waving his hand without looking back.

Mia could not help but laugh, and realized at that very moment, that his words had really come to pass, just as he had prophesized that day by the 40 Building. By saving her that day at her locker from Arthur, their friendship had become etched in stone.

As time passed, both of them were in and out of relationships, yet they still remained solid friends. They had a unique relationship to say the least, staying in touch until Mia married. After Tony had gone away to college, they used to spend hours on the phone; countless late nights as they were both insomniacs. They could and did talk about anything and everything.

Sometimes when Tony came back up from Southern California to visit his family, he visited Mia at her mom's house. Such a peculiar relationship, but it seemed to work for them in an odd sort of way.

Not much kissing, if any at all. And sex, well, it was really only one-sided. Ooh, that magic tongue of Tony's. Mia's nipples hardened at the thought of it. Despite the lack of regular or normal sex, kissing, and especially speaking of their feelings, they shared an incredible and special intimacy. In fact, they had an almost secret relationship, extremely unusual. After he moved back up to the Bay Area and began working in the software field, she could remember visiting him while she was in college at his apartment on Alice Street.

Sometimes they hung out, caught a movie, or just drank wine and listened to jazz and talked. He loved Pat Metheney. Tony's apartment was an eclectic sanctuary of sorts for Mia. He had an affinity for candles; there was always some burning, even in the summer. He had Monet prints hanging, lots of plants, along with rocks, crystals, and agate slices here and there. It became a secret place where Mia could go, and where time seemed to just stand still. There were never any judgments, only acceptance and serenity. Solace during break ups with her on-again off-again boyfriend Myron who she unfortunately went on to marry, despite Tony repeatedly telling her that Myron did not deserve her. Mia figured out many years later, that this special friendship they shared, was an unspoken love. Tony was always there during her times of distress and dismay. His apartment on Alice Street was their Secret Place.

Even after all these years, Mia remembered quite vividly the first time that she and Tony had indulged in taking their relationship on a different twist. Mia's crazy relationship with Myron had driven her overboard with a workout during an "off" time; she was so sore she could barely stand it. She was having trouble sleeping, nothing good on TV, and almost magically her phone rang – it was Tony. What a perfect time for him to call, plus she had not heard from him in a few months and had been wondering what the hell he had been up to.

"So Sexy Mama, tell me something good. What's going on with you, you married yet?" Tony joked.

"Well look who it is, he's still alive. O-M-G. Hmmm, no jealous woman has shanked you yet, I see?" Mia replied laughing.

"Nope."

"So, let me guess, another late shift, you are bored and just hoping I will tell you something good to make time pass, ey? Okay, I will indulge you and keep you company for a minute brotha man, but you owe me. So, what has been going on with your Party Central apartment Mr. T., do tell," Mia teased.

They both laughed.

"Those days are long gone girl, but you know, I still got game though. Shoot, you know how I roll, don't even be getting it twisted now."

"Okay then "Playa", so before you even ask, yes, Myron and I are taking another break. Then my dumbass overdid it again at the gym today, trying not to let it bother me. Stupid, I know, I know, but you can't put the toothpaste back in the tube. Ugh, my thighs and ass are already getting sore, so I know tomorrow will be much worse. I think this time it's really going to be over – like, for real."

"Uh huh, I don't think so Missy, that's what you always say, but you keep taking this idiot back. Why, I will never figure out, but you do. The man is a goddamn fool. He is not going to find anything any better. What he needs, is to be grateful. Damn don't even get me started."

"Yes, I know, I know, I know. You always tell me this."

"Okay then, I'll make you a deal Miss Thing, if you bake me some of those killer chocolate chip cookies and bring 'em over tomorrow, I will give you the most fabulous massage you can ever imagine. Serious biz girl."

"Well wonder of wonders, looks like we're in sync as usual, 'cause guess who made cookies yesterday and there's still dough in the fridge left. I'm hurting pretty bad too, so it's a deal. I have class but no work tomorrow, so what time Mister T?"

"About 3:30 sounds good to me, what say you, girly girl?"

"Sounds like a plan to me man, see you then," Mia replied and hung up with a smile.

It was a gray, drizzly afternoon when Mia got to Tony's place. He buzzed her in, then stood with arms crossed waiting for her at the door.

"What's up, what's up, what's up?" Mia yelled out as soon as she saw him in the doorway.

"What's up with you, Mamacita?" Tony replied, with an upward head nod.

Peering over her glasses, Mia asked, "So tell me kind sir, is that supposed to be your Mack Daddy in Jet magazine pose, or are you just in a Run-DMC mood?"

"Oh girl hush, and get over here," Tony replied with outstretched arms.

He gave her a big bear hug, then they did the French La Bise, kiss-kiss like they always did, before laughing heartily.

"Hey girl, it's so good to see you, come on in," Tony said as he tried to take her coat, but she dodged him, and instead handed him a Safeway, brown paper bag.

"What's this?"

"Well duh, why don't you try looking inside brainiac? I do believe it was part of our deal, you know, those secret negotiations my dear?"

Tony peered in, "Ooh Mia, killer!" he exclaimed as he grabbed a cookie out of the container in the bag. He took a huge bite and rolled his eyes in delight.

"I gave you the rest of the dough too so you can bake them tomorrow or whenevs. Then someone I know can have nice warm cookies whenever he gets ready, because, well, because I am such a wonderfully fabulous woman," she told him while bopping him on the nose.

"Yes. Yes, you are," Tony told her and was finally able to take her coat. He hung it on the brass coat tree near the front door, then gave her another hug.

It was so good to see Tony again, and his embrace felt so comforting. Inside it was clean, nice and warm, with jazz playing as usual. The scent of fresh apples from all the lit candles scattered about permeated the air.

"It's been a while girl, it's so good to see you."

"Thanks, same here. Oh my, look at all these candles you got going on. Must be feeling in touch with your feminine side today or something, 'cause you know I am not one of your hood rats that you use for a sex toy."

"Yeah, yeah, yeah, just get that luscious ass in the tub. Yeah, so I ran a bath for you. I will be out here chillaxing and waiting for you. Take your time, serious biz Mama."

"Say what?" Mia blurted out as she walked into the bathroom.

She tried not to show how happy she was that he drawn a bath for her. With everything that she was going through, feeling pampered was just what the doctor ordered. It smelled wonderful as she walked into the bathroom. She saw a bag of lavender Epsom salt on the counter which had to be what was making the water so fragrant. Mia stripped and slowly slid into the bath. Ahh, the temperature was perfect, more on the hot side as she liked it. How did he know though? Hmm. She luxuriated in the water; it was pure bliss.

She could hear Bob James softly playing in the other room. Mia closed her eyes and began relaxing right away, damn near fell asleep. She lost track of time, but her fingers had become a little pruney, so she knew it was time to get out. She came padding out in a fluffy blue towel that Tony had left out for her, but feeling slightly apprehensive.

"Oh, just stop it now, 'cause you and I both know that I won't do anything to you that you don't want me to do Madame," Tony said with a fake French accent.

"It's Mademoiselle, don't get it twisted Mr. T., and hello, I know that. Do you really think that I'm scared of you boy?

Mimicking throwing him down and stepping on him WWE style,

Mia told him, "'Cause you know that I can whoop yo' ass with one arm tied behind my back," while crooking her neck and snapping her fingers twice.

Tony just waved her off giving her a blank stare, and then rolling his eyes.

Mia took a serious tone, "You know how I feel about my body. I'm very self-conscious, so stop judging me."

"Girl don't make me put you over my knee. Of course, you know I would love to spank that ass anyway, but there is nothing wrong with your bod. You have a beautiful body. Now get your gorgeous ass and the rest of you over here, right now, so I can work some magic and make it feel all better. I opened a bottle of wine last night, so you are going to have a glass right now Mia, no arguing, you hear me? I'm going to go get it for you right now. You need to drink it down really fast. Don't think, just drink. You need to be relaxed first, and your massage will feel all the better, I promise you. After all, I am the older, worldly, and more mature one, so know more about these things than you," he told her with a wink.

She heard glasses clinking in the kitchen and the refrigerator door shut. And just like that, Tony was back from the kitchen. He had a cold glass of white wine in each hand for them, although Mia's glass was noticeably larger. Tony handed Mia her glass. They clinked their glasses together.

"Cheers," Tony said.

"Cheers," Mia replied, and proceeded to drink her wine quickly as instructed. It started hitting her fast, so she headed to Tony's bed, and stretched out, feeling very contented. She could feel the wine working its magic almost instantly since she had not really eaten much all day. The only thing she had eaten for the whole day was a mixed-berry Yoplait yogurt that morning.

She was forever trying to keep her double bubble firm and not jiggly, her abs tight, and those thighs from getting out of control. It seemed to take over at times. It took a lot of work and discipline trying to keep fit and look good. Sometimes she realized that she became a bit obsessive about it, but controlling her body seemed to be about the only control Mia had in her life these days. Yet here she was - totally vulnerable, lying almost completely naked in Tony's bed. Well at least it was an overcast day, so not too bright for him to see her too well she thought.

The warm room only intensified the wine's effect. She lay on the bed with her head resting on her arms behind her head. She could feel herself getting hypnotized while she stared at the flame dancing on one of the candles on the dresser. Faintly, she could hear a Pat

Metheny song playing in the other room but could not figure out the name.

"I think you're ready."

Tony's deep, gravely, voice snapped her back to reality. He grabbed the bottle of massage oil off the black and gold nightstand.

"Come on now, Mia, turn over on your tummy, let's get this party started."

Mia summoned up her strength and rolled over. She felt Tony pull the towel off, but could really care less at that very moment, of lying naked in front of him. Tony was in awe and froze for a second. He was instantly aroused, but knew he had to keep it in check. He poured some oil in his hands, rubbed them together, and began his attack on Mia's exquisite caramel brown body.

The wine continued working its magic, and Mia felt transported to another place, in another realm. And oh my God, Tony's hands were magical. It felt as if no one else in the world knew they were there, just them. They were secluded in their secret room, in their secret place, and it was marvelous.

Trying to make Mia feel more at ease, Tony moved the towel to cover the other parts of her body which he was not massaging, well, at first that is. When Mia turned over on her back, Tony just stopped and stared. Her body was exquisite: firm, round, brown breasts with delectable nipples, which could only be rivaled by a firm, sculpted, and rounded ass, yet Mia had both. Tony wanted her so bad. He could not believe that he finally had her stark naked in his bed. He knew he would not do anything to her that she did not want him to, but maybe, just maybe he thought, he could make her want him to.

He massaged her toes, her feet, her legs, and when he got to her thighs, he took extra care. As he reached her hips near her sweet spot, he used extra caution to make sure not to touch it, but still get close enough to make her want him to touch it, at least he was hoping so. After nearly an hour of massage, Tony told her, "Time for a union break, I am just a bit parched Mademoiselle. I think I'm going to go have that last glass of wine if you don't mind, I will be right back."

Eyes closed, Mia nodded yes.

Tony's dick was beyond hard; he wanted her so bad. How could she not feel the electricity that permeated this room and these very walls he wondered. Mia's demureness brought a newness to it for Tony though, as he had become somewhat jaded about sex. There was an innocence about her that made him want her all the more. He downed his wine in just a few gulps, then walked back to his bed and lay next to her, his head at her navel level.

Looking over at Tony with a big smile, "Wow. That felt so good Tony. You have no idea. Thank you, thank you, thank you! It was so worth the cookies."

"Well, it doesn't have to be over, if you don't want it to be, you know?"

"Huh?" What do you mean?

"I can give you a different type of massage, and if you don't like it, all you have to do is tell me to stop."

Still buzzed and feeling good, "Whateva, Mr. T," Mia agreed closing her eyes.

Music to his ears; Tony wasted no time. Mia felt his tongue licking her ankles, ever so softly. Teeny tiny kisses rained down on her calves, first one then the other as his magical hands massaged her thighs more. He could feel her body responding and welcoming his touch, as he continued on, moving closer to his target. Tony wondered if Myron had ever made Mia feel this way. He doubted that he would make the effort. Tony on the other hand, was trying to ensure that Mia would want this more and more from him, and not ever go back to Myron.

As his tongue slowly traveled up her thighs, his hands massaged her tiny waist until he was finally able to scoop them under her round ass. It was firm and smooth just like he always imagined it would feel. She gasped and wiggled a bit, but the wine overrode her apprehension, allowing the pleasure she was feeling to remain in control.

The slight wiggling left her legs slightly parted, and Tony did not miss his opportune moment to venture to paradise. He began with those soft and slow kisses. Mia tensed momentarily but then he felt her body relax again and accept them. Soft licks came next, and he could tell by her breathing and body language, that she was rolling with it. He knew that now, now, she was his to lick. He finally had his chance, and he planned to lick her like an all-day sucker.

Wow, what was Tony doing down there; it felt so good and so much better than Myron. No matter how many times she told Myron how she liked it, he had to do it his way. He was way too intense, way too soon, and definitely, definitely not gentle enough. She rarely if ever had an orgasm orally from him, and usually preferred that he not even do it. But Tony, damn, he was a different story. Here it was his first time, and he just seemed to know what her body craved, and it was fabulous. Her mind was reveling with all the sensations: the candlelight, the wine, the music. Her body was now literally in Tony's hands, and at his mercy.

As he continued, Mia found that Tony's tongue was even more

magical than his hands. She felt bewitched lying there. She found herself unable to move consciously, her body moving only from reaction to Tony's tongue, his hands, his fingers. He was creating all kinds of marvelous sensations, using just his tongue, or manipulating her with his fingers, or both, with no rhyme or reason. She was under his spell for now; she had no choice but to let her apprehension go. It felt so good, almost loving. Way too hard to describe in her state of mind. And why was she trying to figure any of this out right now she wondered. She stopped and decided to just ride the wave.

The wave rose higher and higher; there was no longer any doubts, Tony had control. He brought her close to the edge and then backed down, then brought her close again backing down again. Teasing her, taunting her, challenging her to the point of her body almost begging for release, until at last she grabbed his hair and held his head. Softly sucking her, he brought the wave crashing against the shore. Mia had not fully recovered, but Tony was relentless as he took her there again and again and again. Her last-ditch efforts to maintain any type of control failed repeatedly.

Knowing she was almost spent, but before she could catch her breath and slow down, Tony slowly, deliberately, and teasingly, crawled up her caramel brown body ending at her breasts. He softly began licking and sucking on them while barely touching her sweet spot.

"Ooh, I love a woman that can let passion take over her body. Mmm, multi-orgasmic. Never knew. So sexy Mia," Tony whispered in her ear.

He felt her momentum building again and lightly bit her right nipple sending her into another tailspin, this time licking his way back down yonder to take her over the edge one more time. Now, he could tell she was totally spent, so crawled back up and lay next to her, stroking her hair for a bit. Eventually her breathing slowed to a normal pattern, as he patiently waited for her to come down from her body high. Time seemed to stand still as they elatedly lay there in solitude.

Tony finally broke the silence, "So girl, I'm hungry. You gonna get dressed so we can go get some burritos and beers or what?! "

They both looked at each other and burst into laughter.

"Before you say anything, I wanted to do it, and am not expecting anything in return. Don't even worry about it. So, come on girlie, let's go eat. Oh yeah, but you're driving," he smirked.

"Not a problem at all Mister Tony, for some reason, I'm in a great mood. Honestly, a fabulous mood right now. Come on now, a girl is trying to get dressed and stuff. Can't have a sista going out naked and stuff. And quit looking at me boy," Mia yelled throwing a pillow at Tony's head, which he dodged easily.

"Oh, it's on now Missy," Tony yelled as he snatched her back to the bed and started tickling her unmercifully.

"Okay Uncle, Uncle. I give up, I give up. Tony, stop. Stop please. Come on Tony," Mia pleaded.

Tony stopped and went to grab his jacket. "Uncle? Uncle? It's Big Daddy babycakes! You done gone and got it twisted. Now get some clothes on girl, we don't have all night. Shoot we got burritos and beer to go get."

He then quickly threw the pillow back, hitting her in the back of the head.

"Booyah."

"Damn you, Tony!"

"That's because Big Daddy is the King around here baby!"

"Oh, shut up, and find my keys why don't you? It won't take me but a minute, Mr. Smarty.

Mia could do nothing but smile re-living that special slice in time with Tony. As she lay on the sofa, she allowed herself to remain in the past with Tony at their Secret Place. Somehow from her thoughts, her hands slowly began travelling over her breasts, pretending it was Tony's magical tongue there. Lying there, she could not help but wonder how and why Tony had chosen to find her after all these years. The previous 48 hours, the drive home, and the bath, finally won over Mia's body; that elusive nap was finally captured. When Mia awoke, she sat up and could not resist the temptation to log onto her laptop. She re-read Tony's email and then replied:

> OMG...You have crossed my mind over the years, but I could never find you! It is so great to hear from you...so how the hell are you?
>
> My second book was self-published last year, another self-help book, but I am still working on a couple of novels. So, guess you have read my bio on my website and found me through the email feature, great! What are you up to these days, and where are you T? We shared special times in your apartment. My mind is racing.
>
> Tag – you're it! Hahaha

Mz Mia

Mia hit send, and felt joy of hopefully re-uniting even if just through email of a past friend, or was it lover? Hmm, none of those really fit what Tony was to her though. She felt excited from hearing from him and hoped he felt the same. She decided to be productive and get her laundry out of the way but while sorting it, thoughts of Tony continued to meander through her thoughts. She could not resist checking her email to see if he had replied even though it had only been a couple of hours. She logged on and there it was – a reply from Tony:

Hey Miss Thing,

Who knows why the world spins the way it does or why we should be chatting now the way we are. I married late, and have two teen daughters, so pray for me haha.

Unfortunately though, my marriage has hit a snag, not sure if we are going to make it. I am sleeping in a separate room.

So, today I was trying to dig into the past to uncover everything we used to do and talk about; a lot is covered up with layers of time particles though. Some things are very clear, some things are barely visible. I definitely have not thought about those things in ages. More significantly our special times in my apartment on Alice Street. So here we are. What the hell was going on with me then, who knows? Might be scary to revisit those times, then again maybe not.

Mind racing, huh? Do tell...
Mr. T

Mia replied right away:

I am sure that I could not pick up a conversation with anyone else I knew 30 years ago, as easily as I am with you right now.

Pretty cool after all this time our paths are crossing again for who knows the reason. All about the journey, right? Yes, I divorced Mr. Asshole aka Myron nearly 20 years ago. I have twin sons, seniors in college this year.

I do look forward to future conversations with you. Yes, I must admit, I was hoping that you would email me back today. The past with you ... hmmm.

So, stored in my memory are various times spent with you. The most memorable and cherished of course are those times after class, coming by your apartment.

The warm baths ready, candlelight, jazz playing, and then you of course worshipping my body with your hands and especially your tongue, for what seemed like forever. It was pure bliss for me.

The first time, I felt bad because I am not normally a "taker", but for some reason I just could not resist taking that. You convinced me that you didn't mind giving it, so it seemed a match made in heaven. It was like Nirvana coming there, you have no idea.

I could tell you whatever was on my mind. There were never any judgments, only acceptance. But the whole feeling of being pampered and appreciated by you, that, was magical for me. It was a secret time and a secret place to escape the stress in my life and just not think. Your tongue was magical by the way also. Most men don't really please me orally, but you were soft and slow just like I like it, and more intense when I needed it. From the beginning, you just seemed to know what my body desired and how to deliver it like I wanted it.

Over the years I have often wondered if I ever crossed your mind. Wondered if you remembered those "burrito" nights/afternoons. I am really happy that you do, and that they are as special to you as they are to me. Once you penetrated during one of those times, but I did not want it that way unless we were truly "together". I asked you to stop, you pulled out, told me that it was only to make me feel good, and never spoke about it again. I was always grateful for your understanding. I never really explained why I did not want you to, so now you know.

And yes, there have been times I wondered what would have happened if we had been together, become a real couple, and I married you instead of Myron.

Mz Mia

She hit send again.

Mia's heart was racing. So, she was now divorced, and he married, but nearing a separation. Well, if nothing else, perhaps those unanswered questions might finally be answered. Her mind began wandering back to the past, specifically the vivid memories of that unseasonably hot day she was working at the nursery:

The bare root roses had just come in and there was a whole lot to do on that hot August morning. Keeping busy with customers and work gave Mia less time to dwell on her less than perfect, so-called boyfriend Myron. Was it just that double standard bullshit that Mama was always talking about or was he just being an asshole? Seems like he was constantly picking fights or trying to start an argument over something to create some distance. He was just overly critical lately. Maybe he would just wake up one morning and

136

have turned into a human asshole, since he was acting like one so much. The thought made her laugh out loud.

"Well, sounds as if the voices in your head must be telling some good jokes today my dear," a familiar voice said snapping Mia back to reality.

She turned around scowling, and there was Tony standing with his arms folded across his chest looking at her with a smug expression on his face. Her scowl was instantly replaced by a big smile.

"Well, well, well, look what the cat dragged in."

"Well, it's good to hear you laughing and not stressing about Mr. Asshole for a change."

Smirking, Mia told him the thought that had just crossed her mind and made her laugh.

"Great minds think alike and all that babygirl. I was hoping you were working today. Moms sent me to pick up some stuff for her latest project, some little rose garden in the backyard. So Miss, may I have some personal service please?"

"Boy, give me that list, I have to hurry 'cause I'm off in about 30 minutes."

"Ooh too cool, so then let's go do lunch somewhere. I've been working my four 10's so got today off. Now ain't that sweet?"

"Would that I could Mister Man, but have a class this afternoon, Parlez vous Francais?" Mia teased.

"You know I love a woman speaking French, you tease. Okay, okay, I see how you are, but you know you're going to be hungry later, and then gonna be calling a guy trying to get you a free lunch girl, mark my words."

"Oh, like you have time for me. What's wrong? All your "bimbi" out of town or something? No one to come over and take care of you? I know, maybe you already went through all of them this week. Poor Little Tony, so very bored and it's only Thursday," Mia teased pretending to wipe a tear away.

"Girl you act like that's all I do," he said throwing his hands up.

Mia gave him a blank stare.

"Okay, okay, maybe I do a lot, but don't be hatin', 'cause a man has game, Missy," Tony told her after blowing on his nails and shining them on his shirt.

"Whatever man, now let me get your mama's stuff so I can get to class. Maybe if you are untied and not gagged by one of your freaks, then maybe, just maybe, if you are able to answer the phone, I can give you a call after class and stop by on the way home?"

"Uh huh, we'll see. Your leash is that long these days, Miss Thing?"

"Please, don't even go there. Now give me that list," Mia said snatching it out of his hands.

She was able to get all of his items before it was time for her to leave, plus made it to class on time. As she was sitting in that hot ass classroom waiting for Madame Lynch to show up, Mia's imagination shifted into overdrive. Her mind began racing from anger at Myron, to curiosity of Tony. There was that electricity they both felt but never spoke of. They somehow remained in touch, but there was that invisible line in the sand.

"Excuse me ladies and gentlemen," an unfamiliar voice boomed, breaking Mia's thoughts.

"Madame Lynch is ill, so class is cancelled today, but she will be here Tuesday," some random person announced, then promptly left the room.

The clatter from people pushing in their chairs, combined with the chatter of words about being pissed-off for time wasting their time filled the air. Well, that was a waste of gas she thought, as she grabbed her backpack and began walking to the parking lot. She was feeling fortunate that she had found a parking space in the closer lot, because the heat had zapped her at work earlier. Even walking to her car seemed a chore now.

Hmmm. Thoughts of Tony flashed through her mind while she was walking to her car. She was grateful for their crazy friendship, but even more, the intimacy they shared. Dammit, he was right again, she laughed to herself. She began driving, but somehow, she found herself heading towards his apartment. I can't just show up though, that would not be too cool, so she pulled into a Mobile gas station and used the pay phone.

As she dialed his number her heart was racing. One, two, three, four rings, and no answer. Her heart began to plummet, and just as she was about to hang up, Tony answered the phone.

"Oh hey, I was just about to hang up. Faites vous voulez la compagnie Monsieur King?"

"Ooh, no fair Mia. Second time with the French today. Don't even be writing checks your body can't cash babydoll. Then again, I don't even know or care what you just asked me, but the answer is ... yes! I just walked in from coming back from the store."

"Well, I just asked if you still wanted company sillyhead. Apparently, I am trying to make your prophecy come true because class was cancelled, and now I am hungry as hell for lunch, so?"

"Seriously? Girl, get your booty over here A.S.A.F.P.!" he laughed and hung up.

Mia was halfway there already, and relieved that Tony answered.

She found herself smiling while she was driving. She turned the music up, blasting Earth, Wind & Fire, Let's Groove Tonight. Too bad it was so hot today, her back had gotten all sweaty at work but it is what it is. Deep down, she knew Tony might tease, but not really care.

For quite some time, but especially after her last visit, unbeknownst to Mia, Tony wanted to make Mia want him completely, but without him telling her how much he desired her. It did not exactly make sense in his mind, though his heart and body would take her however, and whenever, they could get her. He craved every aspect of Mia: her energy, her smell, her taste. Each curve of her body and the velvety smoothness of her skin weighed on his mind when he was not with her. Tony wanted to get Mia to the point of her always being ready for any, and all of his sexual desires. Forever.

With each visit of her visits, Tony was feeling a conversion taking place. He began yearning to be with her more and more, but he needed her to feel the same way. He wanted her to feel it without verbalizing how he felt. He discovered that no matter how many other women he was with, only Mia could stir him to such a deep passion. His erections were so incredibly intense with every touch, every caress of her body. He ached to be inside, not just her body, but also her mind, and most especially, her heart. He wanted all of her. Those passionate sounds which emanated from Mia were so very bittersweet. He so loved hearing them, but was hoping the day would soon come, where her actions would have him making similar sounds.

Tony never felt that intensity before, not with anyone else, and there had been many. He often felt his manhood would split him like a knife, while holding back from doing what he wanted to with Mia's luscious, caramel body. He just could not stop himself hoping for another chance. He would never turn down any opportunity to love her body. His intent was to overwhelm Mia with such an intense passion, that he would be able to get what he wanted. He found himself again hopeful that by her stopping by, would present another chance for him to reach that very goal. As soon as Tony hung up with Mia, he immediately dialed another number.

"Hey Yvette, it's Tony."

"Hey, Tony."

"Uh yeah, so look, I'm going to have to take a rain check on dinner tonight. I think I may have caught some kind of bug. I am living in the damn bathroom. I appreciate the effort and am really sorry about such late notice. I will make it up to you, you know that I will, but ooh, I gotta get back to the bathroom, call you soon, bye," Tony told her, then immediately hanging up without giving her a chance to reply.

He shrugged, then placed the champagne roses he bought to take her for dinner in a vase, filled it with water, then placed them on the chest in the hallway. He hated disappointing Yvette. She may have even begun preparing dinner, but Mia stopping by was a rarity. It was so worth cancelling out any other plans.

As Mia turned onto Alice Street, a car pulled out and she pulled in, what perfect timing. Another close parking spot today. Somehow, the weather seemed even hotter now than when she left school, thank God for air conditioning. As she was walking up to Tony's apartment building, the outer door opened, an elderly lady was walking out, so Mia walked through without having to be buzzed in. All the planets in alignment, the universe opening doors kind of thing, so it would seem. She walked up to Tony's apartment but before she could knock, the door opened and there was Tony holding a bag of trash.

"Whoa, hey girl how did you get here so damn fast? I was just straightening up a little and about to empty the garbage. Go on in and sit down, but don't even think about drinking my wine cooler I just made sitting on the table," he said as he gave her a small kiss on the forehead and popped her on the butt.

Mia began walking in and saw gorgeous champagne roses on the chest in the hallway causing a pang of jealousy. Wow, wonder who gave him those, they look fresh Mia observed. He got a new Ficus tree since the last time she was there too. Then she saw the wine cooler on the table and decided to sneak just a little sip before he came back. She put her purse down and looked over at the door to make sure he wasn't walking in, mmm, it was delicious. Probably more so since it was so damn hot outside, and of course since Tony had warned her not to drink it.

She walked over to the sofa, then decided on taking just one more sip. She stealthily walked back to the table, picked up the glass, and before she knew it, the glass was half empty. Right on cue, in walked Tony. Mia stood there like a deer in headlights.

"Unh, unh, unh. I know you didn't just drink damn near all of my cooler Miss Thing," Tony said with his hand on his hips waving his finger at her.

Mia was caught totally off guard, unable to speak, so just looked down at the floor.

Tony broke into a smile, "I knew you would drink it since I told you not to. I really made it for you. Was just messin' with you girl, I have my own in the fridge, ha!"

"Punk! I was really starting to feel bad."

"Well see now what a stand-up guy I am? But I knew that you would drink it just because I asked you not to. Just think, I could have drugged you and you could be doing all kinds of kinky, sexual things to me at my command, at this very minute. You could be under my total control, my very own little sex slave."

Mia scowled.

"Now bring it in. Come give Big Daddy a hug. I need my props after saving you from dehydration and what not," he told her holding his arms out.

Mia laughed and walked into Tony's big embrace. Ahh, it felt so comforting, it was hard to let go. Tony sensed her reluctance and bent down and kissed her on the lips, softly and then more. Mia responded, which was rare for them. He hugged her again and then kissed her softly on the side of the neck.

"Mmm, yummy, but a little salty there, girl. You been out playing basketball or somethin'?" he joked.

"Boy, you know I was at work today," she said as she pushed him away.

"Yes, I do know this, since I was there, which is why, if you would please follow me Madame, oops … Mademoiselle."

He grabbed her hand with his left hand, while simultaneously grabbing the wine cooler with his right. He led her to his bathroom, where he had once again drawn her a bath.

"Ooh Tony, you didn't. You are spoiling me."

"Uh huh, I know this already Miss Lady, now give me your keys. You do have your gym bag packed in the car like always, do you not?"

"Stop acting like you know me so well, but yes. My keys are on the table," she told him with a mock glare.

"Good, now get naked and get that sweaty body in the tub. I'll be right back with your gym bag."

Before she could answer he grabbed her keys off the table, then pointed to the bathroom before walking out the door. Wow, she could not believe her good fortune. Even though it was hot he still lit a scrumptious smelling pineapple jar candle for her. The sweet smell made her want to be in her favorite place, Hawaii. Hmmm, wonder if he does this for all his girls she wondered while getting undressed. Maybe that is why they keep coming back? Maybe why he got roses? Nah, I just cannot be like the rest of them. She was sure hoping not. Besides how could he do all this for so many like he did for her? And where would he find the time and energy?

Mia laughed to herself as she once again slid in the warm water. She closed her eyes, and imagined being on a beach somewhere standing in the surf of warm, clear, blue water. She started drinking the wine cooler and began to relax. What a day it had been. She did not take as long a bath this time. She finished the wine cooler in the tub, then got out and dried off with the big, blue fluffy towel Tony had once again left for her. It was eerily quiet.

Mia walked out, and there was Tony putting a cd in the stereo.

"I was wondering if you were still alive, it's never that quiet in here, what's up, Playa?"

"It kept skipping, and I tried to clean it, but it's jacked. I am putting in something different if you must know Miss Thing. I just got it. It's by Fourplay. I think you'll like it," he said as the music began playing.

"No complaints here, thanks. Tony, I mean seriously, thank you. You have no idea how nice this is to come to. No idea at all," Mia said looking emotional and shaking her head.

"Whoa now, you called me by my real name, what's up babygirl?" he said walking over to her.

"Just a lot on my mind, trying to transfer to the university system in the fall, ugh. I'm tough though. I will get it done."

"No doubts Mia, no doubts. Stay positive," he told her while holding her tight, then kissing her softly.

The sparks from their electricity hung in the air, as did unspoken words.

"Your bag is in my bedroom if you want to get changed, although I don't mind if you don't. You do wear that towel pretty well, just sayin'," he joked as he began kneading her neck.

"Damn, that feels so good Tony. Let me go change though."

She walked to his bedroom to get her clothes out of her gym bag. As she dropped the towel, she sensed he was standing behind her, and she was correct. Before she could speak, he was kneading her neck again and it felt fabulous. The wine cooler wasn't hurting her state of mind or body either.

"Ooh, Tony."

"Tony's massage service at your disposal Mademoiselle," he said in his fake French accent as he continued kneading.

Mia did not even fight it or even allow herself to think. She just slowly eased down on the bed to allow Tony's magic to continue. She was lying on her stomach and this time she heard Tony's intake of breath, but he never stopped massaging. He worked her neck and shoulders like a pro, then moved down to her back and thighs. He massaged her calves, her heels, and then the soles of her feet. Mia was in heaven. She felt as if she were floating somewhere in space, and it felt wonderful. Tony got up and closed the dark blinds. She opened her mouth to speak, but before she could say anything, "Sshh. Yes, I remember," he whispered.

For that, Mia was extremely grateful. Tony brought the candle in from the bathroom, then turned her over and resumed his massage. The flickering light of the candle was the only light in the otherwise darkened room. He continued his magic on her neck and scalp and front of each arm, down to her fingers which he massaged, and then one by one, slowly sucked on them. She tried to control her breathing and excitement, but her nipples were standing up on her chest rock hard. There was no way that he could not have known he had her in the palm of his hand. Still, he continued working her body with his just his hands, ever the gentleman, until he reached her legs.

Lying there with her eyes closed, Mia felt Tony slowly work his way up her thighs, and then yes - once again, she felt that magic tongue of his. Somehow, some way, her legs parted and Tony's lips, but more importantly his tongue, was kissing her there, again. Oh my God this man, he just seemed to know what her body needed and wanted. Soft, teeny, tiny kisses. Then soft licks, whisper soft, teasing her until she had no choice but to open wider.

The slow and soft licking. The sucking and touching. It was all bringing her closer and closer to the edge. Mia knew there was no longer any reason to fight letting go; she could not even if she wanted to at this point. She was way past the point of no return. That release was imminent now. Her body craved it, needed it - she had to have it.

Tony could not believe his luck, that Mia was allowing him to love her body this way again. He could lick her luscious body all.day.long.

He was so tantalized by her body - it was to die for. That smooth caramel skin, perfectly round full breasts with large chocolatey nipples. That tiny waist and firm round ass was almost more than he could stand. He wanted so bad to be inside of her, yet he knew he would wait until the right time. It was almost impossible for him to not just climb on top and thrust deep inside her. He wanted her more than anything else right now; his dick was hard as blue steel. But he wanted her to ask him, to tell him that she wanted him to fuck her. He also knew that his stubbornness, or perhaps it was his ego, would allow him to continue without penetrating her. It would probably nearly kill him, but so be it. He smiled, cause of death: hard dick.

Tony's tongue had her at the brink and she knew he could feel it after taking her there several times already, but this time she felt his fingers touching her and it pushed her up and over the edge. So intense from the long build up. But before she could level out, he did it again, and again, and again, until she moaned his name. Hearing that pushed him past the point of no return, and he climbed on top of her body.

This time he slowly parted her legs and rubbed his hardness against her slipperiness. He felt her tense for a second, as he carefully pushed through the slight resistance. Tony was savoring the feeling of finally entering that sweet spot he had been aching to for so very long. He ever so slowly continued his penetration inch by inch, until he was completely engulfed within those sweet, wet walls. He dared not move awaiting Mia's response. After a few seconds which felt like several lifetimes, he slowly began to thrust. He was in heaven.

"No. Tony, no. I'm sorry. I can't explain why, I just... I just can't," Mia whispered looking up at him with sad eyes. Tony stopped, and reluctantly pulled out. He pulled his pants up while holding her close in one motion.

"Shh," Tony whispered.

He definitely did not want her if she did not want him. Damn, guess he miscalculated. Her body told him that she was ready for him though, and when she moaned out his name, he thought that was the green light. He tried his best to hold back, but this time, he just could not resist all that lusciousness that was Mia.

"I only did it to make you feel good, but if you don't want it, it's okay," he whispered in her ear.

Mia only clung to him tightly, not uttering a word.

He held her until her sexual body high came down and emotions ebbed. No more words were spoken as they lay there, jazz playing in the other room softly permeating the walls. As Tony lay there, sexually unsatisfied, at the same time he was feeling victorious. He innately knew that he had conquered Mia's body in a way that Myron never had. He hoped that no one else ever would either. Tony wanted her to remember these times with him and someday soon want more. He continued to hold her until her breathing finally slowed down to normal.

Still, he could not shake why she asked him to stop. He could feel that she had wanted him inside of her. She did not try to stop him from penetrating. For the life of him, he could not figure out why she would not ask him not to, but had instead allowed it, then asked him to stop. How shy could you be when you are lying in someone else's bed completely naked, and licked into ecstasy with at least four orgasms? She did have that innocence thing about her; even now, maybe she just could not say it. But maybe she would if he could get her to allow him to love her orally again. Yes, next time he was sure she would ask, he just had to make sure there would be a next time.

Finally breaking the silence, "Tony, I am sorry, I don't know how to ..." Mia began, but Tony silenced her with his finger and then kissed her quickly.

Sitting up, "Well, you know how we roll around here Missy, so get some damn clothes on so we can Go.Get.Me.A. Dayum Burrito - and don't forget the beer!" he laughed, as he got up and put his shirt on.

Mia felt relieved and grateful, "You got it," she said before breaking into laughter and getting dressed. Amazing that Mia kept those memories in her mental rolodex of sorts. Mia ran out and did a few errands, came back home, and headed straight for her laptop. Her heart was pounding, she logged on, and yes – there was a reply from Tony:

Hey Mia,

Wow...I am speechless. I really don't know what to say; that's rare for me.

I read your email 5 or 6 times. I needed to read it and turn it over in my mind again and again to fully comprehend it all. I am sure I will read it several more times before it's all said and done.

My day today has been weird. The day has been surreal actually, and reading your words was like a mind-bending narcotic. It was like going thru an out-of-body experience the whole time reading it. I was transported back in time trying to sense it all again. I am in a stupor. My head is blown.

First thing I want to say, is the fact that you still have such memory of those times amazes me. Truly it does. Yes, I truly enjoyed every bit of it, but I kind of locked it away in a place hidden from me, along with the key hidden in some other place that I didn't know even existed any longer. You see, my life now is so far removed from such things as what we now speak of. Nothing I do now or may do, could bring me such an experience, as it was back then. To have a time now like those of our past would be like a fiction novel of such unreal, impossible events, it would be laughable.

And I also wonder how you could feel those things, yet those times seemed so infrequent. And I wonder too why we never got further into the sensuousness that was at the tip of our tongues, literally, and why we diligently hid our true feelings and deeper desires. We shared such sensuous times together, behind a closed door in a secret room that no one else in the whole world knew we occupied. But there too was an invisible barrier between us that we dare not tear through. How could that be?

It was Nirvana, but then again it was not. There was more to have but we would not have it. I deeply craved to not only taste you but to consume every bit of you...but I dare not do it. Did you cum? Did you hide your ecstasy? Would you come back? Why come back when you had Myron? Did he not please you in ways you wanted, but you needed him just the same? Did you go to him after I brought you to the peak of desire? Those questions were always abound in my mind, but never to be asked. No matter the answers, I would always lick, suck, and touch you just the same the next time, should you come again. Yes, you were that intoxicating.

Those times were very special. Many, many times over the years past I have touched myself remembering one of the last times you let me taste you. Of that one time I was finally able to ease inside of you. Oh my God, the feeling of softly sliding into you, gently, slowly, so as not to violate your trust. To not drive you away and deprive myself the sweetness that you let me have from time to time. You cannot understand the joy and pain I felt of being inside you. Even for just those very few moments. If only I had just touched you more deeply. But still, it was such sweetness. Such pure sweetness.

That memory haunts me too though. I could not find that place you needed to be, that feeling you needed to feel. Why? So now we ask long held questions of each other. Now we face the reality of what transpired and what was left behind, with full clarity and knowledge of what was lost. Now our lives are lived not as we lived them back then behind that door on Alice Street. The memory of you remains with me. So sad that it is only a memory though.

What of now? What of this dialog? I now find myself dealing with so many serious issues; pulling our secrets up out of the dark past has me reeling, staggering.
This fact I will not hide from you now. But 30+ years later...really?

"Mr. T"

Mia immediately replied:

So this morning, I was thinking about the past with you - even back to those high school days when I can remember wondering why a senior was seemingly so attracted and drawn to me. I can always remember that sizzle/chemistry that I felt with you though.

I have a few theories as time has passed as to why you had that "wild child thang" going on back in the day. That was the thing that made me

147

apprehensive to get too close to you, but apparently not enough to stay completely away, huh?

Yes, mind racing last night about men, past and present. My choices, my needs, my desires. Were you included??

Well DUH - hahaha, but that is a whole conversation by itself.

*That slice of time in our lives seemed to help us both, but I am pretty sure, that I got more out of it, *wink, wink. I realized that you were two years older than me, and had much more sexual experience, but for some reason you did not seem to mind my lack of it. It almost seemed as if you rather embraced pleasing me when you sensed I needed it. I can close my eyes and transport back to those days, and I cherish those memories. I always have. I always will.*

Mia

She hit send and regretted it immediately. Had she bared too much of her soul? Would he reply soon or not at all? So many thoughts before bed. She fell asleep with the TV and her glasses on. The sun filtering in through the blinds once again awakened her. She tried to resist checking her email, but after her morning walk, she could just no longer ignore it. With a pounding heart, her breath catching in her chest as her email refreshed, she waited, and there it was, a reply from Tony. Mia's mouth fell wide open as she began reading his latest reply:

Hey Mia,

Yeah, so I am still trippin' hard this morning. There are memories of you that I had buried so deeply. It is crazy that after all these years, that we are actually speaking of the feelings we had so many years ago. Back when we would not and apparently could not, even speak of them. At a time when it would have made a difference. But then again, perhaps this is what the universe demanded of us.

Back then I wanted to overwhelm you with such a passion that you would forever be ready for any and all, of my sexual desires. I wanted to take you the edge of your senses and sexual rationalities, and the pleasure you felt would be part of your feelings for me. I felt the secret to gaining that was to give, like you want to receive. No secret really, it's logical that it is this way.

As I would lick and suck you, I would do so exactly as I wanted to be licked and sucked. I would envision it was me that was laying there, and that your mouth and tongue worked me to orgasm. I would penetrate you with my fingers and moved them to the movements you made, but my desires were that it was me who was arching my back to meet every push forward. I imagined my fingers were my dick. You were fucking my dick, not my fingers or my tongue my dear. I did what I did as to transfer my own desire to have you fuck me in the same manner, as my tongue slid in and out of you.

I worked my tongue slowly or faster as your breathing suggested. I would imagine your tongue sliding up and down my shaft to the same rhythm and movements you made. If I penetrated you, it was my desire to have you raise yourself up and down on my stiffness in the same way.

You tasted so very, sweet - it truly was like exotic nectar. Nothing was sweeter. I could get no harder. I just wanted it to be me being consumed by mouth and touch, with slow tongue and soft hands by you one day. No wait, I am lying – by you, everyday.

Every man, no matter how true to his heart, blinded by machismo or with crystal clarity, desires to know he can use his abilities and sexual senses to bring a woman to pleasure, over and over. I would do so until the light of dawn if the result would be your complete satisfaction. I would stiffen or soften my tongue, move it up over your clit with soft flicks or firmly, to lap up your nectar as a starving man might. I would do so to have you cum like no other man could ever do for you. Each time my mouth sucked you in, it was with the intent that no one could ever, ever bring you the pleasure like I could. It was my selfish intent to have you forever, always laying before me, and ready for me to have you again and again.

Remembering your body now is to remember a perfect moment or beautiful sunset. Firm, smooth, soft. Perfect nipples. Rich color. Perfect proportion. A firm round ass is only rivaled by firm full breasts, you had them both. A slim, curved waist can only be matched by a flat, smooth stomach. I ran my hands over it all, as I moved down to suck and lick in between your legs. Memory of your body makes me ache. To have lived without having experienced such as I did with your body, would be like having lived a life without experiencing fine art, an exquisite dessert, or any moment of complete satisfaction.

I ache too because I was never able to have you fully. I did not thrust madly into your depths. I did not watch you sit atop me, riding me, sliding my dick into you, over and over and over again. I did not take you from behind. We did not confront

taboo. Nor did we exhaust ourselves - fully spent
with hard slapping thrusts and then softly to sleep
with slow, gentle, sweet movements. We did not
experience these things together, but still, what we
did experience together, ahh, those memories have
lasted a lifetime. It was special indeed.

Mr. T

Mia stared at Tony's words, re-reading them at least three times. She sat there stunned and speechless. Talk about a mind-bending narcotic; reading Tony's email had sent her head spinning. Why now she wondered. Why had they kept silent when it appeared that they both wanted each other? Why had she married Myron? Now, in what seemed like the blink of an eye, but in reality, was 30 years and change, were the written words that the walls within their minds would not allow them to speak. Here and now, but why now?

Mia remembered exactly the last time she had seen Tony; it was only a few weeks before getting married to Myron. She had worn her favorite shoes at that time, a pair of metallic purple pumps, a thin purple and black sweater, sheer black hose, and a jean mini skirt. They had met for lunch and chatted like old times for hours. Near the end of lunch, she told him of the wedding date. He seemed somewhat taken aback, but still accepting of her words, as if the proverbial other shoe had finally fallen. It seemed as if all along he knew to prepare for that day when he would hear her speak those words. She knew he wanted more than anything for her to be happy, but apparently never thinking, that just perhaps, her happiness may have been with him.

Deep down part of her wanted him to tell her not to marry Myron, because he had always loved her and wanted her, but he only offered her congratulations. She remembered being disappointed, but then again, she had expected this would be his response. Still, she had hoped that maybe hearing this news, would be what finally broke his silence. But - it was not to be.

She remembered after finishing lunch, they embraced in a long hug, not speaking, just holding each other. That memory of walking away and looking back for that last time - for that last wave goodbye still haunted her. He had not moved, instead, he remained standing there in the same spot, silently watching her walk away. After a few steps she turned and looked back, and he pointed to her legs.

"Killer legs. You're so gorgeous Mia," he had told her before blowing her a kiss.

She smiled, nodded in acknowledgment, and blew a kiss back. This time when she turned to continue walking to her car, she chose not to look back again, fearing she might walk back into his embrace and never want to leave. Just what did they miss out on, Mia had wondered many times over the years. Overcome with emotion, Mia felt compelled to reply:

Hey T,

Talk about speechless, that last email was something else! So here we are decades later and now willing it seems, to say the things we refused to say, so long ago. So where do we go from here? I do feel closure in a way, but at the same time I have new questions. What are you thinking? What are you feeling?

Mia

After she hit Send, Mia closed her laptop and did one of the things she did best, hit the mall! A little Retail Therapy was in order, so it seemed. Besides, what if she and Tony were to meet, or Giovanni? Maybe a sexy new pair of shoes to wear, as if she did not already have enough, she laughed to herself. Tony did love high heels and appreciated lingerie, and it would seem Giovanni as well. Javier liked high heels, but lingerie for him was just, meh. Hmm. Now what the hell was she thinking, but more importantly, why was she thinking it? The anticipation was both delicious and intriguing. She always felt happy, sometimes almost giddy trying on shoes, even if she did not buy any. Plus, it kept her from home and checking her email. Yes, she realized she could check her email on her phone, but quickly put the thought of that out of her head.

No shoes worked out unfortunately, but now Victoria's Secret, that was a different story. She nabbed a nice lacy black bra and thong set, a few animal print thongs, and a sheer white camisole. If Tony or Giovanni ever saw her in any of them, they would love it. She left the mall feeling extra sexy, thinking she was sending a statement out into the universe to bring good times to come her way. Javier actually seemed more excited by her nudity than lingerie. Seeing her naked in a pair of high heels, the man would be more than excited.

By the time Mia returned home, the migraine she had been

fighting off all day, had finally arrived with a vengeance; the pounding was already in effect. She went straight to her medicine cabinet feeling like the old Excedrin commercial jingle, 'I haven't got time, for the pain', and popped one of her pills for migraines. She may have waited too long, since the pounding had become unmerciful, and now could take a day or more to go away. She decided to lie down and try to turn her brain off from so many thoughts of past and present men.

Although Mia tried her best to resist, she found that she just could not help herself, and got out of bed. She grabbed her laptop off the dresser, and logged on to check her email, but nothing from Tony. It did get pretty heavy, so there was a chance he would not reply though. Nah, she thought. It was just a matter of time, she strongly felt that. But what he would say was a whole different thing. She closed the blinds, got back in bed, and crashed out.

Mia woke up at 2 a.m. to go to the bathroom. She was getting back in bed and looked over at her laptop. Hell, she just could not resist the urge to log on. Lordt! Her heart racing, she logged on and held her breath, and then boom, there it was ... Tony's reply from 1 a.m.:

Hey Mia,

Like much of my past, Alice Street is one place that, as you said, still needs some reconciliation. Those four walls and adjoining spaces hold many, many, significant moments in my life. And yes, being there with you is at the top of the list. But for me, so much like you and I, our times there was left unresolved, unsaid, unexplored. You do not know this, but one day I just packed up and left the building without notice. Nothing was said. I left no trace that I was even there, just lingering moments I still carry around with me. I contemplate them still to this day. This seems to fit exactly how things were left between you and I all these years. Alice Street could very well be a metaphor for our entire lives - a place with so much potential but abandoned for reasons we still struggle to understand.

Does anyone besides us even know we were there together? How is that even possible? Without GPS, and the technology we now have to track our whereabouts, no one could even give evidence that you were ever there. You came in and left like a seraph in the night. Did we even speak, or was there only touching? How did we come to the agreement that we should embrace and touch the way we did? How did we apply the rules of our engagement?

We set up walls and other obstacles to keep us from crossing over into each other's lives. There must be some reason for that. My contemplation has brought me some understanding and a kind of acceptance, that if it were not for those times together, I probably would not be sitting where I now am. We were enlightened. We were left longing for more. We came to know ourselves. We understood our weaknesses. From all of that, we made decisions and marched on through our lives.

Do we accept the road we traveled since we left Alice Street? Do we really want to know the answer to that question? Answering it may even force us to look at our children, wondering.

Ahh ... yet another wall stands before us.

I do not have all the answers for Alice Street, like life itself. But one thing is certain, if we could revisit that time and be in that place, I would want to go deeper with you. I would tell you that you fit me well, and that there was something more we could have. I would ask you to explore possibilities and to remove a wall or two. I do think now, that regardless of the circumstances of today, there are things in our lives that also need further examination and consideration of possibilities, and why we may want to revisit our secret place. More than metaphor, more than longing to feel what we felt, our secret place gave us opportunity to connect with something we needed to feel and to have. We just did not know then it would be difficult, if not impossible, to ever go back, regardless of the desire to do so.

This is not to say we will never be secluded together again behind closed doors, nor does is say we could not create something new that is also needed. But we were lean and pure of contaminants all those years ago. Today we would likely only consume, not explore. There would still be limitations and other walls needing to be set. It would be all quite different.

What I desire most, what I miss most, is the wonder and fascination of exploring the possibilities and thinking all things were possible. Our innocence gave us license to have something that could only be felt all those years ago. Touching you was exploration. Imagining what you felt and considering that I was the reason for it, gave me strength and set me off to soar outside myself. In the quiet, listening to your breathing and the soft sounds dripping from your lips, music that you tried to keep secret, so much was said, yet so little was understood. Our senses were ignited full blast and sent us into the ethereal places to careen into each other like embers in a breeze.

I miss it all.
I remember it all.
I cherish it all.

Today our words would squelch your soft sighs. We

would ask for deliverance rather than set off for exploration. We would set sail directly to all that we desired, knowing precisely how to get there. Once satisfied we would instantly realize that we did not arrive where we once did.

Our new secret place is a virtual universe. Memories of our Secret Place with warm baths, candles, jazz, and our own aimless hands; that is all we are allowed from time to time. Words splayed out into electronic white space replacing the sweet sounds of innocence, confirming emotions that we felt, and have held onto and buried all these years.

I wonder, in that secret place we left behind, do the inhabitants there now hear and sense what we shared in private. Do they try to imagine and create it for themselves, unknowing that you and I filled the room with more than they can understand? I feel the room must be still glowing with all the sweet energy we left behind. It was such a special place. Time could not have possibly removed any of what was left behind by us.

The ball is in your court.
T

A life well lived

is not a life of merely existing,

so never stop daydreaming,

Thoughts do create.

Choose love.

Choose happiness

Choose joy.

Choose pleasure.

Never forget,

that you are the hero of your own life.

Own it.

Embrace it,

Live it.

Forever staying mindful,

that lost time can never be replaced.

Time never stops.

Beat the clock.

EENIE,
MEENIE, MINEY ...

I

Mia sat there stunned. Astonished. Validated. Overwhelmed. She read and re-read Tony's last email several times, trying her damndest to wrap her head around it. The ball is in *my* court, is it? Why *my* court she wondered. No way in hell was this an easy call to make, and how in the world could she make it alone? Perhaps it was just best to leave it all unresolved, 30 years and change had already passed by after all. Still, she could not help but wonder if their magic, their unspoken love, that intimacy they once generated - could any or all of that be revived should they arrange to meet? But why was he choosing not to have any input into this decision?

The possibility of what *could* have been, would forever haunt them. Last time they remained silent due to the self-imposed boundaries enacted within each of their minds. Mia realized that it was very unlikely that either one of them would ever be able to figure out just how those rules came to be. Those rules that they somehow both agreed to but never discussed. Was the act of Tony looking for and finding Mia the universe giving them a do-over, or merely the path presented for them to follow to find closure? And why now? What result had Tony desired to come out of tracking her down and contacting her? Did Tony himself even know?

Lordy, so many questions, and no simple answers, if there were any answers to be found at all. Mia's mind was traveling at breakneck speed, without any idea of how to even get on the racetrack, let alone see the checkered flag wave while crossing the finish line to resolution. She could just let it go and leave it buried in the past, but there had to be a reason that Tony found the need to look for, and then find her. Even if flames could arise from these apparently not completely cold embers, as Tony implied, the new fire would burn dissimilarly from the last.

There were way too many unanswered questions, and why in the hell was she even trying to figure all of this out at two in the morning anyway? She felt a bit of relief at having taken the Monday after her vacation time off as she always did, now she had an extra day to absorb what was going on before getting back to the grind. She knew there was no way she was getting to sleep anytime soon, so no telling what time she would wake up tomorrow. The migraine had eased a bit, but it was still there. She took another pill to get rid of it, and then climbed back in bed. She tossed and turned with a parade of thoughts marching through her mind. Eventually drowsiness from the meds let her drop off to sleep around five.

The glaring sunlight streaming in thru the open blinds awakened her. Good thing she had neglected to close them last night or she might still be asleep she concluded. She squinted hard, but found herself still unsuccessful at reading the time on her phone sitting on the nightstand. She let out a heavy sigh and finally rolled over to grab the phone. *Damn* - it was 12:30! Unfortunately, the day was already half gone.

She sat straight up. I need to get up and do *something* today. Maybe go to the nursery or work in the yard? Yes, gardening sounded like a good idea. But her body was telling her no. She lay back down, telling herself she would get up momentarily. Lying there, her mind began reflecting over the past few days. First, Giovanni, *wow.* Now that was some next level shit right there. Then that blast from the past, hearing from Tony after decades. And the final component of her trifecta, was hearing from Javier, after months of mostly silence. Eenie, Meenie, Miney, thank God there was no Mo – she could barely keep those three straight in her mind. Talk about letting chips fall where they may, Lordy Jesus.

Why was life this way Mia lay there mulling over in her mind. No one around for months really, no sex at all – well, technically sex with *another* person she thought, then laughed out loud. But over the past few days, *bam* – three options for sex, and all at once! Feast or famine so to speak. Well, feast is always better, and after all, she did have a healthy appetite. Attempting to quiet her mind, Mia began staring out the window. She found herself caught up watching the blue wind sculpture in her yard spin around and around for a few moments before her inner voice took over again.

> *Okay Mia, take a deep breath, and let it all flow. No one is forcing you to make any type of decision on anything right now.*

She sat up on the side of the bed, grabbed her purple Yeti cup and chugged some water. She decided to go ahead and get up. As she was washing her face, she noticed two very faint lines on her forehead. Ugh. She immediately pulled her hair up into a bun high atop her head, then grabbed the jar of her gold facial out of the medicine cabinet and slathered it on her face.

Still feeling a tinge of the migraine and knowing caffeine was needed, she headed straight to the kitchen for coffee. She put a K-cup in the Keurig choosing 8 ounces instead of her usual 10, hoping less water would make it stronger. While the coffee was brewing, she washed the facial off and applied her serum. Scrutinizing her face in the mirror, she decided she looked a little better and headed back into the kitchen.

The smell of coffee wafting through the air stirred up a bit of nostalgia, conjuring up memories of her daddy making it every morning when he was not on duty at the fire station. She missed him so much, sometimes it seemed her heart would explode. She added milk and sugar to the coffee in her ivory mug that said Queen in gold lettering, then took it outside to the patio.

Ahh, that first sip was bringing life back to her soul. She sat drinking her coffee in one of the glider chairs at the fire pit table, extolling in the serenity she felt, until her attention was drawn to a sparrow. Looked to be the same one from last year and was quite busy building a nest down on the far-left corner of the deck, at the end of the pergola. Mia watched with fascination as the bird worked furiously, traveling back and forth building his home.

"Answer your phone, Answer your phone ..."

Juanita's ringtone broke her concentration from the sparrow's activities. She grabbed her mug, slid the screen door open, and hustled to her bedroom, trying to catch the phone before it rolled over to voicemail. Unfortunately, she got there too late. The message popped, so she listened:

"Hey sis, just checking on you and making sure you got back home safely from your solo weekend. Didn't want nothin'. Give me a holler when you get a chance."

She did not really feel much like talking, plus, she knew Juanita would be all up in her business asking a zillion questions, so decided she would call her back later. She sent a quick text though:

> *"I'm home but feeling lazy and will call you later. It was great, ttyl."*

At least the coffee was accomplishing a minor miracle; her migraine pain seemed to have almost completely dissipated. She threw on some jeans, a purple hoodie, and slipped into a pair of older black Nikes that she wore when working in the yard. Gardening was cathartic so she got in her car and headed to the nursery.

Buzz. Buzz. Buzz. Buzz.

She heard her phone just as she pulled into the parking lot.

> *Good afternoon Ms. Mia, I hope that you are getting some rest. I was hoping that you might feel*

inclined to share your personal email address with me. Texting is great, but in this age of technology, I prefer a good email over lots of texting. Feels more like a conversation.

Please email me at GioE@yahoo.com, this is my personal email, not my business email as on the card I gave you. Hope to hear from you soon. Thinking of you~

Gio

The text brought a smile to her lips. She replied back immediately.

Well hello to you Mr. Giovanni,

I am not home, just got to the nursery when I heard your text, but yes of course, I will email you when I get home. Hope you are having a nice Sunday afternoon.

Thanks again for the most amazing two days ever.
Mia

Giovanni's text pumped her up and she got out her car with a pep in her step. It was impossible to deny that initially, the infatuation phase makes you feel a bit giddy, but for Mia, there was also apprehension about where the relationship might lead. Damn, I must have been a dude in my last life or two because I have serious commitment issues Mia thought, then laughed to herself as she walked towards the nursery entrance. She grabbed a cart even though she was just there to look, you know, for just in case she came across some rare succulent, or something else gorgeous that she might not be able to live without.

Sure enough, she found a quite a few succulents, and a planter with a funny face on it. She could not resist buying it to add to her growing collection of planters with faces. Her collection varied from a glossy ceramic planter of a woman's face with long eyelashes and red lips, to solemn expressions etched in stone, to only the bottom half of a face. As she was heading to the register, she saw a blue ceramic tiki man fountain that would go nicely on her patio by the sliding door. After she stood there mulling it over for a few minutes, she finally decided against buying it, *this* time. Of course, being at the nursery did not compare to hanging out on a beach, but being outside with all the plants, trees, and flowers, was still nourishment to her soul. Mia felt invigorated as she piled all of her goodies into the trunk. Tomorrow the plan of the day would be to plant, weed, and clean up the patio.

She was definitely *not* planning to sleep half the day away again tomorrow. Of course, naps were on a different level, and *always* welcome when and if she could fit them in, she smiled to herself. Still feeling a bit lazy she decided to pick up dinner instead of cooking, and grabbed a salad, chicken gnocchi soup, and breadsticks from Olive Garden. She was barely able to resist the Black-Tie Mousse Cake, but somehow managed. There was that pineapple and vanilla frozen yogurt in the freezer, still carbs, but better than the mousse cake. She knew in her heart of hearts though, that if there was any vanilla Häagen-Dazs in the freezer that would be the winner, since *that*, with fresh sliced strawberries on top was her *very* favorite desert in the world.

She got home, brought her food in the house, and put her salad in the fridge before bringing her haul from the nursery out onto the patio. As she was tending to some of her "babies", pulling off old leaves on her succulents and watering those that were thirsty, she found herself caught up in her garden. She decided to go ahead and pot the new plants she had just bought. There were a few weeds poking through the black mulch, so she pulled those, then fertilized her rose trees and bushes. Still feeling incentivized she swept up the leaves and pine needles from the trees of the damn grumpy-assed neighbor who lived behind her and refused to ever trim them. Finally, she watered the rest of the plants and flowers by hand with the water hose on a light spray setting. She smiled as she watered the last rose tree, feeling extremely uplifted from that instant gratification gained after working in the yard. She stood there surveying her effort and felt pleased. Her yard work now finished, she aimed the hose towards her three-tiered fountain, filled it up, then squirted some bio-degradable chemicals in the water and turned it on.

Feeling tired but accomplished, Mia went back inside, and after washing her hands and scrubbing the grit from her nails, whipped up a double, spicy, bloody mary. She slid a few garlic stuffed olives and cocktail onions onto a bamboo skewer, stuck it in her glass, then grabbed a bag of Lay's Limon Chips and headed back outside. As she stepped onto the patio, the gurgling sound of water emanating from the fountain greeted her ears making her smile. She sat on a chaise watching the water flow for a few moments before taking several large sips of her drink and munching on a few chips. She sat her glass down and lay back on the chaise finally allowing herself to relax.

"It's the simple things," Mia spoke out loud to herself.

At that particular moment, she had not a care in the world. She grabbed her glass, took a few more sips, and could feel her body slowly unwinding. By now sunset was approaching, and Mia felt at peace lying there surrounded by nature and her little patch of heaven. The solar lights began blinking, signaling it would be dark soon. Even with the sun setting, it was still warm, and a lovely evening. Mia drank most of her drink and then settled back and relaxed. All that gardening had kept Mia busy all afternoon and her mind from wandering, but she could feel her imagination reel revving up.

Those early days with Tony came to mind. In junior high Mia had gone the route of cheerleader but did not like how she was perceived. She was amazed that people seemed to associate those in cheer with a lower IQ. She found way too many people were condescending, and some were just downright rude, leading her to decide it was an experience that she would never repeat. When she got to high school, they offered dance, and she was overjoyed, as she loved dance. Throughout elementary school she was in dance every year. She loved dancing of all types but was especially partial to jazz. Being a dancer was the first thing she ever wanted to be when she grew up, specifically, her dream was to be a ballerina on Broadway. She was the youngest from her school to make it into an elite Dance Troupe called the Jr. Honor Society, which focused on modern and African dance.

In high school, every spring there was the annual Dance Showcase in the auditorium. Even in her sophomore year, Mia was in four dances of the 14 in the Showcase. Before the first onstage dress rehearsal, Mia had arrived early and was the first one there. As she was sitting on the floor warming up and stretching, she had the eerie feeling of being watched. She quickly looked over her shoulder but saw no one. It was a little spooky, but she continued warming up. A few moments later she heard the door open and felt relieved as her classmates began trickling in.

The stage began filling with people, and chatter and laughter. The only guy in class, John, arrived and walked over to her. He was a senior, an extremely talented dancer, and one of Mia's favorite people in the class, as well as a good friend. She and John were dancing in a Salsa number, which was the last dance before the show's finale, which had all the dancers in it. But Mr. Diva, *John*, had been given the ultimate privilege of opening the Showcase with a solo dance, a mixture of ballet and jazz dance.

"Hey Missy, it's almost time for us to shine," John said snapping his fingers.

Mia high fived him and smiled," You better know it! You ready G?"

"Quit playin' now, you know how I roll baby," he said striking a pose and they both began laughing.

Although she could not see her, she could hear her teacher Mrs. LaFrance's voice in the distance, way down front by the seats. Suddenly different colored lights on the stage came on shining brightly.

Clap.Clap.Clap.Clap.

Mrs. LaFrance got everyone's attention and the chatter stopped as she began walking towards the stage.

"Okay ladies and, *gentleman,* this is our first rehearsal to get familiar with spacing on the stage and to get the lighting set for each number."

She pointed to the stage, "Behind you are William, Curtis, and Tony, who will be operating our lights and sound. Welcome gentlemen."

Everyone turned around and acknowledged them. It immediately dawned on Mia that it was *not* her imagination after all. Tony was there to work on the Showcase, and he was undoubtedly who she felt staring at her earlier.

"Okay, let's go. Time to warm up people! Curtis, start the tape please."

The music began and the dancers went thru their usual warm-up routine. Mia's first time on stage would be in the third dance on the schedule. She saw Tony talking to who appeared to be William, so surmised that those two were in charge of lighting for the show.

Once again, she heard Mrs. LaFrance's voice, "Dance Number 3. Dancers take your positions now please."

As she was walking from the wings onto the stage, she heard, "Pssst. Pssst"

Mia glanced towards the wings on the other side of the stage where the sound came from, and there was Tony standing there with his arms folded, his head cocked to the side. She looked at him over her glasses, throwing her weight on her right side with her right hand on her right hip for a second. He pointed to her and nodded his head affirmatively. Mia could not help but smile. He smiled back and then winked. She just shook her head, rolled her eyes, and took her position on stage.

There was a slight problem with the music that slowed things down, so practice ran a bit late, but they finally got through the whole schedule. After the finale was done, Mia quickly threw her sweats and slides on, then grabbed her dance bag, and purse. She was trying to hurry and get to the phone booth before there was a line. Her sister Denise was waiting for her call to come and pick her up. She had almost reached the phone booth when she heard, "Hey, you need a ride home?"

She turned around, and who else would it be but Tony. She tried hiding her smile but failed.

"Que se passe-t-il? Are you stalking me or what Monsieur King?" she asked with her hands on her hip once again.

"Damn girl, there you go with the French again, you know that's my Kryptonite."

"Well, I see you still standing, so it must not be that strong. It didn't even knock your ass out, so what about *that*?"

"There it is - that sass...I *like* it!" Tony told her clapping his hands together.

Mia rolled her eyes.

"Serious bizz though, I'm dropping William off, you need a ride? Where do you live? He stays off Freesia on the other side of the hill, you anywhere close?"

"Actually, I'm on Rosario Way, which is near the top of the hill above Freesia. You sure you wouldn't mind?"

"I told you that we would be great friends one day so..." Tony told her pointing to his car with both index fingers.

"I have to call my sister first - she's waiting on me to call her to come pick me up."

"I'm right over there in the blue Celica," he told her walking over to William.

Mia ran to the phone, punched the numbers, and Denise answered on the first ring.

"Hello."

"Hey Denise, it's me. I got a ride home, so you don't need to come pick me up anymore."

"Girl, I've been waiting on you. Where *are* you?"

"I'm at school still. Sorry, practice ran over. I should be home soon, but I'm not the only one getting a ride and not sure who is getting dropped off first, so please let Mama know."

"Lordt! Mama was starting to get all worried - you *know* how she is. No biggie, I get it, but she was seriously getting on my last nerve. I mean it's only been like 15 minutes longer than you said it *might* end and all. Let me go in there and tell her that you did not get kidnapped or killed, and that your bloody body is *not* lying in a gutter somewhere. *Bye Mia*," she said laughing.

"Bye Niecey," Mia said and began laughing too.

She heard Denise yell, "Ma-*maaa*!" before she hung up the phone.

She just shook her head still laughing. She loved her Mama to pieces, but she was so extra - a true *Drama Queen*. She grabbed her stuff, turned around and saw Tony in the first row leaning against his car with his arms crossed as was his usual M.O., waiting for her. As she got closer, he opened the back door for her.

"Do you want to put your bag and backpack in the trunk?"

"Yes, that would be great, thanks."

Tony grabbed them and put them in the trunk as Mia got in the car. Before starting it up, he said, "William this is Mia, Mia - William."

"Hey, what's up Mia?" William said with a head nod.

"Hi William, not much," Mia quietly replied.

Tony started up the car, and Earth Wind & Fire came belting out as he pulled out of the parking lot. *Fantasy was* playing, making Mia wonder if Tony had chosen that particular song on purpose; seemed like something he would do. She smiled at that thought. Well, at least he had good taste in music, or so it seemed, so she just grooved to the music while staring out the window. She heard Tony and William talking but tuned out their chatter, listening to the music with thoughts about the Showcase.

There was pause in between songs when Tony got her attention, "*Hello*. Earth to *Mia*," which snapped her out of her thoughts and back to the present.

"Oh sorry, I didn't hear you."

"Yes, I can see that," Tony said laughing.

"Ha. Ha. Ha. So funny, Tony."

"Look, I'm starving and so is Will, so we're gonna slide to ¼ lb. Burger right quick, just letting you know. It won't take too much time, and we are eating it on the way home, cool?"

"Sure thing, I'm good with that."

"You want something? Will has us all covered," Tony said laughing.

"*Say what?*" Will asked pushing Tony on the shoulder.

Still laughing, Tony said, "Just messin' with you man. I got *you* though Mia, what do you want? All that dancing, you gotta be starving."

"I know I shouldn't, but can I get a burger with no onions, extra lettuce, fries, and a small root beer, *please*? I really am starving, but it will probably just go straight to my butt," Mia said without thinking of all who was in the car.

"Oh, uh..." Mia began but didn't finish because she knew that the genie was already out of the bottle. She did not have to wait but a few seconds to hear the backlash from smart-assed Tony.

True to form, "I don't see a problem with that ...you Will?"

William only nodded no, shrugged, and then smiled. Mia rolled her eyes but said nothing. Tony pulled into ¼ lb. Burger, and he and William got out and ordered at the window. A lady in some Daisy Dukes with a big booty walked up to order at the other window. Mia watched Tony and William checking her out, then they came back and got in the car to wait for the food.

"Too bad *she* wasn't on the menu huh?" Mia asked them when they got in.

William just shook his head and said, "Unh, unh, unh."

"No doubts. You know that your lady would cut you *and* her though. Don't even mess like that with dem hot tempered Puerto Rican women, they ain't *no* joke," Tony replied.

"For reals though. Carmen would kill me, but shoot, I can still look, well, as long as she doesn't see me looking. But got to say, that hot-bloodedness has its advantages too though, feel me?" William asked Tony.

"You know that's right," Tony said as they fist bumped.

Mia shook her head and just sat silently. After about 10 minutes she noticed the man at the food window trying to get Tony's attention.

"*Hello*. Earth to *Tony*. The man is waving at you to come and get the food," Mia said from the backseat.

Tony looked back at Mia who just shrugged and stuck out her tongue. Tony smiled and gave her a wink.

"I got it Will," Tony said opening the door.

"Yo', can you get some salt and ketchup though?"

"And pepper please," Mia threw in.

Tony nodded and got out, grabbed their food then got back in the car. He passed food to Mia first, then handed William his.

"Thanks Tony, it smells so good," Mia told him.

"Yeah man, good call stopping here," William chimed in.

"No thang. This place hits the spot for me, a *lot*."

Tony quickly ate about half of his burger, and then started the car up.

"Don't you want to finish first? Mia asked him.

"Naw, I'm good. I've been thirsty as hell today though," he said taking a long sip out of his large soda.

Mia saw William scarfing his food down too, so just chalked it up to being a guy thing. Tony pulled onto the freeway and was nearly at the exit for her and William by the time she had finally finished her burger. She still had some fries left though. Tony was on the offramp when she asked, "Anyone want the rest of my fries?" holding them toward the front of the car.

Tony was drinking his soda again so did not answer, but William replied, "Heck yeah, I'll take them," while reaching back and grabbing them.

William motioned to Tony who took a few out of the bag, then he ate the rest in mere seconds, and just like that, they were gone. William grabbed his backpack off the floor as Tony slowed down before coming to a stop.

"Okay man, thanks for the ride, catch you at school tomorrow, nice meeting you Mia," William said while getting out.

"Nice meeting you too William," Mia said with a wave.

"*Yuuuuup*. All good, see you man," Tony replied as William got out.

After he closed the door, Tony asked her, "So how do I get to your place Mia?"

"Make a left and go up the hill, make the first right and the address is 101."

"Cool," Tony said as he headed towards Mia's house.

"Hey Mia, I need a favor," Tony said as they were pulling up to her house.

"A favor? Like *what*?" Mia asked apprehensively.

"Uh, I *really* need to use your bathroom. Thought I could hold it, but that large soda after all that water I drank today definitely did not help. Trying to get healthier, so been drinking more water. Hell, I even ate salad twice this week."

"Oh, is that all? Don't be silly of course you can. Water is good for you, I need to drink more myself," Mia said while opening the car door.

Tony popped the trunk, "Great, I'll grab your stuff."

Tony grabbed her bag and backpack, then met her on the porch as Mia was getting her keys out of her purse. She opened the door and they walked in.

"The bathroom is straight down the hallway at the end, "Mia said pointing left.

"Thanks, won't be but a minute."

Mia put her stuff in her room and went back to wait in the living room for Tony. She heard the bathroom door open, "I'm here in the living room by the front door Tony," Mia yelled out.

Tony came back in the room, "I definitely wouldn't have made it home, thanks."

"Mia? Mia, is that you?" Mia's mother Olivia said while walking down the hallway towards the living room where they were.

"Yes, Mom, we're in here."

Olivia, walked into the room. "Oh, so you're the friend that brought Mia home, huh? she asked Tony with a scrutinizing gaze top to bottom.

"Yes ma'am. There weren't that many people left, and I didn't want Mia waiting alone for a ride, so offered to bring her home," Tony replied.

Olivia's demeanor instantly changed after that comment, "Well, that is very nice of you. You are a nice young man, now isn't he Mia?"

Mia rolled her eyes and Tony smiled.

"Well, I have three sisters, so I am mindful of how women are treated. I was at rehearsal working backstage where Mia was, and bringing her home was not too far out of my way. I dropped another friend off too. Was no problem, really ma'am. We did stop to get something to eat which is why it might have taken a little longer. Sorry if you got worried."

"Oh, say you did? Mia, did you have enough money to get something to eat?"

"Tony paid for my food mom."

"Unh. Well let me go get you some money, you just wait right here a minute, will you?" she asked rhetorically, turning to walk back down the hallway.

"It's fine Mrs. Taylor," Tony called out.

"Now you just wait right there. I *said* I will be right back."

Tony looked over at Mia, who just looked down and shook her head, "You're going to have to wait, she does not back down."

Tony shook his head and laughed.

"Hmm, now I wonder where you get your sass from?"

"Now see? I told you that I would be right back," Olivia said walking towards them from the hallway. She walked into the living room and handed Tony a ten-dollar bill.

"Oh, this is too much."

"Well, you used your gas, didn't you? Mia may need another ride sometime, so this will help. Thank you, young man. What was it, *Timmy*?"

"Umm, it's Tony. You're welcome."

"Mmm hmm, okay. Now drive home safely, and Mia, you better go get that homework done. Bye ... *Tony*," she told them and walked back down the hallway, went in her bedroom, then closed the door.

Mia let out the giggle she was holding in, "Well, guess you have some brownie points now, *Timmy*."

"Got jokes huh*?*"

"I couldn't miss that opportunity," Mia said laughing.

Tony just gave her a deadpan stare, "Uh huh, got it all out of your system now?"

"Maybe. But for real, I really did appreciate the ride."

Tony cocked his head to the side and continued staring.

"*And* for dinner, thanks again."

"Uh huh. So, you ready to admit it yet?"

"Admit what?"

"What I told you."

"Boy, you have told me a lot of things with all that talking out of the side of your neck you do."

"Okay Miss Smarty-pants, you know what I'm talking about."

Mia just rolled her eyes and shook her head no.

"I really, really do *not.*"

"Yeah, you do. We, *have* become friends, and it's only getting better, right? *Right*? It's okay, I know I was right."

"Ugh, okay, okay. Yes, we *are* friends. *Yes*, you said that we would be. There, said it - you happy now?"

"Maybe," Tony said laughing.

"Whatever *Timmy*," Mia said making a face.

"Watch it Miss Thing, but look, I best get rolling home, gotta cram for a test 2nd period tomorrow."

"Okay, let me walk you to the door. Seriously, thanks again," Mia told him opening the door.

"All good," Tony told her with a wink while walking out.

She closed the door, feeling really glad they had become friends. They shared a vibe that just did not seem possible to put into words. It was all so long ago, but she could feel that connection still remained. She could talk to him tomorrow, and it would all come back and feel like they just spoke last week instead of decades ago.

Mia drained the rest of her bloody mary, then sat her empty glass on the table. The solar lights were now glowing, and she lay there enjoying the ambience until it got chilly. She turned off the fountain, then grabbed her glass and chips and went back inside. She showered, threw on a nightshirt, a pair of fluffy socks, then padded to the kitchen. As her chicken gnocchi soup was heating up, she began eating her salad, and it dawned on her just how hungry she had become. She ate every last bit of it. All that yard work must have done it she decided. She tried watching TV, but nothing kept her attention, so she turned it off, put the dishes away, then headed to her bedroom.

As she began walking to her room, Giovanni and those past couple of days she spent at the hotel crossed her mind bringing a big smile. She had almost forgotten that she told him she would email him later. She grabbed her laptop, sat on her bed, and quickly logged on:

Hey Mr. Giovanni,

Guess who? Sometimes you get what you ask for, here I am hahaha. Hope you had a nice Sunday. I picked up a few things at the nursery and worked in the yard all afternoon. Very cathartic, but got carried away, so no doubts that I will feel it tomorrow. But it's all good because the yard is looking much better, so well worth the effort. Not sure when I will get a chance to make it back down the coast, but I hope it will be soon. I enjoyed meeting you and even more, spending time with you - immensely.

Tag you're it!
Mia

After she sent the email and closed her laptop, she began feeling the effects from the day. Her bed was began feeling especially comfortable. She turned off the crystal lamp on her nightstand, snuggled under the covers, and began to doze off.

"Ah-oo-gah, Ah-oo-gah ...."

Hearing Javier's ringtone stopped the Sandman from luring Mia to sleep; she turned over and clumsily reached for her phone. In the dark she knocked it off the nightstand and could now hear the ringtone playing underneath her bed, where apparently her phone had slid.

"I don't fucking *believe* this," she said out loud throwing her hands up in exasperation.

Mia turned on the light, looked under the bed and saw her phone. It was still lit up and the ringtone still playing, but damn, it was too far to reach. She went to get the broom out of the pantry, used the handle to slide her phone towards her and was finally able to grab it. Of course, by then, the phone had stopped ringing. As she grabbed it and sat on the side of the bed, the voicemail notification popped so she listened:

"Hey Sexy,

Just thought I would give it a shot to see if I might catch you. Maybe I'll have better luck next time. Anyway, I'm at the airport and about to head back to Cali. Hope you're doing good, sure have missed our rendezvous times, and all of those long talks. Hell, I guess what I am trying to say, is that I have missed you. My brother is doing much, much better, but the time away has helped me think through some things and sort some things out, you know? I'll holler at you when I get settled. Just letting you know that you were on my mind and I'm on the way back. Talk to you soon."

Mia had not heard that sexy voice for months now. She was stunned. For a few moments, all she could do was sit there holding the phone and stare at it, the time read 10:32. Damn, now she was wide awake. Shaking her head with a deep sigh, she tossed her phone on the bed. And the hits just keep on coming she thought sitting there. Mia was glad that Javier left a message though, since she was feeling pretty emotionally conflicted just listening to his voicemail.

She grabbed the broom and took it back to the pantry. As she was walking back through the kitchen, she remembered that frozen yogurt, so took it out of the freezer and stuck a spoon in it. She grabbed a handful of strawberries out of the fridge, rinsed them, sliced them, and threw them on top of the yogurt. She nabbed a bottle of water, grabbed her yogurt, and took it all back to her room.

She turned on the TV hoping that maybe something good was on. She scrolled through the guide and found Princess Bride had just started. She climbed back in bed to watch it while eating her yogurt. The movie was a great distraction, and before she realized it, she was feeling sleepy again. Good thing for all that yardwork, or she would most likely be living through one of her insomniac nights from hell. She turned off the TV and crashed out.

Mia woke up the next day at the regular time as if she were going to work for some reason. Damn, I have a Monday off, and can't even sleep in - *what the fuck?* She lay there for a few moments trying to fall back asleep but could not. She rolled her eyes and with a heavy sigh, sat up in bed. After sitting there for a few seconds, she decided to just go ahead and get out of bed. She was finding out that the older she got, the stiffer her body became, so began doing some light stretches, when a great idea hit her. Mia grabbed her phone and checked the Hot Yoga schedule on her app, then signed up for a class that was scheduled in 30 minutes.

Mia hit the bathroom, got dressed, then gobbled down half of a peanut butter sandwich. She filled her purple Yeti cup with water and ice, then grabbed a hand towel for her face, a bath towel for the mat, and the yoga mat out of the hall closet. She let the garage up, threw it all on the passenger seat, and boom, she was on her way. She threw in a cd and Warren Hill serenaded her all the way there. She found a spot near the back of the lot, getting there with a few minutes to spare. All the *"Yoga Divas"*, with their freakin' perfect form who were *always* there were already down in front. Slightly envious, Mia recognized that she was most definitely not one of those, well, not yet she thought with a smile.

It was a hell of a work-out as usual, but she knew her body would thank her later. She walked out to her car totally drenched from class with the bath towel wrapped around her neck. As soon as she got home, she ran a hot shower then dressed in leggings and an oversized Prince t-shirt. Today was going to be all about comfort.

Mia looked at the clock, it was only 9:14 a.m. She felt quite pleased she had gone to class and was already back home. She could not help smiling knowing that she still had the whole day to kick it. She went into the kitchen to make herself a hot cup of Jasmine tea, then carried it over to the sofa. Hmmm, sipping that tea bought back a vivid memory of Javier. She closed her eyes and let her mind drift back to that erotic filled afternoon:

Javier had lost a sports bet, for what she could not recall, but by *her* winning, she got to decide what would happen the next time he was in her bed. Javier came over, showered as usual, and came walking out of the bathroom with a towel wrapped around his waist.

"Bet you won't talk shit about my Lakers quite so fast anymore *now*, will you Mister Man?

Javier just gave her a blank stare and said nothing.

"So, here's the deal, you are under my control, and there is no talking or touching until or unless I give you permission - or the game is over. We both know that you are not a quitter, so I think you will be a good boy," she told him with a wink.

Javier nodded telling her, "Okay, okay, I lost the bet so let's get this over with."

"Please take off your towel, then lie down on the bed."

Following instructions, Javier unwrapped the towel from his waist, got in bed, and Mia placed a blindfold on him. As he lay there trembling with anticipation, Javier felt her lightly touching his calves, then his thighs. Higher...higher...higher... and then she stopped touching him. His erection was getting stiffer by the minute.

"What are you..." he began.

"The rules are *no* talking until I tell you, or the game is over," Mia sternly told him.

Javier nodded in agreement, and he could only lie there waiting in anticipation of her next touch. Mia could sense his acceptance of his submissive state, so began planting the teeniest, tiniest kisses, on his neck, his shoulders, and his inner arm. She knew his dick was probably screaming to be touched, but she chose to avoid it for now, knowing it would only increase his level of desire. She could tell from his body's reactions that he was enjoying what she was doing to him.

She began kissing his nipples, then licking them, and finally sucking one then the other into her mouth, going from side to side until he was going crazy. She stopped and crawled down in between his legs, but did not touch him yet, knowing that it had to be driving him crazy. It probably seemed to him like an eternity, until he felt her hot breath on his balls and then his dick. His body quivered in anticipation, until she began kissing his inner thighs, alternating between them.

She lightly brushed her breasts along his inner thighs, then against his balls, finally rubbing his dick in between her breasts. She continued her ascent up his body, her nipples grazing his stomach, then his chest, his neck, until they were finally against his lips. She delighted in knowing that he wanted to touch them. She rubbed them on his face, and then told him, "I want you to keep your mouth closed while I do this. Just nod if you understand."

Javier nodded an enthusiastic yes. Mia began kissing him with tiny, soft kisses all over his face ending with his lips. He was trying to keep his mouth closed as agreed; it was much harder than he ever expected, but at the same time, beyond exciting. She softly kissed his lips and then ran her tongue ever so lightly over first the top and then the bottom lip. Then he felt her mouth being replaced by yes - one of those glorious breasts. He could feel her erect nipple and wanted to suck it into his mouth so badly. Mia rubbed first one breast, and then the other breast on his lips, then she took them away.

Next, she began slowly and softly kissing his neck, then softly sucking on the lobe of his right ear. She reached down and wrapped her fingers around his rock-hard dick, and Javier could not help but let out a soft moan. She stroked him and caressed his balls before she rubbed her breasts across his lips again. This time Mia told him, "Lick them for me Javier, they need to be licked please."

Javier wasted no time. He began licking them as if it they were large caramel lollipops.

Breathlessly she said, "Javier, can you please suck them for me now?"

Javier wasted no time sucking those chocolatey nipples into his mouth. She ran her fingers through his hair and then grabbed his head smashing his face into her breasts. Since she was straddled over him, she knew that he could feel her body undulating from all his sucking and licking as well as feel her wetness oozing onto his stomach. Javier's erection was rock hard.

"Touch them now please. Squeeze them, and show me how much you like them Javier, they need your tongue. They want to be licked. They want to be sucked. They want to be nibbled."

As Javier quickly devoured each of her breasts, she touched herself, knowing that his would turn him on even further. She stuck a finger into his mouth which he greedily sucked on. Rewarding him, Mia reached down and yanked off the blindfold, bringing her caramel brown skin, and round full breasts into focus. Javier's heart was beating so hard, she could feel it pounding underneath her body. She looked at him and could tell he wanted so much to speak; she could see it in his eyes. She took pity on him and asked, "You want to say something don't you? You can speak, but only a couple of sentences and then you will have to be silent again, got it?"

Javier nodded, "Mia, I want you so bad, but I want to make *you* feel good even more, will you let me? Please Mia, let me taste you," Javier pleaded.

Mia nodded and Javier quickly threw her on her back and began kissing his way down her smooth, caramel body. He got to her calves, and then began his ascent back up. He reached up and scooped her round ass into his hands, pulling her honeypot to his lips.

"Please, start slowly and softly. Tease me, Javier. Make me want it more and more," she whispered.

Javier began softly licking her lips, which to his pleasure were hairless as usual, and soaking wet. Mia's body began undulating again and he knew she was liking what he was doing. He gave it to her, soft and slow, teasing her, just how she liked it. But when her body begged for it, he devoured her like it was his last meal. She grabbed him by the hair with both hands holding his head still as he sucked her, her body delirious from the pleasure he was giving.

Her orgasm over, Javier pulled back up and lay next to her. After Mia caught her breath but before her body slowed completely down, she rolled over and began with teeny, tiny kisses, all over Javier's chest, then sucking on his nipples as she massaged his dick and balls yet again. She began her descent toward his dick, stopping to stick her tongue in his navel, and lick her way down. At long last she reached her destination. She knew he could feel her hot breath on his dick and balls. His heart was pumping, as the anticipation grew stronger. She knew his dick was aching to be inside of her.

She abruptly stopped and sat on the side of the bed and began sipping a cup of jasmine tea. Javier looked over and saw her drinking it and looked bewildered. She smiled knowing that he had to be wondering why in the hell would she stop to drink tea now, but he had no choice but to lie there silently in suspense. He still was not allowed to speak and did not want to jeopardize any pleasure he was to receive, so just lay there waiting in anticipation, with no idea of what she would do next. He closed his eyes again to make the waiting seem less nerve wrecking. Mia took one last, big sip of tea and held it in her mouth, not swallowing it until she placed the blindfold back on Javier.

Mia smiled knowingly and climbed between his legs, beginning her final assault on his body. She knew that he felt her hot breath on his thighs and balls, and it made his body stiffen in anticipation. She quickly devoured the head of his dick in one motion. Her mouth was oh, *so* hot from that tea, that Javier broke the rules as his body jerked, "Ahh! *Mia!*" he moaned.

This pleased her no end and made her smile, so she did not punish him. She held him in her mouth, knowing that he could feel her tongue slowly moving against it. He was grateful she did not punish him for speaking out, so was not about to speak again without permission and jeopardizing the end to what she was doing. He found himself back to lying there, waiting in anticipation of what she would do to him next. Mia could feel him return to his submissive state, and this turned her on further.

Slowly she began swallowing his dick, inch by inch until she could take no more, his body vacillating from her actions. She pulled him out of her mouth, then reached over, grabbed the cup of tea, and took another large sip, but holding it in her mouth. She reached up and removed his blindfold as she swallowed the tea. She climbed back between his legs knowing her mouth would once more be extra warm from the tea. Their eyes met and locked, and with never breaking eye contact, in one fluid motion she quickly engulfed him in her mouth, sending his body into another spasm. She softly flicked her tongue around the head, then slowly licked the full length up, then down, then back up, then back down, finally just holding him in her mouth, gently sucking.

Before his body slowed back down, she went back to licking him, vigorously this time, as if his dick was a juicy, cherry Popsicle, slowly melting on a hot summer day, and she was not going to allow even one drop to escape *anywhere*, besides her lips and tongue. She felt his body undulating from her passionate assault, until overcome from Mia's stimulation, he left out a soft moan as his body spasmed. He opened his eyes and looked at her as she looked up at him, not stopping, and he was relieved for no punishment again. She could see the gratitude in his eyes. She began kissing his flat, milk chocolate stomach softly, sticking her tongue in his naval, as his breathing slowed down somewhat.

Mia looked up, their eyes locked as she softly asked, "Tell me Javier, what do you want?"

"I want you to climb on top and ride me. I want you to fuck me Mia – fuck me, *hard*."

Mia opened her eyes. She found that her breathing had become a bit labored, her nipples were standing at attention, and that her right hand had traveled down her body and snaked inside of her leggings. Even though Javier's *punishment* had happened a couple of years ago, it seemed like just yesterday; that memory was still so vivid.

She closed her eyes again, and her mind took her right back to that hot, sexy, summer afternoon in her room:

"I promise you Javier, I will milk every last drop out of you," she said to him while straddling his body and climbing into position.

She reached down and grabbed his dick, then slowly began rubbing it along her wet, slippery slit. She slowly and teasingly pushed the head in the mouth of her opening, finally pushing it in. She pulled it back out, and repeated what she did, but saw his eyes silently pleading to end his longing. She began impaling herself very slowly, all the way down, little by little, until every inch was deep inside of her. She began making long strokes all the way down, then back up, back down, back up, with those muscles of hers squeezing and milking his dick, just as she had promised.

She bent down and began passionately kissing his neck, never missing a stroke as he grabbed onto her hips as she slowly rode him. She sat back up and began riding him faster and faster, harder and harder; their sweaty, slippery bodies working in unison like a well-oiled machine. Javier sat partially up, pulling her head back by grabbing her by the hair, before licking and sucking her full brown breasts. He released her hair and they kissed passionately, never missing a stroke. She knew that he could feel her body convulsing from an orgasm. She could not help moaning while they were kissing.

"Damn. Mia why do you feel so good?

"Why do *you* feel so good?"

"I love how you fuck me Mia. I love being deep inside of you. I just can't get enough."

Mia sat up again, grabbing onto the headboard of her sleigh bed with both hands for leverage. Javier grabbed her hips and slammed them down on his dick... *hard*. Over, and over, and over again.

"Yes Javier. Fuck me hard - I want to feel every, fucking, inch."

Their intensity increased as their passion grew more frenzied.

"Damn baby, I can barely hold back."

"Don't hold back. Let go. Show me how good it is to you. *Show me Javier.*"

"I don't want it to end it though, it feels too good."

Mia leaned down and breathlessly whispered in his ear, "You know I can't wait to fuck you again, so give it to me, give it to me *now*, Javier."

Hearing those words sent him over the edge, "Oh Mia. *Mia!*"

As she heard him moaning her name, Mia was pushed over the edge into their now joint explosion of ecstasy. Slowly their bodies began slowing down, and she climbed off and laid across Javier's chest. Javier began drifting to sleep as she gently moved down his body, and slowly enveloped his deflating dick into her mouth. His eyes opened and their eyes met as Mia softly sucked for a few seconds, until Javier spasmed one last time.

"Damn Mia. You're sexy *as fuck*. No wonder I can't get enough of you."

Mia smiled, "I can't get enough of you either, sexy man."

Damn what a flashback; such an intense memory. Mia had to catch her breath thinking back on that one, and it was only one of *many* scintillating memories with Javier. Her age never did seem to factor into their sex life at all, but it did give Mia an incentive to try to stay toned and in shape. Lying there, her body began feeling the effects of that hot yoga class earlier, so she grabbed her fluffy throw and drifted off to slumberland, right there on the sofa.

It ended up being a fairly long nap - almost three hours. Mia woke up starving and decided a change of plans was in order. She threw on a pair of jeans, a Lakers hoodie, and slipped into a pair of black Nikes, then headed out. She decided to treat herself to lunch at The Olive Garden. She dined on the cheese ravioli and salad. Since they did not serve lunch on the weekends, the dinner portion proved too much for her to finish, so she had them pack it up to take home. She could eat the rest for dinner and not have to cook, which pleased her. She decided against stopping at Nordstrom and headed back home.

She put her food in the fridge and decided to do a few loads of laundry. She ended up binge watching Bridgerton while getting her laundry washed, dried, and folded. Looking at the Duke's body made her think of Javier, and how much she longed for his sexy brown body in her bed. Those stolen moments shared in their secret rendezvous times were always, *always* great, but ... would it ever happen again? The odds were against it, but then again you never know. There are those *endless possibilities* she told herself, which brought her a bit of consolation. She considered returning Javier's call, but decided against it, feeling that he still needed to have space.

No longer feeling like eating the leftovers, Mia threw together a small salad instead, and decided to take the leftovers for lunch the next day. As she was getting up from the kitchen table, she looked over at the two baskets of laundry sitting by the couch with dread. Ugh, it was time to put all of it away, which she found to be the very worst part of doing laundry. Somehow, she managed to get it done quickly.

She plopped down on her bed and grabbed her phone to set the alarm for tomorrow when she saw that it was almost 10 p.m. Well thanks to that long nap on the couch she was not feeling the least bit sleepy. She decided to run a warm bath to try to relax, so threw some Epsom salt in the water and lit an aromatherapy three-wick candle sitting on the tub's ledge to add more ambience. She turned off the light then slid into the water and lay back. The first thought that popped into her head was of going back to work tomorrow, but she forced it out of her mind. The water felt so good; it brought back memories of lying in Giovanni's hot tub. Damn, that was an amazing night, and a magical two days.

The bath worked its magic, so Mia dried off and grabbed her nightshirt. She turned off the light, but climbed into the bed naked, still holding the nightshirt in her hand. Feeling her 1000 thread count cotton sheets against her bare skin after a long bath was a glorious feeling that she absolutely relished. She lay there until her body cooled down, then catching a slight chill, she quickly slipped her nightshirt on. With hopes that the dark room would help maintain her serenity, she pulled the covers up and closed her eyes.

Morning came way too fast, as Mia heard her alarm waking her. She could not remember a thing after turning off the light and getting in bed. Wow, I must have been more tired than I thought, she decided. Even with the rest, per her norm, she hit snooze a few times before rolling out of bed to get dressed. First day back, so her vanilla latte was crucial, and she swung by the drive thru on her way to work.

Her girls at work, Ashley, and Kim, were not in the office, but attending seminars until Thursday, so she threw herself into her work. She had only been gone three days, yet there were so many emails to catch up on before she could even get to the files in her queue. Thank God for caffeine she thought sitting there sipping her latte.

Tuesday and Wednesday, proved to be pretty uneventful but terribly busy, preventing her imagination to run wild as it normally would, especially with that *Eenie, Meenie, Miney,* thang going on. As Thursday rolled around Mia was again immersed in her work, and so engrossed in her files that she did not even notice anyone standing in front of the wall of her cubicle. Finally, she looked up when she saw fingers snapping at her on her side of the cubicle wall, and Ashley standing there.

"Hey Mia, I'm *baaaaaaack!* So, whatcha got going on this weekend?"

"Hey Ash-a-lee, what's going on?"

"Umm. I think I need to call in that big favor from taking you to your mechanic all those times," she told her with her hands clasped together in prayer mode.

"Hmm, a favor huh? What *kind* of favor Missy?" she asked peering over her glasses with one eyebrow raised.

"Well, my cousin Barry is getting married on Saturday afternoon, and I kind of *have* to go to the wedding, being family and all, *but*...." she trailed off looking perplexed.

"But? But what?"

"But I need a date. So, will you be my 'And One'? Please oh *please*? I know, I know, it's late notice on a Thursday and all, but I waited too late to ask that guy Brad I met online. He already has plans and will be out of town. Come on Mia, 'cause you know that I am *not* brave like you. I just can't go places alone."

"A wedding huh? What time?"

"It's not until 4:00, so you still have the whole day to yourself pretty much. The reception is going to have prime rib, one of your faves, *plus* a hosted bar," Ashley told her staring at her intently but apprehensively.

"Girl, you know there is nothing wrong with going somewhere alone, come on now Ash," Mia flatly told her.

Ashley's green eyes briefly teared up and she looked away. She turned back giving Mia a sad emoji-like face, before pleading, "Aww come on Mia, if you really don't have plans, it will be good for you to get out. A nice meal and "dranks". And who knows, maybe there might be some hotties there just waiting to meet us," she said winking.

"Girl, you know most people come to weddings in couples, and *hello*, there usually are not too many eligible men at weddings, or should I say men that you or I would *want,*" Mia told her snapping her fingers twice and waving her arm.

Ashley smiled, "See? We can drink and talk shit about what people are wearing, and drink and get our groove on and dance a little bit.... did I mention dancing? Did I mention drinking? *Hello? Hosted bar*??? Come on Mia, say yes ... *pretty please?*"

Rolling her eyes and shaking her head in disbelief, Mia said, "I don't know Ash, I won't even know anybody."

"Ooh, unh-unh. Okay, I know you did *not* just say that. You know *me*. With this ass how did you miss seeing *me*?" Ashley said turning around and pointing to her butt while sticking it out.

"Oh, stop it. You *do* have a sista's booty though," Mia said, and could not help but to laugh.

"Come on Mia, when is the last time you and I just kicked it out somewhere? If you are bored as hell we can leave, I promise - but *after* we eat," Ashley said staring at her with a sad face.

Mia looked at Ashley and rolled her eyes, then told her, "Okay, okay, okay, I will go. I did promise you way back when a big favor, and you know I live by word is bond."

"Coolio! Thanks Mia. I will pick you up like 3ish. It's downtown at the Vizcaya. I don't have any idea of what I'm going to wear. Just gotta go home and try on stuff and see what I can fit. And my hair, Lord only knows," Ashley told her throwing her hands up.

"Girl, try being a sister and deal with this hair," she said pointing to her hair.

"Hey, your hair is very nice. You can wear your natural curl, or flat iron it straight, so be quiet. I would love to have your hair."

"Oh, trust me, it's not easy as you might think. Especially after I *do* flat iron it, then it rains, and it gets all frizzy. You can't even relate, but yeah, okay, you do have a point. Must be that White plantation owner in my ancestral chain huh?"

"Girl, stop it. You are so crazy. See? We are going to have so much fun Saturday, just watch. Thank you, thank you, *thank you*. I am almost looking forward to going now. Shoot, get a few shots of liquor into my, *no filter* friend right here, and who knows what the night may bring," Ashley said laughing.

"True that Ash," Mia said laughing herself.

"Okay I better get back to my desk, thanks *so much* Mia. It's going to be fun and you're going to be telling me later, 'I'm so glad I went with you Ashley', you just mark my words."

"Uh huh, I think you're getting a little carried away now, but whatever makes you sleep at night girl."

"*Sleep at night?* News flash girlfriend – I haven't met him yet – *boom!*" Ashley said while simultaneously pointing both fingers towards Mia and walking backwards.

"Boom is right. Girl, watch where you're walking," Kim said laughing and pushing Ashley back after she backed into her.

Ashley jumped, "Oh *snap* Kim!"

Kim was at least 4 inches taller than either Ashley or Mia, with voluminous black hair and gorgeous, big brown eyes.

"Well excuse *me*, but you need to be watching where you're walking next time Missy," Kim said still laughing.

"Uh huh. See? That's what you get for messing with me," Mia said laughing along with Kim.

"Aww, I see how it is then," Ashley said throwing her hands up and laughing with them.

"So, what's up girlfriends? What ya'll doing this weekend? I'm going to a wedding but not sure about the reception, might ditch. Maybe we can all hang out and have some "dranks" 'n tasty 'lil appetizers and whatnot somewheres, y'all in?" Kim asked them while nodding her head yes with raised eyebrows.

"That's funny, because I'm going to a wedding Saturday too. My cousin Barry is finally getting married to the love of his life, Shelly, and I just twisted Mia's arm into going with me as my date to the wedding and reception," Ashley said winking at Mia.

"Wait, hold up. Not Shelly Jackson and Barry Nixon's wedding?"

"Yes, that one. How did *you* know? That's weird," Ashley said frowning.

"Well, that's because, *you big silly*, it's the same one me and my sister are going to. Shelly is one of my sister Alicia's best friends. She's actually a bridesmaid in the wedding. Hey Mia, you got hella lucky, 'cause the wedding colors are black and white. That color scheme totally works for you since you are like the wife of Zorro, *always* wearing black," Kim told her laughing again.

"Oh, don't hate - Miss Thing," Mia replied with attitude.

"Our family has known Shelly's since we were little kids. Wow, what a trip. Small world for sure. Ooh, so we will all be there? Well, whaddaya know, *heeyyy*," Kim said high fiving Ashley.

"You guys are out of control," Mia said shaking her head and laughing.

"But I do have to admit, the whole wedding thing does sound better being there with two of my girls," Mia said joining in the laughter.

"See? Told you Mia. We can all touch base on Saturday morning, cool?" Ashley said.

Before she could answer, out of the corner of her eye Mia saw Mrs. Johnson, their supervisor coming down the hallway.

"Pssst. Hey, here she comes, you guys better get back to your desks," Mia whispered, quickly putting her earbuds back in.

"Ooh, no joke," Ashley said and turned down the next aisle and Kim walked away in the opposite direction.

Mia pretended to look in her desk drawer when Mrs. Johnson slowed down as she got near her desk. Mia looked up and nodded her head in acknowledgment and Mrs. Johnson smiled, nodded in return, and kept on walking by.

Mia sent a group text to Ashley and Kim:

> *All good, she didn't say anything. Now we have to find something to wear that doesn't make our butts look too big.... may the odds be forever in our favor LOL.*

Ashley and Kim both replied with laughing emojis.

Mia began wondering what shoes to wear. Since according to Kim, she was Zorro's wife, so undoubtedly would be wearing black. Mia always chose her shoes first, then if nothing really matched in her closet, her shoes could always "pop" a black outfit, and frequently did. In her mind she was leaning towards the Steve Madden rhinestone pumps, or her favorites, the candy apple red patent leather Stuart Weitzman pumps, or possibly a pair of T-Strap black patent heels. She smiled thinking about how her dad used to tell her that she and Imelda Marcos would be good friends if they ever met.

The rest of the day passed by uneventfully and finally, it was time to go. As much as Mia wanted to go home, throw on some jammies, and hit the sofa, she decided to go to the gym and hit the U-Jam class. If she had not packed her gym bag and put it in the car this morning, the gym right now would not even be an option. The song list was booming, and Mia was glad she had made the choice to go to class. As she was driving home, she felt proud of herself for at least trying to stick with her resolution to get in better shape while she was on her getaway. Ooh, her getaway, last weekend and Giovanni. The thought of him brought a smile to her face.

After a hot shower Mia slipped into a night shirt and made a chef salad for dinner. She opened her laptop and brought up her email. There was an email from Giovanni from about an hour ago. Damn, we must be on the same wavelength Mia mused. She clicked on it:

My Dearest Mia,

I hope this message finds you doing well. Hard to imagine that it was only a week ago that I had the good fortune for my path to cross yours. It's been a busy week getting things running "under new management", as it were, but as you can probably tell, I enjoy my job and like being busy. Although if my leisure time included you, well, you know, I just might be inclined to work a little less. I just wanted to say hello, and to remind you that someone is thinking of you time to time.

Gio

Mia replied immediately:

Hello Mister Man,

Nice to hear from you, and I have to agree that email is nicer than just sending texts. Since we both have Iphones, who knows, maybe one day soon we can Facetime? Just a thought. But let me know in advance so I don't look a wreck. My week has been okay, but so glad tomorrow is Friday. I have no doubts that you will have things running like a well-oiled machine in your new position in no time, that is, in case you haven't done so already.

Yes, it was a week ago today that the universe had our paths intersect, or was it that one of us manifested the other? Thanks for thinking of me. I cannot say that you haven't crossed my mind time to time as well, *wink, wink.

Mia

Nice to know I was not exactly a one-night stand, and I am still on his mind somewhat. Still, she was glad he was not nearby though. That would most likely lead to spending more time together, which could begin leading down a path to who knows what. Mia was all about the absence makes the heart grow fonder school of thought and such. She decided that at least another month needed to pass before she ventured back down to see Giovanni though, *plus*, it would give her something to look forward to, which she always needed. Ooh, another trek down the coast, and best of all, staying there would be free!

The gym began hitting her, so she shut down her laptop and climbed into bed. Thank the Lord tomorrow was Friday. She had not emailed Tony back yet; she was still at a loss on how to respond. She began wondering when or if she would hear from Javier since he was back now. It was tempting to text him, but she just felt that the next move was still his. Her tired body soon won out over her rambling mind and before she knew it, she was off in slumberland.

II

Mia's ears hearing those familiar nature sounds of waves crashing against the shore woke her up. No, no, no... it just cannot be morning already Mia thought clumsily reaching for her phone to hit snooze. The waves came back again *way* too soon. How is that 10 minutes already Mia thought looking bleary eyed at the time on her phone. If I hit snooze one more time, I can still get to work in time, but will be no time for Starbucks. Deal, she decided, as she hit snooze for the last time.

Damn, the waves again. This time she turned off the alarm and reached over to turn on the crystal lamp on her nightstand. With a deep sigh, she quickly pulled off the comforter. The cooler air hitting her body was working. Ugh. Fucking mornings. She was never a morning person and never would be. She silently gave thanks for her blessings, then slowly rolled over, and sat up on the side of the bed. She grabbed her bottle of Smart Water and chugged down a bunch before stretching and finally dragging her sleepy ass out of bed.

Whoever said, "You're not getting older, you're getting better", needed to be throat punched she decided while grudgingly doing her 25 "girl" pushups. Somehow, she managed a plank - only a pathetic 20 seconds, but hey, it would get better if she stuck with it. She was determined to keep trying to hopefully make *some* sort of difference. Although she took a shower after class last night, there was no way she could even begin to function without another one this morning. She slowly walked into the bathroom and turned the dial all the way to the left to get the water warm while she did her bathroom thing. Even while brushing her teeth and washing her face, she was still feeling groggy, and totally counting on the shower to revive her.

She opened the shower door, feeling the steam immediately hit her face, and putting her at ease. Although the water was only moderately warm, it still felt good splashing over her breasts and running down her body. She could feel it getting warmer by the second until it became fiercely warm, just the way she liked and needed it to be. Ahh, she finally began feeling alive. She pumped some shower gel onto her loofah, lathered up, rinsed off, and wrapped herself into a fluffy white towel.

She went back to the sink to apply moisturizer and lotion her body, then added few spritzes of some Kate Spade cologne. Hurriedly, she wiggled into her undies, slipped into a pair of black slacks and a purple sweater, then slid into a pair of black shootie boots. She pulled her hair into a high bun, then did a quick makeup job – just eyeliner and red lip stain with gloss on top.

She grabbed some fruit out of the fridge on her way out the door to the garage. She let the garage up, jumped in her SUV, and popped in a David Sanborn cd. Her sons teased her about being old school and not streaming, but she had *so* many cds from back in the day, so this is how she rolled. The music kicked in, and she took a deep breath remembering that it was finally Friday, prompting a smile as she backed out. Traffic was so jacked that she barely made it to work on time. Fortunately, she had a Rockstar in the fridge at work, as she had a definite need for it this morning. Right after she logged on to her computer, an email from Ashley popped up.

Hey Missy,

Did you find what you are going to wear
tomorrow? I might be hitting the mall at lunch,
NOTHING FITS! Let me know if you want to come
with.

Ash

Hey Ash,

Nope, I didn't even look, but I have the shoes I
want to wear narrowed down to two, okay maybe
three, so we will see. If all else fails, you know I
have plenty of black dresses and skirts to wear for
them to "pop" my outfit, you know, being like
"Zorro's wife and all LOL

Are you seriously asking me if I want to go to the
mall? *Me*??? Well *DUH*. You know a trip to the mall
is never a bad idea in my book, so, what time you
going to lunch today?

Mia

Hey,

I was thinking 1:00? Meet me at the elevators and see you then.

Ash

Sounds like a plan, seeeee ya.

Mia

The morning dragged, but finally 1:00 rolled around. Mia logged off, grabbed her purse, and dashed to the elevator. Ashley had just gotten in and was holding the door.

"Hurry up!"

"Okay, okay Miss Bossy," Mia said as she sped up her last few steps and jumped in.

"We only have time to go to Macy's probably. Maybe we will get lucky though," Ashley said as the doors closed.

"Guess we will find out," Mia said as the doors opened, and they walked into the parking garage.

Chirp Chirp.

Ashley hit her remote as they reached her car and quickly got in. She started it up, and they were off on their impromptu shopping trip.

"Must be our lucky day, we didn't catch one light and got here in record time," Mia said as they were getting out.

"No doubts. Maybe we should buy a Lotto ticket and see if our luck continues," Ashley said laughing.

They went to the dress section and started browsing. Right away Ashley saw some plum-colored dresses on sale and began looking for her size. She found it and ran over to the mirror and put it up to her body. It had ¾ sleeves, a semi-fitted body, with an A-line bottom.

"Oooh, Mia, whatcha think?"

"I love it, but the real question is ... what *shoes* will you wear with it, hmm?" Mia rhetorically asked laughing.

"Now see, you're so wrong, 'cause excuse *me* Miss Thing, but I recently flipped on a pair of black patent leather pumps, so, *there!*" Ashley said pointing at herself.

"Well now, I just couldn't be prouder," Mia replied laughing.

"I'm going to go pay for it, but not before you find something, get to looking, you know the clock is ticking," Ashley told her pointing to her black Fitbit watch.

"I will probably wear one of my many black dresses, you know I'm already pretty set on wearing those red pumps. Oh-oh, wait - what is *this*?" Mia asked stopping and picking up a muted leopard print dress that caught her eye.

"Damn it's a size 8 too. The universe might be trying to tell me something good right here," she told Ashley as she held it up to her in front of a mirror.

This dress had ¾ sleeves as well, with a V neckline, but had a straight cut instead of A-line like Ashley's dress, and a sexy side-slit.

"Ooh, look at *her*! Girl that is a sexy dress, you *gotta* get it."

"Right? And it's on sale like yours, holla! Hope it fits over the bubble though," she said sticking her booty out and laughing.

"I bet it will. It's okay if it's a little tight, shoot, people pay for an ass like that these days girlfriend. And you know if they don't fit," Ashley said looking at Mia as they were walking to the register, "We will just bring them back!" they said together and started laughing.

"How terrible if we had to bring them back and go shopping yet *again*," Mia said with an exaggerated feigning of wiping sweat off of her forehead with her right hand.

"*Right*? Ashley said before they both broke into laughter again.

As she was getting rung up at the register, Mia saw a really cute sweater but no time to look, they had to get back. They paid for their dresses and raced back to work. Ashley parked and Mia grabbed the bag with her dress in it. They got out and made a mad dash to the elevator, getting in with about five minutes to spare.

"We are lucky the mall is only a few blocks away, and we got our dresses, but no time for food today. I had a Cup-A-Noodles before we left, and I know *you* have some snacks and food Mia."

"You know it."

"Okay, text me when you get home. Maybe we both got lucky, and the dresses will fit, but oh-oh, if yours does fit, you can't wear those red patent leather pumps – *whatever* will you do? I mean Lordy Jesus Mia, you will have to force yourself to find another pair to wear somehow, in your bazillion pairs of shoes huh? Well fuck, *your* life!" Ashley told her laughing as she was walking out of the elevator.

"Well, Mz. Smartypants, I have already recalculated in case this dress fits, and I already know what shoes I will wear, uh, well actually it's narrowed down to two or three pairs. And, just so that you can sleep well tonight, I will have you know that they are all black patent leather, and sexy *as* hell. *Thankyouverymuch*," Mia replied laughing with an exaggerated wink, then turning the opposite way to hurry back to her desk.

The afternoon passed by slowly, and at 5:00 Mia was out of there like a bat out of hell. She never cooked on Friday nights, so grabbed a burrito bowl with chips and guac from Chipotle on the way home. She sat the food on the counter when she got home, and then went straight to her bedroom to try on the dress. She pulled it over her head and wiggled it over her hips. Was a little snug, but it fit! Staring in the mirror, she was especially glad that she was at least somewhat active and not really saggy anywhere.

The closet was calling her, and she walked in and pulled out the three pairs of shoes she had in mind, then tried all of them on. For some reason though, she didn't really care for how any of them looked. Refusing to be defeated, she went back into her closet, looked through the *black* section of her shoes, and then she saw them - the black patent leather heels that crisscrossed over the instep. She tried them on and, *boom*! These were the ones. She looked closer in the mirror at her hair.

Tomorrow she would wash and flat iron it she firmly decided. She took off her shoes and her dress, then hung it up. She quickly stripped off her underwear, threw on a large Magic Johnson t-shirt, and put on some slipper socks. Her stomach grumbled loudly, and she realized that she was starving. Walking to the kitchen, she remembered that she did not really eat much that day at all. Shopping trumped lunch though, and it was well worth the sacrifice to find that dress. She grabbed her phone out of her purse.

Hey Ash,

My dress fit and I got my shoes set too, so not to worry LOL Hope yours fit too!

Almost before she sat her phone down,
Buzz. Buzz. Buzz. Buzz.

What the hell was that Mia wondered. Damn, she had forgotten to take her phone off vibrate after work. She looked, and it was Ashley replying.

Hey,

My dress fit too! And just so you can sleep tonight, I

am wearing black patent leather pumps. Will call
you late tomorrow morning.

Mia smiled, happy that they both found something to wear so fast, and even better, they were on sale! She grabbed her phone and went into the kitchen to get her food. She got a grapefruit Bubbly out of the fridge, then took it all over to the sofa. She turned on the TV and gorged on her food.

Nothing on TV kept her attention, and even though it was dark, she decided to go for a walk. What the hell, the neighborhood was well lit and safe, she thought, but also grabbed her flashlight stun gun and stuck it in her hoodie kangaroo pocket. So often, exercise helped her think things out and clear her mind. She grabbed her earbuds and plugged them into her IPhone, pulled up a playlist, and off she went.

Well didn't I end up with a variety pack of men she thought with a wicked grin. There was Giovanni: Italian, older, extremely financially secure. He was a lovely sort of man that she would enjoy spending time with, but more of a slow burn sexually, although once you reached the "burn" it was totally worth the wait. Then there was Tony: Black, closest to her age, being only two years older, handsome, not especially tall, but tall enough. No idea of how what might play out with his current home situation and all. As far as sex goes, that was still a mystery too, but if the past was any indication, it would work out well. And then of course there was Javier: Black and Hispanic, tall, lean, beyond sexy, and seeming to have that proverbial *hot blood* from his daddy's genes. The mere thought of fucking him again, made her slow her down to catch her breath.

Did it all come down to sex though she wondered? Well, honestly, at this stage of her life, it would absolutely be a crucial component. Some of her friends and her sisters, seemed to have lost almost all interest in sex after menopause, but not Mia. Apparently, she was an anomaly, as she seemed to crave sex much more than when she was younger. When it came down to who though, she was extremely picky. She would much rather go without if there was not someone whom she felt a connection with. Having great chemistry to produce those sparks like she felt with Javier was a definite bonus.

After the divorce, there were quite a few times over the years when she had endured seemingly perpetual sexual droughts. She remembered once living through nearly a year and a half without sex, well, without a partner she smiled. Her toy she kept in her nightstand drawer was handy to have around, rather than some strange guy. Maybe it was the way she was raised, but one-night stands were just not the way she liked to roll.

Of course, there were also many years when her sexuality seemed to be in hibernation. Those years without even having a thought about missing sex or really even having much of a personal life. It could have been from *all* the stress for years in court fighting for custody of Marquis and Russell. Then again, possibly living the life of a single mom and all those long-assed days raising the boys alone, had took its toll.

Mia could remember intermittent and exhausting times when she was working one, sometimes two part-time jobs on the side in order to get the boys through private school. Most likely, it was a combination of those things.

Without enduring that struggle though, she would not have tapped into the inner strength she had unknowingly possessed. In the words of Eleanor Roosevelt, "A woman is like a teabag, you can't tell how strong she is until you put her in hot water."

Mia was certain that she was a living example of that school of thought. Perhaps it had just not been the right time for her true sensuosity to reveal itself. Why the hell am I thinking so hard about all of this right now Mia wondered. What is, *is*. She then realized, as her thoughts had increased in intensity, her walking had become exceptionally brisk, much like an extension of her thoughts.

She had worked up a sweat, so stopped to catch her breath. She looked up and saw she had walked her short walking route nearly twice and was almost back home again, and although she had walked for longer than planned, it felt good. She headed down the last block towards home, no closer to any decisions, but finding herself less agitated and calmer. She walked into the house and turned on some old school jams, then did her pushups. She followed those with 3 sets of crunches and somehow got in 3 sets of bicep curls with her dumbbells before she finally slowed down.

Unfortunately, now she was pumped up and it was nearly 10:00; she knew that sleep would evade her for awhile. She went into the bathroom and turned on the water to start a bath, threw in some Epsom salt, then went into the kitchen and made herself a cup of chamomile tea in her blue and white, Keep Calm and Drink Tea mug, then carried it back to her bathroom. She turned off the water, stripped, then grabbed her tea and slid into the warm bath, exhaling a deep breath. She loved the decadent feeling drinking anything while in the tub. She closed her eyes trying to slow both her body and mind down.

Her thoughts moved to tomorrow and going to the wedding with Ashley. She had owed her big time for all those trips to Javier's and rides to work, but ugh, a wedding? Well, there *was* going to be prime rib, *and* a hosted bar per Ashley, and to be honest, she really had *no* plans whatsoever. Mia drank her tea then slunk down lower in the tub so that the water covered her breasts. The extremely warm water was soothing and felt absolutely glorious. Mia stayed in the tub until her fingers got pruney and the water had cooled off. She got out of the tub feeling much more relaxed than earlier in the evening when she came home. She grabbed a nightshirt out of the dresser drawer, turned off her nightstand lamp, and crawled into bed.

Her body felt somewhat fatigued, yet her mind refused to rest. She decided against turning on the TV again, in hopes that without the distraction, she might fall asleep sooner.

She lay there restless, so tried to focus on something serene, like waves rolling up on a sandy beach. Of course, the beach triggered memories of Giovanni and her fairytale weekend. She decided to email him again when she woke up tomorrow. She was still not sure about reaching out to Tony. And what about Javier? She decided lying there that she would try to keep giving him space until her curiosity got the best of her. Finally feeling some type of closure for the night, she closed her eyes, and finally drifted off into her no longer elusive slumber.

"Answer your phone, Answer your phone ..."

Juanita's ringtone awakened Mia. She lazily rolled over to grab her phone off the nightstand. She squinted to read the time; it was barely 8 a.m. Alarmed that she would be calling so early on a Saturday, she sat up quickly and answered, "Hey sis, what's up?"

Dead silence.

"Juanita, are you there? *Hello*?"

"Hey Mia, sorry to call you so early, just got some scary news is all."

"What? Are you okay? Do you want me to come over?"

"You don't have to do that, I'll be okay, well I hope so. Got a call from Dr. Ainsley late yesterday."

"Stop. Just stop talking. I will be *right* there, just hang tight."

"Really? Sorry to be such a Drama Queen, but I really would appreciate it," Juanita said in a quiet voice.

"I'm about to get dressed right now."

"Thanks sis, bye."

"Bye, see you in a few."

Mia hurried and got dressed throwing on some jeans, a sweatshirt and a baseball cap. As she was backing out, she saw her reflection in the rearview mirror, and realized that she still needed to do something to her hair for that damn wedding later. Mia stopped and got Juanita her favorite, an iced white chocolate mocha, and her vanilla latte, iced this time. As she pulled up to Juanita's house, she saw her sitting in the sun on the front porch, on the blue mosaic bench.

She got out, "I brought you something," she said holding up her mocha.

"Oh Mia, that is just perfect, thank you," Juanita said trying to fight back tears.

Mia looked at Juanita who appeared pretty shaken, "Let's go inside and talk okay?"

Juanita nodded and Mia put her arm around her as they walked into the house and went to the family room. Juanita picked up the remote control and turned the TV off., then came and sat next to Mia on the gray sectional sofa. They sat and sipped their drinks silently.

After a few minutes, Mia looked at her sister, "'Nita, so what's going on?"

Juanita took a deep breath and exhaled, "Well, about a week ago I had my mammogram, and the doctor called me late yesterday afternoon. She said that imaging had found a lump. I have to have a biopsy next week," Juanita told her sadly.

"Oh sis, it's going to be okay, "Mia said moving closer and hugging her.

"Do you think so though? Aunt Maggie May had breast cancer. And one of Mama's other sisters too. It *does* run in the family. That doesn't help my odds at all," she said solemnly looking down and shaking her head.

"Well look, you get a mammogram every year, so even if it is malignant which I don't think it will be, it's early and it's going to be okay. Try not to worry. Do you want me to take you?"

"Thanks, but Gary is taking me. He had to go into the office for something this morning, but will be back a little later. It worked out because I really needed some time to absorb this alone and come to terms with it, you know?"

"Yes, I do."

"I didn't feel it, it's deep in the middle on the right breast. I have dense breast tissue too, so I'm told."

"Yes, so do I. Hmm, I think we all might. But you breast fed the girls, so you know that decreases the odds, right? Did you know that?"

"*Really*? Nope, I wasn't even aware of that. "

"We have to think positive, okay? I know it's gotta be scary though. Is there anything I can do to help?"

"Not really, it's just the waiting that's killing me. Dr. Ainsley got me fast tracked and my biopsy is on Monday. Maybe by this time next weekend, I will have some good news that I'm okay."

"*That's* the way to think," Mia told her hugging her again.

"Thanks Mia. *You* are the baby sister, and look at me acting all scary and shit," Juanita said shaking her head and rolling her eyes.

"I would be scared too," Mia said grabbing and holding her hand.

They sat there in silence for a few moments.

"Hey Mia, are you hungry?"

"So-so."

"Well, I couldn't sleep really, so got up and cooked breakfast for Gary before he left. There's some hash browns like Daddy used to make – fresh potatoes sliced with onions, and there's some bacon too."

Mia raised her eyebrows, "Hmm, did you eat already?"

"Nope, but I need to though. See? You can eat with me. The girls have been gone for years, but I still cook *way* too much, way too often. Come on, let's eat breakfast. I'm going to throw some bread in the toaster you want any?"

"You got any blackberry jam?"

"You know it."

"Okay, then I am *in*," Mia said then smiled.

They walked in the kitchen and sat their coffees on the table. Juanita warmed up the hash browns and threw four slices of bread in the toaster. Mia grabbed the butter, jam, and hot sauce and sat it on the table.

"I'm going to grab some water, want any?" Mia asked opening the refrigerator.

"Yeah, can you grab me one too please?

"Ooh, can we eat some of these strawberries too or are you saving them for something?"

"We had the rest of them last night, so help yourself."

"*Fabulous*," Mia said rinsing a few of them and throwing them in a bowl, then took it over to the table.

Juanita dished up the hash browns, bacon, and two slices of toast for each and brought the plates to the table.

"I didn't think I was hungry, but guess I am after all. I normally can't even think of eating this early."

"Well, you know, it *is* the most important meal of the day and all that."

"So, they say. I do alright without."

"What are you up to today, got any plans? I might go to Macy's One Day Sale; it opens at 9 today."

"I promised a friend I would go to a stupid wedding with her later this afternoon. I *do* owe her though. She was the one who brought me to work when I was having all those issues with my old car, remember those days?"

"Girl, yes. I am *so* glad you finally got a new car a few months ago. Now you don't have to worry about all those car issues, and hell, you deserved it."

"Yeah, I don't have to panic with warning lights and finding wet spots from shit leaking anymore. It was the worst. It was so stressful when I was driving and then all of a sudden hearing, *ding, ding, ding,* or see a red light pop up unexpectedly. My heart would just sink to the pit of my stomach Ugh, it's all over now though. Oh yeah, and before your nephews went back to college after summer, I got them to help me finally clean out the garage, so I can park in there now."

"Well, it's about damn time girl. Wait, look at me, I can't even talk. Mine is bad too, but at least we can still park in there. Just wait until it starts raining, you will be so glad."

"Right?"

They ate in silence and Mia could sense that Juanita was still stressing.

"Hey, it's only 9ish and Ashley isn't picking me up until 3:00, so I can roll with you to Macy's for a minute if you want."

Juanita looked up, "Really? It's not going to mess you up time-wise?"

"As long as I'm back by like one-ish, so I can go home and get ready. I had planned to flat iron my "herr", but who knows? Not like I'm trying to impress anybody. So, we going, or *what*?"

You know it. Let me throw some clothes and shoes on, but..."

"*But*? What now?"

"Will you drive?"

"Well *duh*. You drive like an old lady."

"Be quiet, I do not."

"Oh yes you do. Hurry your butt up then," Mia said laughing.

Juanita stuck her tongue out and made a face.

"It will only take me a minute girl," she said dashing off to her bedroom.

Mia got up to rinse the dishes and put them in the dishwasher. Before she could wash the skillet though, Juanita had walked back into the room, "Let's roll!"

"Oh *snap*. K, we are out!"

They jumped in Mia's car and were off to Macy's.

"Unh, unh, unh," Mia said shaking her head no.

"What?"

"I was just here with Ashley yesterday. I bought a dress for the wedding, and I saw this sweater I liked, but didn't have time to look at, so this is good – it was meant to happen."

"You know that we get this shit straight from Mama, so let's just blame *her*, 'cause that woman *can* shop," Juanita said laughing.

"True that 'Nita, true that."

"Okay this is right up your alley, because I need to go to the shoe department Mia."

"Holla."

Ba-ling. ling. Ba-ling. ling.

Mia grabbed her phone out of her purse, Ashley had texted:

Hey,

You aren't ghosting me, right? Pick you up at 3ish?

Mia replied:

I'm still down. I'm at Macy's with one of my sisters.
See you then.

She stuck her phone back in her purse, "Ooh, I'm going to try these on, what do you think?" Juanita asked her, holding up a pair of black sandals.

"Cute."

Mia looked to see what else was in Juanita's other hand and frowned.

"Wait. Just trying on *one* pair? Unh, *rookie.*"

"Oh, be quiet."

Juanita sat down to wait for the salesperson to bring her size as Mia came bopping over with four pairs of shoes, sitting them on the empty chair next to her.

"What in the actual hell Mia?"

"I am only trying them on, *dang.* Don't be getting your thong all wrong Missy. It doesn't mean that I'm going to buy them all. And so what if I do? I don't have anybody to answer to. *Nobody* is the boss of me. It makes me feel good, *and,* it *a*in't gonna hurt nobody. Divorce has its perks and can sometimes be bliss too, ya know," Mia said crooking her neck and snapping her fingers twice.

"Okay, *okay.* Uh...but apparently it is *you*, with *your* thong all wrong Miss Thing - okay, *wait.*"

"What?" Mia asked holding up her hands.

"Just hold up a minute. Let me see that red shoe you got over there. Hand it to me," Juanita said narrowing her eyes, looking over trying to see the shoe.

Mia grabbed the shoe and held it up. Juanita nodded and motioned with her hand for Mia to hand it to her.

"Uh huh, *see*?"

They looked at each other and laughed, - loud, then quickly looked around slightly embarrassed. No one seemed to be paying them any attention, so they just both shrugged it off. Juanita ended up getting both the black and the red pair. Mia didn't get any of the shoes she tried on after all.

"I can't believe you didn't buy *any* of those shoes."

"Just wasn't feeling any of them, and *hello*, not like I need any."

"Gee, you *think*?"

"Okay Miss Smarty-pants, but I do want to see if I and find that sweater, so let's go upstairs."

"Wait, I need to get some lipstick first, come on over here right quick," Juanita told her.

They both *shopped 'til they dropped*, with Mia ending up with *that* sweater, a pair of jeans, and a couple of nightshirts. In addition to the two pairs of shoes, Juanita got the same pair of jeans as Mia, a dress, a skirt, and a few t-shirts. Since Juanita *always* had to try on her clothes, and she tried on a lot, she spent a considerable time in the dressing room.

"Damn, where did the time go? I'm sorry Mia, we better get going so you can get home, Juanita said as they were paying for their haul.

"No worries, I'm feeling lazy already. I think I'm just going to wear my hair natural or pull it up," Mia told her, knowing that making her sister feel better was far more important than doing her hair for some wedding she didn't really have any interest in going to anyway.

"Aww, okay. Look Mia, thanks for today, for real though," Juanita said hugging her.

"That's what family is for, right? But let's book it so I can at least take a bath," Mia said laughing.

"You got it sis."

Mia dropped Juanita off, got home, and began running a bath. It was already after one, but she had definitely decided that she was not flat ironing her hair, instead choosing to take a long, relaxing bath.

"Ahh," she said out loud as she sank into her glorious bath.

Although she tried to not think, and just relax, thoughts still popped into her head: Life is so strange and unpredictable; everything is going along fine and then something unexpected happens. Or someone pops up unexpectedly, or someone crosses your path. Change is inevitable though - it *is* going to happen. It's just that it seems to happen when you are least expecting it. Usually, it's not what you wanted so you have to adapt, but sometimes, *sometimes,* it can be something good *and* positive Mia thought.

Last week this time she was heading home after a glorious weekend with an unexpected twist – Giovanni. She had not told her girls Ashley and Kim, or even her boy Mark about him, and not sure if she would, unless something more happened between them. She had not seen Tony for decades, so was not even sure how he looked anymore, but doubtful he would have changed too much she decided. Then there was that sexy Javier who may or may not be out of play. Wow, what a variety pack between Tony, Javier, and Giovanni. *Heeyyy,* maybe this girl at 56 *still* has game, she thought making her smile.

Ba-ling. ling. Ba-ling. ling.

Ashley's text tone snapped Mia out of her mind wanderings and back to the day at hand. She had no idea of what time it was but figured she needed to get her ass out of the tub and get ready for this damn wedding. She really felt like taking a nap and flaking but she had given Ashley her word. She got out, dried off, and wrapped the towel around her. She grabbed her phone and read the message:

Hey Mia,

I'm running late, just got home from doing errands and lost track of time. Will be there more like 3:15!

Well, that's a relief, more time was good. If only she hadn't stayed in the bathtub so long, she could have squeezed in a 15-minute power nap. She considered still giving it a shot, it was only 2:20 after all, but decided against it. She knew that the time constraint would prevent her from falling asleep because she had to get up so soon. On a whim, she decided to ditch her glasses for the wedding, and pop in her contacts. She also decided to do more of a glam makeup instead of her minimal work make up, it had been so long. She put on foundation, went with her smokey eye look, but added a little plum and gold eyeshadow, two extra coats of mascara, and a little blush with a cheek highlighter. She went with a matte, deep fuchsia, plum-like lipstick color, no gloss. Fullfed out some curls in front and tendrils in the back and pulled her hair up, securing it with her rhinestone studded clip.

She looked at the time on her phone, it was 3:00, oh snap! Where had the time gone? How do some women do their makeup like this every day she wondered while slathering lotion over her body quickly and putting on her undies. She grabbed a pair of Hane's black pantyhose, then began wiggling into them. She was well aware some called her Old School, but women of a certain age needed to wear pantyhose, especially in the evening. She would have more of a finished look, plus her legs would look sexier, Mia's reflection in the mirror confirmed this fact.

She slipped into her dress, zipped it, then sat down on the bench in front of her bed to fasten the small gold buckles on the sides of her shoes. She got up and scrutinized herself in the mirror one last time, turning both ways. Hmm, the dress hugged her ass just right, but she realized she had forgotten to put on a pair of earrings. She quickly chose a pair of gold, rhinestone infinity hoops.

The thought of a wedding, ugh. Mia went straight to her kitchen, poured a large shot of Pineapple vodka and threw it back. As soon as she sat the glass down, she heard a familiar sound:

Ba-ling. ling. Ba-ling. ling.

Mia looked at her phone:

I'm here! Get your ass in the car!

Mia threw her phone in her purse, grabbed a long black cardigan sweater, and headed outside.

She walked to Ashley's car, and got in.

"Ooh Mommy, look at *you!*"

"Look at *you*, Hot Mama!"

"You workin' some contacts *too*? Ooh, I'm scared of you."

Mia just shook her head and rolled her eyes, and they both laughed.

"Okay smarty, I am your date as promised, so let's roll, soul."

"Let's do it. I can't wait to hit the bar when we get to the reception."

"Well, you're late to the party, I just threw back a shot before you texted, just enough to take the edge off," Mia said laughing.

"Ooh, I'm jelly. Sure hope there's no unexpected traffic that makes us late."

"Girl you know wedding always run late, well at least for us Black folk," Mia said shrugging.

"Kim texted me and was already there around 2:30 because her sister Alicia, needed her to bring some type of lipstick. She's in the wedding and so was already there."

"Yeah, I get it, gotta help your sisters. I was with one of mine today. She is having a biopsy because they found a lump on her mammogram. She was pretty freaked out so I kicked it with her today. She seemed to be in a better place when I dropped her off."

"Oh no. I will pray it will be okay."

"Thanks *Ash-a-lee*."

They got there with 10 minutes to spare, walked in, and was escorted to seating with the family section on the groom's side. They looked over and found Kim on the other side and waved. She made a drinking motion with her hand and they both nodded and laughed. Promptly at 3:05 the ceremony began, the songs, the bridesmaids, the flower girl and ring bearer, and then finally the music signaling the bride. They all stood up and looked back, the bride looked absolutely, beautiful, and her lace and satin gown with a cathedral train, was drop dead gorgeous. Mia was grateful it was a short ceremony with only two songs.

After the happy couple walked out, Ashley looked over at Mia, "Welp, let's head down the street to the reception site, maybe we can park close, then go get us some *damn drinks!*"

"You know what? That idea does not hurt my feelings at all," Mia said following Ashley out the door.

They drove over to the reception hall, nabbed a close parking space, and within a few minutes, was sitting at the table assigned to Ashley. People slowly began trickling in filling the other tables.

"I don't' know about you, but I need something stronger than the wine they're serving, what about you Missy?" Ashley asked Mia.

"I'm not sure yet. What will *your* poison be today though, Hot Mama?"

Before she could answer, Ashley's phone buzzed, "Oh, *hey* Brad. I'm at actually at that wedding reception I told you about right now," she replied with a big smile.

No telling how long Ashley would be chatting, Mia got up from her chair deciding she needed a drink *now.* She began heading to the bar, then looked back, "Ash," she said getting her attention, then pointing towards the bar.

Ashley gave her a thumbs up and kept chatting away. Mia walked over to the bar and began looking at all the alcohol, narrowing it down to two.

"I will be right with you," the bartender told her distracting her from her thoughts.

"Thank you."

Mia stood there, arms crossed, pondering tequila, or vodka, when she felt a presence behind her. Am I trippin'? Nah, I just really need that drink, she decided shrugging it off. Suddenly Mia felt a hand on her shoulder, but before she could react, she was immediately pushed forward, causing her to almost lose her balance.

"Oh, I am *so* very sorry my dear. Please pardon me I nearly tripped. Are you okay?" an elderly man who was walking with a cane behind her said.

Mia looked at him empathetically, thinking of her late father, "It's okay, no worries," she told him.

"I've been standing here thinking about a drink, hmm, maybe not then, huh?" he told her chuckling.

"Nah, go for it," Mia told him with a smile.

He smiled then walked towards the far end of the bar.

She took a deep breath and exhaled, when she felt a presence again, but this time, felt it moving closer to her. Lordy Jesus I need that drink, she mused to herself. She had just decided on sticking with vodka when she felt a gust of hot breath on her neck. She immediately froze, but before she could mouth a single syllable, or react in any way at all, she heard a deep and familiar voice:

"Mmmm. Don't you smell delicious, just like you always do - with your sexy self," softly spoken near her ear.

She quickly turned around to confirm who had just uttered those words, and her suspicions were confirmed, as the person was none other than Javier. She could not hide the look of surprise on her face, which instantly changed to a huge smile. She had never seen him dressed in anything besides shorts and t-shirts, or work clothes at his shop, so now seeing him "dressed", she found herself a bit impressed. He stood there clad in all black - slacks and shirt. But what got Mia's attention and approval were his shoes, which were black of course, but were partially black patent leather on the top of the shoe.

"So, can a brotha get a hug or something sexy lady? It *has* been a minute you know," Javier said opening his arms before she could even speak.

"Oh my God, *Javier*, what the...? Now, what do *you* think?" she said opening her arms and walking into his waiting embrace.

Javier gave her a passionate hug and let his full lips slowly brush across the side of her neck as he was letting go. It immediately set off a familiar chain reaction for Mia: nipples hardening, heart pounding, hard to breathe. That embrace invoked emotions and feelings she had not felt for months. They slowly stepped apart and just stood there staring at each other.

"Evening, may I get you two anything?" the bartender asked before either of them could say another word to each other.

Snapping her back to reality, Mia turned her head to answer the bartender, whose name tag revealed that he was Jack.

She stepped closer to the bar Mia and replied, "I will have a Grey Goose and soda, with a twist please."

"And I will have a double Hennessey, thank you," Javier told him.

"Very good then," Jack told them before stepping away.

Mia slowly turned back around to look at Javier and took a deep breath, "Oh my God, it's so good to see you. I got your message the other night, but, um..."

"Damn, it's so good to see *you* sexy. Now what is this, *but um?*"

"Seriously?" Mia asked before quickly and cautiously looking both ways.

"Come on now Mister Man, are you quite sure that hug was okay, you know, in *public*? 'Cause you know, I don't need a crazy woman stalking me or slashing my tires and whatnot," Mia told him with lips pursed and her head cocked to one side.

Javier stepped closer, setting Mia's heart racing yet again. She tried swallowing with no success. He reached over and took Mia's chin in his hand, then tilted her head upwards giving her no choice but to gaze directly into his eyes. *Come on now Mia, breathe,* she silently told herself. She stood there speechless, making direct eye contact with Javier, who was looking down at her with great intensity. Those electric blue eyes of his seemed to be burrowing straight down into her very soul.

"Yes Mia, it is far more than okay, trust me. I'm flying solo tonight, and looking like there's a good chance, forever."

"Wait... *what?*" Mia asked pulling back and looking confused.

Clunk. Clunk.

"Vodka soda with a twist, and a double Hennessey," was spoken as their drinks were set on the bar, interrupting them from their conversation. Instantly and before the bartender could walk away, Mia grabbed her drink and leaned in closer, "Excuse me, Jack, is it?"

"Yes."

I am going to need one more of these please," she told him holding up her drink with a head nod.

"But of course," Jack told her walking away to get it.

Mia put the glass to her lips, and in a few gulps, that vodka soda with a twist, was history.

Clunk.

Mia sat the empty glass back on the bar, rolled her head both ways, and cracked her neck before looking back at Javier. He had been standing there mesmerized, silently watching her with fascination. His inability to conceal his admiration revealed in his eyes and smile.

"Now, you were saying?" Mia asked him.

Javier chuckled, stepped over to the bar to grab his drink, then took a sip. He swallowed and just stood there without saying a word, slowly undressing Mia with his eyes, top to bottom, then back up again, ending at her face.

Mia slanted her eyes, "Go ahead, take your time why don't you?" she asked him, throwing up her hands.

"Unh. Lordy woman, I sure have missed hanging with you, and I do mean in *every* way," he told her licking his full lips.

Jack brought her second drink, "Perfect timing, thank you, Jack."

Javier pulled out some cash, pointed at him and Mia, and slid the tip on the bar.

"Thank you, appreciate it sir, "Jack told him.

"No problem man," Javier said with a nod.

He turned back to Mia, "This really isn't the place to get into all that, but we will find some time, sooner rather than later."

"I see, okay then," Mia replied with a shrug and looked down.

Javier moved closer to Mia again, "You aren't usually so quiet, you mean you haven't missed me too?" he asked with a concerned look on his face.

Mia's head popped right up, "Now *that* information Mr. Martinez, *that*, is on a need-to-know basis," she told him then adding a slow wink.

"Ahh, there she is. There's my sassy Mia."

His words were hanging in the air as Ashley strode over to Mia tapping her on the shoulder and breaking the silence.

"Hey Girl, what *are* you drinking? Let's get this party started, let's - oh...."

She stopped mid-sentence and looked over at Javier and then back towards Mia, "Oh, *oops*. Did I interrupt something?" she asked grimacing and looking embarrassed.

"No, you're good," Javier said smiling.

Turning her head quickly towards Ashley, "I'm drinking vodka, if you must know Miss Thing," Mia told her, then turned back to Javier.

"This is one of my BFFs and a co-worker, Ashley. She was the one who dropped me off at your shop a bazillion times. Ashley, this is my mechanic, Javier – Javier, Ashley," Mia said motioning with her hands to each of them.

"Hi. Oh, so *you're* the mechanic. Nice to finally meet you," Ashley said holding out her hand with a huge smile.

"Pleasure is all mine," Javier said stepping over to Ashley and shaking her hand.

"I owed her for all those rides to your shop, so I'm officially here as her date," Mia told him.

"I see, well nice meeting you Ashley," Javier said as she stood there speechless, and only nodded.

Javier smiled slightly, "So look, I need to get back to the table, but to partially answer you, I'm here with one of my brothers. I'm actually staying with him right now, well, for the time being."

Mia tried her best to keep her face emotionless, "Oh, okay then."

He stepped closer never breaking that intense eye contact, "Now Mia, don't you even think of leaving here without giving me at least one dance, more like two."

"I just might have a salsa or two for you Mister Man – come find me," Mia told him with a wink.

"Gonna hold you to that," he told her returning her wink, then giving a nod in Ashley's direction before turning to walk back towards the tables.

Ashley stood there watching him walk away for a second then quickly looked back at Mia.

"*Girrrl*, I think my transmission just blew out and something is about to spring a *got*-damn leak, you *know*? I'm thinking that I might be needing to take my car to his shop, A.S.A.*F*.P!"

They both looked at each other and then burst out laughing.

"Ooh, girl - that man is fine, fine, *fine*. Did I mention that he is fine? Not to mention sexy as hell. Ooh *wee!*" Ashley said fanning herself with her right hand.

"*Shh*. True that girlfriend, but that fine and sexy man is also unfortunately married," Mia said with a shrug.

"Well, last time uh, I checked Miss Thing - *you ain't*," Ashley said with attitude.

"Yeah, but..." Mia began.

Before she could say another word, the ever attentive, Jack, returned.

"May I get something for you Miss?" he asked Ashley.

She looked over and cocked her head towards Mia, then told him, "I'll have what *she's* having," with a chuckle.

Jack smiled, "You two got that *When Harry Met Sally* thing going on or what?" he asked referring to the movie.

Mia and Ashley broke out into raucous laughter with Ashley pointing at Jack and nodding her head.

Jack laughed too, "Bingo! I will be right back with your drink," and walked away.

Ashley looked over at Mia, "*So*, back to what we were talking about - *Unh*."

"Right? But for real, we're really good friends though, believe it or not."

"I just bet you are," Ashley said laughing again.

"Come on now, there is more to life than sex."

"Yes, I know this Missy, but with him, that would a big part of *my* life, just sayin'," Ashley said pursing her lips and snapping her fingers twice, then grabbing her drink from Jack.

"Thank you," Ashley told Jack with a nod.

"No problem, please let me know if you ladies desire anything else," he said before walking away.

"Well Mia, do we? Or should I say *you*? Do you desire anyone, uh... I mean *anything* else?"

"I see someone has jokes this afternoon huh?" Mia said turning away, then began heading back to their table. A bit stunned, Ashley watched Mia walking away for a moment.

"Wait. *Mia*. Slow down," Ashley said trying to catch up.

Mia stopped and abruptly turned around, forcing Ashley to stop walking and come to a quick stop. She silently stood there her brows furrowed in apprehension. Mia stepped closer to Ashley and quickly reached out before saying, "Boop!" as she playfully bonked her on the nose.

Relieved, Ashley rolled her eyes and shook her head.

"Oh damn," Ashley said breathing a sigh of relief.

"Gotcha!" Mia said laughing.

"*Girl*, I thought you were mad at me. I'm sorry if I went too far, for real Mia."

"Oh, stop it. What can I say? I totally agree with you, Javier is fine as hell, and sexy doesn't even begin to cover it. But you know, I really don't like to mess with someone I can't have, or more accurately, someone I can't have access to when I want to."

"I feel you on that one."

"Sometimes you just can't help yourself though," Mia said shrugging.

"Wait so what are you saying or trying *not* to say?"

Ignoring Ashley's question, "Besides girl, I am old, I mean like a whole ten years older than him.

"Okay then Mz. Evasive. Well, with the way he was looking at you, I'm willing to bet he doesn't have a problem with that, like none *whatsoever*."

"Yeah well, there are so many younger women he can get with a snap of his fingers if he and the wife ever split, so why would he want *me?*"

"You know like they say, age is nothing but a number girlie."

"But I have two grown sons and am in my 50's."

"Girl, you need to stop it. Stop right now."

"I can only imagine how bad I would look if I didn't go to the gym."

"See, right there though."

"What? Right there? What does that mean?"

"The fact is that you *do* go to the gym, and you don't *even* look your age. Like they say, "Black *don't* crack," Ashley said snapping her fingers twice.

Mia stood there silently giving her a blank stare, before rolling her eyes.

"Besides, there will always be someone younger, richer, thinner etc., etc, but I tell you this – I know what I felt a few minutes ago in the air over there, and that was even after I interrupted and stuff," Ashley said pursing her lips and raising her eyebrows.

"Oh, come on let's go back to our table," Mia said motioning with her arm and beginning to walk towards their table again.

She took a few steps and stopped, then turned around, "Wait. Did you for real Ash?"

Ashley just looked at her with raised eyebrows and pursed lips, "I am *not* making that shit up," she said shaking her head.

"Hmm," Mia said as they started walking. They finally reached their table and who did they find sitting there sipping on a glass of red wine, but Kim. There were two other elderly couples now seated at the table as they sat down.

"Well, there you guys are, I was beginning to wonder, but *hello*, I should have known that you guys were over at the bar," she said laughing and standing up to hug each of them.

"Yes, and so was Mia's mechanic. *Girl*, that man is fine as hell," Ashley blurted out.

"Ooh, where is he?" Kim asked looking around.

"If I see him, I will definitely point him out, but he's not hard to miss; tall, lean, chocolate brown, and the most gorgeous eyes, they're blue!"

"What?" Kim asked frowning and looking around harder.

"His mother is Black, and his father is Mexican, guess he reached back a generation or two from Daddy-O and pulled the blue eyes DNA," Mia said shrugging.

Changing the subject, "So look at you Missy with all that bling going on. I like, I *like* Mommy!" Mia told Kim enthusiastically.

"Yaaasss girl, got it going on. I think Mia is rubbing off on you," Ashley said nodding her head.

"Ooh, well just look at all three of us, Charlie's Angels would be jealous," Mia said, and they all broke into laughter.

Kim looked over at Mia, "Okay, on the real, so where *is* this man?" she asked, still looking frantically around.

"No idea, and I had no idea he was coming. I haven't really spoken to him much lately. But a sista did promise to save a dance or two for him, so we'll see if he reappears. He's been out of state taking care of one of his brothers. He called the other night, and wouldn't you just know it, I was half asleep and knocked my damn phone off the nightstand. And *then*, the damn thing slid under my bed where I couldn't reach it, so missed the goddamn call, but he left a voicemail."

Ashley looked at her pursing her lips and frowning, "Uh huh, so what did he *say* Miss Thing? Do tell," Ashley said.

"Yes, do tell," Kim chimed in.

"You guys need to quit it. He just said he was coming back and would be in touch. It was a complete surprise seeing him here. I don't think our dear friend Ashley informed you that he's married, now did she?" Mia said giving Ashley a deadpan look.

"Nope, but *hello*, you ain't," Kim said.

"That's what I told her ass too," Ashley said laughing.

"Okay, you guys are just a hot mess. Y'all seriously need to quit it and learn to let shit go. That's why if anything happened in the past or in the future I wouldn't even say," Mia said laughing.

Ashley and Kim looked at each other with questioned expressions.

"Well, I'm sorry that he's married, but you're not trying to marry him, right? I haven't even seen the man, but if he's half as hot as Ashley *says* he is... "

Mia just looked at her, folded her arms and rolled her eyes.

"Look, life is short, and every now and then you just might need to go to your mechanic – you know for a full service, or at least an oil change is all I'm saying. Can I get an Amen up in here?" Kim asked looking side to side with her arms outstretched.

"Amen!" Ashley said holding up her hand.

"I swear y'all been hanging with me too long, you guys are beginning to sound Black," Mia said laughing.

Ashley and Kim joined Mia's laughter as a waiter brought them their salads and bread. Mia downed her drink, trying to put Javier out of her mind, definitely not an easy thing to do. It had been months without him, and then seeing him for just a few minutes, it all came flooding right back. All those months apart, yet and still a mere few moments ago, they were emitting sparks from the electricity they apparently still generated.

They were all eating in silence until Kim broke it, "Guess we were all starving, no one is saying a goddamned thing," she said laughing.

213

"For real, I know I was," Ashley said.

"Me too, "Mia said grabbing a roll out of the basket on the table.

Mia got lost in her thoughts again, until she heard, "Are you finished Miss?" from the server.

"Oh, yes, thank you."

Ashley and Kim were in their own world texting on their phones. Mia was just about to try to get Kim's attention, but the entrée beginning to be served at the table got her attention instead.

"Looks like we all got the prime rib. I sure hope it's good as it looks, 'cause I am *still* starving," Kim said enthusiastically.

"Well one way to find out," Mia said cutting into hers with her knife and putting a forkful in her mouth.

"Well?" Ashley said.

Mia stopped chewing and just gave her a condescending look and rolled her eyes. She continued chewing and nodded her head yes. She finally swallowed, "Delicious you guys," she told them as she cut another piece.

"Fabulous," Kim said cutting into her own prime rib.

Ashley watched Kim's face as she smiled nodding yes, before she dug into hers. They ate in silence until Kim grabbed the wine bottle on the table, topped off her glass and then, "Anyone else want?" she asked.

"None for me," Mia said.

"I'll pass, red wine gives me a headache sometimes," Ashley told her.

"Well, there's a little left," Kim said still holding the bottle.

The woman sitting next to Mia held her glass up, "I will take those last few drops if you don't mind, please. Hi, my name is Myrna," she said as she passed her glass to Mia to give to Kim.

Kim poured what was left in Myrna's glass, and passed it back.

"Thank you my dear," Myrna said.

"I'm Mia, and that's Ashley and Kim," Mia said motioning to both women.

"Hi," they both said at the same time.

"Nice meeting you, and this is my husband Kent," Myrna said elbowing him to look up from his plate.

"Hello, nice to meet you," Kent said pausing for a brief moment, then resumed eating with gusto.

"The only way I got him to come with me, was to promise that there would be a good meal," Myrna said chuckling.

Leaning over towards Mia, Myrna said, "Wasn't it just a beautiful ceremony?"

"Yes, it really was, and her gown was absolutely gorgeous."

"Yes, yes it was, just beautiful. Are you a friend of the bride?"

"Actually, my friend Ashley is a cousin of the groom, I'm just her date," Mia said nodding her head towards Ashley.

"Yes, I confess, I am his crazy cousin," Ashley said holding up her hand and smiling.

"Really? Well, I was Barry and his brother Larry's, piano teacher. I have watched them both grow up into fine young men. I've known the family for what seems like forever."

"How nice," Mia told her.

"I am so glad they finally got married," Ashley told Myrna.

Their chit chatting slowed down as they followed Kent's lead, and finished their meals. The servers began bringing out glasses of champagne for the toast.

"Well, it's just about done, almost time to toast the happy couple," Myrna said happily, clasping her hands together.

"Yes, it sure looks like it Myrna," Mia replied.

Clink. Clink. Clink. Clink. Clink.

"Ladies and gentlemen, may I have your attention please," the Best Man said after tapping a glass with a knife to gain everyone's attention.

"It is time for the Official toast..." he began.

Mia tuned him out and got lost in thoughts of wondering if she and Javier were going to dance. The Maid of Honor's speech escaped Mia's ears as well.

"Mia, *Mia*. Stand up, we're toasting," Kim told her nudging her with her elbow.

"Oh damn, I was zoned the hell out," Mia said embarrassed.

"Gee, you *think*?" Kim said with lips pursed and eyebrows raised.

"My oh my, I wonder what your mind could have been wandering off to?" Ashley said sticking out her tongue.

"Lookee here, you two just mind your biddness"," Mia said standing up but could not help but to laugh a little.

The toast done, they all clapped and sat down. Mia drained her champagne in one long gulp.

"Dayum babygirl, you want mine too?" Kim teased.

"Pony it up," Mia said motioning with her fingers.

"Booyah! Here ya go then girlfriend," Kim sad.

Kim and Ashley looked at each other and nodded to each other, then looked over at Mia.

Ashley slid her glass over, "Go 'head dahling, I mean what would be the point of stopping now? It's said things go in 3's, and it's just champagne. Dancing is coming up after they cut the cake and serve it," she said pointing to Barry and Shelly standing by the wedding cake getting ready to cut it.

"*Kill it girl*," Kim said nudging her with her elbow again.

Mia looked at them both, shrugged and then slammed Ashley's glass of champagne too.

"Ooh, I need to go to the bathroom," Mia said standing up.

"Ooh, me too," Ashley and Kim said together.

They all laughed, then got up to go with Mia, I sure hope the line isn't real long, I have to go pretty bad, now that I stood up let's go. Come on hurry up," Kim said.

"Oh *snap*, that champagne hit me kinda hard when I stood up - I hope I don't fall," Mia said laughing.

"Not to worry Mia, we will walk right behind you and catch you ... well, *maybe*!" Kim said laughing and high fiving with Ashley.

"Yep, girl we got you, well after we stop laughing," Ashley added still laughing.

"Lord help me, I am surrounded by wannabe comedians tonight. What *is* a girl to do I ask you?" Mia asked rhetorically shaking her head and throwing up her hands.

They all laughed and made it to the bathroom.

"Ooh, no line yet, cool!" Kim said.

They handled their business, then touched up their lipstick and began heading back to their table. As they were walking, Ashley saw Javier, stopping abruptly to point him out to Kim. They both stopped and stood there gawking. As if he somehow felt their gaze, he turned towards them.

"Oh hell, let's go!" Kim said tapping Ashley on the back.

They quickly turned around and began walking briskly until they caught up to Mia, giggling like little schoolgirls nodding to each other. Mia glanced back quizzically, having been completely oblivious to their slight semi-detour. They immediately stopped laughing and presented straight faces. Mia frowned and then just shrugged it off and kept walking. As soon as she turned around Ashley and Kim began laughing again, almost hysterically this time. Mia just shook her head, rolled her eyes, and continued walking straight on to their table. They had missed the cake cutting by the newlyweds, and their cake slices were being placed on the table as they arrived.

"Ooh, perfect timing, I need a sugar pick me up," Mia said. Ashley and Kim looked at each other and shrugged.

"Excuse me, are you serving coffee as well?" Mia asked one of the servers.

"Yes, we are. Would you care for a cup?" he answered.

"Yes please. You guys want coffee?" Mia asked motioning to Kim and Ashley.

"Nah, I'm good," Kim said.

"Yeah, I'll have a cup please," Ashley said.

"Okay two coffees, cream and sugar?"

"Yes please," Mia replied.

The server nodded and walked away.

The Best Man spoke, "Ladies and gentlemen, the First Dance."

Mia looked over and saw that most of the table was empty, the other couples seemed to have left already since there was no longer any trace of a purse or jacket on the back of any chair.

"Miss, your coffee," the server said handing Mia a cup.

"Oh, thank you. I need this right now," Mia said smiling.

"I have the cream and sugar over here Mia," Ashley said stirring creamer in her coffee and then handed the creamer and sugar to Kim to pass over to Mia.

"Thanks, babygirl," Mia said with a wink, busy stirring in the sugar and creamer in her coffee.

Ashley looked up, quickly elbowing Kim, nodding her head upwards in Mia's direction, and putting a finger over her lips to shush her.

Kim frowned, but Ashley gave her more intense head motions, so Kim turned and looked in the direction of Ashley's head motions, and her mouth fell open as she saw Javier walking up to the table. Mia's back was to him, so she had no idea.

"I know I said we could leave after we eat, but um, are you still saving that dance or two?" Ashley asked.

"Girl, Javier's probably..."

"Javier's probably *what*?" his deep voice reverberated near her ear as he simultaneously pulled out the chair next to her at the table and sat down.

Mia jumped, "Lordy Jesus man, what are you doing sneaking up on me like that?" she said with a mock frown while Ashley and Kim laughed.

Mia looked at all three of them suspiciously for a moment then just shrugged it off,

"Hey Javier, this is another one of my girls, another co-worker, Kim – Kim, this is Javier," she said motioning to both with her hands.

"Hey, how are you doing? Nice to meet you Kim, and hi again ... Ashley, *right*?" Javier said snapping his fingers twice.

"*Really* nice to meet you too," Kim said with a big smile nodding her head.

"Yup, you got it right, it's Ashley, good memory," she told him with a head nod in his direction.

"I bet that's not all that's good though," Kim whispered to Ashley and they started laughing,

"See? I just can't go anywhere with you guys, *Lordt*. Ignore them Javier, they are a just a hot mess," Mia said turning to Javier, rolling her eyes and shaking her head no, but still smiling.

"So, Mia, I know I've been MIA, but there has been a lot of stuff that has been going on, I will have to fill you in. Damn, it is *so* good seeing you though. Crazy how we both showed up at a wedding reception though right? I mean, what are the odds?"

"Yeah, it's been a minute. But you do know I'm glad you're back, right? By the way, I bought a new SUV while you've been MIA, so shouldn't be having any car issues for a while."

"Well, don't let that stop you from coming by every now and then, you should bring it by the shop. What did you get? I'd like to see it."

"A Lexus RX, pearly white."

"Nice, you deserve something like that for yourself, you know how we grind all the time."

"Yup, that's how we roll alright."

Ashley and Kim were delighted sitting there riveted, listening to their conversation and wondering what might transpire from it.

"So, like I told you, I came with my brother Alejandro, and we aren't going to hang much longer, but someone I know said they would save a dance for me," Javier said with eyebrows raised.

"Yeah, but listen to this music they're playing, really? *Come on.*"

No sooner than those words were spoken:

"We're going to take it back right now, let's get some 'Ol School going on," the DJ said, giving Mia pause as she began hearing familiar music.

"*Uh. Uh, uh, uh, owww.* Brick House began playing.

"Ooh, no you didn't," Mia said looking down shaking her head no, before finally resting her forehead in her hand.

Javier stood up and held out his hand, "Come on Mia, it brings back great memories, doesn't it? Let's go make another one," he said with a wink.

"Damn you Javier Martinez," Mia said narrowing her eyes as she took his hand and stood up.

Javier smiled, and they walked out to the dance floor together. As they started dancing, Kim and Ashley who were watching and listening to the entire exchange, high fived each other.

"Ooh girl, you were right, that man is even more "*foine*" up close. Our girl *better* get some of that," Kim leaned over telling Ashley.

"You *know*?" Ashley said before they both started laughing again.

They sat and watched Javier and Mia on the dance floor.

"Come on Kim, let's go dance next to them," Ashley said getting up.

"Hells yes," Kim said as they found their way to the floor next to Mia and Javier.

"*Heeey*," Kim said making Mia smile.

Kim and Ashley nodded to each other and then began dancing with Mia and Javier surrounding them.

"Ooh, look like you got game right here Playa. Rolling three deep," Mia said laughing.

"What can I say?" Javier said laughing.

The song ended, so Kim and Ashley headed off the floor, and a Santana song, Amorè, came on.

Mia paused, then looked at Javier, "You once told me that you can salsa, let's see Mister Man."

Javier did not say a single word, just walked closer and put one hand on the small of Mia's back, and pulled her closer.

"I do, now show me what *you* got," he said licking his lips in his seductive way.

They started moving slowly to the music and easily found rhythm and movements in unison right away.

"Mmm. You *know* I like how you're moving those hips, and you know what I'm thinking about. Just so you know, you done set the bar so high, I doubt there is anyone else who can reach it. I may have been gone, but I still thought about you, I hope you know that. I can't explain what you do to me, but I love it. I've missed it."

Mia said nothing as they continued dancing in perfect unison, her body matching his moves automatically. Javier leaned in closer to her ear and whispered, "You are *so* fucking sexy Mia."

As per the norm, Mia's breath caught in her throat and her nipples instantly hardened. Hearing Javier's sexy voice whispering those words in her ear was verbal Astro Glide. Fortunately, the coffee and food had not completely wiped out her buzz from all the vodka and champagne she had earlier imbibed, which enabled her to stop thinking and enjoy dancing to the song. The song came to an end and a slow song began playing.

"Let's not push the envelope, you still have your wedding band on," Mia said biting her lower lip and raising her eyebrows.

"True that, but damn girl, you standing over there looking like a *snack*," Javier said undressing her with his eyes yet again before licking his lips.

"Man, come on," Mia said turning around and beginning to walk back to the table. Before she reached the table, she saw a tall, handsome man walking towards her, so she stopped.

"Hello," he said to Mia.

"Hello?" she answered back.

"Hey Jav, I hate to break up this Saturday Night Fever thang you got going on and all, but we need to roll," the man said pointing at his watch but smirking.

"Mia, this is my brother Dro ...well really Alejandro. Alejandro - Mia," Javier said gesturing with his hands to each of them.

"Oh, *Mia*. Nice to meet you," Dro said with a slight smile.

"Same here Alejandro, uh, Dro," Mia said nodding her head towards him.

"Okay Dro, give me a minute and I'll meet you at the car," Javier told him.

He looked over at Mia, "Well, as you can see, I need to go. Let's talk next week, but when I call, you going to answer this time?"

Mia shook her head and smiled, "Yes. I would have last time but believe it or not, I knocked the damn phone off my nightstand, then it slid under my bed. I had to get the broom to reach it," Mia said shaking her head.

"Well, I *was* kind of hoping you would call back, but running into you like this and seeing you after so long – this is so much better."

"Oh, is it, now?"

Stepping closer to her ear he whispered, "Alright now, don't make me snatch you up in some broom closet around here and fuck you to show you just how much," then stepped back and folded his arms across his chest.

Mia couldn't help smiling, "You know Alejandro is waiting on you. Call me, and I *promise* to answer so we can chat. Thanks for the dances Mister Man."

"Anytime - but you should know that already."

"Hmm. Well, *see* ya."

"I'm hoping sooner rather than later, sexy," he whispered in her ear as he walked past her.

"Hey, those endless possibilities," Mia replied making him pause.

Javier nodded his head affirmatively and then turned back towards Mia, "Next week?" he asked pointing at her with eyebrows raised.

Mia used his line, "You already know."

Javier pursed his lips and smiled, then turned to walk out of the door.

Mia walked back to her table where Ashley and Kim were sitting with their arms crossed waiting for her.

"Before you say anything, the man is still married, well wait ... I guess separated. We are supposed to talk next week."

"Talk? *Talk*? You mean like the Bar Kays: *She Talks To Me, With Her Body*, talk Mia? Kim asked laughing.

"Well, after she was acting all Beyonce out there, *Getting Bodied* and stuff, what else kind of talking do *you* think?" Ashley chimed in elbowing Kim.

"Okay, y'all need to stop," Mia said rolling her eyes.

Kim and Ashley stopped laughing abruptly and looked at Mia. Mia looked at Kim, then at Ashley. Ashley looked at Kim then Mia. Kim looked at Ashley then Mia. They all turned their heads and looked both ways at each other, then they all burst out laughing.

"Okay look, before you even ask, if anything happens when he calls, I will let you know, well *maybe*, 'cause I see how y'all act," Mia said with a wink.

"Okay but *girl*, Ashley was right! That man is fine as hell, do you hear me? And sexy as fuck," Kim said shaking her head.

"No Kim, I hadn't even noticed, *DUH*," Mia said laughing.

"I've known him for a few years, he has worked on my car and the boy's cars. He's a great mechanic. Ash has dropped me off several times over the years."

"True that, but I never saw what he looked like, *until tonight*," Ashley said throwing her hands up.

"Just to think, neither one of you knew the other one was coming to this wedding and reception. Hmm. Sure does seem like it was supposed to happen, you know like all that manifesting stuff you're always talking about Mia. I'm just sayin' girl," Kim told her with a shrug and shaking her head.

Ashley nodded in agreement.

"Well time will tell. Oaky, so we ate and danced, *now* can we go Ash?" Mia asked with praying hands.

"Yes, ma'am. And even though I had to share my date, I didn't mind," Ashley told her sticking out her tongue.

"And *I* need to go find my sister. I dropped her off at the hotel last night, and I'm dropping her off at home tonight. I will see you two chickadees at work Monday," Kim said winking with great exaggeration.

"Okay see you then," Mia told her waving.

"Bye Kim," Ashley said as she and Mia grabbed their purses and headed to the door.

"I'm so glad we parked close, my feet want out of these shoes right damn now," Mia said.

"Well, you *were* tearing up the dance floor doing the salsa girl. And here we are," Ashley said.

Chirp. Chirp.

221

"Thank you, *Jesus*," Mia said getting in the car and taking her shoes off.

Ashley took hers off too and tossed them in the backseat.

"See? I *told* you we would have fun, and uh, excuse me, but some of us had more fun than others," Ashley said pulling out of the parking lot.

"Seriously though, thanks for going with me Mia, and see? The universe wanted you two to run into each other. Didn't you say he's been gone for awhile?"

"Yup, been gone several months to take care of another brother who lives back east."

"Well maybe he's back to stay?"

"Guess I will find out pretty soon. As fine as he is though, I don't think I feel up to being in a relationship. Sometimes I wonder if I ever will."

"Well, what do you always say? Time will tell."

"Mmm hmm," Mia said as her eyes slowly closed.

"Sleeping Beauty, your carriage ride is over," Ashley said gently shaking Mia.

Mia awoke startled, then looked around to get her bearings.

"Oh damn, I dozed off huh?"

"That you did. Well after all, you did have a busy night babycakes," Ashley said laughing.

"Oh, be quiet. But for real Ash, I did have fun just like you said, and the food was dee-lish. Thanks for twisting my arm and making me go," Mia said sticking out her tongue.

"I'm so glad you came."

"K. Girl, my ass is tired as hell. I drank a lot without eating much first, so I'm 'bout to go crash the hell out. Text me you got home alright, okay? Mia said grabbing her shoes and purse.

"You got it. See you Monday."

"Not unless you're in L.A., you forgot I'm on vacay next week Playa."

"Oh yeah, well have a safe flight and have a few drinks for me."

"You know I will, and for Kim, and for Mark and...."

"You are so crazy," Mia said laughing.

She got out, opened her front door, and waved. Ashley waved back and took off.

Mia headed straight to her room and flopped on the bed. She was dozing off when she heard Russell's text tone. She immediately sat up to dig through her purse to find her phone.

Hi Mom, sorry haven't called lately, but I'm good.

Love you.

Mia smiled, and texted back.

I love you more. We will chat soon. Yo' Mama

Before she could put her phone down, she got another text.

Hey Mama, cramming for a test, but just wanted to say hi, and I love you!

Mia smiled again and replied:

I love you more, kill that test! LOL

That twinning thing was in full effect it seemed, since they were both feeling that Mama wavelength or something Mia mused.

She lay back on the bed for a minute, then rolled over and looked at the time on her phone, it was barely 9:00. There was the text from Ashley, she didn't even hear it. She looked and saw that she had somehow had again put her phone on vibrate.

Hey Mia, I'm home safe and sound. Finishing packing for L.A. Leaving early in the morning to visit Grammy and kick it with some old friends. I will sleep on the plane hahaha. We will definitely talk when I get back! Luv ya.

Mia replied:

Have fun! Tell your Grammy I said hi, have fun but be careful, and you know what I mean! Luv ya back~

The Grey Goose had long worn off, but for some reason Mia was still feeling a bit emboldened, so logged onto her laptop, pulled up her email and typed:

Hey Mr. T,

Honestly, my head was pretty much blown after your last email. Has taken me a minute to know how to respond. Not sure why you are leaving the ball in my court, but as such, I think it would be great to talk on the phone, you know like we used to those late nights when insomnia was hitting us hard. Who knows, maybe I could tell you a bedtime story one of these nights LOL.

Mz Mia

She closed her laptop and felt some type of satisfaction. *Finally*, after about a week of wondering, there was now a resolution of sorts. Where her email would lead, who even knows? She washed her make up off and stripped to take a quick shower. Not surprising, she found that the crotch in her thong was pretty, damn wet. Like the song, Javier made her *love come down* more than anyone, as was evident in her leopard thong she had just stepped out of. It sure was a good thing that neither she, nor Javier drove, but instead were at the mercy of Ashley and Alejandro to take them home. Who knows what might have happened? Javier might have really dragged her off into some broom closet and fucked the shit out of her without anyone there who would wonder about their whereabouts. That thought brought a wicked smile. The passion they generated was off the chain.

She dried off and slipped into a nightshirt as usual, turned on the TV, then got into bed. When Harry Met Sally had just come on, but somehow, she didn't really end up watching too much of it. Her mind wandered back to Javier - of course it would. She was trying to stay strong and not get caught up again, but nothing in life was guaranteed, so how careful should one be? That was her last thought of the night.

Tick Tock, Tick Tock.

Time keeps moving.

Time cannot be re-captured,

nor replaced.

Overanalyzing can make you miss out,

or get left behind.

Emotions, people, and thoughts are all temporary.

Nothing is permanent.

Learn to adapt and flow,

with whom and whatever,

brings you happiness and joy.

Life is full of choices we make.

Choose to live, not merely exist.

Dare to go out on the limb -

that's where all the fruit is.

GET IN

WHERE

YOU

FIT

IN

"*A*h-oo-gah, Ah-oo-gah ...."

Javier's ringtone woke Mia up. She somehow summoned up enough strength to roll over and grab her phone off the nightstand. It was a text message, and for that she felt grateful; she definitely did not feel like talking to *anyone*. And all that drinking last night. Ugh. She reached over to her nightstand again and grabbed her glasses as well as the bottle of Smart Water she had the brilliant foresight to leave there last night. Feeling somewhat dehydrated, she sat up and slammed half of the water down. She looked at the time on her phone, not *too* terribly late, only 9:27.

She opened the text:

> *Hey Sexy, it was so good running into you last night. We need to talk soon, like this week. Think you can make some time to talk or hopefully meet up?*

Mia sat there re-reading the message a few times. Although she hated mornings she had to admit, this was definitely a great way to begin one. His text was probably a result of that out of sight - out of mind thing Mia had accused him of a few times; he saw her again last night then realized he missed her. The last time she said it though, he unequivocally told her that it was *not* true, saying he had no choice but to compartmentalize his life which included her. Translation: he could not talk to or see her as much as he wanted to - there were definite self-imposed limits.

It was true, Mia *was* the one who was free with no one to answer to, and yet, Javier continued to risk it all by meeting for their *secret rendezvous* and seeing Mia as often as he could. Maria had become suspicious when Javier was working late nights at the shop for a while, but even through that, he still chose to live his double life refusing to give Mia up. He *always* desired her body; it did not matter what she weighed. Since his shop was demanding of his time, he often reminded Mia that if she ever felt herself jonesin' for some of his "Chocolate", all she had to do was let him know. True to his word, whenever she did, he made time for her without hesitation, *always*. As with Tony, she and Javier also had their own unspoken agreement for a "line" in the sand which they had chosen not to cross. But even if Javier did become single and up for grabs, there was always that commitment issue for Mia.

More than once he told her that she had no idea of how often she crossed his mind; her smile, her kindness, her sensuality, and her spirit. It seemed apparent that he was torn and trying to figure out his next step since he was staying with his brother and not at home. Was it best to stay, or best to go? Mia had lived that existence for quite some time herself once upon a time. That reality, of the confusion and drama which Javier was living through was the catalyst which caused her to walk away all those months ago. Then there was Tony; what about that? And why now after all this time were they both wondering, *what if*, from decades ago? Giovanni did seem to be the most stable one, but where would that lead? And what stage was his Parkinson's in?

Aaagh. Too many thoughts, and *way* too early. Why even wonder when it was not possible to come up with any answers? She decided to get up and go for a walk, so hit the bathroom and threw on some sweatpants, a t-shirt, and a hoodie. She twisted her hair up into a baseball cap, then slipped into a pair of white Nikes. As she was tying her shoes, it dawned on her that she had on a purple cap, navy sweatpants, white shoes, and a green hoodie. She was totally mismatched, but at that precise moment, she did not really give a fuck. She saw her reflection in the mirror and simply shrugged it off. Whatevs. She went into the kitchen and ate a quick half of a peanut butter sandwich before grabbing her earbuds, phone, and keys, then heading out the front door.

Mia selected a high energy playlist and was on her way. She was feeling so full of angst, that she found herself walking at a pretty brisk clip as soon as she began. Even the slight headache she felt from last night's drinking took a backseat. Those endorphins being released after a few blocks of feeling the fresh air rushing against her face truly invigorated her. She was feeling much better, well, better physically that is.

Apparently, it was impossible for Mia's mind to remain silent and faded to black. She could feel the imagination and random thoughts projector of her mind revving up. Of course, once the reels began spinning, the first memories and images which flickered into her mind's eye were of the most recent incident in her mind. And just what or who could that possibly be of? It was most definitely thoughts of seeing and dancing with that sexy ass Javier at the reception.

Wow, last night. That was a stone ta-*rip* Unh. Never, not even in her wildest dreams, would she think that she would run into of all people, *Javier*. And, without the wife. *And,* at a wedding reception nonetheless, go figure. That electricity generated between them was still undeniably and strongly felt. It may have been months since she had last seen him, but it felt as if it had only been yesterday. The distance and time apart did nothing to suppress the sensuosity they shared. Apparently, it would *always* be there, perhaps that is why Javier told her they could never just be friends. Hmm.

She stopped walking, pulled her phone out and was just about to reply to his text, but caught herself. Shaking her head no, she stuck the phone right back in her pocket, deciding against replying just yet. She needed to go back to her *CrazySexyCool* mode, and not seem too anxious. Besides, she had not really decided how she felt about possibly starting things up again.

She looked up to get her bearings and realized that she had somehow walked her longest route. She was only at the halfway mark, so decided to stop the mind chatter and get back to her walking. She cranked up the volume, got lost in the music, and made it back home. She went straight to the refrigerator first thing, grabbed a cold bottle of water and downed half of it down before stopping. She carried the water with her into the bathroom and turned on the shower. She did her pushups, and yet another pathetic attempt at planks before stripping. As she reached over to pick up her water, she glanced at her reflection in the mirror. Hmm, not too horrible for a woman my age, but I definitely gotta keep working on it she decided.

In the week or so since her getaway, things were toning and tightening she concluded as she turned and looked at her butt in the mirror. She took a few deep breaths then exhaled slowly. She began to feel her body slowing down. The effects of the last 24 hours began hitting her. Juanita's dilemma concerned her greatly and affected her the most, weighing heavily on both her mind and her heart. She continued to silently pray that everything would turn out okay.

She finished the bottle of water and opened the shower door. The hot steam from the water immediately hit her in the face, and it felt wonderful. She stood there letting the hot water rain down her back for quite some time before finally squeezing some aromatherapy gel on her loofah and scrubbing until she once again felt revitalized. She got out, wrapped herself in a fluffy gray towel, and just lay on the bed for a few moments.

After dressing and pulling her hair up, she felt her tummy rumbling.

Honk-Honk. Honk-Honk.

A text from Kim popped:

Hey – Wanna go grab some lunch or brunch somewhere? Let me know either way PLEEZE.

Talk about perfect timing. She knew Kim would be asking more questions about Javier, but lunch did sound like a great thing do to right now, besides, she was starving after that long walk.

She instantly replied:

You name when and where and I'm down.

Before she even sat her phone down Kim had replied:

Let's hit the Cheesecake Factory. Pick you up - 15 minutes?

Mia replied:

Let's do it. I'll be waiting out front. C ya.

She threw on a pair of jeans, a purple tie-dye t-shirt and slipped into her pair of lavender Uggs.

She pulled her hair up in a clip, grabbed a sweat jacket and her purse, then went outside and sat in her black Adirondack chair on the porch to wait. She pulled up her email on her phone and saw Giovanni had sent her a message:

Mio Tesoro,

I hope you are having a wonderful weekend. I am hoping I can call you so we can chat soon. I need to explain something to you that is weighing heavily on my mind. I don't mean to sound too ominous, but honestly, I had no idea that I would meet anyone in which my condition would need to be disclosed. As I previously told you, I have been quite reserved with women, but you have made me feel more alive than I have in years. I would like to explain. If you have time this evening, I would like to give you a call, say around 7? If you are busy,

234

please text me and let me know, otherwise, I look
forward to chatting with you later. Enjoy your day,

Gio

Whoa, ominous does not even begin to cover it. What could possibly
be going on? And it seemed to be something that was going on before
he met her, because he said *my condition.* Hmm, what kind of medical
condition Mia wondered. First Juanita, and now Giovanni in the same
weekend. He seemed pretty healthy, but who knows? She
immediately replied:

Hey Mr. E,

I'm about to have lunch with a friend/co-worker
and would be dishonest if I didn't say I am a bit
alarmed. I sincerely hope you are okay, and yes, I
would love to chat tonight, and looking forward to
your call. Let's Facetime~

She hit send, closed her email, and put the phone in her purse. She
sat in silence for a few moments absorbing the last 48 hours. Finally
finding the words to email Tony back, running into Javier last night,
Giovanni's cryptic medical issue message, but most importantly,
Juanita's biopsy tomorrow. It was a lot to take in over such a short
amount of time. Mia was sure hoping that there would not be a third
person with some medical issues.
   Honk. Honk.
   The sound of Kim's horn snapped Mia back to the day. She waved
to Kim, and then slung her purse over her shoulder and walked
down the driveway to her car. As she was getting in Kim looked at
her concerned.
   "I was sitting there for a minute, and you didn't even look my way
so that's why I honked. You okay?"
   "Oh, hey Kim. Yeah, I'm okay. Well, I think so. Just have a lot going
on."
   "Uh huh. I can't help but ask you then, did something more
happen with Javier after you got home? You don't have to go into
detail if it did, I'm just concerned about you."
   "Oh no, that's not it, nothing happened with him overnight.
Although he did text me this morning and asked if we could talk later

this week."

"*Girrrl*, I'm buying you a drink or two, or three, come on let's fly," Kim said driving off.

"Yes, a drink sounds really, *really* good right now."

"Yes, I know this Miss Thing, that's why I said it, *hello*," Kim said chuckling.

"So, what made you get out and about today?"

"Well, I would be lying if I told you that I didn't want to hear more about Javier, but honestly, I just was bored and hungry at home. Then seeing you outside of work last night made me realize that we really hadn't just kicked it for a really, long time, you know?"

"Yeah, I guess you're right. When I got back last week, you and Ashley were attending that seminar, and then the rest of the week was a blur until last night. It's like everything has just - boom - happened all of a sudden," Mia said shrugging and shaking her head in disbelief.

"Life is so strange, isn't it?"

"Oh yeah, fo'. *sho*'," Mia replied enunciating dramatically while nodding affirmatively.

"Well traffic is flowing smooth as hell, so we're almost there. I already know what I want too. I have been craving their meat loaf and mashed potatoes for days."

"Hmm, I'm not sure if I want appetizers, small plates, or a big entrée. Ooh, maybe a big salad."

"And don't forget drinks. Notice I said *drinks*, plural, not *a* drink," Kim said as they pulled into a parking spot.

"Yes Missy, I caught that," Mia said as they got out and began walking in.

"Two for Kim," she said at the desk and got the pager.

"Let's go to the bar and wait."

"Smart girl," Mia said winking.

They surprisingly found two seats at the end of the bar.

"Must have caught the lull right before the lunch rush," Kim said looking at the drink menu.

"Lady Luck is on our side it seems. Traffic was smooth too."

"What may I get you ladies? The bartender James asked.

"Um..." Mia began.

"We will take two Stoli bloody marys, spicy please," Kim told him.

Mia shrugged and nodded, "That will work, thanks Kim."

"Answer your phone, Answer your phone...."

Mia jumped and grabbed her phone, since Juanita's text tone was also her ringtone.

She was relieved to see it was a text:

Hey Mia, I just wanted to say thank you again for yesterday, thanks for being there like always. I will let you know when I get the results, love you.

Mia replied immediately:

I love you too. I am always here for you, any time day or night. Hang in there sis, it's going to be okay. Out at lunch with Kim. Will talk to you later, and tomorrow will be okay. Call me if you need ANYTHING!!!

"Woosa, woosa," Mia said taking a deep breath.

Kim looked at her with a confused expression.

"Where *are* those drinks?" Kim said sensing Mia could really use her drink quick, fast, and in a hurry.

As if on cue, "Ladies," James the bartender said as he sat their two drinks in front of them.

"Perfect timing, thanks," Kim told him.

James continued, "So, the couple that was sitting at the other end ordered the fried zucchini strips and sweet tamale cakes appetizers, but got a call and had to leave on an emergency. They already paid for them and asked me to give them to the next people who sat at the bar – are you interested? The zucchini just came out from the kitchen, and are sitting in the back right there," he told them pointing at the end of the bar.

"Wow, *what*? That is just too fabulous. Yes, yes, we will take them please," Mia said nodding at Kim.

They both grabbed their drinks.

"Here is to happier days," Mia held up her drink to toast.

"And good luck!" Kim said as she held up her glass to toast.

Clink.

Kim took a long sip, Mia took two.

"Enjoy. The sweet tamale cakes are on their way as well," James said sitting the basket of fried zucchini slices with ranch dressing in front of them.

"Thank you, "Mia replied.

Kim nodded in his direction.

"Now that's what I'm talking about, right here," Mia said as she dunked a zucchini slice into the ranch and bit into it.

Kim took another big gulp of her drink but didn't take her eyes off

Mia who looked worried, "Mia, you okay?"

"That text I just got, it was from my sister."

"Which one?"

"Juanita. She called me yesterday morning and told me that they found a lump on her mammogram. She's having a biopsy tomorrow. I went over there yesterday morning and we had breakfast, then ended up going to the Macy's One Day Sale before the wedding. I had quite the full day," Mia said with raised eyebrows.

"Oh Mia. *Mia,* I am so sorry. I will add her to my prayers that it won't be cancer. How scary though," Kim said shaking her head, then taking another big gulp of her drink.

"Right? She has a mammogram every year though, all five of us do, so I think even if it the worst happens, and it *does* turn out to be cancer, she will be okay. It would be caught early so her odds of survival are pretty high," Mia replied taking a big gulp of her drink as well.

"Well damn, it does sound like you had a full day, but you should have had a full night too, I'm just sayin'," Kim said elbowing her.

"You just need to quit it, you…"

Buzz. Buzz. Buzz. Buzz.

They both jumped, startled from the pager.

"Saved by the bell, uh buzzer?" Kim asked laughing as she grabbed their drinks and Mia grabbed the zucchini and ranch. They walked back to the hostess desk.

"Kim?" the hostess asked.

"Yes."

"If you would please follow me," she said as she led them to the table and handed them menus as they sat down.

"Your server will be with you shortly ladies."

"Thank you," they both told her.

"Well, I already know what I want, but what about that other appetizer?" Kim said pushing the menu toward the front of the table without opening it.

No sooner than the words were out of Kim's mouth, "Sweet tamale cakes?"

"Hi, yes, from the bar order?" Mia asked.

"Yes Miss, there is no bill, they have already been paid for. Did you need anything else from the bar?"

Kim piped up, "Yes, we *both* need another drink, so two more spicy Stoli bloody marys please. And can I get extra celery in mine, *please*?"

"Not a problem, I will have those over to you in a few moments."

Mia nodded, "Thank you," she told him.

She grabbed one of the small plates and scooped some tamale cake on hers, and Kim followed suit.

"Ooh, this is *so* good Mia."

"Right? I'm wondering if I should even order food with these appetizers, but I suppose I can always take the leftovers home for dinner."

Before either of them could say another word, they were interrupted, "Hi, I'm Diane, your server. Are you ready to order, or do you need more time?"

"I'm ready. I will have the meat loaf, lunch portion size please.

"Of course, and for you?" Diane asked looking at Mia.

I would like the factory chopped salad with no blue cheese, and the dressing on the side please."

"Very good. Fresh bread will be out shortly," Diane said while collecting their menus.

They both smiled and Kim drained the rest of her drink.

"Ooh, I needed that," Kim said sitting her empty glass down and rolling her head slowly side to side.

"I wonder if Ash has made it to the beach yet," Mia asked.

"More like a bar somewhere. Ooh, and look who is talking - I have *some* nerve, huh? It *is* what it is though," Kim said laughing.

"Two spicy, Stoli bloody marys?"

"Yes indeedy," Mia said, taking a last sip to finish off her first one, then setting the glass back down.

"Atta girl," Kim said winking.

The server from the bar sat their fresh drinks on the table and removed the empty glasses.

"To good health," Kim held her glass up.

"Here, here," Mia replied holding her glass up and nodding.

They both sipped their drinks in silence for a few minutes before Mia said, "Okay, so on my little getaway, I met this older man, a one Mr. *Giovanni Esposito*. I had dinner both nights I was there with him. And girl, I am talking fucking, fabulous dinners – and I do mean like *to die for* fabulous. That weekend was out of a goddamn fairytale."

"Well go on with your bad self then. Dinner huh? What about *desert* though? Kim asked with a smirk.

"I'm getting to that. *But wait,* when I was checking out, I was shocked to find out that my room had been comped by management. He had left me a card telling me he was the President of the damn hotel chain! He had just gotten the promotion and told me that Friday night's dinner with me was a celebration for him."

"*What* the fucking fuck Mia?! A celebration huh? *Do tell.*"

"Okay, so the first night we had dinner in the hotel restaurant, the best table there, with a perfect view of the beach. The food and service was, well, it was extraordinary. The second night we had dinner in his penthouse, well, actually it was outside, on the patio. It was all catered from the kitchen. There was the sunset, and the fairy lights, and lots of drinks," Mia told her with a faint smile from the fond memory.

"Uh... I know I didn't stutter earlier - *desert though*?"

Mia just looked at her stoically before saying, "Well, I'm not one to kiss and tell, but let's just say a sista can still have game even in her 50's. Only did it once though, and not until the second night. Now you know that is *not* how I roll, but everything just felt so magical, so, I rode the wave," Mia said mock brushing dust off one of her shoulders.

"Yaaaasss," Kim said snapping her fingers twice.

"We exchanged phone numbers and emails. When you came to pick me up, I had just replied to one of his emails. It sounded like he has some sort of medical issues though. I'm a little concerned. He wants to talk on the phone tonight."

"Oh wow. So *hello*, how was the desert?"

Mia rolled her eyes, Kim..."

"Oh, come on Mia, spill."

"Okay, well, it was extremely sensual. It wasn't that *rip your clothes off I can't wait to fuck you* kind of sex, but after the drought I've been in, it worked out just great. More like a slow burn, know what I mean? Started off slow, but it intensified over time and got really hot."

Kim opened her mouth to reply but was interrupted, "Lunch portion meatloaf and a factory chopped salad, no bleu cheese with dressing on the side?" Diane asked.

Kim and Mia both nodded yes.

Can I get either of you anything else?" Diane asked after setting the salad in front of Mia and the meatloaf and potatoes in front of Kim.

"Two waters with lemon please," Kim said nodding to Mia.

"Yes, please," Mia chimed in.

"You got it," Diane responded before walking away.

"Great service, she needs a good tip," Mia said watching the server walk away.

"Yeah, yeah, *yeah*, continue please," Kim said motioning Mia to keep it moving with her left hand while eating with her right.

"Girl, it was like two fairytale dates. Cristal champagne and delicious seafood the first night, and tequila and a catered, buffet style dinner on his penthouse patio the second night. He must be a hopeless romantic, it was all so perfect, the lights, the sunset, the hot tub."

"Hot tub? *Hot tub?* Well god*damn* Mia. How did you meet this man?"

"I was sitting on the beach right after I got there and he walked up and introduced himself, and then the brave soul asked me to have dinner with him that night - just like that. It was something about his confidence and energy that intrigued me; he was a different type of man that I hadn't experienced before. I found myself digging his vibe, so I accepted his invite. He got a call and had to leave town for business after the first night's dinner, so I thought that dinner was it. But when I got back from the hotel gym the next morning, *girl*, there was room service breakfast, and a dozen roses waiting for me in my room!"

"Get the fuck *outta* here. Ooh Mia! Does he have a brother? An uncle? *Somebody?*" Kim asked laughing.

"So, what does he look like? Come on now, spill it."

"He is a well preserved 64-year-old Italian man. Tall, lean, olive skin, hazel eyes, with gorgeous white hair and one of those manicured close shaved white beards. *Very* sexy."

"Ooh Mia."

"I know, *right?*"

"Dayum girl, you are on a roll."

"Go figure, been in a sexual desert and then all of a sudden – *BAM!*"

"Well, it definitely is 'raining men' these days for you Miss Thing, but..."

"But what?"

"You know, that 3's thing you always talk about. Sorry sister, looks like you're one short," Kim said shrugging her shoulders and nodding her head in Mia's direction.

Mia quickly looked down to avoid Kim's prying eyes.

"Wait. What is that? Mia, you holding out on me or what?"

Mia looked up with a sheepish look on her face.

"No way. There *is* another one? There *is* three? Okay, quit playin' and fess up. Slam that damn drink and spill. Come on now, details, *details!*" Kim said tapping her hand on the table.

"Shh," Mia said looking around.

"I am *not* trying to care what these people think. You know that I don't give two shits. You better start talking or..." Kim said, before opening her mouth wide, then sharply slanting her eyes toward Mia.

"Okay, okay, okay."

"Now that's more like it, the floor is yours, Miss Thing," Kim said motioning to Mia with her palm upward.

"Okay, so when I got home last Saturday from my getaway, I decided to check my email, and there was an email from this old friend from high school. Well, um, more than a friend. I have not been in contact with him for like 30 years. And before you ask, yes, he's married," Mia said rolling her eyes and pursing her lips.

"More than friends, huh? Please feel free to continue at any time Miss Thing."

"After high school we stayed in touch, and let's just say there were a few times during those break-ups with evil ass Myron, that well, how do I say it, we connected in a *different* way."

"Wait, hold up here. So, you did or *didn't* have sex with him then?"

"Well kind of."

"Mia, come on now."

"It's a little complicated, just calm yourself and let me try to explain. So check it, he is two years older than me and after high school he moved to southern Cal, but after a couple of years, he moved back up to the Bay Area. There were times when he stopped by to visit me at my mom's house, but he had this apartment downtown, and sometimes on the way back from school I stopped by. A few of those times when I stopped at his place though, two, maybe three of those times..." Mia trailed off, took a deep breath and began shaking her head in disbelief at the memories.

"Drink some more of this so you can go on with the story," Kim said pushing Mia's drink towards her. "Here now, g'head."

Mia drank half of it, then sat her glass down.

"Yeah, now that's what I'm talkin' about, now let's go," Kim said as she picked up her drink and took a long sip as well.

"Well, that *first time*, I had overdone it at the gym. That night on the phone he promised me a killer massage if I made him some chocolate chip cookies. I was probably maybe, 21 or 22, back around that time, and so I go over there after class the next day. I brought him some of the cookies I baked, and the rest of the cookie dough that was left over. And *girl*, he had drawn a bath for me, and had candles lit *everywhere*, do you hear me? I remember it being overcast and the candles made it feel so warm and cozy. My mind was blown."

"Ooh Mia."

"Right? I remember having a glass of wine before my bath, and by the time I got out of that tub, trust me, I was feeling absolutely *no* pain. And that man had magic hands, and I was feeling so good, and then he told me that he could give me a different kind of massage. I was confused but he said he would show me, and if I didn't like it, then he would stop. He did it, and I did *not* ask him to stop."

Mia took another sip, and looked over her glasses at Kim, "Girlfriend, I will tell you this, his tongue was even more magical than his hands!"

"Unh, unh, *unh!*"

"Right? He's still my all-time favorite for *that*. It's like he just read my body language and knew exactly what to do and how to do it, and *unh*. Girl, it was the best...*ever*."

"But you guys were never a couple? Did you ever have regular sex? You did nothing for him, like, *ever*? Come on finish the story."

"How are you two doing? Can I get you anything else? Drink refills perhaps?" Diane asked interrupting Mia's story telling.

"Oh no, we're just fine thanks," Mia replied.

"Yeah, we're good," Kim added, rolling her eyes as Diane walked away.

Mia began eating her salad with gusto. After a few forkfuls, she realized that Kim was not eating, and instead, just staring her down. She looked up before taking another forkful, "What? I'm *starving*. I'm going to tell you the rest, but can't we eat though?"

Kim laughed, "Okay then, don't want my mashed potatoes to get cold, but it would have been worth it."

Mia ate a bit more then drained the rest of her bloody mary.

"So, there's not really much more left to tell you about Tony though. We only shared a few of those *times*. We actually talked on the phone more, and sometimes just hung out with no physical contact, but the intimacy was always there. It's like we had this secret place and shared this secret type of relationship, but never spoke of it, and never went any farther with it. It was pretty much like we both adhered to this secret agreement, the terms of which were never spoken aloud. I don't even know Kim, it just seemed to work for us at the time. But now we're both looking back and questioning as to why it was the way it was."

"Wow," Kim said finishing the rest of her bloody mary as well.

"I know. I'm still trippin' kinda hard on how like 10 days ago there was not a damn thing going on men wise, and now look."

"*Facts.*"

"It gets confusing sometimes though, trying to decide what to do. Yes, I am trying my best *not* to overthink, to go with my soul, and you know, just *ride* the wave."

"Ride the, *who*?" Kim asked laughing.

"Girl you need to stop," Mia said laughing along with her and picking at her salad.

"I'm going to take the rest of mine home, I am *so* full," Kim told her.

"Yeah, same here, I'm full too. That's another reason why I always get my dressing on the side, so my lettuce doesn't get all soggy from the dressing, and I can eat the rest later at home," Mia said winking and clicking her tongue twice.

Kim saw Diane walking in their direction and got her attention.

"Can we please get boxes and bags?"

"Of course. Would either of you care for dessert?"

"No thanks," they both said at the same time and laughed.

Diane smiled, "No worries, I will be right back with the containers, a couple of bags, and the bill."

"Thanks for suggesting lunch. It was good getting out, although Ashley will be mad when she gets back from L.A. to find out about the storm raging, caused by all my *raining men*," Mia said laughing.

"Yeah, but she will be glad like me, 'cause I don't have much going on, so I'm living vicariously through you right now. Your next book should be about your love life," Kim told her nodding her head.

"I'll think about it, who knows?" Mia replied with a shrug.

Diane came back and brought the boxes for their food and two bags. She sat the wallet with the lunch check in between Kim and Mia.

"The tab from the bar is separate but included inside. Thank you, please come back, and have a good rest of your day, "she told them before walking away.

Mia grabbed the bill first.

"How much Missy?" Kim asked while beginning to dig in her purse.

Mia quickly placed the money she had in her hand inside the wallet.

"Huh? Did you hear something? I thought I did, but hmmm, guess it was just my imagination," Mia said looking up and around, then shrugging with her arms outstretched.

"Ooh, unh unh. Come on Mia, how much?" Kim asked frowning.

"Look, I didn't really spend anything on my weekend get-away, so it's my treat. Plus, you drove. Better take advantage girlfriend," Mia told her winking.

"Aww Mia, are you *sure*?

Mia just gave her a deadpan stare, pursing her lips before rolling her eyes.

"I know it was a lot with the drinks, but at least the appetizers were free, huh? Well thank you, a million times, thank you," Kim told her, clasping her hands in prayer mode and bowing her head down.

"No thang, but I feel lazy as hell. I'm so ready for a nap. And holla, I don't have to cook dinner because I got the rest of my salad for later."

"For reals, thanks again. We are outta here then," Kim said getting up.

By the time they got back to Mia's house, Kim said, "I think I'm going to take a nap too," nodding her head yes.

"Naps are worth gold," Mia told her.

"They certainly are today," Kim said stifling a yawn.

"Well good thing you don't live too far. Drive safely, see you at work tomorrow."

"Got another conference this week, but we will catch up. Okay, bye... *Playa*," Kim said then stuck out her tongue and laughed.

"Don't hate the player, hate the game," Mia said pointing and winking at her before she got out.

They both laughed. Kim drove off as Mia waved back before walking into the house. She put her salad away and flopped on the couch, then grabbed the chenille throw lying on the back of the sofa and wrapped herself in. And the hits just keep on coming she thought lying there with a slight smile on her face. Her tummy was full, and fatigue from the walk earlier in the morning was hitting her.

Mia had no idea of how any of the relationships with Javier, Giovanni, or Tony would work out or possibly end. It *was* exciting though. Through the divorce from hell with Myron, Mia had learned that all you can do is try your best, use your best judgement, and always, *always*, listen to your gut feeling, because that is your soul speaking to you. Worrying about what *may* happen is never going to solve anything, and although it is difficult to let go and stop worrying, it is very necessary, because stress can eat you alive.

Eenie, meenie, miney indeed. And all three men brought something different to the table. Their sexuality was a variety pack as well, all of them bringing satiation for Mia in a myriad of ways. She grabbed her phone intending to text Giovanni, but somehow her body won out and she fell asleep with it in her hand.

Buzz. Buzz. Buzz.Buzz.

Mia awoke startled from her phone vibrating in her hand. She checked quickly in case it was Juanita. She was relieved to see a text from Giovanni.

> *Hello my dear, was hoping perhaps we can chat soon? Still up for Facetime? Please let me know.*

Mia checked the time - 5:57. She had been asleep nearly two hours. Wow. She decided to text Juanita before it got any later:

Hey Sis, please let me know when you get home and how everything goes tomorrow.
Prayers and sending nothing but positive vibes. Love you!

Juanita immediately replied:

Thanks Sis. Renee, Jean, and Denise know all about it too. I don't know what I would do without my sisters. I wish they lived close as you do. Will text or call you tomorrow, or Gary will for me. Love you more.

Mia felt relieved that Juanita seemed at peace with tomorrow. Now she responded to Giovanni:

Hey Mister E., yes, we can Facetime, how about 6:30ish? Not sure if you are on the west coast or if that is too late for you, please let me know or talk to you then.

Damn, I need to add a lot of make-up kind of fast Mia thought as she tossed off the throw and dashed to her bathroom. She got out her cosmetic bag and promptly got to work. She filled in her brows, added a little gold shimmer underneath them, then she added black eyeliner on her top lids, and lined the bottom with a deep brown pencil. She added two coats of black mascara, then finished by lining her lips with a plum lip liner and filled them in with a clear plum colored gloss. She took her hair down and brushed it, then put it back up in a high bun. She looked at the time, 6:26.

Mia grabbed her phone, went back in the family room, sat down at the kitchen table and propped it up. She took a couple of deep breaths, but her heart was still pounding in her chest. She got up, went straight to the freezer, and pulled out her bottle of Grey Goose. She poured a generous shot and threw it back.

Buzz. Buzz. Buzz. Buzz.

She rushed over and answered the FaceTime call. Giovanni's face popped up which made her smile.

"Buona Sera Miss Mia."

"Hey Mr. Esposito, how are you? Are you okay? I would be lying if I told you that your last message did not have me concerned."

"My apologies, it was not my intention to alarm you, but I just wanted to explain something to you. Not assuming that we will develop a relationship, but I am a man who puts all his cards on the table, you know?"

"I could tell that about you, and I do appreciate it."

"Technology these days, I love it. It is so nice to see you. You look beautiful, which is no surprise to me, but first, let me tell you that I have thought of you often since those two glorious nights with you," he told her with a smile and eyebrows raised for emphasis.

"You are too kind my dear sir, but may I say, you are also looking your regular dapper self."

"Now you are the one being too kind, but I need to clear my conscience if you don't mind, please."

"Of course, please tell me what it is that you want me to know."

"Well about 10 years ago, when I was about your age, I was diagnosed with Parkinson's disease."

"Oh no, I am so sorry Giovanni, are you okay? Is there anything I can do?" Mia asked looking alarmed.

"Thank you my dear, but there is nothing you can do. It seems the disease is progressing, and unfortunately, I am finding that I am not quite spry as I once was. I walk a bit slower and there are times my head shakes without me being able to control it too well."

"Oh Gio, are you in pain? I wish I could help you."

"No, no, I am not telling you this for sympathy. I had just gotten a Botox shot in my neck a week or so before I met you, so I was in great shape those evenings I spent with you. However, I felt that I owed you an explanation were you to ever return, and I was *not* in such great shape. Of course, due to my disclosure tonight, I can completely understand if it bothers you, and we become relegated to being modern day pen pals. So how are things going up there?"

"It's going well. Listen, I appreciate your honesty, I really do. But a disease or condition does not define a person unless you allow it to. You are still the same kind, witty, and intelligent man I met nearly two weeks ago. It is your soul which matters most."

Giovanni exhaled loudly, "I wasn't sure how you would feel after I disclosed this. I honestly did not know I would become so smitten and want to monopolize some of your time. As I told you before, I have been a loner more-or-less since becoming a widower. It is quite rare to find the combination of intelligence, beauty, and sexiness in one woman, but you my dear seemed to have accomplished it."

"Well, that's a helluva compliment, thank you. Are you feeling alright now though?"

"I've become adjusted to the pain, and I have meds which help. So, am I to presume that based on your previous answer, that you might come back to visit 'Ol Giovanni Esposito?" he asked with his head cocked to the side and one eyebrow raised.

"Well, of course sillyhead! No to mention you have racked up quite a few of those brownie points ya know," Mia said pointing at him and shaking her finger.

"You have no idea of how relieved I feel my dear," Giovanni said clasping his hands together and looking up towards the sky.

"Well, I appreciate you confiding in me, but I wish there was something more I could do for you. I had an aunt who had Parkinson's and she used to get massages pretty often, and said they helped quite a bit. I would offer, but as man of your means, I am sure it is no problem and probably best to get a professional who knows precisely how to help you."

"Good point, but I am quite sure they would not be so sexy!" Giovanni said laughing and shaking his finger back at Mia.

"I think you might be a bit biased," Mia replied with a shrug.

"I think that would be a correct assessment. So, listen, I have business coming up in Davis and Sacramento, in a couple of weeks on the 11th and 12th. Since Sacramento is your neck of the woods, I was hoping to maybe see you, even if briefly. Perhaps you might be inclined to pencil a guy in for dinner on the 12th? It's a Wednesday, so would be an early evening, I know you have to work the next day. I'll be staying downtown at the Kimpton Sawyer. I would look forward to seeing that beautiful face in person, but no pressure," he said waving his hands and then winking.

"Well, I said it from the beginning, you *are* a smoothy. Yes, of course I would love to have dinner with you. I will rush home to change and can meet you there around 6:30?"

"6:30 sounds just fine. I will be in touch before that. As always, I have fires to extinguish so I must dash, but I appreciate your graciousness and acceptance to overlook my condition."

"Like I said, it doesn't change who you are - it doesn't change your soul. I will talk with you soon, sleep well, *Vanni*," Mia said looking over her glasses.

"Ha! *Vanni* is it now? I like it. You sleep well too. Buono note."

"Nite," Mia said with a wave goodbye, then disconnected.

Mia sat there feeling warm and fuzzy. Poor Giovanni, Parkinson's was pretty serious, but it seemed that he had it under control, well at least for now. There are things that you just don't have control over, so you do what you can, and find as much happiness while you are able. That very thought made Mia think about her present status. Did she really have to choose just one if she didn't really want a serious relationship though? Hmm, maybe I can just act like a dude and stay unattached and keep all three she pondered.

Mia looked out the sliding glass door to the patio and the solar lights were coming on. She went into the kitchen and poured some ice water in a glass and dropped both a slice of cucumber and lemon in, then grabbed her left over salad out of the fridge. She pulled the throw off the couch, wrapped it around her shoulders and took her water and salad out to the patio. She hit the switch on the fountain and relaxed on one of the chaises. Lying back and listening to the gurgling water made her soul feel happy. It was the end to a great weekend, and possibly the beginning of new adventures: she would be chatting with and possibly seeing Javier sometime this coming week, she would have more conversations with Tony one way or another this week, and the following week she would be having dinner with Giovanni ... *whew*.

"My dance card is full," Mia shouted out loud to no one and holding her glass up towards the heavens with a smug smile.

Well now, maybe being a single woman in her 50's wasn't too bad she decided. Lately, she was enjoying some fantastic perks indeed. She finished her water and salad, then went inside to watch TV in bed, but was fast asleep within minutes.

As always, morning came way too fast, and Mia hit snooze several times before dragging her ass out of bed to get ready for work. Hitting snooze that last time caused her to sacrifice stopping at Starbucks, but shrugged it off, knowing that it was probably good to be skipping the carbs and sugars. She got to work, grabbed a Punch, Sugar-Free Rockstar out of the fridge and logged onto her computer. After putting her makeup on in the bathroom as she did nearly everyday, Kim stopped by Mia's desk on the way back to her own.

"Hey Missy, I am hella dragging today."

"Girl same."

"Got some training going on so I better get over to it. What time you doing lunch?"

"I don't *even* know. Email or text me."

"You got it, see ya."

Will today never end Mia thought, as the files in her queue almost doubled during the course of the day. Usually being busy helped time pass faster, but unfortunately, that scenario did not seem to be working well today. Never got an email or text from Kim, so she warmed up a Lean Cuisine and ate lunch at her desk. At least tonight was her U-Jam class at the gym, thank the Lord. She sent a text to Juanita:

Been praying for ya sis, it will be okay. Love you.

She instantly got a reply.

> *Hey Mia, it's Gary. We are back home. Juanita is resting, and it went okay. Took about an hour. Should have the results in a few days.*

Mia replied:

> *Thanks Gary. I will wait to hear. I know how she's nervous and probably doesn't feel up to chatting. Love you guys ttyl.*

The day dragged, but at 5:00 on the dot, Mia was outta there. She headed straight to the gym to work off some stress and angst. After she changed and warmed up on the bike, she did four sets of lunges with the 30 lb. barbell. Then she managed to hit the machines for a few sets of leg curls, leg press, and hack squats. She got it all done before class, walked into the room, and was able to get her favorite spot in the middle of the floor by the mirror. The class was slamming as usual, and she drove home from the gym feeling tired but accomplished.

She found that she was starving, so threw together a salad with some chicken strips from Trader Joe's on top. Damn those lunges, she could feel the soreness setting in her hamstrings already. Too bad there would be no Tony massage for them though. She sat there smiling at that thought. To slow down her mind and chill a bit, she poured herself a glass of Petite Syrah. After finishing her salad, she grabbed her wine, and as her per her norm, she settled on the chaise of the couch and turned on the TV. Nothing really held her attention for long. She picked up her phone, pulled up her email, and saw that she had an email from Tony. Still on the same wavelength, or so it would seem.

> Hey Miss Thing,
>
> Hope things are going well for you. I'm going on a business trip Thursday thru Saturday in Colorado, closer to you but not close enough to meet up. So if I can't sleep, still going to tell me a bedtime story

or what? Here's my number, 210-569-7431. Why
don't you give me a text and maybe we can chat. It
will be great to hear your voice again after so many
years.

Mr. T

Oh my God, why had I said that about telling him a bedtime story? At
the same time though, the thought of telling Tony something sexy
was definitely a turn on. Maybe she could help make up for never
doing anything sexually pleasurable for him. Where would all this
lead, she had no idea whatsoever, but decided to just continue riding
the wave which seemed to be swelling. She replied right back:

Hey Mr. T,

Things are busy at work, and I hit the gym tonight,
but lying here on the sofa, I can feel I went too
hard - it will be a good sore in the coming
days, hahaha. I've grown accustomed to not having
a personal masseuse to help me out, (wink, wink),
but yes, let's chat soon. Not sure what I may be
doing this weekend, text me when you can, and
maybe we can see what shakes out. 916-684-4344.

"Miss Thing"

She hit send, and soon as she lifted her fingers off the key, she began
wondering if she had accepted too fast or too easily. Nah, life is far
too short, more chips to fall where they may she decided. She lay
there with Tony on her mind and felt excited at the thought of
hearing his voice again too. But damn, it was only Monday, ugh.
    Tony remembered her body from back in the day, not as it was
now, more mature and softer, plus her skin was definitely not as firm
after the pregnancy with the boys. Of course, there was also the age
factor. Perhaps it would be best to leave it alone, and just let him
remember how she was back in the day. Allowing him to remain
enamored of that seemingly near perfect image of Mia he had in his
mind was pretty tempting. However, Pandora's Box had been

opened, and Mia was not one to shy away from adventure, so that was just not a viable option. After all these years why had he found her though? The universe knew, but apparently wanted Mia to find out on her own. She would have to be brave enough to search and find the answer so it would seem.

She closed her eyes and let her mind transport her back there, back to their Secret Place. She lay there imagining being in a warm bath with candles about, jazz playing in the other room, and Tony patiently waiting for her. The naivete of her, and the much more experienced Tony, hmm, what a combination. Mia finished her wine, then feeling the day and gym had caught up with her, headed to the shower. Still with Tony on her mind she caressed her breasts under the water, and found herself wishing her hands were Tony's, as well as his lips and tongue.

Mia got out and threw on the nightshirt she had just bought. She got in bed with Tony still on her mind, but hoping that he wouldn't want to Facetime. Only time would tell though. She found that her reasoning skills were non-existent, as the gym had taken its toll, and the wine topped it off. As she felt herself drifting off to sleep, she was in hopes that her increased workload at work would cause her to stay busy and help the week pass faster. More importantly though, she was hoping the busy week would help to keep her mind from wandering too much, which was usually an impossible feat. She decided to close her eyes to try and still her mind, once she did, sleep came nearly instantly.

The next morning as Mia logged onto her computer at work, she wondered how she had even gotten there. She had absolutely no idea whatsoever of how she had even got out of bed and dressed, let alone drove all the way to work. It was one of those days she realized that she was operating on autopilot, and all she could do was to hope for the best. She saw there was still lots of work to do, so decided to throw herself into it, but of course found her mind wandering. She stopped typing and sat there with her head resting on her palm, thoughts of those magical dates with Giovanni began running through her mind. Everything was done so perfectly - the food, the attention, the ambience created - she felt so special. She closed her eyes as she felt her imagination about to hit overdrive.

Clap. Clap. Clap. Clap.

Startled, Mia opened her eyes, looked up quickly, and saw her boy Mark standing in front of her cubicle.

"Craig ..."

Clap. Clap. Clap.

"*Craig!* I need to borrow your VCR right quick," Mark animatedly told her by throwing down one of their favorite movie lines.

Mia could not help but laugh.

"*Bye* Felicia," Mia replied with a wave of her hand.

They both giggled.

Mark had once told her that he was a Black woman stuck in a small, White man's body. He was all of about 5' 6", around 160ish, with devilish green eyes, and a contagious laugh. His heart was enormously huge; he was truly a loving and giving person. He was always volunteering to help out with various charitable organizations and the elderly on the weekends.

He was right about one thing though, culturally he *was* Black. They connected right off the bat years ago at the title company they both used to work for. Mia remembered being at her desk and hearing a voice on the other side of her cubicle:

"Cause you *know* that's what they do. They will drag a brotha behind a car like a dog in a damn minute down in the south - now quit playin'," and she found herself sitting there wondering just who in the hell had said it.

She poked her head around the cubicle wall over at Christy's desk. Mark looked over at her, "Oh hey Boo, what's up? I'm Mark. Sorry, my bad - my voice carries, *huh?*"

Mia remembered smiling, "No worries, was just an unfamiliar voice, but all good."

Mark winked at Mia and smiled.

"Thanks anyway Christy," Mark told her as he stood up to leave her desk.

"Hey Mark, this is Mia, she actually knows more than I do, so she can probably answer you."

Mia remembered helping him with some underwriting issue. They bonded instantly, became great friends, and had been kicking it ever since. They were both stoked a few years ago, when they saw each other again at this job, and found out that they worked in the same building, on the same floor. That memory made her smile.

"What's shakin'?" Mark asked bringing Mia back to the present moment.

"Not much, you are *so* crazy, thank you for making me laugh."

"You know the *dill...* pickle. So *chirrl,* what you know that's good?"

"Nothin', just living the dream," Mia replied dryly.

"Uh huh, sho' aint't what the girls done told me, so ... what's *up*?" The wedding reception? Gorgeous man? *Hello*?"

"Oh *snap*. Some people just can't keep quiet," Mia said rolling her eyes.

"So, kitten, *where* did you meet this man? Who *is* he? The fo'-one-

one, *if you please?*"

"Welp, you might know who he is, actually," Mia said snapping her fingers and pointing at him.

"Get outta here."

"Didn't you once tell me that you had car problems, and went to a shop that you liked a lot, Martinez Auto Repair?"

"Yep. Sure did. The owner took good care of me and that T-Bird I used to have. Why are you bringing *that* up though Miss Thing?"

Mia just looked at him over her glasses with her lips pursed. Mark frowned and shrugged. Mia could see the thought processes running through his mind, then his green eyes lit up like a pinball machine.

"Wait a minute now. Hold *up.* The owner? No way. *Javier?*" he asked slanting his eyes towards her.

Mia looked up at the ceiling and then back at Mark with raised eyebrows.

"*Shut up!* That gorgeous milk chocolate drink of water with those gorgeous blue eyes?"

"*Shhh,* keep it down. Not proud of it, he *is* married you know."

"Uh, well last time I looked, hah, *you* ain't," he told her matter-of-factly with attitude.

Mia just shook her head.

"Betta' get in, where you fit in babygirl. You know I ain't judging nobody, but look, I have a meeting to get to. We need to hook up with some *dranks,* and uh, I do mean soon, so we can chew the fat."

"Hells yes we do. Maybe this weekend?"

"That's it, muffin. I'll holler at you later and we can set it up. You know a pimp is dying to find out the scoop. See ya later."

Mia was sitting at her desk a couple of days later trying not to doze off from lack of caffeine, it being morning and all, when a group text popped from Mark.

> *Hey "Playa", so me 'n Kim were talking about meeting at my place Saturday night for drinks and such. Ashley is in, she will be back Friday afternoon. Don't even think of saying no - and make some of your dee-lish guacamole please. We're doing a light potluck. Oh yeah, and bring your suit, we're getting in the hot tub. Holla right back.*

The text perked Mia up. It was only Thursday, and honestly, she really had no weekend plans, other than maybe a Facetime call or two, and no way was she going to sit around waiting on that. Another

Saturday night drinking seemed imminent, and she did have fun last Saturday at the reception, but this time she would be kicking it with her boy Mark too. She quickly replied:

> *Allrighty then y'all, I'm in. What time? Only guacamole?*

Almost instantly she got a reply from Mark:

> *Fab-u-lous! See you at 6, my place.*

Kim:

> *Sweet, I will bring wings!*

Ashley chimed in from L.A.:

> *I'm bringing potato skins. My feelings would not be hurt if you made some of that killer salsa too Mia, just sayin'...*

Mark:

> *Looks like it's on and kickin' ya'll. I got the alcohol and mixers and a few more eats 'n treats. P-A-R-T-Y? Because I, GOTTA!*

Mia laughed; he was worse than her with the movie lines.

Mia:

> *Okay Ash, I will throw down on some salsa too. See you guys @6 on Saturday at Mark's.*

Kim:

> *Can barely wait, seeeeeee ya!*

Ashley:

> *Yay! See you guys soon, 'bout to head to the beach. Don't hate me too much lol.*

Mia quickly jotted a grocery list on Notes on her phone for what she needed to pick up at the store to take to Mark's. It had been a long time since all of them had cut it up, a good time was imminent.

About noon, she got a text from Juanita:

> *Biopsy was benign, all good! Love you sis, thank you for being there!*

Mia took a deep breath, silently thanked God, and instantly replied:

> *I am so happy and relieved. That's what family is for. We will talk soon. Hella busy at work, but if you need to call you know you can. Love you!*

The rest of the day and week passed by uneventfully, and Friday after work found Mia sitting in the In 'N Out drive thru line, getting a burger, fries, and root beer for dinner. The boys were grown and away, but her rule of not cooking on Fridays was still in effect. The week had dragged, and her back was aching after the gym the other day, so she popped a muscle relaxer and got in bed after eating and was soon in slumberland.

She woke up Saturday morning later than planned after a night of broken sleep with weird dreams, so decided to skip the gym. Her back was feeling better, but she was still dragging ass from the muscle relaxer. She made herself a cup of ginger–lemon tea, got dressed, and then headed to the grocery store to get supplies for the shindig later that evening at Mark's. At least that was a bright spot; kicking it with Mark and her "Girlz", was a guaranteed good time.

Mia found some wonderfully ripe avocados for the guacamole, as well as tomatoes on the juicy side for the salsa which Miss Ashley had requested. She grabbed the rest of the ingredients, as well as her groceries for the next week, put them in the back seat, and then headed to the nursery. She felt like surprising Mark and making him a little somethin' somethin', so grabbed a white rustic planter to put a few echeverias, an agave, and a kalanchoe in. She knew he was partial to succulents and that he would be surprised at what she was putting together for him.

Mia returned home and got busy working on Mark's arrangement. She added a couple of the painted rocks she had made for her arrangements and flower beds. One had a peace sign and the other said Love. She was pleased with how it turned out, and pretty sure that Mark would like it as well. She threw together a bag with her towel and toiletries, then put it on the floor behind her seat in the car, and the box with Mark's surprise behind the passenger seat.

She glanced at the clock; it was barely 3:00. She decided to set an alarm and sneak in a quick nap. She woke up feeling rested, then rolled over to grab her phone off the nightstand, thinking she had awakened before the alarm went off, but was shocked to see it was 4:55! What in the actual hell? She looked and saw that she *had* set the alarm, but had mistakenly set it for a.m. instead of p.m.

"Well fuck *my* life," she shouted out loud, then rushed to turn the shower on.

She showered, wiggled into her swimsuit, threw a black maxi dress over it, then slipped into a pair of black flip flops with patent leather straps. She pulled her hair up in a high bun, and being in a rush, decided to skip make up except for just a little berry lip stain and gloss. She decided it would be better to drive to Mark's and make the guacamole and salsa there rather than being late, so quickly threw all the stuff she bought in a bag then headed out. She was grateful that she had the foresight to put Mark's succulent arrangement and her bag in the car earlier.

Mia hated being late but fortunately Mark didn't live too far away. She pulled up at exactly 5:47.

Bing Bong. Bing Bong.

Mark came to the door in black flip flops, dark red shorts, and a red and white striped t-shirt.

"Hey Pimpin'," Mia said handing him the planter.

"Ooh, what's this? It's for *me*?"

"No, it's for the *other* Mark. I was on the creative tip earlier, so decided to hook my boy up is all."

"Ooh, thanks love, this is way groovy. You know me too well," he said giving her a kiss on the check.

"Come on in. Now, not that I mind babydoll, but we're a little early, aren't we? What... you runnin' from the Po-Po or somepin'? Mark asked with his eyes narrowed to slits, in a mock scrutinizing stare for a second.

Mia quickly looked both ways twice before replying, "Yeah, but ... *fuck da police!*" then crossed her arms in a rapper's pose with a mean mug expression.

They both broke out laughing.

"Lordt Mark, I set my alarm for a.m. instead of p.m. and woke up late from my nap, so decided to make the dips here and brought all the stuff with me."

"No thang, chiile. Follow me into the kitchen and let's get you set up. I see you got the black flip flop memo though, *hey*."

"You know that's right," Mia replied chuckling.

Mark got some bowls, utensils, and a cutting board out for Mia. She washed her hands and got to work.

"The girls aren't here yet, but let's have us a shot. What's your poison tonight babygirl? I got some of that pineapple vodka in the freezer that you like, just sayin'."

"Let's do it then, bring it."

Mia began chopping and Mark poured them two shots and handed her a glass. He held his up, "Here's to good friends."

"And *Old* friends," Mia added.

Clink.

They threw the shots back without chasers, then sat the glasses down.

"Ooh. Now that's what I'm talking about right there," Mia said rolling her head side to side.

"You ain't neva lied. I am so glad you're here. It has been like *forever,* since we kicked it."

"It really has, we must vow to not let that happen ever again."

"Done," Mark said bumping fists with Mia.

Mia quickly put together the guacamole and salsa while Mark set up the cooler with water and sodas.

"The salsa might be a little spicy. I hope I didn't add too much jalapeno," Mia said looking a bit perplexed.

Mark picked up a chip, dipped it into the salsa, and put it in his mouth.

"Mmm, yummy. It's got a little bite, but not bad. I love hot stuff though, it's all good babygirl."

"Fabulous. Where should I sit this?"

"On the breakfast bar right there on the tray with ice. This is where all the food is going. Now, we have a few minutes before the rest of the posse gets here, and you need to get real with your boy...*so?*"

"About which one?"

"Wait – what do you mean, *which one?*"

"I thought Kim had blabbed as usual and told you everything."

"She told me about the reception and that sexy Javier. Go 'head on you little Cougar. So, what you sayin'? There's *more* to tell? I mean, are you saying that there's *another* man?"

Mia looked over her glasses, then held up two fingers.

"Slow your roll now, two men, or two *more* men?"

Mia just gave him a deadpan stare and then raised her eyebrows, pursed her lips, and turned to walk out of the kitchen.

"Ooh, no you dii-*ent,*" Mark said grabbing her by the arm.

Mia turned around and shrugged.

"Spill it Missy," he demanded with his hand on one hip and head cocked to the side.

"Okay, there are actually two *more* men. 1+1+1=3," Mia said using her fingers to count to three.

"Shut.The.Fuck.Up."

"Well, I mean, what's a girl to do?" Mia asked throwing up her hands.

Bing bong. Bing bong. Bing bong

"Oh damn, we was just about to get dem juicy parts too."

"I'm going to go get changed while you answer the door."

Mark went to the door and Kim was standing there. Ashley was walking up the driveway.

"Hey y'all come on in. Mizz Mia is already here."

Ashley and Kim walked in. Mia came out with a towel wrapped around her waist.

"Hey y'all," Kim said as they all exchanged hugs and greetings.

"Where do we put the food?"

"Over there on the warming tray Mark has plugged in. See? Next to the salsa and guac on the breakfast bar," Mia said pointing.

"Okay, now that we all had our Kum Ba Ya moment, we need to get this party started, so we're all having a shot of pineapple vodka," Mark told them as he set down four shot glasses.

"Sounds good to me," Kim said.

"Let's do it," Ashley added.

Mark poured them all drinks.

"Here's to good friends, and making some fabulous *got*-damn memories," Mark said as they all clinked glasses and threw the shots back.

"There's water and sodas in the cooler too right over there," Mark said pointing to the far corner.

"I'm about to get in the tub y'all, I need this *so* bad you don't even know," Mia said as she made her way to the hot tub.

"I have my suit on under my clothes," Kim said.

"Me too! Great minds think alike," Ashley said.

"Lawd have mercy," Mark said chuckling.

Ashley and Kim went into the bathroom and came out with towels wrapped around their waists as well. Mia had already gotten in the hot tub. Mark came out last and ever being the host with the most, "I made a big ass pitcher of bloody marys - y'all down?" he asked while setting four glasses down.

"Oh, *hells yeah*," Ashley replied.

"Well, *duh,*" Mia added.

"Bring it," Kim said.

He went to the kitchen, came back with a huge pitcher, and filled their glasses before getting in the hot tub himself.

"This is heaven, thanks for the invite," Ashley said.

"Yes, you and Kim did well, I am so glad to be here with you guys," Mia told them.

"Here's to some real OG's," Mark said lifting his glass, and they all clinked and toasted with him.

"Okay, I know you guys want to be all in my business, but let's just enjoy this right now, and we'll chat when we eat – *cool*?" Mia asked.

"All good," Kim said and the other two nodded in agreement.

"We need to be kicking it like this with our boy Marky Mark a little more often. It's been way, *way* too long." Ashley said.

"*For* reals," Kim chimed in.

"I've just been so busy with all these projects, but we ain't neva going this long ever again, pinky swear," Mark said hooking pinkies with Mia, Ashley, and Kim.

Fighting back tears, Mia blurted out, "Kim and Ashley know this already, but my sister Juanita had a scare in the past week or so. They found a lump in her breast, and it was pretty scary for a few days, but it turned out okay, *thank you Jesus*. But it also made me realize how short life is, and... I'm just so glad to be here with you guys right now."

"Aww Mia, I'm so glad she's okay. You hadn't said anything, so I didn't want to ask."

Ashley hugged her.

"Sorry, I just got emotional, I'm good now," Mia said draining most of her drink before sitting her glass back down.

"Damn girl, take it to the head why don't you," Kim said laughing.

"*Speaking of head* – oh...right - *my bad*! We agreed to wait until we eat to speak of such things, huh *babydoll*?" Mark asked, gently elbowing Mia in the ribs and winking.

Mia burst into laughter.

"*You* are beyond a hot mess, but I love you lots," Mia told him.

"Ditto babes."

"Oh, hold up. Did you guys see Mrs. Johnson call that skank Lisa in her office late yesterday afternoon?" Kim asked them.

Mia and Ashley shook their heads no.

"Who is this, Lisa?" Mark asked.

"This chick who wears really short skirts and low-cut tops. I mean forget business casual; she looks like she should be out on the damn corner. You know, I don't think she has even been there 90 days yet, so wonder if she will still be there on Monday. Word is, she sent a nasty picture to some guy in another department on her computer," Kim told them.

"Unh, unh, unh. What a fucking idiot, 'cause you know Mrs. Johnson does *not* play," Mia added.

"She sure in the hell doesn't," Kim said shaking her head.

"Speaking of playing, you know what? We should all go on one of those all-inclusive vacations to somewhere like Cabo or something," Ashley said.

"I could definitely get used to this for a week, *on the real*," Mark added.

"Same," Mia and Kim said together and burst into laughter again.

"You know, that is a fabulous idea *Ash-a-lee*," Mia told her.

"Do this every night for a week? Quit playin' and sign my ass up, *right.damn.now*," Mark said waving his arm in the air.

They all laughed and nodded in agreement as they finished their drinks, then just chilled in the warm water for awhile.

"So, this feels great and all, and I don't know about you chickens, but I'm 'bout hungry as a mofo," Mark said looking around at everyone.

"Now, you *know* I can eat," Kim said.

"I'm always hungry," Ashley chimed in.

"So, we're all ready to get out and eat then?" Mia asked.

No one answered, but apparently everyone was in agreement, since they all grabbed their glasses and climbed out of the hot tub.

Mark shut it down and put the cover on. The girls went into the bathroom to change, and he went to his bedroom.

Mia dried off and threw her Maxi dress back on.

"I am totally going commando," she said giggling.

"Well, what's the point of putting underwear back on at this point? I'm with you Mia," Kim said.

"Yup, me too. I feel free!" Ashley giggled.

They walked back out into the family room/kitchen area.

"I am starving, and this sista is about to get her grub on," Mia said grabbing a plate from the stack and getting her utensils.

"Girl me too," Kim chimed in.

"For reals. Where oh where is our Marky Mark? We could sure use some refills on our *dranks*," Ashley said laughing.

"*I heard that*," Mark yelled from the kitchen.

They all looked at each other with surprised expressions, but before they could say another word, Mark had already walked into the room holding a fresh pitcher of bloody marys, then struck a pose before saying one word - "*Bam!*"

They all laughed.

"You are just the best," Kim said before hugging him.

"Oh, you go on," he replied and started re-filling everyone's glasses.

They all got their food then sat down to eat. No one spoke a single word for several minutes.

"Sure got mighty quiet up in these parts," Mark said giggling.

"I think we were all starving, and the water always makes you hungrier for some reason," Kim told him.

"Facts," Mia answered.

They all laughed and nodded in agreement.

"Girl... this salsa is - the bomb," Kim told Mia.

"See? Told you Mia," Ashley added.

"I do what I can."

"Oh *really*? Uh, then why oh why, ain't you fillin' us in *Miss Thing?* Just what is going on in Mia's world these days? Do tell," Mark said with attitude.

"I can't believe Kim hasn't spilled everything," Mia replied.

"Wait, how come Kim knows and I don't?" Ashley asked with a frown.

"Because your little partying ass was in L.A., and Kim and I had lunch," Mia said as she bonked her on the nose.

"Oh yeah," Ashley said rolling her eyes and shaking her head.

"Okay, okay, here is the 411 y'all. So, on my getaway I met this man, Giovanni. He's an older Italian gentleman, 64, very handsome. Tall, lean body, and is a hopeless romantic. We had dinner both nights I was there."

"*And* desert the 2nd night!" Kim interjected.

A collective, "*Ooh. Mia*," filled the room.

Rolling her eyes and shaking her head Mia continued, "Yeah, well yeah. It was like a fairytale date each night. And the second day when I came back from the hotel gym, he had room service delivered to my room with a dozen roses."

"Oh damn," Ashley said.

"But wait - when I checked out, I found out he is the President of the hotel chain, had comped my stay, *and* ...he's coming up to Sacramento on business and wants to have an early dinner on the 12th."

"Go 'head," Mark told her before high fiving her.

"But appears there's a bit of bad news too. We Facetimed last week, and he told me he had Parkinson's, so I think he wants to talk more about that, I don't know. He seemed to be okay then though. At least it will be a great dinner because the man does *not* skimp - only the best. That definitely does *not* hurt my feelings," Mia said sticking out her tongue.

"Okay, uh, now serving number 2. *Next?*" Mark asked then clapped his hands quickly two times.

"Calm yourself," Mia said taking two long sips of her bloody mary.

"Okay, so I met this guy, a brotha, Tony, in high school, and we became good friends. He's two years older than me, I was a sophomore, and he was a senior. Well, recently he tracked me down thru my website, and we have been emailing. He's married but unhappy. Lives out of state. Anyways, we were really solid friends but, umm, how do I say this? There *were* a few times back in the day when I was in college at his apartment, you know? Well, actually it was really one-sided, and only for me," Mia said shrugging.

"And what exactly does that mean?" Ashely asked.

"Can I get some fries with that shake though? *Details please?*" Mark added.

"Okay so, let's just say the man has magic hands and an even more magical tongue - Lordy Jesus," Mia said shaking her head, then drained the rest of her drink.

"Mark give her another one, she's our entertainment for tonight," Kim said tapping him on the arm.

"Y'all need to quit it. I'm good. I gotta drive home ya know," Mia said waving off another drink.

"Now where was I before I got interrupted? Oh yeah, so we are supposed to talk sometime this week. We have been going back in time and examining why we had this invisible line in the sand that we wouldn't cross way back when."

"Hmm, well that's different. So wait now, you never had *real* sex? Like, just lip service for this sista right over *herr* and whatnot?" Mark asked sipping on his drink.

"Exactly, and like I said it only happened a few times, but he always drew me a bath, and there were always candles lit, and jazz playing. We call it our Secret Place," Mia replied.

"Wait - so how did those times end? He never expected to get his turn or said anything about not getting any?" Kim asked her.

"You're not going to believe this, but after each of those times, he wanted to go get burritos and beer," Mia said laughing and shaking her head.

"The *fuck?*" Ashley said frowning.

"Hey, that's what worked for us at the time. I can't explain it, and neither can he. That's what we've been discussing. But I can tell you this, that intimacy that we created decades ago, surprisingly it's *still* there. Whenever we text or email it's like I just spoke to him yesterday, same for him. Conversation just flows. I have no idea what will happen when we talk on the phone this coming week," Mia said shrugging.

"Well, well, well, looks like we are getting the best for last. What 'chu know about a good lube job girl? *Is there a mechanic in the house?*" Mark yelled rubbing his palms together.

Everyone burst into laughter.

"You are just wrong," Mia said rolling her eyes but still laughing.

"It was simply an innocent question though," Mark said fluttering his eyes.

"Exactly," Ashley said co-signing on Mark's response.

"I am admitting nothing about Javier," Mia stated flippantly.

"Aww come on now, we could feel that vibe grooving way over where we were sitting, huh Kim?" Ashley said.

"Straight up. *Facts,*" Kim replied nodding affirmatively.

"Really?" Mia asked, surprised that she and Javier's electricity was palpable by others.

Kim and Ashley just stared at her, then looked at each other, then back at Mia without saying a word.

"Okay, okay, but he's married, *well*, he was when I met him. He's been away taking care of a brother who was ill."

Mark reached over, grabbed Mia's left hand, held it up showing no ring, shrugged, then let it drop to the sofa.

"*And?*" Mark asked crooking his neck with outstretched arms.

"Well, he told me that he's staying with another brother right now. You guys saw Alejandro at the reception, right?"

"I saw him alright. He's not fine as Javier, but dude can eat crackers in *my* bed," Kim said laughing as she and Ashley high fived.

"You guys, Javier is like 10 years and change younger than me," Mia said pursing her lips.

"*So,*" Ashley replied with a steely look.

"But the real question here, and the ultimate deal breaker would be - does his *dick* care though?" Mark bluntly asked.

Kim had just taken a big sip of her drink and almost spit it out. Everyone burst into laughter.

"Unh, unh, *unh*. You did *not* just say that," Mia said shaking her head and rolling her eyes.

"Oh, but I did. And I do *not* recall stuttering, whatsoever. Let's be real here *chirrl*, from what I've heard, that age thang don't seem to be mattering a damn bit. In fact, it is seeming to *moi*, that particular dick must be digging on a Cougar these days, uh more specifically, a certain one who is in our presence this evening. *Can I get a witness?*" Mark said holding up his right hand before breaking into laughter.

"Testify," Kim said holding up her right hand and bowing her head, then joined in Mark's laughter.

Ashley sat there nodding yes while sipping her on her drink and smiling.

"It's *not* the right thing to do though," Mia said solemnly.

"Look Mia, I know you feel bad that he's married, but who knows what his status is now. And from what I know of you, you are not trying to break up his marriage and steal him away, you are just trying to have some fun now and then. Hell, men, especially older men, have been doing this to younger women forever, so ..." Ashley told her shrugging.

"Yes, I know this, but it doesn't make it any less wrong," Mia replied.

"But it doesn't make it *feel,* any less right!" Kim said laughing.

Mia could not help but laugh.

"I think I'm speaking for everyone else in this damn room tonight girl - we would *all* fuck that man in a heartbeat. The fact that you are ten years older says a lot for you honey. You still got it goin' on. Am I right or am I *right* ladies?" Mark asked.

Ashley held up her glass, "Hells yeah. Here, here!"

Kim and Mark held up their glasses as well, "Here's to Mia and her harem. Go 'head with your bad self Mamas!" Kim yelled.

"*Go Mia, Go Mia, Go Mia*," they chanted as Mia just shook her head and laughed.

"And that concludes the entertainment portion of our evening," Mia said bowing her head.

They all laughed and began throwing their plates away.

Mark looked around, "Oh hol-*up*, something's missing."

He got up and turned on some Old School music, Rick James Super Freak came on.

"Ooh yeah," Mia said.

Mark grabbed Mia's hand and pulled her out into the middle of the floor and started dancing. Feeling no pain after all the drinks, Mia started dancing with him. Not to be left out, Ashley and Kim joined them, and they all danced for three or four more songs before collapsing on the couch in laughter.

"Ooh wee, that was fun," Mia said gulping down some water.

"I think we need something more than water to revive us though," Mark said walking into the kitchen.

The girls heard silverware clinking and plates clattering. They all looked at each other frowning and confused.

"What in the hell is that man *doing* in there? Ashley asked.

Kim and Mia just shrugged and shook their heads.

"Ain't no tellin', you know Mark," Mia said.

"*Okay now, y'all just give a pimp a minute,*" Mark yelled from the kitchen.

They all smiled, rolled their eyes, and shook their heads at Mark's outburst.

"So Ashley, what's up with the Brad guy?" Mia asked.

"Well, we met for drinks when I got in last night."

"Uh huh, just drinks? Kim asked.

"Yup. He ain't no Javier, so didn't get it, but a good chance he will," she said laughing.

"Ooh, you nasty," Kim said pushing on Ashley's shoulder.

"Look who's talking, I remember your beach thang one night awhile back Miss Thing, so don't even," Ashley shot back sticking out her tongue.

"Good point Ash," Mia said laughing and pointing at Kim.

"And look who is talking. Mia you cannot say *shit*!" Kim yelled.

"Facts," Ashley added.

"I'll give you that," Mia said looking down shaking her head.

"Brad is really nice though, gonna take it slow and see what happens."

"Desert is served," Mark said while pushing his little liquor caddy into the family room.

"Oh damn, my thighs are excited," Kim said.

"Mine too, and this bubble butt - *Holla*", Mia chimed in.

"Whatcha got going on over there Marky Mark?" Ashley asked.

Mark brought the cart closer.

"So, ladies, we have a bowl of fresh strawberries and melons, whipped cream, turtle brownies, and some lemon pound cake," he said pointing to each desert as he announced them.

Then pointing to Mia, "And for our resident *Playa-Playa,* our very own "Pimpette" of the evening... I'm talkin' about my home girl Mia right *herr,* we got some *got*-damn, vanilla Häagen-Dazs! Y'all are welcome, and good night," Mark said, then dropped an imaginary microphone before taking a dramatic bow.

Mia blew him a kiss, which he pretended to catch.

"Oh Mark, you didn't! God bless you man!" Ashley yelled.

"And the winner for host of the year goes to ...our very own Marky Mark!" Kim yelled, then got up and hugged him.

"Oh, y'all stop it. I am just doing me; you know that's how I roll. Anybody want coffee? I can throw some K-Cups in the Keurig right quick," Mark asked hand on his hip and eyebrows raised looking from Mia to Kim to Ashley.

"Yes please, Mister Man," Mia said holding her hand up.

Ashley and Kim looked at each other and both said, "Nope", at the same time then laughed.

"I'm not ready to get rid of my buzz just yet," Kim said.

"Right?!" Ashley replied.

"Okay got you Mia. Milk and 2 sugars for me 'n you babes. Be right back."

Kim and Ashley got up and began piling their plates with deserts. They looked over at Mia standing there with her plate in her hand quizzically.

"I'm just trying to decide," Mia told them finally grabbing the tongs.

"Life is short babygirl. You've been working out. Go on and get you *some*," Ashley said winking at Kim.

"Yeah, get you *some*," Kim answered.

"Both of you are just *nasty*, " Mia said laughing.

"We're nasty? Us?" Kim asked, pointing to her and Ashley and shaking her head no.

"Uh, last time I looked, we ain't the ones with a harem Miss Thing, so you go right ahead on and check, *yourself*," Ashley said pointing at Mia then snapping her fingers twice and laughing.

Looking pleased, she walked away from the breakfast bar and took her desert to the sofa and sat next to Kim.

"Fair enough," Mia responded laughing and shrugging.

"I'm having some of everything, it all looks so good," Ashley said while heaping one more spoonful of fruit on her plate before sitting down next to Kim.

"Damn, I have *no* will power whatsoever," Mia said while getting just a small slice of cake, half of a brownie, but putting ice cream in a bowl and adding some of those sliced strawberries on top with a few pieces of melon.

"Oh, you can work it off though, no doubts girlfriend" Ashley said laughing and elbowing Kim who laughed with her.

"See? That's why I shouldn't be telling you guys *shit*," Mia said laughing, rolling her eyes and shaking her head.

At that very moment Mark walked back in and handed Mia her coffee.

"To the host with the most," Mia said raising her coffee.

"Here's to Mark," the girls chimed in raising their drinks.

"Oh, you guys," Mark said blushing and walked over to get his desert.

Mia took a sip of her coffee.

"Ooh, this coffee just hit's the spot. I love coffee with ice cream," Mia said.

"Freak," Kim said and laughed.

Oh, shut up, what do you know anyways?" Mia asked and threw a pillow off the sofa at her head but missed.

"She don't know what's good muffin, she don't know what time it is. I feel you on that," Mark said sipping his coffee.

"Tonight has been so good hanging with you guys," Mia told them.

They all shook their heads in agreement.

"But that vacation would be the bomb though. We really gotta get that going dude," Kim told Mark.

"I'm on it," he replied.

"I am not even trying to take that guac and salsa home. I made *way* too much. Y'all work it out amongst yourselves," Mia said getting up to take her dishes to the kitchen.

"You don't need to do that kitten," Mark called out.

"You just be quiet in there. I am a grown ass woman, so there," Mia yelled back.

She quickly rinsed her dishes along with the dishes she saw in the sink, then put them all in the dishwasher before Mark walked in with his and the other two's dishes.

"Thanks, you're a doll, but you really didn't have to," Mark said before kissing her on the cheek.

"I know, but you went above and beyond, as usual," Mia told him linking her arm in Mark's and walking back into the family room with him.

"Look guys, it's way past this old lady's, excuse me – this *Cougar's,* bedtime, so I'm 'bout to head on out, " Mia said before hugging Ashley and Kim.

"You sure you're good to drive? Cause you all can crash right here tonight, if need be," Mark told them.

I'm good to go Pimpin'," Mia told him.

"I'm not," Ashley said.

"Me either," Kim chimed in.

"No worries. Let me get y'all some blankets and pillows while I walk Miss Thing to the door," Mark told them.

Mia hugged Mark one more time as he opened the door.

"Now text me and let you know you got home in one piece babes," Mark called out to her.

"You got it," Mia said before getting into her car.

Mia drove home feeling good. She was glad that Mark and Kim had decided on their somewhat little impromptu soirée of sorts. It was so good hanging with her posse and catching up on things and reconnecting. She had not laughed that hard for so long, it was so needed.

She pulled into her garage a little after midnight, went straight to her room and threw her purse and bag on the bed. She jumped in the shower and took a nice hot one, dried off, and lotioned up. She sauntered into her bedroom and slid her window open a bit for some fresh air, then turned on her electric blanket.

Mia stripped off the towel and lay on her bed on top of the covers, without a care in the world. She could feel the heat from the blanket at the same time feeling a slight breeze from the fresh air, and it felt glorious. She should be tired but for some reason, was not. A night of insomnia seemed imminent. Although she hoped that it was not going to happen, there was nothing that could be done to stop it. She did not feel like moving to turn on music or the TV, instead she just lay there contentedly, doing absolutely nothing, stark naked.

She remembered that she told Mark she would text that she got home safely. Ashley and Kim had done some serious damage drinking, so were probably crashed out on his couch by now for the night. She grabbed her phone and texted in the group:

I'm home safe. Tonight was so much fun. Love y'all.

Before she could even set her phone down, Mark replied:

Glad to hear it, luv u Boo.

As she lay there with the phone in her hand, she felt it vibrate, thinking it was another message from Mark with some movie line, she glanced at her phone, but it was a text from Tony:

*Hey Mia, it's late, hoping I am not waking you, and
that you are awake and can't sleep too. If you are,
hit me back...*

Mia sat up almost not believing her eyes. She started shaking her head and broke out into a huge smile.

She replied:

*Well, well, well. It appears that we are still on the
same wavelength, just like old times back in the
day. At least we are still consistent. I am currently
wide awake, what's up Mr. T?*

Before her imagination could even begin lacing up its running shoes and get going...

Buzz. Buzz. Buzz. Buzz.

"Hello."

"Wow, your voice still sounds the same."

"Well, was it supposed to change? Yours sounds the same too," Mia replied laughing.

"Hi Mia."

"Hi Tony."

"Been a long time huh? How the hell are you?"

"I'm alright, and you?"

"I'm good."

"What are you up to?"

"Would you believe me if I told you?"

"Try me.

"Well, I got home not too long ago, and I'm lying on top of the covers on my bed, stark naked."

Silence.

"Hello? *Are we all still here*? Mia asked.

"Helluva way to start a conversation after more than 30 years, but from you, I would expect nothing less. Still intriguing, I will give you that."

"Welp, I'm just being me."

"Yes, you are, thank the Lord. My mind is racing - conjuring up images of you lying there naked, you do know that, right?"

"Yes, I can imagine that you might be. So...about those images you're conjuring, hmm, how should I say it? The curves are still there but the road has widened?"

"I would imagine so. But then again, your younger you had that P.Y.T, pretty young thing with a killer body, so the older you will have evolved into a *P.M.T.*, pretty mature thing. I have no doubts that you have a mature killer body."

"You think so, do you?"

"Absolutely."

"I don't know, things change, become a bit different over time."

"Yes, they do, but I bet your skin still feels like satin, your body is still firm, and undoubtedly, you still have the same intoxicating taste."

Mia swallowed hard.

"Too bad we aren't Facetiming, but then again, I do remember someone I know being modest about being seen, even though she *was* seen. And I loved each, and every inch of what I saw, what I felt, and especially, what I tasted."

Mia's nipples instantly hardened from hearing Tony's words.

"Hello? *Are we all still here?*" Tony said mocking Mia.

"Hey..."

"Was my turn Missy."

Mia took a deep breath and exhaled.

"Well apparently, we have gone from zero to sixty in 5.0 seconds."

"Well, it's all your fault, talking about lying there all naked and stuff."

"You asked."

"So I did, so I did.

"Moving on then, how are you Mr. T?

"I'm doing okay. So in a nutshell, have a son and daughter 26 and 24."

"I have twin sons, almost 21. Okay, so yeah, remember how all those times you told me about Myron? I admit it, *yes*, you were right. But at least he did give me two beautiful sons whom I love more than my life, so..."

"He didn't deserve you, but looks like you have moved on, how long has it been?"

"About 16 years."

"I'm guessing you didn't re-marry, but what's your status now? I mean, are you in a relationship right now?"

"I have a couple of uh, *friends*, but nope - not in a monogamous relationship. I have commitment issues still I guess you can say. I do go to therapy before you have anything smart-assed to say about it though."

"I get it, I get it. Hell, I'm in therapy myself, so you get a free pass Miss Lady."

"Okay decades have gone by, and so I'm extremely curious, what made you try to find me after all this time?"

"Well, it's not like you haven't crossed my mind over the years, but I don't know, one day I just decided I wanted to find you and talk to you – I just wanted to hear your voice again. I'm guessing you didn't mind since you responded."

"Well *duh*. I tried finding you a few times over the years with no luck, so I sent it out in the universe, and now look, years later, here you are. As it is said, delays are not always denials."

"So, I have no idea of why we had this secret type of understanding that we both agreed to without ever speaking of it, do you?"

"I most definitely do not."

"Well, there's that."

"Well, to be honest, like I said in an earlier email, over the years I wondered what would have happened had we ever broken our silence."

"Yes, so have I. But I figured you were still married, so left it alone, well that is, until now. It's really good to hear your voice."

"Yes, I feel the same.

"Maybe we can get more into my current situation, but to sum it up, I'm questioning where I want to be and who I want to be with right now."

"I see. Well, I'm not that sexually naïve woman I once was, but still probably nowhere close to you with all your wild parties. You know your apartment had a bi-polar personality, you and your friends of all types, and then, well, then there was me."

"Good point."

"Okay, but there's a question that I've been dying to know the answer to for years, actually - decades."

"You know me Mia, shoot."

"Okay well, you know those *burrito and beer* times we shared?"

"Now, you know the answer to that."

"Just wait and let me finish the question Mister Man."

"Okay, okay, go ahead."

Mia took a deep breath, then exhaled.

"What *is* it? Just ask me already Mia."

"Well, I've always wondered if you did all that for all of your other women, too? I mean like the baths, the candles, and the massages?" Mia asked holding her breath, her eyes tightly shut waiting to hear the answer.

Silence.

Mia opened her eyes.

"No."

Mia exhaled and sat up, "Really?"

"*Really, really.* You were the only one."

Mia felt relieved and could not help but smile.

"I know this probably sounds weird, but I was *so* hoping that would be what you said."

"Is that right? And why is that?"

"Because, well because, I was just hoping that I was treated differently than all the others. I mean, you definitely made me feel special, like, I don't know. I guess like I was the center of your universe at that moment in time - in that secret place that only you and I knew about."

Silence.

"You were."

"Oh."

"Like I told you, I locked those memories away long ago, and hid

272

the key so well that I didn't know where it was. These past days emailing with you has helped me find it and unlock them."

"Yes, I've relived some of those times myself. And yes, it would be different now, but for you it would be better, at least I would hope so."

"What do you mean?"

"I mean that it wouldn't be so one-sided, or maybe it would be, but this time, it would be for you."

"Mmm, really?"

"Yes."

"Care to elaborate?"

"I just thought that it would be exciting to reciprocate after all this time, or maybe *because* of all this time."

"Hmmm."

"I mean if I could even come close to making you feel like I did, and I'm pretty confident that I could, the circle would be complete, so to speak."

"I like the way you think."

"Is that right?"

"You know you could still elaborate more. In fact, someone I know mentioned something about a bedtime story? Not sure if it will put me to sleep, but I'm up for listening, that is, if you are up to telling it."

"Sounds like a challenge Mister Man. I can spin a story for you, no idea of what may pop into my head though."

"I'm ready if you are."

Mia took a deep breath and began spinning her tale:

Tony planned to get there much earlier, but still made it there two minutes early and saw Mia, cool as a cucumber standing at the bar waiting for her drink. The bartender handed her a dirty Martini, and she took a sip. Tony quietly walked up behind her, her head turning ever so slightly sideways for a quick second, but she did not move. She took another sip of her drink; he sensed that she felt his presence. He walked right up behind her, then pulled her long hair to one side over her shoulder, her scent instantly wafting up and tickling his nostrils making them flare. He breathed in deeply and could feel himself getting aroused without even a single touch from her. He kissed her neck lightly and felt her body respond to him by backing up into him. Her rounded ass was against his crotch and his arousal began to grow, he hoped she could feel it.

"Hmm, this is starting off better than I hoped for," Tony told her.

"Shh, no interrupting the story," Mia scolded Tony.

"Sorry, please continue".

Mia cleared her throat.

"I was wondering where you were Lover Man," Mia told him without looking back at him.

"And how did you know it was me? I could have been some stranger kissing on your neck," he whispered in her ear.

She replied, "Don't worry how I knew, I knew. I ordered you a glass of wine and look, I wore your favorite skirt."

Tony looked down and saw that "little black skirt" that hugged her ass just right that he liked so much.

"Aww, but you wore pantyhose."

Leaning in and whispering in her ear, "I was hoping to cop a feel since you got waxed yesterday baby."

"Well, things are not always as they may seem my dear. After all, what fun is life without a little mystery or surprise?" Mia replied with a wink.

Since they were standing at the end of the crowded bar in a corner, with no one really paying attention, Tony seized the opportunity to reach down and underneath Mia's skirt. He ran his fingers slowly along her thigh encased in the nylon hose, but as his hands got near the top of her thigh, he felt smooth skin, then a bit farther up was yes, the smoothness of that firm, round ass he loved to nibble on so much. He reached around under her skirt to the front, his fingers slipping underneath her thong, and finally found what he was in dire search of, those lips of hers. Ooh, they felt soft and silky - completely smooth from her waxing yesterday, bringing a smile to his face.

"Damn, you are just the sexiest woman I know, and such a tease," he whispered in her ear.

This time she turned around, "Am I now? I do walk my talk, after a bit of teasing time to time, but tonight I haven't spoken a word. I honestly do not know whatever you could mean my dear sir," Mia taunted.

"On the contrary my dear, you are *screaming* with this outfit, and I cannot wait to get you alone on the boat after dinner."

"Well, we are going to have drinks and dinner as planned, and of course I am going to tease you as much as humanly possible during both," she told him.

Tony looked down and kissed her lightly on the lips, "I wouldn't expect anything less coming from you, and you know that I am so counting on it. So go ahead and have your fun, because I have no doubts that I will thoroughly enjoy it, but when it's done, then you, you are *all* mine my dear."

Mia said nothing, merely smiling slyly.

The bartender brought Tony a glass of one of his favorite wines at the same time they were called to their table for dinner. Mia winked at him and said, "Timing is everything in life, yes?"

"You are something else, thank you."

Mia followed the waitress with Tony following behind her to the table. Mia had pre-ordered one of their favorite meals and desert. They sat down and the food was served. They feasted on huge salads filled with shrimp, crab, lobster, a dish of assorted veggies, along with some crusty French bread. They sat next to each other European style and Tony could not stop looking down Mia's top, ogling her cleavage.

"May I help you Mister?" she asked when she caught his eye.

"I'm beginning to believe that you are wicked as you say you are - I'm loving every moment of it by the way," he whispered in her ear.

Mia picked a large chunk of lobster out of her salad, and hand fed it to Tony, making sure that her fingers got into his mouth. Tony took her cue by grabbing her hand, dipping her fingers in the dressing, before first licking, then sucking her fingers clean, one by one. He could see her body gently undulating and wondered if her juices were already beginning to flow. She finally pulled her hand away, sitting it right in his lap.

"Mmm, is it possible there's another course for dining tonight Mr. K? Feels more like desert though."

"I don't know what to do with you and haven't for some time, but I absolutely love this about you, it's one of my favorite facets of your personality. It's a fantastically warm night, the sun hasn't set yet, so we can still take a short ride on the boat, if you're game that is."

Mia just looked at Tony as she stuck her finger in the whipped cream left from the desert, and then slowly slid the whole finger in her mouth, and very slowly sucked it clean. As Tony watched her, he could feel his mouth fall open. That was his breaking point. He quickly left money for the check, grabbed her by the hand telling her, "Let's go, let's go right now!"

Fortunately, his boat was docked within walking distance of the restaurant and within five minutes they were aboard. It was a beautiful night and Tony was checking things and getting the boat running. Mia stood near the side and let the breeze blow thru her hair. She watched Tony at the wheel, then slid in between him and the wheel. She looked back over her shoulder and demurely asked, "May I drive?"

"Well, it appears you already have the car warming up, so why stop now?"

She put her hands on the wheel and Tony stayed there pressed firmly against her, needing her, wanting her.

"So, Mr. K., everything checked out and running properly, yes?"

"Well...." Tony began his answer, but Mia turned around and shh'd him with her fingers. She put her arms around his neck and softly and lightly, ran her tongue over his top lip, and nibbled on his bottom lip. Tony put his arms around her waist and pulled her into him, hard, squeezing her ass. He began kissing Mia passionately, his tongue finding hers over and over again. Mia reached up and began undoing his tie. She flung it onto the floor, then began unbuttoning his shirt. She unbuckled his belt, unzipped his pants, then pushed them down as he kicked off his shoes and stepped out of them. She stepped back and stepped out of her own skirt then pulled her top off, tossing it on the growing heap of clothes piled on the floor. Tony turned the engine off, knowing now, there would be no cruise on the water slowly making love, because tonight was going to be raw, hot, sex.

Mia was clad now, in only a black lacy bra, black thong, thigh high stockings and high heels. She began kissing her way down until she reached her prize. She held his manhood in her hand and gave it teeny tiny kisses before she began to softly start licking. Up one side and down the other, licking the front, then the back of his dick. Slowly and softly swirling the head around and around until she looked up at him, their eyes locked, and she devoured the head of his dick at the same moment. Mia felt Tony's body tremble, but she continued inching more and more of his dick into her mouth, until it was full. She caressed his balls as she continued her licking and began sucking him, then stroking him in time to her sucking.

"Oh my God Mia.," Tony breathlessly said grabbing a handful of her hair and holding her head still.

Mia was undeterred and resumed her passionate assault on his dick until Tony was overcome and told her, "Mia, please, I want to be inside of you. I want to taste you. Let me taste that bare "kitty." It's my turn to make *you* squirm."

Reluctantly Mia let go, and Tony laid her atop a table. He knelt in front of the table where Mia's body lay before him like a feast, waiting for him to devour. She was so incredibly wet and smooth. Her juices had run down to the tops of her thighs and Tony loved it. He began at her knee, and softly kissed his way upwards on one leg, then skipping her kitty and beginning on her other knee, teasing her. He knew she wanted to feel his tongue and lips there; she, her breath having grown labored. Finally, he pushed her legs up, and began soft tiny kisses, and felt her body responding to his efforts. He licked her softly and slowly, just like she liked it, teasing her to want more. He slowly increased his tempo and intensity and was rewarded by feeling her body trembling and undulating. Mia reached down with both hands and grabbed him by the hair.

"Oh, Tony...you're going to make me cum," she warned.

"Yes Mia, I want you to cum over and over and over again. Cum now. Cum for me Mia, *cum for me now,*" he told her and then licked her bottom to top and held his mouth over her clit softly sucking until he felt her body spasm. She held his head there as she cried out, "Oh Tony...oh yesss," as her orgasm took over.

Tony could barely contain himself and when her spasm ended, he flipped her over on all fours; the table was the perfect height for him to enter her from behind. He slapped her ass on both cheeks making her recoil a bit but immediately kissed and licked them both, then nibbled on the round part of her ass the way she liked. He stood up still caressing her ass and felt her pushing it back in search of his body and his dick.

"Do you want this Mia"? he asked as he rubbed his dick along her wet slit, teasingly.

"Yes. I want you. I want you *so bad,*" she told him.

Tony wanted to just ram into her and pound her until she screamed for mercy, but he wanted her to tell him to do it. He continued rubbing his dick along her soaked, slippery slit, letting the head push against her opening and then not moving. His dick was pulsating with need.

Mia looked back over her shoulder, "You know I want it, give it to me now."

"What is it you want Mia? Tell me, tell me now."

"I want you deep inside of me. I want you to fuck me, fuck me hard Tony, and make me cum all over you."

Tony did not hesitate, and slid every inch in, pausing for a second reveling in Mia's velvety wetness. He could feel her squeezing him with her muscles and he loved it.

"Oh Mia, you feel so damn good. I'm going to give you what you asked for, are you ready?" he asked as he slowly began thrusting.

"I am so ready," Mia said pushing her ass back in reaction to his thrusts.

"Don't move, let me do it for awhile," she told him, "I want you to want it as much as I do."

Tony stood there balls deep and felt Mia pull away and then back her "kitty" against him, swallowing more and more of his dick until he was once again balls deep inside of her. She continued to move back and forth almost in a circular motion and Tony was in ecstasy, he could no longer help himself, and grabbed her hips like handles, and began thrusting and pounding into her over and over until she cried out, "Yes. Oh yes...Fuck meee Tony."

Her words spurned Tony to pick up his tempo.

"You are *so* damn wet. Feels so good," he told her feeling himself getting closer but not ready to let the pleasure go just yet. He pulled out, then flipped Mia onto her back, grabbed her legs throwing them atop his shoulders and jumped right back in, almost in one fluid motion.

His hard thrusting made the "Girlz" jiggle, turning him on even further. When Mia grabbed her breasts and squeezed them together, Tony could barely hold on. He allowed her to put her legs down as he held her arms above her head. He grabbed her hands and intertwined his fingers with hers, but never stopped pounding her. Mia wrapped her legs around his back, then leaned up to lick his chest. She licked a nipple then nibbled it sending Tony into overdrive; he was in the zone now. He put Mia's legs back on his shoulders, reached under and grabbed that round ass and started thrusting with long strokes.

"Ooh, those long strokes, you know they make me cum so hard," Mia moaned.

Hearing Mia's words, feeling her slippery, hot wetness, and watching her breasts jiggle finally proved to be too much for Tony.

"Oh Mia, Mia. I can't hold back anymore. Oh damn. Oh *Mia*!!"

Tony's words pushed Mia over the edge yet again, and she joined his explosion.

"*Ohhh.*"

The sound snapped Mia out of her author mode.

"Tony, um, everything okay?"

"Well, it is now. Wow. Now that, that was a helluva bedtime story Mizz Mia. Kudos for your imagination."

"Wait. You didn't - *did* you?" Mia asked while at that moment realizing her fingers were resting on her clit, and that she was nearly dripping wet herself.

"Well, you did want your story to have a realistic ending, didn't you?"

"I guess I hadn't really thought about it, but glad that it worked out so well for you. I guess I hadn't realized that after all this time we would have phone sex for me to finally make you cum."

"Mia, you can't be serious, *right*?"

"What do you mean? You know that we have never done this before."

"Well, it's a variation on a theme. You probably have no idea of how many times I masturbated to you and fantasies of what I would love to do to you, and you to me, now do you? Hell, I don't even know how many times. What I do know is, hearing you tell me that scenario tonight was fucking great."

"Oh."

"Damn, I had taken a muscle relaxer two hours before calling you, and usually they knock me out, but not tonight. After your story though, I feel so much more relaxed, just like a typical man who wants to sleep after sex," Tony said laughing.

"You weren't so typical, as I recall, you always wanted to eat, *not* sleep"

"Aha, but I wasn't the one who actually had sex, I was the one who gave the pleasure my dear. Makes a guy work up an appetite."

"Point goes to Mr. Tony King," Mia said laughing.

"So, there is no question if I liked your bedtime story or not, right? Now, do you really get waxed, or was that just a lovely feature of your amazing story?"

"Yes, I really do. A past friend asked me to try waxing once for him, and I loved how it felt, was so worth the pain. Plus, it's so much better than shaving. It feels extra good if the man is shaved too by the way, total smoothness. Anyways, as the years passed, the grays began popping up and had to go, so I continued with waxing."

"Mmm, nice fun fact of Mia, thanks for sharing."

"I do what I can."

They both laughed.

"Wow, after over 30 years what a conversation we've had."

"That's just how we roll, but look, that muscle relaxer has really taken over. I can't even keep my eyes open, and I can barely form sentences. I'm about to crash, as much as I would love to continue this conversation."

"So, I can get all your secrets out of you then," Mia said laughing.

"As if I wouldn't tell you anything that you asked me."

"Another good point. Okay Mr. King, I will allow you the luxury of sleep, provided you call me again, and soon, but for a regular conversation, deal?"

"All your definition of what a regular conversation is though, but yes, I will call you soon. I loved talking to you tonight."

"Me too. Now hang up and get some rest Mister Man."

"Okay, dream about me though."

"I think that's a given."

"Great. Goodnight Mia," Tony told her drowsily.

"Nite Tony."

Mia ended the call and threw the phone on the bed. Wow, wow, *wow*! She had no idea the call with Tony would go this way. Hmm, great imagination huh? Well maybe, but Mia had partly drawn on some of her Javier times. He loved restraining her to some degree and challenging her to have an orgasm before relenting any control he had. Keeping her legs on his shoulders was one of Mr. Alpha Male's favorite teases. Oh well, all is fair in love and... *sex*?

Mia shrugged and just chalked it up to another example of endless possibilities. She closed her eyes and let her mind lead her back to their secret place on Alice Street and Tony's magic hands, and especially his tongue. Her hand crept down, and found the wetness leftover from Tony's bedtime tale, and those memories and her fingers, helped her to find the satisfaction that no dream would.

II

After opening her eyes the next morning, Mia lay in bed trying to summon the energy to move. She did not have a restful night due to all the alcohol at Mark's shindig, so was up for several bathroom visits. At least she did not wake with a headache; she would hate to be Kim or Ashley right now, as they most likely woke up hating life this morning. Mia looked at her phone, damn, 11:37. Oh well, not like she had big plans for the day anyways. She sat up and drank half of the bottle of Smart Water on her nightstand, then went into the kitchen and ate a bowl of Corn Pops and some fruit.

Feeling lazy, she walked back to her bedroom and lay across the bed on her tummy. Thoughts of talking to Tony overtook her brain. That conversation last night before bed had been something else. What would happen if they actually did decide to meet, she lay there wondering, since that story she told him came so easily to her. The ol' imagination reel was beginning to warm up and then:

"Ah-oo-gah, Ah-oo-gah ...."

Surprised hearing Javier's ringtone, Mia quickly grabbed her phone and looked at it. Oh snap - it wasn't a text this time, so she took a deep breath and answered, "Hello Sexy Man."

"Hello yourself, you know that you are the sexier one though, *right?*"

"Uh huh. Now you know telling me that, your eyes should be brown."

"Yeah, yeah, so you say. Anyways, I'm really calling to see what you got going on today."

"Me? *Today?*"

"No, your evil twin sister who is also named Mia. Yes *you,* and yes today," Javier said laughing.

Lordt. His voice was so goddamn deep and sexy. She had not realized how much she had missed hearing it.

"Got a few errands to run, nothing life changing. On Sundays, I usually like to take it slow. Why... what's up?" Mia replied, as usual trying to play the ever cool and aloof one.

"Well, you always said you wanted to taste some of my meat... uh, well more specifically barbeque from the pictures you saw on Facebook, right?" Javier asked chuckling.

"Smartass. Yes."

"Well, Dro asked me to throw down on some barbeque today, and I just wondered if you might feel up to coming by. Going to be *a lot* of meat to eat, just sayin'."

"Unh, Is that right?"

"Yes. Hopefully I will have your favorite," Javier said then cleared his throat.

"Okay so wait, it's cool for me to come over *there*? Alejandro isn't tripping?"

"Nah. He and Lisa, my sister-in-law, are cool with it. They know what's up, well with Maria, not with us - well they know a little bit about you. Dro thinks you're sexy as hell too. He couldn't believe your age."

"Hmm. So I see you told him that his little brother has become Cougar prey hmm? Well thanks for the compliment I guess?"

"I think he might be envious his little brother could get all that you got, what 'chu think about that, huh? So, what are you thinking? Might have a little time to slide by and chat with a guy, and get some uh ...*meat*?"

"You are something else," Mia chuckled. She continued on, "Well, it *is* a distinct possibility. If I do come, what should I bring?"

"*If* you come? You don't have to bring anything but your lovely self. Like you always used to tell me, it's a yes or no, and if it's no, that's fine, I just need to know either way."

"*Hey now*, my Mama gave me proper home training, thankyouverymuch. You just don't show up empty handed for dinner, so what else are you having with your, uh ...*meat*?

"Let me ask Dro, hold on a sec."

"Sure."

Immediately questions began popping up in Mia's overanalytical brain. Oh my God, am I really going over there? What will I even wear? I do *not* feel like doing my hair. There's really not much time anyway. Should I try though? It's his brother's house so I can't look *too* sexy, but I still gotta look sexy. Will I be able to have dinner and not want to just fuck the hell out of him? Mia, still holding on the phone, went to her closet and began frantically looking for something to wear with no success. What will in the hell will I wear? What ...

Javier came back on the line interrupting her rambling thoughts.

"Hey Mia, Dro said a salad would be great. Macaroni or potato salad would be preferred if you feel up to making one and can swing it. Lisa is grateful for your donation and says to tell you thank you in advance."

"How many people?"

"Not many, maybe a few more of Lisa's family might pop over, so maybe 7 at most."

"Time?"

"About 5 is good. So, sounds like you're coming then?"

"Looks like it, and yes, I will bring potato salad."

"*Nice.* Can't wait to see you."

"Is that right?"

"Yes."

"Hmm, I like hearing that but, words without action and all that," Mia said chuckling.

"Okay now, you better be careful, 'cause you know what happens to me anytime I'm around you.

"Well, it *has* been a minute."

"You might be paying for that remark later."

"Uh huh. *Whatever* man. Looks like I will be seeing you in a few hours then."

"Okay I'm about to text you the address. See you a little later."

"Yes you will. See ya Sexy Man."

"Bye."

Mia hung up and a line from Ferris Bueller popped into her head: *"Life moves pretty fast."*

That was an understatement for Mia's life right now; her life was moving *way* beyond fast, but she was kind of digging it though. Gave her less time to overanalyze and more time to live and enjoy. She finally found a leopard top which had crisscross straps on the chest, and a black jersey maxi skirt with splits down both sides to wear. She laid them out on the bed, then threw on a pair of sweats and a t-shirt so she could dash to the store to get the fixings to make the potato salad.

She got back from the store and threw the potato salad together, then set it in the fridge to get cold. She glanced at the time - 2:27 - she still had time to catch her breath and get ready. She decided to chillax in a nice hot bath, so turned the water on then pumped some Amazing Grace gel in the water. She was due for a waxing and too much gray down "there", so had to resort to doing her combo thing with Nair and shaving instead, because, well, because you just never know where the evening might lead.

She used the electric shaver to closely trim those lower lips, then applied Nair on top of her "kitty". She turned the water off in the tub, and while the Nair was working, plucked a few strays from her eyebrows, then brushed her teeth again. She grabbed some Kleenex and wiped off the Nair and loose hair, then jumped into the shower just to lather up and get off any Nair residue. She looked down, hmm, not perfect, but a vast improvement. Most importantly no gray hairs, and for the most part, it was all smooth down there now.

She wrapped herself in a towel, and feeling a bit of anxiety creeping up, went to the fridge and poured herself half a glass of white wine that was left over from the other night. She came back to the bathroom and sat the glass on the tub's rim. She applied a moisturizing facial mask and dropped the towel. She stepped into her bath, then slid deep into the bathwater until it covered her breasts, reveling in the luxurious feeling from the warm scented water for a few moments. She sat up slightly and reached over to grab her glass of wine. She quickly drank more than half of it before setting it back down.

"Oh yeah, I most definitely needed *that*," Mia said out loud to herself as she rolled her head around side to side a couple of times, finally cracking her neck then delving back into the steamy bathwater.

Going to see Javier later set Mia's mind on a sprint. Maybe tonight would be when those falling chips would finally land. Maybe, Mia would get the status on Javier and Maria's relationship, or at least where it was headed. Yikes, what if he told her that he and Maria were done, what *then*? Mia knew in her heart of hearts, that Javier would be better off leaving Maria, she was taking advantage of him financially, and provided no type of emotional support really. They shared no intimacy. It was not just their lack of sex either - Javier and Maria did not seem to share much of anything at all. Mia also sensed that Maria appeared to be that type of woman who wouldn't want anyone else to have Javier, unless and until she had someone else to ride off into the sunset with.

Feeling a little self-righteous, Mia's thoughts continued down this path. How in the world did she not want sex from Javier was well beyond anything Mia could even fathom. If Maria had been on her j-o-b, then Mia would *not* be playing the role of the *Clean Up Woman*, and be going to see Javier later this afternoon now, would she? Mia knew more about Javier's shop, his dreams and goals, than Maria ever dared to. Of course, this did not make their affair morally right, but facts are facts.

Deep down, she knew that Javier was actually, "boyfriend" or even "husband" material. Unfortunately though, Mia was not sure if she could handle a relationship, even as deeply as she cared for Javier. Damn, commitment issues still ran deep with her. What the fucking *fuck*? Would Myron's tentacles never loosen their grip on her? She forced herself to stop thinking, then drained the rest of the wine and lay back in the tub again, trying to still her mind, and nearly fell asleep.

She had no sense of time or how long she was in the tub, so quickly got out. She checked the time, whew, it was only 3:39, thank goodness. Alejandro's house was about 20 minutes away, so no need to rush, she still had time. She washed off the facial, dried off, wrapped herself in the towel, and lay on her back on the bed. The wine had done its job, and her brain had finally shut down the random thought reel from rolling, which was very much appreciated. I'm going to get up get dressed, go have a good time, and whatever happens, happens. No more overthinking and overanalyzing the situation, I will just roll with it Mia firmly decided. She unwrapped the towel and decided to get up to ensure she had time to do her make up.

She applied moisturizer, then pumped some Kiehl's into her hand and slathered the lotion all over her body and feet. She chose a lacy black bra with a matching thong to wear, then put on the leopard top and slipped into the black maxi skirt. She stared at her reflection, scrutinizing her face in the mirror. Hmm, she didn't want to go too heavy on the make-up, but she still wanted to have a sexy look tonight.

Usually, she was wearing minimal makeup when Javier saw her. She decided on keeping that look but adding a little more oomph. She decided on going with black liquid eyeliner on her top lids, and dark brown pencil on the lower lids. She added a light dusting of gold shadow on the eyelids and under her brows. Next, she penciled and brushed her brows, then finished with two coats of black mascara.

Now for her hair, *ugh*. Welp, looked like it was going to be an up-do hairstyle tonight, so she pulled it up, and then fastened it with her rhinestone studded clip, leaving a few tendrils around her face and at the nape of her neck. She lined her lips with a deep red liner, red lip stain, then added a coat of red matte lipstick on top of that. She knew eating barbeque would take her lipstick off, but the stain would still leave some color on, even after eating that. Almost done, she sprayed one short spritz of Pleasures, then added a pair of silver, bling, U shaped hoops. Finally, she slipped into her black leather wedge slides, and she was ready to go.

She grabbed the blue Tupperware bowl containing the potato salad out of the fridge, slipped it into a bag, and then sat it on the floor behind her seat. She threw in a Michael Franks cd, took a deep breath, and was on her way. *One Bad Habit* began playing. How appropriate and timely; it was sure hitting home at that very moment. Not counting ice cream and shoe shopping, Javier was truly her only one bad habit – she definitely did not possess the willpower to turn down his invitation today. What else would she not have the willpower to turn down later? She would find out shortly she decided with a shrug.

As she was sitting at a red light, she realized that she had missed not just having sex with her favorite lover, but almost as much, she had missed their conversations and the intimacy that they had shared. She decided that she was going to try to be strong and not let her emotions take over. She was going to be a good friend by just listening to what he wanted to tell her and talk about. It was not likely that they would have sex at his brother's anyway, but then again, you just never know, those endless possibilities were always abound, you just needed to be open to them.

Traffic got a bit snarly, but she still made it there with 5 minutes to spare. She turned off the car and sat there for a moment, then took a few deep breaths trying to calm herself. Just before she opened the car door, a wicked 'lil thought crossed her mind. With a sly smile, she lifted her hips off the seat, reached under her skirt, pulled off her thong, and then quickly stuck it in her purse. She slung her purse over her shoulder before grabbing the potato salad and sauntered up to the front door feeling exceptionally sexy. She rang the bell and almost immediately Alejandro answered the door.

"Hi. It's Mia, right?

"Hi, yes. And you're Alejandro, correct?"

"Yup. Feel free to just call me *Dro*. Come on in. Thanks a lot for making the potato salad. Here, let me take that from you," he told her grabbing the bag out of her hands.

"Oh no worries, this is how my mama taught me to roll - you just don't show up to dinner empty handed."

"Well thank your mama for me, I'm looking forward to eating some. I love potato salad," he said flashing a familiar smile.

Unlike Javier, Dro had large dark brown eyes, but like Javier, he also had those killer, long black eyelashes. Must be a family thing. She could see why Kim had been so attracted to him now.

"Why don't you follow me this way," Alejandro told her as he began walking to the kitchen.

They walked in and Lisa walked over to Mia and held out her hand.

"Hi, I'm Lisa."

"Hi, I'm Mia, nice to meet you."

Lisa was wearing a purple maxi dress. She had a beautiful honey brown complexion, and not much make up on, just some gloss. Her thick black hair was piled in a bun on top of her head, and she was wearing huge, Jody Watley style gold hoops.

"Javier is out there at the grill if you want to go on out. Did you want anything to drink?" Dro asked Mia.

"Maybe later, I'm good for now, but thank you," she replied.

Mia opened the sliding door and began walking toward the grill when Javier looked up.

"You made it. Wow, you look nice," Javier told her with a big smile.

"Thanks. Yes, I gave Alejandro, I mean *Dro - he told me to call him Dro -* the potato salad. I met Lisa already."

"Great. Want something to drink? Javier asked taking a sip out of his beer.

Mia shrugged.

"You can have a taste of *mine*," he told her winking and holding his bottle of beer close to her face.

Mia rolled her eyes and shook her head. Then immediately re-thinking her decision, quickly grabbed the bottle out of Javier's hand, wrapped her lips around the top of the bottle, sliding them down the neck and then back up, before taking a big gulp.

Javier stood there staring with raised eyebrows. His mouth fell wide open. He took a step back before saying "Well damn."

Mia handed the beer back with a slight smirk on her face, "What? Something wrong?

"No baby, you are just being you, just being Mia. *Thank the Lord,*" he said looking up at the sky.

Before she could reply, they heard the door slide open, so they both turned around.

"Hey Jav, how much longer? I'm starvin' like Marvin up in this bitch – oh… sorry Mia."

Mia just laughed then told him, "I'm a big girl and trust me, I've heard worse. Besides, I'm no saint myself, so it's all good."

"Okay, cool then, thanks Mia," Dro told her nodding affirmatively.

"Relax Big bruh, I got you, I'm about to take the links off right now, just give me a few."

Dro nodded again and replied, "Solid," then closed the door.

Still holding onto the bottle of beer, Javier drained the rest of it.

"So Mister Man, what *other* meat you got there?"

Javier smirked. "*So* much meat for you Mia".

They stared at each other feeling that familiar vibe they generated.

"I even got some ribs, and a tri-tip too."

"Well damn, you really weren't messing around."

"You know I don't," he said while picking up the last link with the tongs and adding it to the rest of the meat in the pan.

"Would you mind getting the door for me please?"

"But of course, *my life is but to serve you my liege,*" Mia said in her best Jafar from Aladdin voice as she walked to the sliding door.

As Mia was sliding the door open, and right before he walked through it, Javier bent down and whispered in her ear, "I can think of *quite* a few things, that I would love to have you do as my servant."

Mia's nipples instantly hardened hearing his words, and she stood there like a deer in headlights, momentarily frozen still. She took a deep breath, regained her composure, and then slid the door closed. As she began walking towards the kitchen table, she could not help but wonder if taking her thong off before coming to the front door had been such a great idea after all. Javier sat the pan on the counter and began brushing sauce on the meat. Dro walked to the refrigerator and pulled out a beer, "You still good Mia, or want anything? Maybe a soda?" he asked.

"A beer sounds *great*, I will take one, thank you."

"805 work for you?"

"Sure does, it's one of my favorites actually," she answered as she walked over to him.

Dro took the cap off and handed her the bottle, then did the same for Lisa and handed her a beer too.

"Thanks babe," she said with a wink.

"Can I help with anything?" Mia asked Lisa.

"Nope, I have everything but the meat on the table already. Thank you for asking though. You are a guest, so just have a seat and relax, let Javier do all the work," Lisa said chuckling.

"Will do," Mia said with a nervous laugh.

"Anybody want me to slice up some tri tip"? Javier asked.

"*Me*," Dro answered.

"Got it."

Mia sat down and took two big swigs of beer.

"No need to be nervous Mia. The only one who has the right to judge is," Dro told her pointing up at the ceiling.

Mia nodded in confirmation.

"True that," she replied back.

"Besides, life is short, you gotta do what you can to be happy."

Mia took another long sip of beer.

"And get away from those crazy ass bitches," Lisa added with attitude.

Immediately her eyes grew large before she covered her mouth with her hand.

"*Lis*," Dro said rolling his eyes.

"I am a very direct person, without much of a filter myself. As you said life is short, and who has time to wonder about things. Might as well speak your mind and move on, well, that's how I roll anyway. As the years have passed, I find that more and more often, I just have *no* fucks to give, none whatsoever," Mia told them with a shrug.

Lisa smiled, nodding her head in agreement, and looked relieved.

"That's it right there. Here, here," Dro said holding up his bottle to Mia.

Clink.

"Yeah, that woman over there doesn't have much of a filter," Javier said as he walked to the table with a platter of links, ribs, and some tri tip sliced for him and Dro.

"Ooh, that looks so good Jav, dig in Mia, you go first," Lisa told her.

Mia took a hot link and two ribs off the plate. She skipped the rolls but spooned some barbeque beans and potato salad on her plate. Everyone followed suit, although Dro went pretty heavy on the meat.

"Do you think you have enough meat or what Dro? Lordy Jesus man. Well hell, maybe I should increase your damn life insurance policy," Lisa said shaking her head.

Dro just waved her off, "Whatever woman."

"And they're *still* together," Javier said laughing.

Before anyone took a bite of food, Dro held his head down and said, "Lord we are grateful for this food, thank you for blessing us all."

"Amen," was said by the rest.

Mia took a bite of a rib and was pleasantly surprised, "Mmm. Ooh, this is *so* good Javier," she told him with raised eyebrows peering over her glasses.

"I just do what I do, you know," Javier said cocking his head to one side with a shrug of his shoulders.

"Yeah bro, you threw down like usual. And Mia, this potato salad is da-bomb," Dro said.

"Yes, to *all* of that. Thanks again Mia, your potato salad is *really* good, and I'm very picky about my potato salad. You passed the secret test," Lisa added laughing,

As they were all finishing eating, Lisa looked over at Dro, caught his eye, "Hey Jav, you and Mia really did most of the cooking, so you guys are excused from kitchen duty. See ya," she told them fanning her hand forward gesturing for them to shoo, then gave Javier a quick wink.

Javier smiled at Lisa then glanced over at Dro, "Cool, thanks. Hey Mia, let me show you Lisa's succulents, she likes them too."

"I just got into them, let me know what you think," Lisa told her as Mia walked to the door.

"Sure thing."

Mia and Javier walked outside to Lisa's table of succulents.

"She has a nice collection, but she needs to be careful not to overwater, and let them dry out between waterings."

"I will tell her what you said."

As they began walking around the yard, Javier saw Mia shiver a little. He walked over to her and pulled her close to him.

"Looks like someone is getting cold. Let's go in, I need to talk to you anyway. Sure have missed having my muse."

Mia smiled and shook her head.

"Seriously though, I have missed our conversations, more than you can know."

Mia looked up at him and nodded, "Same."

Javier hugged her tightly and she hugged him back. They stood there for a moment in a tight embrace before Javier bent down and kissed her softly on the lips.

"Come on, let's go inside," he told her taking her by the hand and leading her to the door.

They went inside. Dro and Lisa were nowhere to be seen. Javier went to the freezer and pulled out a bottle of Grey Goose.

"It's Dro's drink too. I'm going to have a shot, join me?"

Mia was feeling some tension from the apparent trajectory of the evening, and instantly decided she would need it for their talk, "Yes," she answered him nodding.

Javier poured two generous shots and they both threw them back. He took her by the hand then led her down the hall to his room.

"Have a seat," he told her as he sat down on his bed.

Mia climbed onto the bed next to him, then lay back on her elbows.

"Feels like whatever it is you're about to tell me, it's something heavy. The Grey Goose is doing its job, so bring it."

Nodding, Javier began, "Helping take care of my brother Carlos gave me a good deal of time to think about things. Maria flew out a couple of times, but honestly, by the time it was her day to leave, I was looking forward to seeing her go. We just don't seem to connect so well at all now, in almost *any* way. Plus, you just might have spoiled me with all that good sex," he added with a sly smile.

Mia shook her head and rolled her eyes. She grabbed his hand, and looked at him, "You know you can tell me anything, right? So why don't you just tell me what it is that you need to say. You know that I don't do drama."

"Well, I thought I had it figured out, but Maria doesn't seem to want, or is ready, to let go. I saw a few signs, and felt like she had an affair years ago, but I didn't pursue it. Not sure if I wasn't ready to handle the fallout and hurt the kids at that time, or if it just wasn't important enough to find out because, well, maybe I just didn't care enough. You and I had already met by then, but not taken it to this level yet, so it wasn't because of you at that time. But you know, over the past few years, our relationship has made me realize what is missing in my marriage. I am not happy, and I know that she isn't happy either. I really have no idea why she is digging in and acting possessive, *way* too much. I know what I need though."

"Sometimes people don't like to be or can't be alone. It could be an ego thing; she doesn't want to feel rejected. Maybe if she had someone else, then she would let go. But look Javier, like I told you before, *I* would never want to be the reason that you leave. If you leave it should be because you feel the need to get away from a toxic relationship, or from one that no longer works for you. Yes, I realize that I've been the catalyst to help you see how it feels to be treated differently, how you really deserve to be treated, and for that I give no apologies. Perhaps this was my purpose in our paths crossing, then again, maybe there's more, time will tell. If you do decide to leave, please realize that you need to take time to get grounded and become whole again. I know you don't like going to doctors and all, but therapy would be great for you, whether you leave *or* stay."

"Hmmm. Ironic that you should mention therapy, because that's what is on the table now. She asked me to move back home, then begin going to therapy."

"Okay, but that actually does sound reasonable for your situation. How do *you* feel about that?"

"Honestly, I don't know. I mean, I'm so tired of all the damn drama. But I also feel like if I do this, but it doesn't help to save our marriage, I can leave knowing that I tried everything. Like I said, I know what I need."

"Well, looks like the time apart may have given you time to think and figure things out."

"It most definitely has, and what I need... is to be single again."

Mia was stunned, but she tried not to react from his last words.

"Well, if you try what she suggested and it doesn't work, then you will know you gave it your all, right? Maybe go through therapy whether you move back home or not and see what shakes out before making the final decision? At this point could it hurt?"

"Damn Mia. You are a really good person, and very persuasive. You could have easily just told me that you thought it was over, and told me to stay here with Dro, and then move on. You know how much I value your opinion, on *everything*. The thing is though, I already put down a deposit on renting a house last week."

"Well, if you forfeit the deposit, but things are working out, wouldn't that be better and worth losing the money?"

"Good point. I did tell her that even if we try again, I may be living separately for awhile, especially in the beginning. You are correct though, if I was happy, the money wouldn't mean anything if I lost it. Damn, intelligence will win me over every time. One of the many great things about you."

"Well, just been my experience that money comes and goes, and always will. Sometimes you are a fat cat sitting on a pile of money, and other times, not so much. But the thing is, time and people are not replaceable, money is, so you should follow what your gut feeling is telling you, because that is your soul talking to you."

"Damn, I know you're right, I guess I just don't want you to be."

"Yes, I can see that."

"I *am* having mixed feelings you aren't trying to get dibbs on me though, since it's a high probability that I will be back on the market in the near future - I'm not even going to lie."

"Well then, what I'm about to tell you might make you feel better. Some nights lying in my bed, thoughts of you cross my mind, more specifically, me craving our stolen moments when you are lying there too. So many times over the last few months, my body has ached for your kiss, for your touch, and, for that tongue. I've caught myself wondering how it would feel waking up to your deep voice in my ear telling me how bad you wanted to fuck me, right before you did just that."

"Unh," was all Javier could manage to say looking pleasantly surprised.

"I'm telling you this because I don't want you to think or to feel in any way, that it's easy for me to just walk away. From what you have just told me though, we both know that I would interfere with you trying to give it your all. But should that fail, then your next step is to get centered and take time to re-discover yourself. Remember now, I've walked down this path before."

"Yes."

"Javier, you know how I feel about you."

"Yes, I do, and you know that the feeling is mutual."

Mia sat up and grabbed his hand and stared into his eyes, "I also feel that if we are truly destined to be together, it will happen. I don't feel that this is the time to try that, and timing is everything in life is it not? Don't forget about that open invitation though Mister Man."

"Open invitation?"

"Umm, that may be the wrong terminology, I guess it's more of an offer. Remember me telling you that if you find yourself needing space after a night of arguing, or for whatever reason, that spare bed at my place is yours with a simple call, and without having to explain yourself. No matter what time of day or night."

Javier pulled Mia's hand up to his mouth, kissed it, and then told her, "I appreciate that more than you can know. And Mia, thank you for being so honest."

"Well, feel any better since we've had our talk?"

"It needed to be said, but I don't know about the feeling better part."

"Well, I think you know what you are going to do. And by the way, your "meat", *was* delicious, thanks for inviting me over," Mia told him with a wink, before getting off the bed and walking to the door.

"Wait, where are you going? You're ready to leave?" Javier asked as he quickly got up and walked over to her.

"Well, I thought that we've discussed what it is you wanted to talk about, or am I wrong? Was there more?"

"Not really, no," Javier said shaking his head no.

They stood silently, both standing there stiff and unmoving. Almost seeming to be waiting in anticipation of an unknown force, like chess pieces sitting on squares while the player decides on the next move. Mia finally broke the logjam as it were, turned around, and then grabbed the doorknob to open the door. Javier quickly put his hand over hers before she could turn the knob, then pushed her up against the door with his body. Her heart began pounding furiously as she attempted to take a deep breath, but it caught in her chest.

"I told you before that you don't know how often you cross my mind. You have no idea of how much I've wanted to feel your body next to mine over the last few months, and even more than that, to be deep inside of you again," his deep, sexy voice reverberated near her ear.

He quickly bent down to Mia's neck and inhaled deeply.

"Mmm. You always smell so good, good enough to eat, and you know how much I like doing that," he whispered softly in her ear.

Mia tried swallowing which did not work at all, and her voice was nowhere to be found. She stood there feeling powerless, knowing that Javier was in control of both her mind and body at that very moment. And in all of his Alpha Male prowess, Javier began his passionate assault by grabbing Mia's free hand as well as the hand on the doorknob, raising and pinning both arms above her head against the door, simultaneously pressing her body against the door by pressing his body against hers.

She could feel his hardness pressing against her, finding herself once again second guessing taking her thong off earlier. Pinned against the door, their hearts pounding wildly, Javier ground on her ass, causing both their bodies to undulate against each other. Mia could feel her excitement flowing as their bodies began searching for a release of the passion so quickly overtaking them.

Javier kept Mia's arms pinned above her head with one hand as he reached into her hair with the other one, squeezed the rhinestone clip, pulled it out, and tossed it towards the bed where it landed on the floor. Mia's hair spilled wildly down upon her shoulders.

"Javier, after what you just told me, should we really be doing this because......" Mia breathlessly began.

"So...you *don't* want this, Mia? Javier interrupted, his deep voice reverberating again in her ear as he continued grinding against her ass.

"Uh, I don't know anymore, I just ..." Mia mumbled trying to find reason between her mind and what Javier was doing to her body.

"You really don't want me to fuck you right now? Because if you don't, you just tell me, and I will stop right now."

Words escaped Mia, as it took every ounce of her strength just to be able to breathe.

"I'm willing to bet that pretty pussy you got is already all nice and wet for me," Javier whispered in her ear as he reached down under her skirt.

He pulled her skirt up while searching for the sweet spot. Mia's breath once again caught in her chest as she felt Javier's hand slowly sliding up between both legs, his search coming to an end when his hand found her smooth ass - naked. Mia heard a quick intake of breath then, "Oh fuck! *No* panties. You *know* that I love this right?"

"Yes. I know," Mia replied finding her voice and nodding her head yes.

Javier nudged her legs father apart with his knee as his hand explored her naked body underneath her skirt, "Mmm, smooth and so juicy baby, just like I knew it would be - just how I like it," he told her, his voice growing husky, as he slowly ran his finger along her wet slit, sending Mia's body into a quick spasm.

He let her skirt fall back down, and then put the finger that was touching her into his mouth. He slowly sucked on the finger and with his mouth full told her, "Mmm. I have sure missed all that sweetness. But it's no surprise to me that you're still so delicious."

She heard him slurp and smack his lips before that hand went in search of her breasts under her top, expertly unhooking her bra within seconds. He delighted in their liberation by passionately squeezing them and pinching her nipples.

Mia's legs had grown weak, and she could barely stand at this point. Any resistance she could initially provide was now completely obliterated.

"Tell me Mia, tell me to stop, or tell me not to, I need to know," his baritone voice spoke near her ear as he began to softly suck on the bottom of her ear lobe.

"I ... I can't think right now, but I, I just can't lie. I have *never* stopped wanting to fuck you Javier," Mia told him the words coming out in a breathless rush.

As soon as her words were spoken, Javier quickly grabbed a handful of her hair, pulling her head back exposing her neck, which he attacked with his lips and tongue. She could feel his hardness pressing against her ass even more. Mia now knew that she was now totally under his control; she wanted to fuck Javier as much as Javier wanted to fuck her.

"Can you feel how bad I want to fuck you?" his voice having grown even huskier, as his body ground harder into her ass.

"Yes," Mia answered in mostly a whisper as her voice got lost somewhere yet again.

"These past few months, it's been all you Mia. You have been the star in *all* of my fantasies. Tell me to stop...tell me Mia," he breathlessly spoke in her ear.

"Javier, no, I... I *can't*," Mia said shaking her head no.

Shocked hearing her words, Javier instantly let go of his hold on her. Before he could say anything, she turned around and looked him in the eye and told him, "Javier, I *can't* say it. I can't tell you to stop because I *can't* stop myself. I *do* want you to fuck me, fuck me *hard*, just like you fantasized about. I want to fuck you too. I want to fuck you right now," she told him as she grabbed him by the waist of his jeans.

She began pulling him towards her and unzipping his jeans. Never breaking eye contact, she reached inside his underwear and wrapped her hand around his rock-hard dick, softly stroking and squeezing it.

Javier reflexively closed his eyes as his body instantly spasmed from her touch, "Oh yeah, go on and take it Mia ...*take it!*" he said closing his eyes for a few seconds while nodding his head yes.

He began pulling Mia towards him while walking backwards. She was still holding onto his dick, as he led her to his bed. As soon as she pulled her hand out of his jeans, he turned her around and playfully pushed her face down onto the end of the bed. In almost the same motion, he pulled her back up by her waist until she was on all fours at the edge. He lifted her skirt, leaving it bunched up on her back, then pushed his jeans and underwear down to his knees with one motion.

"Say it again Mia, tell me what you want," he told her rubbing his dick along her slippery, wet slit.

Mia looked back over her shoulder, "You, Javier. I want *you*. I want you to fuck me. Fuck me *right now*."

With his hands encircling her waist, he slammed into her with one hard thrust.

"*Ahh*. Oh, damn Javier. Damn," Mia moaned loudly.

"Oh yeah. Unh," he said reaching under her top and squeezing her breasts, causing him to increase his tempo.

"I have missed fucking you *so* much. Damn, why is this pussy so good?"

"Why is this *dick* so good?"

Javier slowed down, changing to longer, slower strokes which he knew Mia's body loved, "You gonna cum for me Mia?"

"You know that you're gonna make me," Mia's words spilled out, barely audible at this point.

"Come on baby, give it to me," Javier told her while tightening his grip around her waist and slamming her body into him harder and faster again.

They were both breathing hard and fast, reveling in ecstasy, yet still fully clothed.

"Oh, damn Javier. I've missed this too. You feel so good... I ... I can't hold on anymore," she moaned to him, as Javier's unrelenting thrusting pushed her over the edge.

"Oh yeah. I love making you cum Mia, come on, give me one more," Javier told her while pounding her harder and grabbing a handful of her hair.

"Give it to me Mia," he moaned as he slapped her on her right ass check making her body spasm again.

"I love fucking this pussy," he moaned loudly.

"Then show me. Show me how good it is to you. Give it to me Javier. Give me what you been wanting to do all these months. Come on... Javier. Fuck. *Me*."

"Oh Mia, you got me, *you got me*," Javier said finally succumbing to the frenzied pleasure they had created, bringing Mia along with him.

They both fell onto Javier's bed trying to catch their breath, unable to speak for a few moments. Finally regaining her composure, Mia slowly rolled onto her side and looked at Javier, and before he could speak, she softly halfway sang a few lines from Gigolos Get Lonely too:

Javier looked at her quizzically, "Well, we did have all of our clothes on ya know," she said winking.

He burst into laughter, "You are something else woman, but you know that happened way too fast. You know I don't like when that happens," he told her cupping her face in his hand.

"Sometimes our passion is in control babycakes. We are both satisfied, and we both know you can be the Energizer Bunny, so it's all good in my book," she replied with an exaggerated wink.

Javier smiled, then looked up at the ceiling shaking his head, "You may have a point. Stay right there, let me go get you a wet towel to help you clean up, be right back," he said as Mia reached around to fasten her bra.

After they cleaned up and adjusted their clothes, Mia looked at the time; it was only 9:37.

"Hey Mister Man, that was something else, but then again it always is when we do what we do. But look, I'm gonna need to go ahead and be the "guy" right now, 'cause I really need to get going. Sorry baby, can't spoon with you and hold you all night," Mia said making an exaggerated sad face, then smiling.

"Why, you scared of round two? We really need to do that ya know."

Mia shook her head. "Maybe we will one day, but for real though, I didn't sleep well *at all* last night, and tomorrow is going to be a heavy day at work. I sincerely doubt if I will have a problem sleeping *tonight* though, thanks to a certain, *extremely*, sexy man," she told him mouthing a kiss.

"Me either, thanks to an *exceptionally*, sexy and sensual woman I have the pleasure of knowing. Tonight, will probably be the best sleep that I've had in weeks. Well, so damn, it's looking like I'm going to have to hold my teddy bear tonight then," he told her with a mock sad face before laughing, then grabbing her hand and leading her to the bedroom door.

"Come on and follow me sexy lady, I'll walk you out," he told her opening the door.

Mia followed him down the hall, grabbed her purse off the hall table, and fished her keys out before they reached the front door.

"I will definitely be in touch," Javier said before giving her a long, soulful hug.

"And I will be sending you positive vibes," Mia told him before giving him a soft kiss on the lips.

Javier stood in the doorway watching her as she walked to her car. She gave him a wave before getting in and driving off. He closed the door, then walked down the hall back to his room. He stripped down to his underwear then sat on the bed with a heavy sigh. He looked over at the end to the exact spot where he and Mia were in the throes of ecstasy just moments ago. Although it was still early,

Javier turned off the light and pulled the comforter over him. He lay there quietly in the dark trying to still his mind. It was only a momentary effort though, as he drifted off to sleep almost instantly; his body having been satisfied, but not his soul.

Mia drove home, feeling pretty damn tired but still content. Between last night's shindig at Mark's, the late-night conversation with Tony, and tonight's "after dinner activity" with Javier, she found herself exhausted, both mentally and physically. It was a good type of tired though she thought with a smile. The fatigue seemed to have rendered her mind incapable of its usual questions and thoughts, and for that, she was truly grateful.

She walked into the house and immediately took a hot, soapy shower. She put on an old Jimi Hendrix t-shirt Marquis bought her years ago, then made a beeline straight for bed. She made sure the alarm on her phone was set for work in the morning, then sent a text to Marquis and Russell, telling them that she loved them. She turned off the lamp on her nightstand, then grabbed the remote to turn on the TV, but the Sandman had other plans; Mia fell asleep within moments, the remote still in her hand, the TV never turned on.

The next morning brought Monday, Mia's least favorite day of the week, and which did not disappoint in being a crappy day. It began when she accidentally hit "End" instead of "Snooze" when her alarm went off. She overslept, and had to rush getting dressed, feeling grateful that she had the forethought to take her shower the night before. Definitely no time for her Monday Starbucks, so was going to be a Rockstar morning apparently. There was a serious accident on the freeway, leaving traffic at a crawl, and she ended up being 15 minutes late. She had emailed Mrs. Johnson, about the traffic, and fortunately she understood. Of course, she had offered to work until 5:15 to make up for it since they were so busy, which seemed to appease her.

Both Kim and Ashley had called in sick. Mia was somewhat relieved so as not to be further grilled to talk about her "men". She decided right then and there that she was not going to let them, or even Mark, know about going over to see Javier last night. Well, that is unless and until, she felt that they needed to know. She knew Mark was teaching some sort of training this week which actually served her well, because she was not feeling too social today. She took a nap in her car at lunch and felt much more refreshed when she awoke. She began feeling more hopeful things were going to get better in the second half of the day, that is until she received a text from Javier around 2:30:

Hey Sexy, I thought about what you said, and I am going to give it one more try with Maria. I feel like I'm only going thru the motions, my heart just isn't in it. Thank you for last night, thank you for being you. I will be in touch, and you know I am still your mechanic.

Her heart sank, even though deep down, Mia had been expecting this to happen for quite some time now, those chips to finally land.

She immediately replied:

Hey Stud, so been there, done that. I do relate and understand. You know where to find me, and yes, last night was great, but it always is.
"It" never disappoints.
Sending positive vibes. Follow your soul.

Although the rest of the day she had a heavy heart, she also realized that Javier's decision was really inevitable. It had been a few years, and they had more than a great run. His text seemed to make the day drag ass even more somehow, but at 5:15 sharp, Mia left work and headed straight to the gym to work off some angst with Javier remaining heavy on her mind. Okay, so it's done, well, maybe - maybe not, Mia thought, as she made her way through the traffic.

She finally got to the gym, and wouldn't you just know it, the damn Monday Murphy's Law reign had not ceased. There was no class tonight – Cancelled - the sign at the front desk read. What a fucked-up Monday Mia thought shaking her head. She was already there, so got dressed and got on the elliptical instead. Thoughts of her and Javier in her bed, bent over his desk, in that chair in the bathroom at the shop, their long talks, his eyes, his voice, his touch, plus so many more, ran wildly rampant through her mind, no matter how hard she tried to push them out.

Well, looks like I can add "Cougar" to my résumé now I suppose, Mia thought with a sly smile. Even though their relationship was "wrong", her being the "Side Chick" for a few years more-or-less, she still had no regrets. She knew that she would always cherish both the experience and their relationship. She only did a cardio workout and then headed home.

She threw a lasagna Lean Cuisine in the microwave. She was more tired than hungry, and was only eating out of necessity, not hunger.

She let it cool for a few moments and scarfed it down standing right there at the sink, then tossed the container in the trash. She began stripping as she walked down the hall to her bedroom and was nearly naked by the time she got there. She turned on the light and tossed her clothes into the laundry hamper in her closet. She walked into the bathroom, turned on that light and stared at her reflection for a few moments. Still much work to do she decided, then ran a bath and got in.

As she lay back in the water, it dawned on her, that in two more nights she would be seeing Giovanni, and wondered what *that* evening would bring. He was such a hopeless romantic, so there really was no telling what to expect. Unfortunately, she had a feeling that it would be more on the serious side, further discussion of his illness. Well, all she could do was to be a friend, listen, and try to offer support. She got out, dried off, then snuggled into a David Bowie t-shirt and climbed into bed. It was another night that Mia fell asleep almost as soon as her head hit the pillow.

She had not set her phone on vibrate, yet when she hit snooze after the alarm went off the next morning, she saw that Marquis had sent her a text around 10 last night:

> *Hey Mama Bear, just saying hi, maybe we can FaceTime soon. Luv you.*

She replied:

> *Apparently I was in a deep sleep and didn't even hear the phone. Yes, let's FaceTime soon. Love you more!*

Wow, she must have been sleeping hard, and although the volume was not turned up exceptionally high, she still should have heard it. She shrugged it off and lay there smiling, feeling that the day was definitely beginning much better than yesterday. She decided that when she got home, she would flat iron her hair, giving her a different look for dinner tomorrow night with Giovanni. She pulled into the Starbucks drive-thru and somehow managed to make it to work almost 10 minutes early. As she was logging in on her computer, she once again caught herself wondering how she managed to even get dressed, let alone drive to work - it was all a mystery. She took a sip of her extra hot vanilla latte and could feel her soul coming to life.

The thought, "Hello, my name is Mia, and I am addicted to caffeine," popped into her head and made her smile. Kim walking back from her daily make up ritual in the bathroom stopped at her desk.

"Ooh, and what are you smiling about Miss Thing?"

"My coffee," she dryly replied then took another sip.

"Uh huh. Too late to try to keep secrets *now*."

"Welp, just like a line from one of my faves, *Get Shorty: "Never say more than you have to,"* Mia told her with a wink.

"So not fair, but no time... I better get to my desk, catch you later."

"Mm hmm," Mia said nodding while sipping on her latte, completely unperturbed.

The morning seemed to fly by. It was nearing lunch time, so Mia sent a text to the girls and set off a chain:

> *I'm going walking at lunch, 1:00, holler, if you wanna come with.*

Ashley:

> *Aunt Flo is visiting, gonna skip, plus I'm a bitch...I need a Snickers! LMAO*

Kim:
> *No shoes to walk in, next time.*

Mia:
> *Okay. Catch you guys another time.*

Secretly Mia was pleased they didn't want to go. Today she felt like using the time on her walk to think things out, and there was a lot weighing heavily on her mind right now. She had put on her cross-training shoes earlier, and 1:00 found her getting on the elevator to go outside. Nice day to walk, not too hot, not too cold, hmm kind of like Giovanni. He was agreeable and sexy but not overly, just smack dab in the middle in the scheme of things. She had not heard back from Tony again, and once again Javier appeared to be out of the picture. To top off her present situation, she was still unsure of what tomorrow night would bring with Giovanni. Well damn, only about 10 days or so ago, all three seemed to be in play, and now, all three were a toss-up. Well, as they say, what a difference a day makes Mia thought with a shrug. At least her life certainly was not boring these days.

She got in a little over 3.5 miles over lunch and returned to the office with a few minutes to spare. She got her lunch bag out of the fridge in the break room, grabbed a Granny Smith apple out, washed it, and sliced it. She squeezed a little lemon juice on top, added a dash of Sea Salt, and took it back to her desk. Not much of an appetite, so her snack hit the spot.

As 5:00 finally rolled around, Mia logged off and decided to head straight home, no gym tonight, since she had decided to do her hair. As soon as she got home, she washed her hair, added conditioner, and put on a disposable shower cap. Still not having much of an appetite, she threw together a small salad for dinner. After she ate, she rinsed her hair, then put her terry turban on and ran water for her bath. She lit an aromatherapy candle, turned off the light, then slid into the tub. She took several deep breaths and exhaled, then closed her eyes in search of some type of solitude of which she unfortunately did not find.

Life was certainly teaching her the lesson of patience, but even more so, of realizing that all you really had the power to do, was to control your *reaction* to what happens, not have the power to control what *does* happen. Much easier said than done, but then again there was really no choice if you wanted inner peace. She decided lying there in the bathtub that she had to think more positively in order to attract more positivity into her life. After her bath, Mia got out of the tub, put on her leopard robe, then rinsed, blow dried, and flat ironed her hair. She pinned it up, pretty sure that Giovanni would notice and hoping that he would like the different look. She picked up her phone to text Mark, and a text from Russell popped:

> *Hi Mama, hope you are doing good. I'm studying for a big test, and I thought of you. Love you.*

She instantly replied:

> *Nice... believe that you will do well, and you WILL! I love you more...yo' Mama*

Next, she texted Mark:

> *Hey, so trying not to stress about tomorrow night with Giovanni. I just did my "herr" so at least I will be looking kinda good. I'm thinking maybe I'm too*

old for this shit and just need to stick to my succulents and writing...NAH! Hahahahahaha XOXO

She smiled after she sent it, then decided to get in bed and call it an early night again, once again, it was barely 9 p.m. As she snuggled under the covers:

Boing. Boing. Boing. Boing

She reached over to her nightstand and grabbed her phone, it was Mark replying.

Babygirl, don't you worry about a damn thing. "Let go and let love", I mean it's not love, but you get what I'm saying. Go with the flow cuz it's gonna be all good. But you KNOW on Thursday I want ALL the details. XOXO

Mia smiled, set the phone back down then sneezed. She felt another one coming on, so sat up and sneezed again, four more times in succession. Hmm, must have come across something on that walk at lunch and stirred up her allergies. She went to her medicine cabinet, popped a Benadryl, and then quickly got back in bed. She lay there wondering how Javier was doing, and if they would ever be able to see each other, and *not* end up tearing each other's clothes off. Ooh, but wait - last time they did not take *any* clothes off and *still* did the damn thing. She would definitely miss all that, but it is what it is. If she didn't hear from Tony by Friday, she would email him on the weekend she decided. She seemed to have sorted through her Trifecta, and thankfully began feeling drowsy from the Benadryl.

The next thing she knew it was a new day as she awoke from the familiar sound of waves from her phone alarm. She laid out a little black dress and her favorite red patent leather pumps to wear for her dinner date later. Once at work her day seemed to fly by as there were so many emails and fires to put out. Ashley and Kim seemed to sense her anxiety so decided to hang back, as Kim put it, *"We will leave you alone today, but tomorrow morning we will be vultures circling you trying to get that 411."*

Mia was out of the door at 5 straight up, and rushed home to get ready for her dinner date with Giovanni. She made it home by 5:25, tossed her phone and purse on her bed, then stripped and took a quick, hot shower. She got out, rushing to get ready since she had no idea how traffic would flow. She slipped into the dress, matching undies of course, and a pair of sheer black pantyhose. Flat ironing her hair last night was definitely one of her more brilliant ideas, it saved so much time since she only had to touch it up. Giovanni had only seen her hair in its natural, curly state, well, until tonight she thought smugly. She could barely wait to see his reaction, hoping that he would like the change up. She ran the flat iron over her hair, then fluffed it a bit.

She re-lined her eyes with black on top and navy on the bottom, added some blue-grey eyeshadow to the outer corners, and two coats of mascara. She applied red lip stain, Lancôme red matte lipstick on top, then added a pair of linear rhinestone earrings. A spritz of Pleasures, and all she needed now was to put her shoes on. She glanced at her Fit Bit sitting on the bathroom counter, it read 5:55. She could feel anxiety knocking on the door wanting to come in. She took a deep breath then sat down on the edge of the bed to put her shoes on.

Buzz. Buzz Buzz. Buzz.

Startled, Mia jumped from the vibration of her phone she had tossed on her bed earlier. She picked up her phone to read the message. It was from Giovanni. Her breath caught in her throat as she began reading:

> *My Dear Mia, there's been a slight change in plans for tonight. No need for you to rush to try to meet me at 6:30 after a long day at work. I will be picking you up about 6:30 instead. App says 15 minutes away. See you shortly.*

Mia took a deep breath and exhaled, feeling relieved. She had been rushing around since 5:00; this was a welcome modification in the evening's plans. Now that the rushing was over, she remained sitting on her bed, then took another deep breath and exhaled, then repeated it. More than likely, there would be more heavy conversation about his condition. She wanted to be supportive, he was such a genuinely caring person, still, she was not exactly sure what to expect.

Mia bent down and slipped into her shoes, grabbed a long black cardigan out of her closet and put it on. She went back to check herself in the mirror one more time. Well, not going to get any better at this point she decided after fluffing her hair a bit more. Feeling a headache coming on, she put her phone in her purse and took it with her to the kitchen where she popped a couple of Excedrin to head off trouble at the pass, so to speak.

Knock. Knock. Knock.

Mia went to the door and peered through the peephole; Giovanni was standing on her porch which immediately made her smile.

"Well, well, well, look who it is," she said as she opened the door.

Giovanni stepped into the foyer, "A bit ahead of schedule, but look at you - you look beautiful Ms. Mia, but that is no surprise," he said giving her a quick embrace, and soft kiss on the lips, then pulling back and looking harder, "I am loving your hair, aren't *you* just full of surprises?"

"Oh my, look who is talking... the Master of Surprises right here," Mia said as they both laughed.

"The car is waiting for us, reservations are at 7:00 Miss Lady, shall we?" he asked his palm extended towards the black Mercedes sitting in front of her house.

"Yes, we should," Mia said as they both stepped back onto the porch, and she locked the door.

As they approached the car, a driver stepped out and opened the door for them. They both got in and were on their way.

"I chose Italian, I hope that sits well with you."

"I've become pretty partial to Italian lately, in case you hadn't noticed," Mia replied with a wink.

Giovanni smiled nodding his head yes.

"I trust your judgment, I'm sure it will be delicious."

"So, my dear how was your day? Good I hope?"

"It was busy, which was a good thing; helped the day pass faster. To be honest, I was a little preoccupied thinking about seeing you tonight."

"Hmm, were you now? I hope this midweek "date" didn't throw a monkey wrench into any plans."

"Not at all, the most I do after work is hit the gym, so this is a definitely a treat. Now you know that I can't help but ask, are you okay? Facetiming with you had me very concerned about your health."

"My apologies, it was not my desire to alarm you, but I felt that you deserved to know about my health. Now, I don't presume to figure into your life, but just in case that you would care to spend some time with me, I thought it prudent for you to know."

"I appreciate that. Honesty is crucial."

"Yes, I agree," he paused before continuing, "I feel a bit of tension, is everything alright my dear?"

"Yes, it's just, well, sometimes when I'm with you, and I see how you live, your lifestyle, well, it just makes me feel so behind the times, as it were," Mia told him then stared out the window.

"So, I make you uncomfortable then?"

Mia quickly turned back towards Giovanni, "Oh not at all, quite the contrary – it makes me want to do better, so I can live as well as you," she told him squeezing his hand.

Giovanni took a deep breath and exhaled, then took Mia's hand that was squeezing his, and never breaking eye contact, brought it up to his lips and softly kissed it.

Mia smiled, "Told you that you were a smoothy from day one," she told him nodding her head.

"Sir, we have arrived," the driver told Giovanni, interrupting his dialogue with Mia.

"Thank you," Giovanni replied as the door was opened and they both got out.

Giovanni opened the door to the restaurant and they walked in.

"Reservations for two, Esposito," Giovanni told the hostess.

"Yes, your table is ready, please follow me," she said grabbing two menus.

As they were escorted to their table, Mia told him, "I'm actually starving."

"So am I," Giovanni told her smiling.

They sat down, this time facing each other.

"Your server will be right with you,"' the Hostess said before walking away.

Giovanni looked at Mia and smiled, "You know, I'm so glad that you are not one of those women who kill themselves over every calorie, but instead seem to have found a balance and enjoy yourself. We all overindulge time to time, and that's okay."

"Oh, look at you, Mr. Flat Stomach talking," Mia said wagging a finger at him.

"Well, not to sound misogynistic, but I think that a woman should have some soft spots. I mean abs on a woman are great, but if she's a little soft there, I'm good with that."

"Well God bless you," Mia said laughing.

Giovanni joined in her laughter as they both perused the menu.

"Believe it or not, I was once a hard body myself. The proverbial 36-24-36 for a few years before I married. Now after years of mileage, I like to say that the curves are still there, but the road has widened," Mia said shrugging,

"Well, we should toast to those, might I say *dangerous* curves."

No sooner than the words were out of Giovanni's mouth, than the server came to their table.

"Good evening, my name is Aubrey, may I get either of you

something to drink or perhaps appetizers before dinner?"

"Why yes you may, I will have a glass of your best Remy," Giovanni replied.

"I will have a Grey Goose Martini with two olives and two onions, dirty ...*very dirty* please."

"Anything else?"

"Two waters with lemon please, "Giovanni told Aubrey as he winked at Mia.

"Did you need more time to look at the menu to decide on dinner?"

"Do you?" Mia asked Giovanni.

"No, not really."

Turning towards Mia, "And what will you have tonight Miss?"

"I will have the Caprese salad and the seafood risotto please."

"And for you sir?"

"I will have a Cesar salad, and the Grigliata Di Pesce Misto thank you."

"Did you want your salads before or with dinner?"

Giovanni replied, "Before," while looking at Mia for her approval which she gave shaking her head yes.

"I will have all that out to you momentarily," Aubrey said then walked away.

"You know, I am quite pleased that you are a direct person and don't need things sugar-coated. Sometimes you just need to rip the band-aid off and see where things go, know what I mean?"

"I do," Mia said nodding her head in agreement.

"Before I go any further though, I must compliment you once again, your hair is striking my dear. I had no idea you could change it up like that, but then again you seem to be a woman of many talents."

"Well okay *Mr. Smooth*, I will just say thank you and leave it at that. I am really pleased that you like it so much. So how did your business meetings go – productive I hope?"

"Yes, they did, thank you. We are doing a bit of restructuring as you can well imagine."

"A glass of Remy and a dirty Grey Goose Martini," Aubrey said before sliding the glass of Remy to Giovanni and the martini to Mia, then placing a glass of water in front of each of them.

"Thank you for the exceptional service," Giovanni told Aubrey with a nod.

"My pleasure sir, your salads and entrees won't be much longer. Can I get you two anything else?"

Mia and Giovanni looked at each other and Mia shook her head no.

"We are good for now, thank you."

"Enjoy," Aubrey said smiling and walked away.

Giovanni raised his glass and Mia did likewise.

"Here's to a lovely evening, a lovely woman, and some very dangerous curves," Giovanni said winking at Mia.

"And those endless possibilities," Mia added before they clinked their glasses.

They both took a sip, Mia taking a larger one as she felt something heavy was about to be said.

"You know over the past week or so, you have crossed my mind, and it came to my attention that perhaps a man of my age, and now my condition, might not be so appealing to you. I am nearly 10 years older you know," he told her with his hazel eyes searching her soul.

Hearing his words made Mia realize how Javier probably felt when she told him the same. She sat there speechless for a few seconds before telling him, "Yes, I realize the age difference, but when two souls connect, does that really even matter? I have been single for so long, that I cannot imagine that a prince will now appear and take me riding off into the sunset. At this point in my life, I don't want or need drama, or necessarily commitments, but I do enjoy having friends like you."

"Very good then. I did not harbor any fantasies that a woman of your quality and beauty would be lonely."

"I am extremely picky of the company I keep, there are *very* few in case you are wondering."

"Caprese salad Miss, and Cesar salad, sir. Here is fresh bread, olive oil, and balsamic vinegar. Would either of you care for cheese?" Aubrey inquired and interrupting their conversation.

"No thank you," they both answered.

Giovanni looked over at Mia's glass which was now more than half empty.

"Can you bring the lady another martini please?" Giovanni responded.

Aubrey nodded seeming to sense she interrupted a somewhat intense conversation, and discretely walked away.

Mia looked down and smiled before picking up her glass and drinking the rest, as well as eating her last olive.

Giovanni just stared admiringly.

"Care for bread?" Giovanni asked as he was slicing the loaf on the table.

"It's damn near impossible for me to resist fresh bread, and with the olive oil and balsamic vinegar? *Fuggedaboutit.*"

Giovanni smiled at her words, while slicing up bread for both. He slid the dish with the olive oil and balsamic vinegar in between them, "Dig in."

"I have to keep my thighs balanced, so two pieces are quite necessary," Mia told him picking up two slices of bread with a small shrug.

Chuckling, Giovanni picked up two slices as well.

"Thank you for the martini, I guess I could use it, huh?" Mia asked with raised eyebrows.

"One is good, but I think due to the tone of our conversation, two may be better. I have no doubts had you not agreed with my decision, you would have interjected. Now shall we eat a bit before continuing our conversation?"

Mia smiled nodding in agreement, picked up her fork, and began eating. They ate in silence for a few moments. Mia began feeling a bit relieved now that another Martini was on its way. She had begun feeling a bit of anxiety creeping up, since she had absolutely no idea which way their conversation was heading. They were halfway through their salads when, "Dirty, Grey Goose martini," was spoken by Aubrey as she swapped out Mia's glasses.

"Are you still fine sir?" Aubrey asked Giovanni.

"Yes, I am good for now, thank you."

"Great, let me go check on your entrees, they should be out momentarily."

"Sounds wonderful," Giovanni said with a nod.

Mia took a couple of sips of her Martini, helping to fend off that anxiety trying to sneak in. She sat her glass down, "You know, this dinner date was excellent timing. I needed a little break from the daily work routine right about now," she told Giovanni.

"I'm glad I could be of service Madame," Giovanni replied in a terrible French accent, and they both burst out laughing.

"I better stop eating this delicious salad, or I will be *way* too full to eat my dinner," Mia said pushing the salad plate to the side, then picked up her martini.

"You are behind Mister Man," Mia told Giovanni tipping her glass towards him.

"Yes, I will probably stay behind, as I still have a bit of work to do later, but this is a wonderful diversion for a few hours, I can think of none better."

Mia took another sip of her martini before telling Giovanni, "You are far too kind, I'm not always so nice ya know," with a mock frown.

"I am sure that mood would be warranted, but not to worry, I will keep our secret that you are not the meenie that you make yourself out to be. I can only imagine that being a single mother makes you tougher. From what you have shared with me of your sons, it appears that any time that you were not so nice, served you and your sons well," Giovanni told her before taking a sip of cognac.

"You most definitely have the gift of gab to diffuse me now don't you, *Vanni*?"

Before he could answer, Aubrey was back, "Seafood risotto," she said placing the dish in front of Mia.

"And Grigliata Di Pesce Misto, for you," she said to Giovanni placing his plate in front of him.

"Do you require anything else?"

"No, I'm fine, this looks so delicious," Mia replied with a smile.

"Yes, mine looks fine as well."

"Very good then, I will leave you to enjoy your meal and check in a little later."

After the first forkful of risotto, Mia looked up and rolled her eyes, "Oh my God, this is heavenly, you should taste it."

Giovanni ate a forkful of his food, "Oh yes, mine too. Well, I will taste yours, but *only* if you taste mine," Giovanni told her feigning a surprised look with his hand over his mouth.

"Oh-oh … am I rubbing off on you *already*?"

"Maybe. If so, I *like* it."

They both took forkfuls of each other's dishes and agreed on they were equally delectable.

"Lordy, there will be no way I can finish all of this."

They looked at each other, "Lunch tomorrow," they both said at the same time and smiled.

They ate in silence for a bit, but Mia felt tension emanating from Giovanni.

"So, I am 99% sure that you have not said all that you intended to tell and/or ask me this evening, am I correct?"

"Quite astute you are."

"Okay then, *Yoda*," Mia said laughing.

Giovanni joined her laugher.

"You are intelligent, sexy, and funny too. No wonder I could not stay away from you."

"So, what are you saying Mister Man? That I'm your new drug? "

"Absolutely."

"I see."

"Like you, I am of the mind to ask, get the answer, and respond accordingly. Hopefully, I am correctly gleaning from our conversation a bit earlier, that you might not mind fitting me onto your dance card as it were?"

Mia looked at him a bit puzzled.

"I would think a man of your stature would draw women of all types and have your choice."

"Many are drawn to my stature and income, yes, but I have found that those relationships are quite superficial for the most part. From the moment I laid eyes on you lying on that chaise, I felt a strong magnetism that drew me to you. There are so many facets to you - your intelligence, your sensuality, your quick wit - I could go on," he told her before taking a sip of his cognac.

Sensing Giovanni was about to say something monumental, Mia picked up her martini and drank the rest in two gulps.

Giovanni smiled and continued, "In a nutshell, I find you beautiful both inside and out, and I so enjoy your company. There is one thing though, I do not know how this condition of mine will affect me, and am concerned about, well, I think you may glean from my words, my meaning," he told her with eyebrows raised, his eyes searching Mia's face for a glimmer of recognition.

After a beat Mia nodded, "I believe that I get what you are saying, or actually *not* saying."

"I realize that this is not the ideal place to broach this portion of our conversation, but I have been holding it in for a couple of weeks now, so could no longer wait."

"Giovanni, you know that I thoroughly enjoy sex, but that is not all there is between us. I felt a connection with you that day on the beach as well, which is why I agreed to dinner that first night. From our short tenure, I already feel a special intimacy with you. Trust me, that is extremely rare, and I find that it is, well, that it is simply priceless."

Giovanni exhaled, "I have to say that I am so relieved. I do so enjoy spending time with you, which took me by surprise, but makes it all the more special."

"Can I tempt you with desert or coffee?" Aubrey asked.

Before Mia could answer, "Yes, may we have a slice of the Chocolate-Caramel mousse cake to share, and two coffees please? That is, if it is fine with you Miss Mia?" Giovanni asked cocking his head to one side.

"I am full, but I suppose I can squeeze it in," Mia replied looking up at the ceiling and rolling her eyes in mock submission.

"Boxes for you either of you? I can package it up for you if you would like."

"Yes please, thank you so much," Mia replied.

"Not for me, thank you," Giovanni answered.

"Very good. I will be right back with your desert and coffees,"

Aubrey said whisking their plates away.

Giovanni nodded his approval. He looked at Mia, then reached over the table and holding both of her hands told her, "I cannot begin to tell you how pleased I am that our paths have crossed. You are a piece of my puzzle that I did not know was missing. I cherish spending time with you."

"Wow, that's a helluva compliment Mr. Esposito, thank you."

"Your boxed food Miss, two plates, one slice of Chocolate Caramel mouse cake, and two coffees. There is also a small bag with bread. Thank you for dining with us tonight, and have a good rest of your night," Aubrey told them setting the wallet for the bill on the table, and with a nod walked away.

Giovanni cut half the cake and put it on one of the small plates before taking a forkful, "Mmm, this cake is delicious, wait until you taste it. It seems my affinity for chocolate and caramel has grown of late," Giovanni said pushing the other half of the cake in front of Mia.

"Has it now? Well, you know what? I find white chocolate a bit more mellow, a little sweeter, but equally as delicious," Mia responded returning a wink.

Giovanni smiled, "You are a jewel, now eat up, so I can get you home since tomorrow is a workday after all."

Peering over her glasses Mia told him with a scowl, "Excuse me, *Vanni*, it is only 8:03, so ...*seriously*? I live maybe 20-25 minutes away."

"Is it really? Time flies so fast when I'm with you that I thought we had already talked the evening away."

Mia put a forkful of the mousse cake in her mouth and fell in love.

"Oh my God, delicious is an understatement, this is heaven. Mmm, mmm, *scrumptious.* I may as well save time and spread it all over my thighs right now," Mia told him rolling her eyes.

Giovanni chuckled. They finished the cake and coffee and headed back to Mia's place.

As they drove up to her house Giovanni told her, "I do not expect to come in, please don't feel obligated."

"That my dear sir, is entirely up to you."

"I must walk you to your door though," he told her as they got out, slightly wincing.

Once at the door, Mia looked over at Giovanni, "You are more than welcome to pop in, but it's up to you."

"Actually, I should have taken some medication earlier, so I will take you up on your kind offer. Might I cash in on some of those "brownie points" you informed me that I have accrued for a glass of water, kind lady?"

"You got it, come on in," Mia told him turning on the light in the foyer.

She sat her purse down on the Bombay chest, "Follow me please sir," she said walking into the kitchen and turning on more lights. She put her risotto in the fridge and got a bottle of water out for Giovanni.

She reached into the cabinet to get a glass, "That will not be necessary. I can just take the rest with me to drink on the way back to the hotel."

"As you wish," Mia replied handing him the bottle of water.

He grabbed a pill box out of his jacket pocket and quickly swallowed the pills with a few sips of water.

"You sure you don't want to sit down for a moment?"

Mia hadn't closed the blinds on her sliding door and the solar lights on the flower beds were on which caught Giovanni's attention.

"May we step outside a moment before I go?"

"Of course," Mia told him walking towards the sliding door and opening it for him.

"How lovely. It's almost as enchanting as you my dear."

"It's even better when the fountain is on. I love the sound of water. I spend a lot of time out here. Drinking tea, drinking coffee, drinking wine, drinking vodka," Mia said laughing.

"I know we had coffee, but I would say that second Martini is still lingering a bit," he said laughing before wincing.

"Giovanni, what's wrong? I can see that you are in pain. Come and sit down on the sofa, and no arguing."

He nodded in agreement holding his neck, followed her over to the couch, and sat down on the edge of a cushion.

Looking concerned Mia asked him, "Can I get you anything?"

"No but thank you for asking. The meds will kick in soon."

Mia kicked off her red pumps, hit the remote on her Bose player and Art Porter began softly serenading them. She hit the dimmer on the lights, then climbed behind him on the couch and began gently massaging his neck and shoulders.

"Oh, that feels so good Mia," he told her as he felt his body responding to Mia's kneading.

"Now you know Mr. E., I hear tell of a fabulous hotel down the coast that has a spa with massage packages ...*just saying*," Mia whispered in his ear.

Giovanni smiled, reaching back and patting one of Mia's hands, "Great idea, I will get one tomorrow when I return before my trip back east. I'm flying out Friday."

"Such a busy, busy man. Well, I think someone that I know with a

Type-A personality may need to slow down for a minute and take care of himself just a little more. Maybe plan a nice vacation somewhere and relax a little?"

"Hmm, not a bad idea."

Mia began kneading his neck more aggressively and felt his body responding positively as the muscles in his neck began relaxing more.

"Oh my, this feels wonderful. No doubt it is due to you being the masseuse though."

"I do what I can," Mia told him while reaching her head around and kissing him softly on the cheek before resuming her makeshift massage through his shirt.

"If I were a dog, I would be wagging my tail."

Mia laughed, then scooted back on the chaise section, "I know there are a million fires for you to put out, but what say you take just a few moments and lay back and relax?" she asked him while motioning for him to lay his head in her lap.

Giovanni hesitated but did just as he was asked.

"Now take a deep breath and exhale."

Giovanni breathed in and out.

"One more time."

He repeated.

She softly began to massage his temples, then moved to the back of his head near his nape.

"Ooh. This feels magical. You are so very special; do you know that?"

"Nah, my one day a year."

"Well lucky me."

"If you say so."

"I do."

"So, let's re-cap, shall we? You aren't sure how your condition will affect you physically. I feel that our new relationship is not based on sex, therefore it is not a prerequisite for it to continue. If it occurs, fabulous, if not, it's not the end of the world, because I still enjoy your company. Footnote to this, is that you will book a vacation in the near future. Now, did I miss anything?"

"It appears that you have not. Although, if, excuse me, *when*, I decide to book a vacation, might you be open to joining me for a part of it? With technology these days, it's a breeze to get you an e-ticket to join me for a few days somewhere and you can relax as well?"

"If the timing can work out, I think that would be absolutely lovely. Time will tell, will it not?"

"Indeed, it will. I must tell you that I was very apprehensive when this evening began, thinking you might not want to endure hanging out with an older guy with health issues. I'm sure you can have your pick of a quite a wide range of men. I am more than content to be lying here with you right now, but more than that, happy that you haven not written me off."

"Sillyhead," she told him playfully pulling a tuft of hair.

"I am actually serious. Life is so short and unpredictable. When you find something or someone who enhances your life, it would be wise for you to hold onto that for as long as you can."

"Agreed."

"So, as you can see, I travel quite a bit with work, but just giving you fair warning, whenever I find myself closer to you, I will be reaching out."

"Thank you for the warning, I shall be prepared."

"You know, I could lie in this spot forever, it's so very lovely and relaxing, but I should go now, or I fear I may never leave."

"Well, since you were only going to walk me to the door, I have no complaints."

Giovanni sat up and stretched his arms. Mia scooted to the end of the couch and sat next to him. He wrapped an arm around her and gave her a hug.

"Thank you for a most enjoyable evening."

"Thank you for a wonderful dinner, and excellent company," Mia said with a wink.

They stood up and she walked him to the door.

"Sleep well, and have a safe trip," Mia told him before softly kissing him on the lips.

"I shall, and you sleep well, I will be in touch."

Mia opened the door and Giovanni stepped out, then abruptly turned around to face her and gave her another kiss.

"Okay, off I go."

"Goodnight, and thanks again for a lovely evening," Mia told him smiling as she stood watching in the doorway.

Giovanni walked to the waiting car and waved before getting in. Mia waved back then closed the door. She turned off the Bose and lights in the family room, then headed to her bedroom feeling relieved. Not that she or Giovanni knew the extent or what to expect at this point from his Parkinson's, but he had disclosed information about his condition nearly immediately, allowing her the option of continuing to see him or not.

She changed into a nightshirt, washed her makeup off, and put her hair up in a ponytail. She picked up the remote to turn on the TV, but wasn't much in the mood, so grabbed her laptop instead, threw some pillows behind her and logged on. She opened Word to work on an idea she had for a story, but somehow, just could not resist the temptation to check her emails first. Lo and behold, there was an email from Tony.

> Hey Mia,
>
> So, your story the other night has been on my mind, A LOT. I love that your imagination is so sensual, as it appears you have become even more so over the past decades. I can feel it emanating from you even though thousands of miles away - but then again, we have always shared a special connection. The past couple of days, I have felt like a moth drawn to the proverbial flame, which is you, and you seem to be burning very hot. I know nothing has been decided about meeting, but it does seem to me that the direction we are heading towards is to meet up, and hopefully soon. Just thought I would throw that out there.
>
> TK

Mia immediately replied:

> So Mr. T., I had no idea my impromptu story would have such an effect on you, glad I could be of service (Wink, Wink). It does seem that the universe is aligning to bring us together. I am still open to it, guess time will tell, yes?
>
> Mz Mia

Mia sat there shaking her head with a smile, feeling overwhelmed but in a good way. She closed her laptop, slid it to the other side of the bed, then reached over and turned off the light, finally snuggling down under the covers. Not that she had really given much thought to her personal life after the boys grew up, but certainly not imagined it might be like this. She really had no complaints. Where would any of this lead with *any* of them though? None of them knew, but it did feel kind of amazing to be desired at this level. And what a variety pack she had: younger, older, and about the same age. One who was Black and Hispanic, one who was Italian, and the other Black. Endless possibilities indeed. Mia drifted off to sleep, dreaming of jazz playing as she lay in in Tony's bed.

The sound of waves woke Mia up. She immediately sat up, thinking she was still back in time lying in Tony's bed. She sat there for a few seconds slowly looking around the room as the realization dawned on her that that she was in her own bed, and all alone. Sometimes dreams seemed so real she thought sitting there shaking her head. She reached over to her phone sitting on her nightstand, hit snooze, and lay back down.

Damn, it's only Thursday Mia lay there thinking, and considered calling in sick. As her alarm went off again though, she decided to get up and get dressed for work. After brushing her teeth, she did her pushups and added some crunches. Aging sure wasn't making staying shape any easier, that's for sure she thought, rolling her eyes. She threw on a floral maxi dress, a black shrug, and slipped into some black sandals.

After driving a few blocks, she realized that she forgot to get her risotto from dinner last night out of the fridge, well, at least she knew what was for dinner tonight. Those synapses were apparently not firing in her brain, so most definitely a Starbucks morning. She got her usual, but a venti today. After a couple of miles on the freeway, traffic slowed. Ugh, must be an accident. Good thing she got up when she did, or she would definitely be late again.

She sipped on her latte and thoughts of her "Variety Pack" popped into her head. She couldn't help but smile. So far, her 50's had not been too dreary as she thought they might be, well man wise anyway. Finally, she got to the slow-down on the freeway, there was no accident, but CHP had 3 vehicles pulled over on the shoulder causing major rubbernecking. She got to work with 10 minutes to spare, despite the snag in traffic. She logged in early and sat there enjoying her latte.

Boing. Boing. Boing. Boing.

She heard Mark's ringtone realizing that she had not set her phone to vibrate since she was at work, so quickly pulled it out of her purse intending to answer and stop the sound:

> *So how did it go last night? You know I'm chompin' at the bits to find out. Let's do lunch. The deli on the corner at 1? Holla back.*

Mia:

There's not a whole lot to tell but sure, I will meet you for lunch, if you're buying hahaha.

Mark:

I got you "Playa", meet you there at 1 then.

Mia:

Deal

She smiled, but before she could switch it to vibrate:
Ring-ring. Ring-ring. Ring-ring.
Mia froze. She had given that text tone to Tony after their last conversation, but somehow had never really expected to hear it. She grabbed her phone and read the text:

Morning Miss Thing. Guess where I am? Give up? I'm in Oakland. Flew in last night. My uncle was in a car accident and rushed to surgery. We were at the hospital all night, but fortunately he pulled thru. Going to leave tomorrow and was about to book my flight home. I didn't rent a car, my cousin picked me up, but I was thinking of catching the train to Sacramento, and if a certain someone I know is willing to give me a ride to the airport, I could fly home out of there instead. Maybe we could have a drink or two and see what shakes out. Sorry such short notice, but if you could let me know as soon as you can, yes or no, I can book my flight home. I would appreciate it. Of course, if I don't hear from you in a few hours, I will just consider it a no and fly back out of Oakland. Hope to hear back. You have been heavy on my mind.

Mia sat there holding her phone with her mouth open. Definitely not what she expected to read, but then again, was *anything* lately what she was expecting? Maybe it would be better for that other shoe to fall though, so she could stop wondering, but then again, did she *really* want to find out? She was sitting there in deep thought, so deep that she didn't hear Kim trying to get her attention on her way back from her morning make-up ritual, well, when she wasn't running late.

"Earth to Mia, come in. *Hello?*"

Mia still deep in though heard nothing.

Snap. Snap. Snap.

The noise broke her concentration and she looked up.

"Oh, hey Kim. Sorry, I had zoned the hell out for a second."

"Gee... ya *think*? Everything okay though?" Kim asked apprehensively.

"Yeah, for the most part. I'm just, um, like... *busy*? Wait, not sure that's really the right word."

"Still raining men girl?"

"Apparently, and my dumbass didn't bring her umbrella today."

"Well look, I gotta book it to my desk and log in, I will catch you later for the scoop," Kim told her waving as she dashed off to her desk.

Mia picked up her phone and re-read Tony's text again. She decided not to overthink, so replied:

> *Hey Mr. T, sorry to hear about your uncle, but glad he's going to be okay. So, here's the dealio - I work downtown and that is where the train station is. I get off work at 5, don't know what your timing is, but if you can book a train ride up here after 5, I got you covered. Let me know if that works for you.*

Mia sent the text, finally switched her phone to vibrate, then took a few sips of her latte. With a deep sigh, she went into her queue on the computer and pulled up a file. Mark is going to trip out when I tell him about Tony at lunch, she thought with a smile. She took a file from the queue but before she could even open it:

Buzz. Buzz. Buzz. Buzz.

Tony had replied again:

> *Hey, so look, I will make it work and get to Sacramento. TBH, I can't seem to get you out of my mind lately. I am looking forward to seeing you tomorrow night, even if for 15 minutes, I don't care. I need to see you in person at this point, not sure how you feel about it. I will let you know as soon as I get it all booked what time I get in.*

Mia took a deep breath and exhaled hard. She drained what was left of her latte and decided to throw herself into her work in an attempt to stay dry from the downpour of men raining down on her. The next time she glanced at the clock it was 11:45, so staying busy was working, and for that she was grateful. She could not help letting her mind drift from work a little bit, with all she had on her mind.

Giovanni would be more for intimacy than hot, passionate, consistent sex. She was pretty sure that sex with Tony would be great, but was unsure of the intensity, other than the one-sided way from the past. Javier was definitely at the top of the list for sexiness and passion, but regrettably, he was out of the picture. She wished the best for him, but strongly felt that the best for him was *not* Maria. Apparently, Lisa, Dro's wife, did not either. Mia knew that snide remark at dinner on Sunday was directed towards her.

So, what was the deal then? Giovanni was such a thoughtful and caring man - not too exciting, yet they shared a comfortable vibe. Tony at this point seemed to be a hybrid of Javier and Giovanni, but she would know for sure tomorrow night. Yes, but *then* what? Mia felt herself getting all wound up, so got up, went to the restroom, then popped by Ashley's desk on the way back to hers.

"Hey Ash," Mia said while lightly tapping on the top of her cubicle wall.

Ashley looked up and took her earbuds out, "Well look who it is, our very own Miss Popularity," she said smiling.

"Yeah, well it feels like it's taking its toll though. I guess it will all unfold the way it's supposed to, but it's hard not getting wiped out riding that wave sometimes."

"I can imagine, but it's gotta be better than just sitting on the beach all alone though, *right*?"

"You do have a point."

"Yes, I know this, which is why I said it.... *Playa*. How was your dinner last night?

"It was delicious, and his Parkinson's is under control for now but he's not sure what will happen in the future. I told him I was fine with it, and he told me he was relieved and pleased I would stick around. Just dinner before you ask. He picked me up and dropped me off and will be in touch soon. So, what's up with you? How's Brad?"

"He's okay, kinda wondering if he's married or something. Maybe he's just cautious. Like you always say, time will tell. We are supposed to have dinner tomorrow night at Ruth Chris, so for now, in the words of Mark - *get in where you fit in*."

"Facts."

"What are you going to wear?"

"Girl, no fucking idea. You know I'm going home tonight and try on a bunch of stuff."

"You could always wear the dress you wore to wedding, he hasn't seen that, right?"

"Ooh, clever Mia. How the hell did I miss thinking of that?"

"That's why you have me. Of course, maybe there could be a shopping trip at lunch tomorrow?"

"Hmm. That's a possibility as well."

"Well, I will be checking back with you to see," Mia said looking over the top of her glasses.

"I know you will."

"Okay, I better get my ass back to my desk, catch you later Missy."

"Bye Mia," Ashley said putting her earbuds back in.

On the way back to her desk, Mia decided that she was going to put her earbuds in and try to disappear into her files, and not let her "Variety Pack" thoughts trickle in. When she got back to her desk, she was just about to sit down and get started when:

Bing-Bing. Bing-Bing.

Mia picked up her phone, "Hi, Marci," she said to the receptionist.

"Mia, can you please come up to the reception desk? There is something here for you. I would bring it to your desk, but the phones are crazy today."

"Of course, I will be right there."

Mia began walking to the reception desk figuring Mark left something funny for her they could talk about over lunch. As she turned the corner and began walking up the aisle to the receptionist's desk, for the second time that morning her mouth fell wide open for a few seconds, and she paused her walking. She recovered from the shock and slowly walked the rest of the way to Marci's desk.

"Hey Mia, looks like you're someone's favorite today," Marci told her smiling.

"Wow, I guess so", Mia said shaking her head.

"Lucky you," Marci told her.

"Uh huh. I mean thanks… I think," Mia said while trying to recover from the unexpected surprise. She picked up the vase of Colombian long stemmed red roses and baby's breath and began walking back to her desk. She sat the vase down on her desk and opened the small card attached:

Thank you for another delightful evening.

Thank you for understanding.

Thank you for just being you.

"Vanni"

Mia stood there staring at the gorgeous roses and briefly teared up. She took a picture of them and sent it to Giovanni with a text:

These are so gorgeous - you spoil me! Thank you so much, I would be lying if I said I didn't love them. You made my day.
Mz Mia

She continued staring at them for a few minutes, and then put her earbuds in to try to get back into her work groove. Thank God it was almost time to meet Mark for lunch. She barely finished the file she had been working on, when she looked at the time on the computer screen, 12:57. She grabbed her purse and headed to the elevator. As she walked into the deli, she saw Mark already standing in line and waving her over.

"I am *so* starving right now. Shoot, I already know what I want. What you gettin' ... *kitten?*" Mark asked chuckling.

"I'm pretty damn hungry too. I was supposed to be eating my leftover seafood risotto from dinner last night about now, but someone forgot it this morning. *Lordt!*" Mia told him mock slapping her forehead.

"Well, I'm getting a hot pastrami and cheese."

"Hmm, that sounds good. I think I'm going to go for a cold ham and turkey hoagie though, pickles and peppers on the side, please."

"Got it, and what you drinking, Coke?"

"You know it."

"Hey, lookee over there. Go snag that table from that cute old couple getting up right quick," he told her pointing to a table.

"I'm on it," Mia said and headed to the table.

"Good timing, we are just leaving," the man told Mia.

"Yes, lucky me, thank you."

Mia sat down and waved at Mark who saw her and gave her a thumbs up. She had only sat there for a few seconds before:

Buzz. Buzz. Buzz. Buzz.

Mia pulled her phone out of her purse and saw a text from Tony:

Booked my flight, train should be in Sac at 5:25 tomorrow night. Flight is at 8:20 Not much time, but still better than nothing. Can't wait to see you, it's been so long.

Mia immediately responded:

Sounds good. Yes, it has been a VERY long time - see you tomorrow night!

Mia sat her phone down and looked up as Mark walked up holding a tray full of food.

"Oh snap! What's all *this*?"

"Well, I got our sandwiches and our drinks, and then I wanted some macaroni salad, so thought you might share with. And *then*...I saw these *got*-damn slices of carrot cake, and chirrl, I just knew they were our destiny. *Boom*!"

"Oh my God. Well, it looks delicious, you did good."

"Well speaking of *good*, in the words of Bootsy Collins, your hair looks, *uh, extravaganza, baby bubba,*" Mark said imitating the singer.

Mia laughed, "Guess we will see who gets, *funked up*!"

"And not just Knee-Deep, but If It Don't Fit, Don't Force It, and we'll see who is *Up* ... For the Down Stroke," Mark said snapping his fingers twice with attitude.

"Now you know it's just One Nation Under a Groove, up in this bitch," Mia added, then burst into laughter with Mark joining her.

"Shoot, talking 'bout all them Parliament and Funkadelic songs makes a pimp want to go out dancing and whatnot, but let's eat," he said before placing the food on the table then walking over to stack the tray with the others.

Mia was already unwrapping her sandwich when Mark sat down, and he quickly jumped into his food. After a few bites they looked at each other and laughed.

"Guess we were both starving, huh?" Mia said laughing.

"Girl, quit playin', you *know* we were."

Mia pulled out her phone and brought up the picture of her roses and sat in on the table in front of Mark.

A sharp intake of breath, "You got these?"

"Yes."

"Today?"

"Yes."

"Uh, from which one Playa-Playa?"

"These would be from Mr. Giovanni. We had a lovely dinner and long talk last night. I told him that I would still love to see him time to time, and that his Parkinson's was not a deterrent for me. After dinner he came in for a short while, I gave him a mini massage, then he left."

Mark's eyebrows shot up; he sat his sandwich down on his plate, then cocked his head to one side, "Excuse me, what? *Massage*? You gave him a *massage*? Massaged *what*? All over? Happy ending? Come on girl, details, *details!*" he told her clapping his hands together for emphasis.

"Slow your roll. I saw he was in pain, so I just massaged his neck a little while we sat on the couch. And yes, we remained fully clothed."

"Mm hmm," Mark said looking at her disbelieving while picking up his sandwich.

"Serious bizz. And the other day, Javier texted me and told me he was going to give it one more try with Maria," Mia told him resignedly with a big shrug.

"Damn girl, anything else?"

"Actually, there is. Tony flew into Oakland yesterday to see family; his uncle was in a car accident. He texted me this morning asking if I would pick him up from the train station and take him to the airport, so we can have a drink and talk in between. Tomorrow night after work, you know what I'll be doing."

"*Girrrl*, your life is like a Lifetime movie."

"Facts."

"Okay, but you know it's probably best for Javier to give it that last try to see what shakes out. Chiile, that is a sexy man though, I mean *dayum*," he told her fanning himself like he was hot.

"Right? And I know you've been wondering, and trust me when I tell you this, all that sexiness translated into satisfaction – it was *always* good - feel me?" Mia told him peering over her glasses.

"That. Is. My. *Girl! Shee-it*, you might be older, but that fine ass man was sure getting after *that.* My girl *still* got it goin' on. *Yay-Yaayy.*"

Mark held his fist out and they fist bumped.

"I haven't told Kim or Ashley yet, but feel free to let them know if you feel so inclined. I just don't have the energy to be honest. Thanks for lunch too Pimpin'. This is really hitting the spot. I didn't realize how much that I needed to get away from the office," Mia said, scooping some macaroni salad onto her plate.

"No thang. I am curious though, if you had to pick one of them, which one would it be?"

"I've thought about that myself a lot lately. They all bring something unique to the table, and I don't actually know how "real" sex with Tony would be, but from what I do know of him, it would be amazing. They are all financially independent so that's great because I've already raised two men, and you know I am *not* trying to raise another one."

"I know that's right."

"Giovanni is way straight with that though G, I mean take last night for example, he had a driver in a 'Benz, dined on a top-shelf fabulous dinner, then roses this morning, not to mention all the perks at the hotel those two days. Tony is an IT manager, so he's got to be doing well financially as well. Javier's shop is probably getting back on track, so there's that."

"Well, that's saying a lot."

"If I could waive a magic wand, of course I would fuse all three: Giovanni's money and lifestyle, the intimacy with Tony, and sex with Javier."

"*Right?*"

"Why can't I just be an OP and keep all three though?"

Pulling back at looking at Mia with raised eyebrows, "Unh. Well look at *her*. I'm skirred of you chirrl."

Clap.Clap.Clap.Clap

Mark quickly clapped his hands, "Excuse me ladies and gentlemen, but we now have an OP, Original, *Playa,* right here in the *howwse*."

"Shh."

"Girl these people ain't paid a bit of attention."

Mia rolled her eyes and shook her head, "I just hope I don't have to choose anytime soon, but not lose my mind either. Just wanna keep riding this wave for a little longer."

"Aww *Suki-Suki now*, go 'head on with your bad self. Now what did you just say? Ride the, *who*?" Mark said laughing.

"Oh, be quiet. Men do it and have done it, forever … so you know, maybe a sista can get hers too."

"Legit right there."

"No idea what I'm going to wear to work tomorrow though. It's Friday, so we can wear jeans, so maybe I will just change into a sexy top, and different shoes after work before I pick Tony up at the train station, whatchu think?"

"Yes – that," Mark said pointing his index finger at her and nodding yes.

"I think I'm going to save my carrot cake for later G, I'm stuffed. Thanks again for lunch, this is just what I needed."

"For reals, I feel like I'm about to pop my damn self. And you're welcome Boo, you know how we do."

They bussed their dishes, grabbed their cake, and began walking back to their building.

Mia looked over at Mark, "Honestly, my life right now feels surreal, but despite not knowing how anything will end, it *is* pretty damn exciting."

Mark stopped walking and looked over at Mia who stopped too.

"Who are you telling? *Hellooo*, who is standing right here all up in your *biddness* and whatnot?" he asked her with his hand on his hip.

They both broke into laughter. Mia gave him a one-armed hug as they walked up to their building and Mark opened the door. They walked to the elevator and stepped in, still giggling until Mark got off on the 3rd floor. He stepped out, quickly turned around, then told her with attitude, "Now remember that all your "mens" are good, so you just go 'head on, and... *work it*," adding two snaps of his fingers right before the doors closed.

Mia stood there laughing and shaking her head. As she approached her desk, she could not help but to break into a big smile; she had forgotten about the gorgeous roses Giovanni sent earlier. She stood there smelling and admiring them for a minute before jumping back into her files. Lunch with Mark had snapped her out of worrying over the unknown for a while, thank goodness. 5:00 finally rolled around, but Mia decided to hang back for a few, so less chance of nosey people on the elevator in her business. Since she was picking Tony up tomorrow night, she needed to bring her beautiful roses home tonight, and not have them in the car when she picked him up at the train station tomorrow. About 5:10 she headed to the elevator, and made it to her car uneventfully. She put the vase on the floor, let the passenger seat all the way up, then stuffed a hoody she had in the backseat on the side of them, so they wouldn't slide while she drove home.

She sat her roses on the opposite nightstand when she got home. The underwire in her bra had been bugging her all day, so the first thing she did was take off her top, then yank the damn bra off, flinging it on her bed by her purse.

"Ahh, what a goddamn relief," she said out loud while massaging her breasts for a few seconds, then threw on an oversized Lakers t-shirt that one of the boys had outgrown and passed down to her.

She took the carrot cake out of her purse and sat it on the breakfast bar in the kitchen. Unfortunately, the anxiety monkey was trying to creep up her back, so she decided to make a quick bloody mary. She grabbed the throw off the couch, then took it outside along

326

with her drink. She clicked the remote to turn on the fountain, wrapped the throw around her shoulders, and took two long sips of her drink, before lying back on one of the chaises.

Tony was the last leg of her "Trifecta" that she needed more information on, and the one she was most curious about. So many questions from their past, but then again, there was a good chance they may never come up with the answers. Still, having the conversation would be a good thing. Mia took a few long sips of her bloody mary to hurry and take the edge off. Damn, if being in anticipation could help you lose weight, then she would be Super Model thin by now, she mused.

She lay back again trying to still her active mind, but to no avail, so sat up and slammed the rest of her drink. Now, what in the world will I wear she began wondering. Maybe her burgundy Timberlands with that burgundy sweater that zipped in front, and a pair of black jeans? Yup, that would work. She closed her eyes and listened to the water sounds emanating from the fountain, and finally began feeling the effects from her drink.

Hopefully, when she woke up Saturday morning, the dust will have mostly settled, Tony being the wild card as it were. When they chatted the other night, it definitely did not feel as if it had been decades, more like only a few days since they last spoke. She still felt that electricity they once shared and had no doubts that they would feel comfortable with each other, even after all this time. She grabbed her phone and pulled up emails from Tony. She re-read the end of his last one several times:

> I wonder, in that secret place we left behind, do
> the inhabitants there now, hear and sense what we
> shared in private. Do they try to imagine and create
> it for themselves, unknowing that you and I filled
> the room with more than they can understand? I
> feel the room must be still glowing with the sweet
> energy we left behind. It was such a special place.
> Time could not have possibly removed any of what
> was left behind by us.
>
> The ball is in your court.
>
> T

Her mind felt blown again re-reading his words. She clicked the remote turning the fountain off, grabbed her empty glass, and went inside. Mia heated up her left-over risotto and ate it in silence - no TV, no music.

Buzz. Buzz. Buzz. Buzz.

Her phone broke the silence. She grabbed it off the breakfast bar, it was a text from Giovanni:

> *Ms. Mia, I am so glad you liked your "surprise". Sorry, I was in meeting after meeting and did not have a chance to do much besides work today. Perhaps I will catch you on the weekend. Sleep well — "Vanni"*

She smiled, then rinsed her dishes, adding them and her glass from earlier into the dishwasher before heading to her bedroom. She set her clothes and undies out for tomorrow, then flopped onto her bed. That drink and full tummy made her feel lazy. She had no idea of what time it was and did not care. She reached over and turned her lamp off, then reached down and wiggled out of her pants and panties. She snuggled under the covers and was out like a light.

Mia awoke the next morning and quickly sat up thinking she overslept, but had actually awakened before her alarm, which almost never happened. Must have needed that extra sleep she decided with a shrug. She was relieved to see no texts or missed calls when she checked her phone. She got up, plugged in her electric rollers, and began running a bath. She decided to do a quick rosewater mask as she scrutinized her face while she brushed her teeth. She did her morning push-ups, put the rollers in, and slathered on the mask before she slid into the bathtub. She sat in the tub feeling somewhat accomplished from being a bit productive in the morning for once, which was most definitely an anomaly, since mornings were certainly *not* her groove.

After getting out and dressing, she added an extra coat of mascara, gold eyeshadow under her brows, and a brownish-burgundy shadow in the outer corners, then went with all black eyeliner - top and bottom lids. She fluffed her hair, spritzed on some Pleasures, and was ready to roll. With the extra sleep she decided to forego her Starbucks and drank some ginger-lemon tea instead when she got to work. Besides, her stomach was on the nervous side about seeing Tony later, so coffee was probably not the best choice. There was no Kim passing by her desk this morning, must be running late Mia figured. As soon as she changed her phone to vibrate:

Buzz. Buzz. Buzz. Buzz.

> *Morning "Miss Thing", looking forward to seeing you later this afternoon. Thanks for picking a guy up. Will text you while I'm on my way up from the train.*

Mia replied:

> *Looking forward to seeing you too after all these years. See you soon Mr. T.*

Mia wasn't sure if Mark had told the girls about tonight, but was pretty sure if he had, they would have said something to her by now. She decided to let sleeping dogs lie, and if it came up, then she would talk about it, if not she would tell them after it was all done. She had a meeting that would take up most of the morning, and hopefully keep her mind focused on work. The meeting was over at about noon, and she sent a text to the group chat:

> *Hey Peeps, I'm in a weird space, will explain later. Going to walk again for lunch, need to sort some things out in my head.*

Mark:

> *All good, handle your "biddness" ☺*

Kim:

> *Okay, try not to stress*

Ashley:

> *We will be here when the dust settles.*

Mia felt relieved, then switched into her walking shoes and left the building about 1:00. Too bad Mama was on a trip with Aunt Jewel in Hawaii, she sure would love to hear what she thought about Mia's situation. Then again on the other hand, she didn't *really* want her to know all that was going on, judging her, and asking too many questions. The afternoon passed uneventfully, thank the Lord.

Around 3.30, Mia got a text from Tony:

On the train, on my way up to you

Mia replied:

See you soon

Her inner self: *Breathe Mia, breathe.*

Around 4:30, Mia made a dash to the bathroom to freshen up her makeup, and in popped Kim.

"Hey Girl, you all good? Mark told me and Ashley that you're seeing Tony tonight?"

"Girl yes. He had flown into Oakland for family issues, but he is catching the train up to Sac to fly out of SMF back home. I'm going to pick him up from the train station and give him a ride to the airport. We're going to have a drink or something quick to eat, depending on how long he has. I think his flight leaves around 8 and he gets here around 5:30."

"Well just remember, you will be no worse off if nothing shakes out, but you might get some closure about the past."

"Good point."

"I know it's probably fun with your variety pack and all, but I know you, and I know you're probably a little stressed because there are so many unknowns, am I right?"

"You are."

"Okay, but just remember, a few weeks ago none of this was really in play too much, and you were fine, so even if they all went away, you would be fine again. At worse, you would have had fun and got you some girl," Kim said giving Mia a half hug.

"Thanks for that. I just didn't have the energy to go into all of this with everyone, not like I was trying to keep anything from you or Ashley."

"We get it Mia, it's probably fun, but at the same time, it's a lot, because you do have different levels of caring for each of them."

"That's *exactly* it. Not trying to figure it out is easier said than done, because you want to try, but you really can't."

Kim stood back and looked Mia quickly up and down and began nodding her head affirmatively, "Well, I think what you chose to wear is just right – it doesn't look like you got dressed up, but at the same time, you can let that zipper on your top down a little and let the "Girlz" shine a bit. And then of course, there's always that double-bubble you got back there, *Playa*," Kim said popping her on the butt.

Mia laughed, "Thanks babygirl."

"I will text or call you tomorrow, okay?"

"Sounds good, and thanks again."

Kim winked and walked out. Mia applied more lipstick then fluffed her hair a bit before giving herself one last look, "Well this is good as it's gonna get," she said to herself out loud, then walked back to her desk. Only about 15 minutes left. She took a deep breath and exhaled, then closed out the last file she was working on. Finally, she began closing down the open applications. By the time 5:00 hit, Mia had already logged off and was standing at the elevator.

She jumped into her car and got to the train station at 5:17. She parked as close to the doors as possible.

Buzz. Buzz. Buzz. Buzz.

Text from Tony:

> *Pulling into the station. After decades we will be seeing each other in 10 minutes or so. I have on black jeans and a black sweater*

Mia replied:

> *No Gardenia behind your ear though? Hahaha. I'm sitting here near the entrance. White Lexus SUV. Should be fairly easy to spot. I will be on the lookout for you*

Mia sat the phone down, popped a wintergreen lifesaver, and began watching the door. Her heart began pounding fast and she could barely take a breath. She was seeing lots of people walking out when she spotted him; she managed to take a deep breath and exhaled hard. She quickly opened the door and got out to wave him over. He saw her, waved back, and began walking towards her. She let up the back door for him, then moved a few things for space for his bag, when she stood back and turned around, Tony was standing right there.

"Well, well, well, look who it is. I see you got the black jeans memo," she said to him standing there with her hands on her hips.

"Yes Ma'am, it's Mr. T., *in the flesh,*" Tony replied holding out his arms for a hug.

They embraced, and he kissed her on the check as they were pulling apart. They stood there staring at each other for a moment before Tony threw his bag in the back, and Mia clicked the remote to close the door. The electric current they created so long ago was palpable and present again, even after decades apart.

"I don't know about you, but I need a damn drink," Mia told him while strapping her seat belt on.

"Sounds like an excellent idea to me."

"Well let's roll, soul," Mia said pulling out of the parking lot.

"Let's do it," Tony said smiling but not able to take his eyes off of Mia.

"It's Friday night, so figured restaurants and bars will be packed - I'm thinking a hotel bar is the way to go, plus a lot quieter," Mia said glancing over at Tony.

"You are asking *me*, Miss Know It All?" Tony asked glancing at her with his head cocked to the side and eyebrows raised.

"Well, I see time has not changed your smartassedness," Mia said laughing.

"Well, hey, at least I'm consistent, you gotta give me that, right?"

"Yes, you definitely have that going for you Mister Man."

"You know, the last time I was in the car with you driving, we were going to the Burrito Shop on College Ave," Tony said nodding his head up and down slowly and pursing his lips.

"Wow," Mia said as she pulled out of the parking lot and into traffic towards the Kimpton Sawyer. Giovanni really liked his stay there; he told her they had a nice bar.

"I seriously can't believe I'm sitting in your car again. It's been *so* long. Damn, like what - 30 years at least, right?"

"Yes, actually a little more than that, but I don't want to think about how old we've gotten."

"Good point."

Mia drove to the front and the valet walked to her window.

"We are dining and shouldn't be more than a couple of hours," she told him.

"Very good Miss," he told her handing her a ticket to reclaim her car.

They got out and went inside. As they began heading towards the bar area, Tony looked over at Mia several times.

"*What?*" she finally said, slowing down and peering over her glasses but not completely stopping.

"You're awfully quiet."

"*Hello.* I have a lot going through my mind, you don't?"

"I do."

"It will be easier when I have that drink, though," Mia told him laughing.

"How far is the airport from here? I need to be there around 8:30ish I took a slightly later flight to give me a bit more time with a certain someone."

"Umm, about 15 minutes in good traffic. So, it looks like we have a couple of hours and change to catch up on *thangs*."

"Why do I feel like I could talk to you all night and it still wouldn't be enough time though?"

"Maybe because a lot of time has passed by already?"

"Well, we did used to have those long, late night phone calls ya know."

"Well *duh*, as if I forgot about all of those, brainiac."

"I don't think anyone else has ever called me that but you."

Mia looked over at him and smiled.

"I'm glad I had this brainstorm to ask about flying out of Sacramento and could see you. Seems surreal to be walking alongside you right now."

"*Right?*"

"Well looks like we're here, "Tony said pulling out a chair for her.

They both sat down and grabbed the menus. Almost instantly a waiter came over.

"Evening folks, I'm Ryan, can I get you something or do you need more time?"

Mia spoke up immediately, "I'm ready. Can I have a double Grey Goose martini, dirty - with two olives and two onions please?"

"Of course, and you sir?"

"Michter's bourbon, neat. Also, we need some appetizers, do you have some sort of sampler? Or Mia do you want anything else?"

"I'll go with your lead, but can we have two waters with lemon please?"

"I'm sorry, we don't have a sampler, but you can add one to three appetizers together for a reduced price," Ryan told Tony.

"Great, so we will have the hot artichoke dip, bone-in wings, and pot stickers."

"Very good. I will get the order into the kitchen, and get your drinks right out," Ryan said with a nod to both before walking away.

Mia took a deep breath, "Your hair is looking like Obama's. Got a little gray going on, but it fits you though. Men look distinguished, women look like hags, well for the most part. Very few can pull the gray look off without it making them look old. I'm gonna dye mine like my mama does when the time comes."

"Well, I would say you seem to be aging pretty damn gracefully."

"Yeah, but don't have that 24 or 25-inch waist anymore."

"But at least you can say you did once, how many can say that?

Besides, you may no longer have it, but I have the most marvelous memories of that waist, and much, *much* more."

Mia instantly froze, feeling like a deer in headlights, "Double Grey Goose martini, *dirty*, with two olives and two onions, a Michter's bourbon neat, and two waters with lemon. Your appetizers will be out shortly," Ryan told them breaking the uncomfortable moment for Mia, as he set the glasses down on the table in front of them.

"Thanks man," Tony told Ryan who smiled and walked away.

Mia immediately grabbed her drink and lifted it to her lips.

"Now slow down, sista girl," Tony told Mia stopping her from taking the first sip.

She looked over at him as he raised his glass, "Sorry, here's to old friends," Mia said clinking her glass to his.

"Here's to special friends and extraordinary people," Tony added and clinked his glass to Mia's once again.

Mia took two long sips of her Martini as Tony silently sat there admiring her.

"Still got the gift of gab I see," she told him with a wink.

"As I recall, it never worked on you though Miss Thing. But you know, sitting here and watching you drink that right now, brings back memories of you sneaking my wine coolers and stuff," Tony said chuckling and nodding his head.

Mia's heart began pounding faster as memories of Alice Street began swirling about her head.

"Yes, I did get buzzed a few times at your place," Mia managed to eke out before taking another long sip.

Tony continued to watch her with fascination.

"Like you're about to do now if you don't slow your roll."

"Excuse me Mister T., but I think I know how to roll with drinking and driving. I have been flying solo for quite a few years now, *thankyouverymuch*."

"Yes, yes you have. What about that? I'm wondering as to why."

"Hot artichoke dip, wings, pot stickers, and two plates. Can I get either of you anything else?"

"Nope, we're good, "Tony told Ryan.

"Enjoy," Ryan said before walking away.

In the distance Mia saw a couple walking to the elevator. The lady looked somewhat familiar. She nudged the man she was with who turned to look in Mia's direction as the elevator door opened. He waved. It dawned on her that it was Dro and Lisa; she smiled and waved back before the doors closed.

Tony looked at her then looked back to see who Mia was waving to, but they were already gone.

"Waving to your imaginary friends again?"

"They already got on the elevator so be quiet."

"Uh huh. Well, I'm hungry as hell," Tony told her helping himself to the appetizers and heaping them on one of the small plates.

This time it was Mia who was watching with fascination and a smile.

"You *did* have a hearty appetite. I remember you wolfing those burritos down."

As soon as the words tumbled out of her mouth, she regretted saying them, and immediately looked down, tightly squeezing her eyes shut.

"Well, let's just say I had worked up a bit of an appetite on those burrito nights, wouldn't you say?" Tony asked her with a wink before laughing.

Mia looked up shaking her head, "Lordy *Jee*-zas, why in the hell did I just say that? Unh, unh, unh," she said before lowering her forehead into her hand.

"I would gather to say two words – *Grey Goose?*" Tony said laughing.

"Smartass."

"Someone told me I was consistent right?"

Mia didn't break eye contact as she picked up her glass, drank the rest of her Martini in a few gulps, then sat it back down and began eating one of the olives.

"Well damn girl."

"It's all *your* fault ya know."

"Is it now?"

"Yes sir. Since you emailed me and we brought up Alice Street, I have racked my brain trying to figure out why we chose not to cross some invisible line in the sand, that line that we somehow both agreed and adhered to, yet neither one of us ever spoke the words."

"Well, did you come up with an answer?"

"I did not," Mia said shaking her head no with a shrug then pulled off an onion on the skewer from her glass and ate it.

Tony grabbed the other plate, scooped some of the artichoke dip, a few chips, and then added a wing and a couple of pot stickers to it, and slid it in front of Mia.

"As I'm still the older and wiser one, I'm advising you that you need to eat this right now, Miss Double Martini."

Mia peered at him over the top of her glasses, "I hate it when you're right."

"Yes, I know this, but..." Tony said with eyebrows raised and pointing towards the plate.

Mia dipped a chip in the dip and ate it.

"Satisfied?"

"Hardly, but it's a start."

Mia smiled and not being able to hold back began laughing. Tony looked at her quizzically, "What's so funny?"

"What the *fucking* fuck Tony? Decades have passed, and we have both experienced so much apart, yet here we are together, sitting and talking like none of that has even transpired - like we are still back in the day."

Tony just nodded, "Because, like I've always told you, our friendship was part of our destiny. Now, whether that's all it was meant to be, that was not foretold."

"I see old wise one."

Tony laughed and Mia began eating more of the appetizers he had given her.

"You know, I honestly don't know many people who I haven't seen in over 30 years that I could just fall back into conversation with so effortlessly, and definitely not *any* other woman that comes to my mind."

"Well, I doubt if you could have gone through your mental rolodex of all the women in your past besides me that quickly, that would be quite a vast list wouldn't you say?"

"Not of women worth thinking of, let alone speaking to Miss Thing, so there."

"Hmm, I see."

"Come on now Mia, you had to know you were treated differently."

"You don't say."

"I *do* say. Like I told you before, I never ran a bath or pampered others the way I did for you – *ever*. Once, I even had a date, someone was making dinner for me, but guess who cancelled it at the very last minute, because *you* asked to come over."

Mia could not hide her reaction - her mouth fell open. She sat there stunned, but secretly pleased.

"And before you make a smart-assed comment, I have never regretted those decisions."

"You know that I cherish those memories," Mia told him briefly squeezing his hand.

"I'm glad that you remembered them and feel that way, you already know that I do too."

"Sometimes when I think back, I wish I had, umm, for lack of better terminology, the *skills*, to make you feel the same pleasure I did. I wish I could have reciprocated at least once, to bring you to the level of pleasure that you brought me to."

Tony could not hide his smile as he took a deep breath and exhaled.

"You have no idea of how much I longed for you to crave me the way I did for you. Maybe it was my pride, my ego, hell, I still don't know, but I wanted you so damn bad. I wanted you to want me too, but it had to come from *you*, never from my request."

Mia looked down shrugging, "Back in those days I was pretty naïve about sex, and shy as well."

"Yes, yes you were, but I have to say, that was part of your allure for me."

"Well, I would like to think I have evolved over time. As in your email, were it ever to happen again, there would be different walls, different expectations, but I would still feel a sense of closure, since *I* would be the one running the show."

Tony looked at Mia speechless, and he was the one who drained the rest of his drink this time. He signaled to Ryan for another.

"Uh huh, see? I knew what I was doing with my double martini Mr. T.," Mia said pursing her lips.

"Now where did I hear this earlier? I hate it when you're right," Tony said laughing.

"You know, you told me the ball was in my court, but I would beg to differ since I am free to indulge in whatever I choose, whereas you are not."

"Michter's sir, and may I bring you another martini Miss" Ryan asked sitting the drink in front of Tony and interrupting the conversation.

"I'm good, but thank you," Mia told Ryan.

"Very well, enjoy the rest of your evening, and thank you," Ryan told them and left the bill in the wallet on the table.

Before Ryan was out of Mia's eyesight, Tony drank half of his bourbon, "As I recall, I was asking you earlier about you staying single, all these years."

"Well, I will let you in on something Mister Man, being a single mother trying to raise two boys alone takes *everything* you've got. I honestly did not have the time nor the energy to *look* for a man while I was trying to *raise,* two men. Besides, I was constantly in and out of court for over 13 years fighting to retain custody, so a relationship wasn't high on my list."

"That's fair."

"Yet we are here, right here, right now."

"So we are," Tony told her nodding before draining the rest of his drink.

Mia looked at the clock on her phone, "Wow, time is flying. Can you believe we have been here over an hour already?"

"To be honest, I'm really not surprised. Look at how naturally we fell back into conversation. Totally effortless."

"To finish what I was saying earlier, relationships have not been my thing, but I've had a few male friends over the years, and that's been enough."

"I can imagine that you have."

"Look Tony, I honestly don't know what, if anything was supposed to be accomplished by us meeting tonight, but I have to say, I do feel a small sense of closure. There was a bond formed all those years ago, along with some sort of unspoken love that we chose not to completely acknowledge, but do now, am I right?"

"You are."

"I really am glad that it weighed on your mind, and you took advantage of the opportunity of being so close to fly out of Sacramento. And for that, here we are, physically present in this moment."

"I felt we needed to see each other."

"So did I, but like I said, I have freedom, you do not, so didn't want to ask."

"Yes, but there seems to be a force greater than you and I drawing us together."

"Agreed."

They sat in silence, both of their imaginations flying.

"Damn Mia, I've missed you, but in a strange way, you've never completely left me. I know that sounds weird, but..."

"No, no, you don't have to explain, I get you," Mia interjected.

"It's always been this way though."

"It has."

"Of course, I will replay this evening over and over in my head on the plane ride home, and in the days to come."

"As will I."

"There is not complete closure, and I cannot say if this will be enough for me, you do realize that right?"

"I do."

"If you ever find yourself feeling the same, I am asking you this time, to let me know. Will you do that for me Mia? Please don't hesitate."

"Yes."

Mia looked down at her phone again.

"Oh damn, time really is flying, we better get the car and get out of here."

Tony grabbed the bar tab, pulled some money out of a money clip and stuck it inside the wallet Ryan left on the table.

"Okay then Pimp Daddy with the money clip going on and whatnot," Mia said laughing.

"Girl be quiet. When I travel, I don't like pulling my wallet out a lot, so put some ready cash in my clip. You just be quiet. Let's go Missy."

"Okay... *Big Daddy*," Mia replied still laughing.

They walked out to the front and Mia gave the ticket to the valet.

"I'm really glad we met up tonight," Tony told Mia with a one-armed hug.

"Same," Mia told him hugging him back.

The car came, Tony handed the valet some cash, and they headed to the airport.

"No traffic tonight, but better to get there early rather than late."

"True that."

"You know if I don't hear from you right away, it's fine. I think we both have a bit to digest from tonight."

"Yeah, well you never know about these things. As someone I know used to always say, *time will tell*."

Mia smiled, "Oh, so you actually paid attention to me did ya?"

"More than you could ever know."

Tony's words hung in the air, and they rode the rest of the way in silence with only Brian Culbertson serenading them until they reached the airport. Mia pulled up and popped the back. Tony got out to get his bag; Mia got out and met him there.

"You have a safe trip home; it was *so* good to see you again, you have no idea," Mia told him with a big hug before he could grab his bag out of the back.

Tony hugged her back - hard, then bent down and softly kissed her on the lips, then grabbed his bag.

"At least now we can both admit how we felt back then. Take care of yourself Miss Thing," he replied before walking away with a wave of his hand, and not looking back.

Mia stood there frozen for a few seconds, then took a deep breath. After decades apart, the feelings and intimacy they had shared, all came back; it still all felt the same. She watched the sliding doors open, and just like that, Tony was gone. She got back into her car and drove home feeling a myriad of emotions. Nothing was completely resolved, but somehow, she felt a slight sense of closure from the past. Tony *had* treated her differently than his other women; he went into a bit more detail about it, and it made her heart feel happy. Their special connection was still very much intact even after all these years, it all feel into place so effortlessly. They were both feeling their vibe pretty strongly tonight, but of course the future was uncertain.

Once home Mia grabbed a bottle of water out of the fridge and chugged half of it on the way to her bedroom. Good thing Tony made her eat something, because she didn't feel like eating anything else right now. Wow, what a night, and what an ending to the week. She hit the bathroom, washed her makeup off, and then slipped into a nightshirt. She grabbed her phone out of her purse and saw that Tony had texted her:

> *I'm about to board, but happy to have seen you.*
> *Feel free to dream about me*

Mia replied:

> *Really good to see you too. Feel free to think about*
> *me in the shower *Wink, wink.*

She was still feeling somewhat elated from her evening with Tony, but it wasn't even 9 yet, so Mia grabbed the remote and turned on the TV. Another fave was on, Smokey and the Bandit, so she climbed in bed to watch it, but by the time Buford T. Justice showed up, she was already out like a light again; she pretty much missed the whole movie. When she woke the next morning, both the TV and the lamp on her nightstand was still on.

Wow, I must have needed that sleep she thought as she rolled over and grabbed her phone off the nightstand. Yay, no messages. She got up, showered, and decided while getting dressed to splurge and go grab a Starbucks. She looked at the time, 9:20. On a whim, she texted Juanita:

> *Hey, you up? I feel like getting out of the house and*
> *going to Denio's or the mall, maybe lunch*
> *somewhere, wanna come with? I'm about to go*
> *grab a Starbucks, so let me know.*

She had barely set her phone down.
'Answer your phone, Answer your phone ..."
Juanita had instantly replied:

> *I'm down if you're driving hahaha. I can throw on*

340

some clothes right quick. I will be ready when you get here, but can we get Dutch Bros instead?

Mia replied:

On my way, and yes on the Dutch Bros.

Mia drove up to Juanita's and saw her watering her potted flowers and plants on the porch. She turned off the water when she saw Mia, then grabbed her purse sitting on the blue mosaic stone bench and made a beeline for Mia's car. She opened the door, "Hey sis, what's shakin'?"

"Just my big 'ol booty," Mia told her laughing.

"Girl, stop. Thanks for the invite. Gary went to the office as usual, so I was just home watching TV. Girl you know I can always shop. We must have got that shit from Mama."

"*Right*? I think she will be back from Hawaii next week. I've wanted to call her over the last few weeks about stuff, but she deserves to not worry about any of us, especially me."

"Something wrong?" Juanita asked looking concerned as Mia pulled into the drive thru.

"Not really, just get confused at times. You know, just stuff, men, life. What you want?"

Juanita's eyebrows shot up.

"Did you say men? Does somebody have a secret? Somebody finally take Mia off the market?"

Mia just pointed towards the lady walking towards the car to take their order with no reply.

"Okay, *okay*. Just get me a vanilla latte like you."

Mia ordered their coffees then looked over at Juanita, "Nah, not really, just juggling a few, you know, being that *Mack Mama*."

"*Right*," Juanita replied, then looked over at Mia, wondering if there was any truth to what she had just said.

"I do *not* have a man, stop looking at me like that. You know I have commitment issues. I have always had *friends* though, if that's what you're wondering right now."

"Now how did you know I was wondering that?"

"I got that witch-like sixth-sense like Mama," Mia told Juanita while handing her latte over.

They both took a sip, "Ooh that first sip though," they both said at the same time and laughed.

"So, what are we doing sis?" Mia asked.

"Denio's is cool and all, but I could go for the mall and lunch a little more. If you're not crunched for time, maybe we can get a pedi after? *My treat.*"

"Well hell, let's do it. I want to go in Nordstrom and see if they have an Yves Saint Laurent lipstick in stock anyway."

"I'm good with that."

Juanita pulled out her phone and called the nail salon.

"Can I speak to Lisa? Hey Lisa, how are you? It's Juanita. Do you have any time left for a pedicure this afternoon, and I need another appointment for my sister."

"Okay, hold on," Juanita said holding the phone away from her ear.

"Hey Mia, we can get in at 2:00, that work for you?"

"Sure does, I'm down, thanks 'Nita."

"Okay Lisa, yes, put us down, we will see you then. Thank you."

They got to the mall and did some slight damage. Mia not only found her lipstick, but picked up another bottle of Pleasures, a pair of faded wash jeans, and a pair of white sandals. Juanita bought two pairs of Michael Kors shoes, and the same pair of white sandals as Mia.

"Unh, unh, uh. This is all your fault. Look what you've done to me. I've become a *got*-damn shoe addict," Juanita alleged as the cashier rang up her purchase.

"And your point *is*?" Mia rhetorically asked dismissing her comment.

Juanita stood there rolling her eyes and shaking her head.

"The real question of the day is, what are we going to eat? Japanese maybe? I vote for Mikuni's or a good burger somewhere."

"Ooh, Mikuni's. I could go for some sushi."

"I want that ginger pork, I love theirs," Mia told her as they got into her car.

"Oh yeah, good idea."

They pulled into Mikuni's parking lot and Mia looked at over at Juanita, "All of a sudden, I am fucking starving,"

"I'm with you sis."

The bar was the way to go since there was immediate seating. They each ordered pineapple mules, a spicy tuna roll to share, and the Bento Box with double ginger pork. When their drinks arrived, Juanita grabbed hers and offered up a toast, "Here's to sisters."

"Yes, because they make the best of friends," Mia added before clinking her glass to Juanita's.

"Hey, you know what? We need to do a sister's trip, and all go somewhere so we can hang out sometime soon," Mia said snapping her fingers twice.

"That's a great idea Mia."

"Excuse me, can I please get another one of these?" Juanita asked when their food arrived.

"Ooh. Look at you."

"Hey, I'm not driving, I can get my buzz on Missy, but you can't," Juanita replied sticking out her tongue.

"True that. Go 'head on sis."

They finished their lunch, "This was so good, I am *so* full," Juanita said rubbing her tummy.

"I'm with you there, oh snap - what time is it?"

"Ooh, it's almost 1:30, lets book it so we won't be late to the nail shop," Juanita said pulling out cash for lunch.

They made it to the nail salon with 5 minutes to spare.

"Hi Lisa, I'm here. I'm treating my sister Mia today."

"Hi Juanita, follow me, we are the two on the end. This is Lucy who will be doing your sister."

"Hi, I'm Mia."

"Hi, Mia. Do either of you want water?" Lucy asked.

"Yes, please," they both answered.

They sat down and put their feet in the tubs filling with water.

"*Ahh.* Now this is what I'm talking about right here," Mia said closing her eyes.

Lisa looked at Mia, "So *you're* Mia. Your sister has told me a little about you."

"Oh, has she now?" Mia replied opening her eyes and glancing over at Juanita.

Lisa smiled, "All good things. She's very proud of you."

Mia just shook her head and turned on the massage feature. Lucy returned with their waters.

"Here are some color samples Mia," Lucy told her handing her a bowl.

"Thanks Lucy, but I won't need them. I just want a gel pedicure - French with clear pink please."

"Sounds good. You want the basic, with massage, or deluxe pedicure?"

"Give her the deluxe like me please," Juanita interjected.

"Got it," she said turning off the water then turning on the aeration.

"I will be right back with your polish," Lucy told her.

"Lisa, I'm going to have a French gel too, but can I have a pearly base instead of clear please?"

"Of course."

"Either of you ladies want a manicure too?" Lisa asked.

"Not me, I'm going home to work in the garden," Mia told her.

"Maybe next time, I'm going to do some painting around the house," Juanita added.

Lisa smiled, "No worries."

"This feels so good, huh?" Juanita said with her eyes closed, relishing the warm water.

"Girl quit playin', you know it does. If I ever win millions in the Lotto, I'm going to get this once a week. This was really a *great* idea. Thanks again sis."

"No worries, I needed to get out of the house, but we should do this more often. One day we are going to do it with Rene, Jean, and Denise. That would be so much fun!"

"Wouldn't it though?"

"Maybe one day we can drag Mama out with us too."

"Hey, we should all go on a vacation together, but maybe without your husbands," Mia said somewhat rhetorically, peering at Juanita over the top of her glasses anticipating her reaction.

"Works for me either way, don't know about the others," Juanita replied shrugging.

After the pedicures, they were pampered with a hot stone massage, mask, and hot paraffin wax.

As Lucy and Lisa rolled down Mia's and Juanita's pants legs, they admired each other's pedicures.

"Thank you, Lucy. My feet feel good and look *so* much better."

"Me too Lisa," Juanita chimed in.

"Hey, can we swing by Sprouts for a minute? I need to grab a few things. Do you mind?" Juanita asked as they got in the car.

"Sprouts it is Miss Ma'am. I have *no* plans today, I'm just *rolling with the homies,*" Mia said, her right-hand emulating wave motions.

They walked into Sprouts, Juanita grabbed a shopping cart, then started throwing food in it like it was her *job.*

"A few things? *Only* a few?"

"Oh, be quiet. You said you ain't got nothin'' goin' on, so there," Juanita replied with attitude.

Mia smiled as she grabbed a ready-made salmon meal for dinner later, and some fruit and veggies. She was finding it increasingly difficult not to confide in Juanita about all that was going on, but she knew without a doubt that if she did, her mom and sisters would be *all* up in her business with a quickness. No way did she want that, so resisted the urge to share.

"Can you put it all in the least number of bags as possible please?" Juanita asked the cashier while Mia looked at her sheepishly.

Juanita pointed her finger at Mia as she sternly told her, "Don't you *even* start with me."

"What? I didn't say even say nothin', *Miss Bossy*," Mia said laughing as the bags were loaded into the cart.

Mia pulled into the Juanita's driveway, looked over and told her, "Really sis, thanks. It was a fabulous day."

"Shoot, I got new shoes, so you know it was," Juanita said nodding her head towards Mia before opening the door.

"And you know this, *man*."

Juanita laughed and began grabbing all of her bags from the back.

"You need some help?"

"Nah, I got it. You should see how I bring a bazillion bags of groceries in the house, 'cause I *hate* to make more than one trip. I texted Gary when we left Sprout's; he's home and going to help me at the door. Look at me, Daddy would be so proud," Juanita said holding the bags then closing the door with her hip.

Mia let the passenger window down, "Thanks again, catch you later."

"See ya Mia," Juanita yelled back while walking to the front door that Gary opened.

Gary waved to Mia before grabbing some bags out of Juanita's hands as she walked into the house. Mia waved back at Gary, then backed out of the driveway and headed straight home. Once there, she made a cup of ginger-lemon tea, took it outside, and turned on the fountain. The day with Juanita had been great. She lay back on the chaise, slowly sipping her tea and a sense of calm came over her; she was feeling relaxed and at ease for a change. She looked down at her feet and smiled, admiring her fresh pedicure.

After weeks of feeling like she was on a roller coaster ride, her personal life seemed to have finally hit a smooth stride. She took a deep breath exhaling loudly. Nothing was completely decided, but it did appear that Javier was now out of the picture, Giovanni was on a see you sometimes mode, and Tony was on a wait and see mode. This reality was probably best with her commitment issues, so it seemed to have all worked out. Life is so damn unpredictable; you think you have it all planned out and then *zing* – you get thrown a curve ball with no warning. You either swing and luckily hit the ball, swing and miss, or stand there and do nothing, missing an opportunity.

Regretfully, Mia wished she had been able to spend time with Javier without having to sneak around or watch the clock so much. Then again, the secrecy was also part of the excitement she supposed. It was unfortunate they would not become the real estate moguls together they aspired to become, but it was not to be, or so it would seem. Several times she told Javier that they could have a purely business relationship - that she could separate their sexual/emotional side, but he told her that he could not. He said that there was just *no* way he could go from where they were, back to the *Friend Zone*.

Innately, Mia knew that she would ultimately find a path to success in the real estate game, because she would not stop grinding until she did. She had always depended on herself, it seemed to be the best way, well actually the *only* way for her. She got that from her daddy no doubt; he was definitely a man of action and very little words. But the thing was, she and Javier's goals and aspirations were so much in sync. They seemed to be aligned in most everything, sex being no exception.

Ahh yes, the sex. That raw passion they generated was something she had never experienced on a consistent basis before. Sex with Javier had been absolutely amazing for five years at least. Even the "quickies" were intensely pleasurable. Whether it was in her bed, bent over his desk, some chair in his shop, or *other* places in his shop, it was *always* exciting and passionate. The sexual facet of their duo seemed to cement the friendship they had formed. They had both enhanced each other's lives in various ways, and although their relationship was morally wrong, she had no regrets. But unlike her and Tony, she and Javier had both admitted they "caught feelings" at some point and loved each other. After that initial confession they never spoke of it again, as there did not seem a need to.

With all three of the men, the egotistical side of Mia knew that she had carved out a unique place in their sexual rolodex, and possibly their hearts. Giovanni told her that she had awakened a part of him that he thought died years ago along with his wife. She knew from Tony's words that he had longed for more and would always wonder what he missed. He cherished what they had shared, but he had never completely shaken the fantasy of having Mia all to himself. It all made sense now, as to why after all these years he had searched for, found, and ultimately met with her last night.

Probably the largest impact she had on any of her Trifecta, was on Javier. Their ability to talk about anything and everything, including plans for the future, captivated them both. He often told her how much it meant for him to have someone who understood and supported his ideas and goals, and it was reciprocated. And the fact that Javier and Maria's sex life had gone from him *never* telling her no, to him *rarely* saying yes, spoke volumes. It caused him and Mia to have more of an active sex life than what he and Maria shared, quite often. The fact that Mia was a little over ten years older made it feel surreal at times, but most definitely made it all the more, even sweeter. She felt especially gratified to experience all three of these relationships, and she cherished them all.

Mia finished her tea, turned off the fountain and went inside. It was nearly five, but she was not too hungry, so just plopped down on her favorite spot on the sofa, then snuggled under the throw. Sleep felt imminent, so she allowed herself the luxury of what she thought would be a short nap. She awoke and was alarmed to see it was 7:37; she had slept over two hours! Oh well, she was a night person anyway. She realized that she would be up late now, and just accepted that fact. At least it was Saturday she thought with a shrug. She would sleep in tomorrow, and Sunday would just be a "Lazy Day" as the boys called it.

She decided on snacking instead of eating a real dinner, so made herself a plate with cheese, crackers, prosciutto, grapes, and strawberries. She grabbed a cold bottle of water and poured a large glass of sangria. She put all of her goodies on a tray and took it back over to the couch, then found some cooking shows to binge watch. She resisted the urge to check her email until tomorrow, deciding that she was going to have a *man-free* day. Well damn, that was egotistical of her she thought, to just assume that there would be emails from at least one of the men. But being honest with herself, she would be surprised if there were not. And if that *were* the case, she really would not care.

As a result of her earlier reflecting, Mia sat there feeling a sense of empowerment, and as Tony had said about her waist, at least she could say that she *had* made some great memories. Hell, there were even recent ones, and guess what? She made them in her *fucking* 50's. But wait, there's more - she had also become a Cougar. Watch out world ... I may be a divorced woman who decided to remain single, *and* in her 50's, but make no mistake, *Mia.Is.Still.Fierce*!

Feeling some satisfaction from those thoughts, and after vowing to make at least five of the mouth-watering dishes she had seen, Mia found herself channel-surfing once again. She came across the 50 Shades trilogy, which she watched in its entirety. As the last movie was ending, she glanced over at her phone and saw the time - 1:55 a.m. She stretched out like a contented cat, then stood up and turned off the TV. She grabbed the tray, took her dishes to the kitchen, and feeling lazy, left them sitting on the counter to deal with tomorrow.

She got to her bedroom knowing that sleep would still evade her, so turned on the television and tossed the remote on the bed. She stripped, slipped into one of Russell's old tank tops and a pair of capri leggings, then lay on top of the covers on the bed. She found,

You've Got Mail, and began watching it when she heard a familiar sound:

"*Ah-oo-gah, Ah-oo-gah....*"

Mia instantly sat up, grabbed her phone, and saw that she had a text from Javier:

> *Hey Mia, I am finding myself in need of that offer for somewhere to sleep tonight. I'm sorry if I'm waking you, but you are literally saving my ass right now, you have no idea. I'm in the car outside, and about to walk to your door.*

Mia replied:

> *I am actually awake, all good. Word is bond~*

Fuck, fuck, *fuck*! Mia dashed into the bathroom, brushed her hair, and pulled it up into a high bun. She turned on the light in the entrance hall and rushed to open the front door. Javier was already on the porch bending over picking up his backpack. He looked up when the door opened, slung the backpack over his right shoulder, and then stood straight up.

He was wearing faded jeans and a black hoodie with the hood pulled up over his head. Mia stood there mesmerized as Javier pushed the hood back, revealing a nearly shaved head. His luminous blue eyes fixated on Mia's, delivering a soulful gaze with raised eyebrows. He shrugged his shoulders and exhaled loudly before reflexively licking his full, sexy lips. Transfixed, Mia continued to stand there speechless, her breath catching in her chest as she tried desperately to breathe. They both stood there in silence staring at each other spellbound, in one of their electrically charged pauses. Finally breaking the spell, Javier gave Mia a small smile. He slowly cocked his head to one side giving a slight nod. With his deep voice sounding slightly raspy, he softly spoke two words, "Hey Mia."

Mia responded with her own small smile, and emulating Javier, cocked her head to one side with a slight nod as well. Somehow, she had finally managed to find her voice and breathlessly replied, "Hey yourself."

Javier stepped into the house and Mia closed the door.

About the Author

J.D. Laster's love of books started at a young age; she became an avid reader. After taking a creative writing class while in college, she began writing poetry and short stories. Her writing took a backseat as she travelled through the many twists and turns on the path of life, but the spark never burned out. As years passed, her life experiences in concert with her vivid imagination helped her to find her voice and begin writing again. Sensuosity is one of the stories she wanted to tell.

Made in United States
Orlando, FL
16 January 2022

13590977R00221